# The MX Book
## of
# New Sherlock Holmes Stories

Part XVIII
Whatever Remains . . .
Must Be the Truth
(1899-1925)

THE MX BOOK OF NEW
SHERLOCK HOLMES
STORIES

PART XVIII
WHATEVER REMAINS . . .
MUST BE THE TRUTH
(1899-1925)

SOUTHAMPTON
STREET

359

EDITED
By
David
Marcum

OFFICES

TRADITIONAL HOLMES
ADVENTURES
COMPILED FOR THE
BENEFIT OF THE
RESTORATION OF
UNDERSHAW

ISBN Hardback 978-1-78705-510-0
ISBN Paperback 978-1-78705-511-7
AUK ePub ISBN 978-1-78705-512-4
AUK PDF ISBN 978-1-78705-513-1

Published in the UK by
**MX Publishing**
335 Princess Park Manor, Royal Drive,
London, N11 3GX
www.mxpublishing.co.uk

David Marcum can be reached at:
*thepapersofsherlockholmes@gmail.com*

Cover design by Brian Belanger
*www.belangerbooks.com* and *www.redbubble.com/people/zhahadun*

# CONTENTS

## Forewords

## Adventures

*(Continued on the next page . . . .)*

The following can be found in the companion volumes
# The MX Book of New Sherlock Holmes Stories
# Whatever Remains . . . Must Be the Truth

## Part XVI – (1881-1890)

*and*
## Part XVII – (1891-1898)

*(Continued on the next page . . . .)*

*(Continued on the next page . . . .)*

## PART III: 1896-1929

## PART IV – 2016 Annual

*(Continued on the next page . . . .)*

## PART V – Christmas Adventures

*(Continued on the next page . . . .)*

## PART VI – 2017 Annual

*(Continued on the next page . . . .)*

## PART VII – Eliminate the Impossible: 1880-1891

## PART VIII – Eliminate the Impossible: 1892-1905

*(Continued on the next page . . . .)*

## Part IX – 2018 Annual (1879-1895)

*(Continued on the next page . . . .)*

*(Continued on the next page . . . .)*

*(Continued on the next page . . . .)*

## PART XIV: 2019 Annual (1891 -1897)

*(Continued on the next page . . . .)*

## PART XV: 2019 Annual (1898-1917)

*The following contributions appear in the companion volumes:*
**The MX Book of New Sherlock Holmes Stories**
**Whatever Remains . . . Must Be the Truth**
**Part XVI – (1881-1890)**
**Part XVII – (1891-1898)**

# Editor's Introduction:
# *"Whatever Remains . . . ."*
## by David Marcum

People like mysteries. We read books about them. We watch films and television shows about them. We look for them in real life. The daily unfolding of the news – *What's the real story? What is the truth behind these events that I'm following? What will happen next? What will tomorrow bring?* – is just another form of mystery.

Some people claim that they don't like mystery stories, instead preferring other genres. But consider for instance how often a mystery figures in a science-fiction story. I've been a *Star Trek* fan since I was two or three years old in the late 1960's and saw an Original Series episode on television, and I can say for sure that many – if not most – *Star Trek* television episodes or films have strong elements of mystery somewhere within the story, and in most cases the characters serve as detectives, leading us from the unknown puzzle at the beginning of the story to the solution at the end, working step-by-step and clue-by-clue to find out what happened, or to identify a hidden villain. *Is that harmless old actor really Kodos the Executioner? How exactly does Edith Keeler die? Why does God need a starship?*

To extend the Sci-Fi theme a bit: I don't like *Star Wars*, although I guess that one way or another I've seen just about all of it, so I'm certainly aware of the mysterious elements throughout the story. *What did the hints imply about Luke's father, before the answer was provided? What exactly was the emperor up to before all was revealed? Who are Rey's parents?* It's all a mystery, cloaked in space battles and pseudo-religion Force-chatter and light-sabre fights. In *Dune*, which I do like, mysteries abound as the story unfolds, with questions that must be answered, followed by more questions. These stories may not be a typical "mystery story" – a murder or a jewel theft, with a ratiocinating detective or a lonely private eye making his way down the mean streets, but they are mysteries none-the-less.

Look at other genres: Romance books and films? Who is the tall dark stranger, and how can his background be discovered by the heroine, layer-by-layer, using detective-like methods? The Dirk Pitt books by Clive Cussler, along with books about Pitt's associates "co-authored" by others, are most definitely mysteries, although clothed in incredible world-shaking plots. (I've lost track of the Sherlockian references that

1

continually pop up in the adventures of Pitt and his friends.) The original James Bond books, before Bond became so currently complicated and far from his origins, were each labelled as *A James Bond Mystery*. Stephen King, known for his supernaturally-tinged masterpieces, writes stories that are full of mysteries, and sometimes with actual detectives, showing just how much influence that the early mystery writers like John D. MacDonald had on him. Television shows like *Lost* or *Dallas* or *How I Met Your Mother* respectively asked questions like *What is the Island?* or *Who shot J.R?* or *Who is the mother?* None of these were specifically mysteries, and they are draped in all sorts of other trappings – time-shifting castaways, oil-baron shenanigans, or a typical sit-com group's antics – but the plot points that drive the shows are no different than what would be found in a mystery story. It's the same for stories that are nominally for kids like *Gravity Falls* or *A Series of Unfortunate Events* ask *What's Grunkle Stan's story?* and *What's up with that ankle tattoo and the VFD?*

And liking mysteries is just a step away from pondering greater unknowns. It's a human trait, as shown in cultures around the world. No matter what place, and no matter what era, we find stories of ghosts, and monsters, and questions raised about the nature of death, and whether there is more going on all around us than can ever perceived. It was that way thousands of years ago, when mankind squatted in caves around fires, waiting for the dangerous night outside to pass, and it's that way right now, as we hide in our fragile constructs of civilization and wires and thin walls and fool ourselves into believing that we've pushed back the night. (Look around. We haven't. The night is here.)

The Victorian Era, with its rapid strides in scientific knowledge, brought science crashing up against superstition and religion and spiritualism. Scientists had been gaining an understanding of the workings of the universe, and our little speck of it, for decades – chemistry, physics, astronomy, and so on – but the means for spreading that knowledge and educating the ignorant was very limited. Many people still lived much as their ancestors had a hundred years before, or longer, close to the land and nature, and uninterested in explanations about weather patterns or how atoms and molecules interacted. It was much easier to rely on superstitious explanations for natural phenomena, in the same way that the ancient Greeks and Romans had created their gods to explain the sun and moon and lightning. In daylight, all might be rational and modern, but when the sun went down, it was much easier to believe that *there was something out there* . . . .

The Victorians were gradually becoming educated, but the skin of knowledge was still thin, which allowed such things as the fascination with death and the spiritualism crazes of the late 1800's to take such a strong hold, even luring in those who wouldn't be thought to be so gullible – Dr. Watson's *first* Literary Agent, Sir Arthur Conan Doyle, for example. It's common knowledge how he ruined his reputation during his later years by going over so whole-heartedly to the spiritualists. Additionally, he was shamed for his avid and naïve support of the Cottingley Fairies hoax. It can be taken as a fact that Mr. Sherlock Holmes, indirectly associated with Sir Arthur by way of Dr. John H. Watson's writings, was not happy that his reputation might be linked to such foolishness. Fortunately, there is ample evidence that Holmes forsook neither his beliefs nor his dignity.

Many people brought cases to Holmes throughout his career that seemed to have hints of the supernatural or the impossible about them. A few of these were published by way of the Literary Agent: "The Creeping Man" begins with the story of a girl's father who is seemingly changing into some sort of beast. "The Sussex Vampire" finds a woman accused of sucking the blood from her own baby. "The Adventure of Wisteria Lodge" has voodoo intruding into the supposedly modern English countryside. And of course there is *The Hound of the Baskervilles*, in which a curse from centuries past seems to have reawakened, killing a respected Dartmoor resident and threatening to destroy his heir as well.

These tales are part of the pitifully few sixty adventures that make up The Canon. It contains references to many other "Untold Cases", some of which have seemingly impossible aspects – a giant rat and a remarkable worm and a ship that vanishes into the mist. We can be sure that Holmes handled each of these with his customary excellence, and that any sort of supernatural explanation that might have been encountered along the way was debunked. For Holmes, the world was big enough, and there was no need for him to serve as a substitute Van Helsing.

Holmes's stated his rule, with minor variations, for getting to the bottom of seemingly impossible situations several times within The Canon:

- "How often have I said to you that when you have eliminated the impossible whatever remains, however improbable, must be the truth." (*The Sign of the Four*)
- "It is an old maxim of mine that when you have excluded the impossible, whatever remains, however improbable, must be the truth." ("The Beryl Coronet")
- "We must fall back upon the old axiom that when all other contingencies fail, whatever remains, however improbable, must be the truth. ("The Bruce-Partington Plans")

- "That process . . . starts upon the supposition that when you have eliminated all which is impossible, then whatever remains, however improbable, must be the truth." ("The Blanched Soldier")
- "That is the case as it appears to the police, and improbable as it is, all other explanations are more improbable still." ("Silver Blaze")

Thus, the first part of the process is actually *eliminating the impossible*. And to a man with a scientific and logical mind such as Sherlock Holmes, this means that the baseline is established that "*No ghosts need apply*." So Holmes explains to Watson at the beginning of "The Sussex Vampire", asking, "*. . . are we to give serious attention to such things? This agency stands flat-footed upon the ground, and there it must remain. The world is big enough for us.*"

If Holmes were to start every investigation with all possibilities as available options, including those beyond our human understanding, he would be finished before he even started. Imagine Holmes saying, "*This man may have been murdered – or he may have been possessed by a demon, overwhelming the limits of his body and simply causing him to expire. I'll sent you my bill.*" Think of the time wasted if Holmes were an occult detective, with nothing considered impossible, all possibilities on the table, and virtually nothing that could be eliminated in order to establish whatever truth remains. The Literary Agent, Sir Arthur Conan Doyle, was willing to accept ridiculous claims about spiritualism and fairies and all sorts of nonsense. Not so for Sherlock Holmes – and thank goodness.

That's not to say that Holmes was closed-minded. There were many intelligent men in the Victorian and Edwardian eras who mistakenly believed that all that *could* be discovered *had* been discovered – but Holmes wasn't one of them. There is an apocryphal tale where Charles H. Duell, the Commissioner of U.S. patent office in 1899, stated that "*everything that can be invented has been invented.*" In *A Study in Scarlet*, while discussing crime, Holmes himself paraphrased *Ecclesiastes* 1:9 when he told Watson, "*There is nothing new under the sun. It has all been done before.*" And yet, with a curious scientific mind and an exceptional intelligence, Holmes would have certainly realized that there *was* more to be discovered, and that things are always going on around us that are beyond what we can necessarily perceive or understand – invisible forces and patterns of interaction on a grand scale beyond our comprehension. In relation to his own work, Holmes explained:

*". . . life is infinitely stranger than anything which the mind of man could invent. We would not dare to conceive the things which are really mere commonplaces of existence. If we could fly out of that window hand in hand, hover over this great city, gently remove the roofs, and peep in at the queer things which are going on, the strange coincidences, the plannings, the cross-purposes, the wonderful chains of events, working through generations, and leading to the most* outrè *results, it would make all fiction with its conventionalities and foreseen conclusions most stale and unprofitable."*

Thus, in spite of his statements that *"[t]here is nothing new under the sun"* or *"the world is big enough"*, Sherlock Holmes would have been open-minded enough to realize that – with our limited perspectives – the impossible isn't always easily eliminated when identifying the truthful improbable.

Sometime in late 2016, when these MX anthologies were showing signs of continued and increasing success, it was time to determine what the theme would be for the Fall 2017 collection. When I had the idea for a new Holmes anthology in early 2015, it was originally planned to be a single book of a dozen or so new Holmes adventures, probably published as a paperback. By the fall of that year, it had grown to three massive simultaneous hardcovers with sixty-three new adventures, the largest collection of its kind ever – until we surpassed that in the spring of 2019 with sixty-six stories, and a total of nearly four-hundred.

Initially, in 2015, I thought that it would be a one-time event. But then people wanted to know when the *next* book would appear, and authors – both those in the original collection and others who hadn't been – wanted to contribute more stories. So of course the original plan was amended, and it became an ongoing series.

It was announced that a fourth volume would be published in the Spring of 2016, *Part IV: 2016 Annual* – with the word *"Annual"* confidently assuming that it would be a yearly event. But there was such great interest by participating authors that I realized a Fall collection in that same year was necessary, beginning a pattern of two collections per year that has continued to the present – an *"Annual"* in the spring and a themed set in the autumn. And so I announced and began to receive stories for *Part V: Christmas Adventures*, published later in 2016.

These types of books have to be planned with plenty of advance notice for authors to actually write the stories. So halfway through 2016, the book for the following Spring, *Part XVI: 2017 Annual*, was announced,

5

and very soon it was necessary to figure out what the Fall 2017 collection's theme would be.

That came to me while I was mowing my yard, where I do some of my best thinking. We have 2/3's of an acre, and I still have a push-mower, so that's good for a couple of hours of intense perspiration and pondering. And on that day, I had only been mowing for five or ten minutes when the idea of *Eliminate the Impossible* popped into my mind.

That title, *Eliminate the Impossible*, had been used before by Alistair Duncan for an MX book in 2010, something of a catch-all examination of Holmes in both page and screen. (In fact, this was the first Sherlockian title published by MX, and look what that led to!) This new anthology, however, would feature stories wherein Holmes's cases initially seemed to have supernatural or impossible aspects, but would absolutely have to have rational explanations – *"No ghosts need apply."* And yet, after the rational solution was explained and the case resolved, it would be acceptable if there was perhaps a hint that something more was going on beyond Our Heroes' understanding. I explained by paraphrasing Hamlet when soliciting stories from the various authors: *"There are more things in heaven and earth, [Watson], Than are dreamt of in your philosophy."* For instance, after the culprit is revealed, and Holmes and Watson could be departing, the investigation complete. Watson might look back and see . . . *something impossible.*

> *"Holmes,"* (he might say.) *"Do you see it?"*
> *"It is nothing, Watson,"* (would be Holmes's reply.)
> *"Mist. A mere trick of the light."*
> *"But still . . . ."*

And so the rational ending would be preserved, but the idea that there are more things in heaven and earth would be possible as well.

When I had the idea for the theme of the first MX collection of this sort, 2017's *Eliminate the Impossible*, I wasn't sure how it would go. I received a bit of sarcastic push-back from one person who referred to this as a "Scooby Doo book". I was disappointed at his reaction, and I'm glad to report that the success of both simultaneous volumes of *Eliminate the Impossible* proved that his assessment was incorrect.

Still, a few people were surprised that I would encourage a book of this sort. They shouldn't have been. I make it very clear that I'm a strict Holmesian traditionalist. I want to read more and more Canonical-type stories about Holmes and Watson – and nothing whatsoever never ever in any form about *"Sherlock and John"*! – with no parodies or anachronisms or non-heroic behaviours. That's what I collect, read, chronologicize, write, and edit, and also what encourage in others as well. There have been many times when I've started reading a new Holmes story, only to realize that, no matter how authentic the first part is, the end has veered off into one-hundred-percent no-coming-back supernatural territory – Holmes is battling a real monster, or facing a full-fledged vampire or wolfman, or perhaps a brain-eating fungus from another planet. There is a misguided belief that, just because someone wishes it to be so, Holmes can be plugged in anywhere like Doctor Who, or that he's is interchangeable with Abraham Van Helsing – and he most definitely is not.

As someone who has collected, read, and chronologicized literally thousands of Canonical Holmes adventures for almost forty-five years – and that certainly passed quickly! – I'm dismayed when this happens. As I make notes for each story to be listed in the massive overall Canon and Pastiche chronology that I've constructed over the last quarter-century, I generally indicate when a story has included "incorrect" statements or segments, and I include notes identifying those parts that were really and truly written by Watson, as compared with paragraphs or pages or chapters that were clearly composed and added by some later editor who has taken Watson's notes and either changed parts, or stuck in completely fictional middles and endings to fulfil his or her own agenda. Sometimes the story goes so far off into the weeds that even pulled-out pieces of it can't be judged as authentically Watsonian, and the whole thing is lost.

But the stories of *Eliminate the Impossible* – and now this collection as well – are fully traditional in the best Canonical way.

The idea of a story where Holmes and Watson were presented with circumstances that initially seemed supernatural but ended up having a rational solution was not new, and I can claim no originality for thinking of it. Before those volumes in the ongoing MX series appeared in late 2017 – *Eliminate the Impossible Part VII (1880-1891)* and *Part VIII (1892-1905)* – there were many other tales of that type. In my foreword to *Eliminate the Impossible,* I listed a number of them, and since then there have been more. As I explained then, there are far too many stories of that type to catalogue in this essay . . . but here are some of them for friends of Mr. Holmes to locate.

First, I have to recommend the stories in *Eliminate the Impossible,* Parts VII and VIII of this ongoing anthology series. They are some of the finest Sherlockian adventures to be found, and *Publishers Weekly* wrote of the two volumes: "*Sherlockians eager for faithful-to-the-canon plots and characters will be delighted*" and "*The imagination of the contributors in coming up with variations on the volume's theme is matched by their ingenious resolutions.*" Other MX anthologies in this series also have stories along these lines, although they are mixed in with more general Canonical adventures, in the way that "The Sussex Vampire" and "The Creeping Man" were included with Holmes's other non-*outrè* investigations.

While assembling the three-volume set that immediately preceded this current collection, the *Spring 2019 Annual*, containing general Canonical tales in *Part XIII: (1881-1890)*, *Part XIV (1891-1897)*, and *Part XV (1898-1917)*, I received a number of stories that could have just as easily fit into this current collection. I considered whether I should contact the contributors and see if they wished to hold those stories for publication in this Fall 2019 collection, *Whatever Remains . . . Must Be the Truth* (Parts XVI, XVII, and XVIII), but in the end decided to go ahead and use them in Parts XIII, XIV, and XV instead. And I'm glad that I did, because the inclusion of those narratives in the Spring 2019 books made for a really excellent set of adventures.

Among the many other places that one can find Holmes stories – some full-on supernatural and some that fit my own requirements – are *The Irregular Casebook of Sherlock Holmes* by Ron Weighell (2000), *Ghosts in Baker Street* (2006), the Lovecraftian-themed *Shadows Over Baker Street* (2003), and the ongoing *Gaslight* series edited by Charles Prepolec and J.R. Campbell. These titles include, *Gaslight Grimoire* (2008), *Gaslight Grotesque* (2009), *Gaslight Arcanum* (2011), and most recently *Gaslight Gothic* (2018). John Linwood Grant is editing a forthcoming book in which Holmes will team with noted occult detectives, such as Thomas Carnacki, or tangentially with Alton Peake, an occult investigator of my own invention who has appeared in some of my Holmes narratives, although always off-screen.

Holmes battled the supposedly supernatural in countless old radio shows, including "The Limping Ghost" (September 1945), "The Stuttering Ghost" (October 1946), "The Bleeding Chandelier" (June 1948), "The Haunting of Sherlock Holmes" (May 1946), and "The Uddington Witch" (October 1948). An especially good radio episode with supernatural overtones was "The Haunted Bagpipes" by Edith Meiser, (February 1947), later presented in comic form as illustrated by Frank Giacoia, and then again adapted for print by Carla Coupe in *Sherlock Holmes Mystery Magazine* (Vol. 2, No. 1, 2011)

And of course, one mustn't forget the six truly amazing radio episodes of John Taylor's *The Uncovered Casebook of Sherlock Holmes* (1993), and then published soon after as a very fine companion book. Then there's George Mann's audio drama "The Reification of Hans Gerber"

(2011), later novelized as part of *Sherlock Holmes: The Will of the Dead* (2013).

In addition to numerous radio broadcasts, there were similar "impossible" films with Holmes facing something with other-worldly overtones, including *The Scarlet Claw* (1944) and *Sherlock Holmes* (2009). Television episodes have tackled this type of story. The old 1950's television show *Sherlock Holmes* with Ronald Howard had "The Belligerent Ghost", "The Haunted Gainsborough", and "The Laughing Mummy". The show was rebooted in 1980 with Geoffrey Whitehead as Holmes, and had an episode called "The Other Ghost".

In 2002, Matt Frewer starred as Holmes in the supernatural-feeling *The Case of the Whitechapel Vampire*. Nearly a decade earlier, Jeremy Brett performed in a pastiche that was loosely tied to "The Sussex Vampire" entitled *The Last Vampyre* (1993). The supernatural elements were greatly played up in that film, although it had a rational ending. Brett's performance was extremely painful to watch, as at that point he had foisted his own personal illnesses – both mental and physical – so heavily onto his portrayal of Holmes and there was really nothing of Holmes left, but other aspects of the film were tolerable, if one looks past the acting and accepts that this was a separate story entirely from "The Sussex Vampire".

Brett's tenure as Holmes limped to an end the following year, and since that time, except for a few stand-alone films – three more Matt Frewer adaptations, a curiously odd and unpleasant version of *The Hound of the Baskervilles* (2002) starring Richard Roxburgh, a mild effort starring Jonathan Pryce called *Sherlock Holmes and the Baker Street Irregulars* (2007), and Rupert Everett's emotionless Holmes in *The Case of the Silk Stocking* (2007) – there have been no other versions of Sherlock Holmes on television whatsoever. (It's hoped that Holmes will return to television sooner rather than later, since it's been a very long time since 1994, when the last Holmes series was on television – not counting a few Russian efforts – and it's sure that when he does, a few seemingly supernatural stories will certainly be included as part of the line-up.)

In print, there are many other examples of this type of story. From the massive list of similarly themed fan-fictions, one might choose "The Mottled Eyes", "The Case of the Vengeful Ghost", "The Japanese Ghost", "The Adventure of the Grasping Ghost", "Sherlock Holmes and the Seven Ghosts", "The Adventure of the Haunting Bride", "The Problem of the Phantom Prowler", *That Whiter Host*, or "The Vampire's Kiss". There are countless novels, such as the six short works by Kel Richards, or Val Andrews' *The Longacre Vampire*, or *Draco, Draconis* by Spencer Brett and David Dorian. One shouldn't ignore the narratives brought to us by

Sam Siciliano, narrated by Holmes's annoying cousin Dr. Henry Vernier, all featuring supposedly supernatural encounters. Check out Bonnie MacBird's second Holmes adventure, *Unquiet Spirits*, and David Wilson's *Sherlock Holmes and the Case of the Edinburgh Haunting*. Then there are several by David Stuart Davies, including *The Devil's Promise*, *The Shadow of the Rat*, and *The Scroll of the Dead*. One can read Carol Buggé's *The Haunting of Torre Abbey* and Randall Collins' *The Case of the Philosopher's Ring*, and the different sequels to *The Hound*, including Rick Boyer's most amazing *The Giant Rat of Sumatra*, Teresa Collard's *The Baskerville Inheritance*, and Kelvin Jones' *The Baskerville Papers*.

Holmes has battled Count Dracula in too many encounters to list, but in almost every one of them, he finds himself ridiculously facing a real undead Transylvanian vampire who can change into a bat. Often, Holmes is simply inserted into the Van Helsing role within the plot of the original *Dracula* story. Although I own each of these, I've always ignored them, as the *real* historical Holmes would never encounter an *imaginary* creature such as this. The one exception so far that I've enjoyed and been able to finish has been Mark Latham's remarkable *A Betrayal in Blood*– finally, a Holmes-Dracula encounter that I can highly recommend.

A list of this sort is really too long to compile, and this shouldn't be taken as anywhere close to the last word. There are numerous supposedly impossible circumstances or supernatural encounters of one sort or another contained in many Holmes collections, tucked in with the more "normal" cases, and these are but a few of them:

- "The Deptford Horror", *The Exploits of Sherlock Holmes* – Adrian Conan Doyle and John Dickson Carr
- "The Shadows on the Lawn", *The New Adventures of Sherlock Holmes* – Barry Jones
- "The Adventure of the Talking Ghost", *Alias Simon Hawkes* – Philip J. Carraher
- "Lord Garnett's Skulls", *The MX Book of New Sherlock Holmes Stories – Part II: 1890-1895* – J.R. Campbell
- "The Bramley Court Devil", *The Adventures of the Second Mrs. Watson* – Michael Mallory
- "The Ghost of Gordon Square", *The Chemical Adventures of Sherlock Holmes* – Thomas G. Waddell and Thomas R. Rybolt
- "The Ghost of Christmas Past", *The Strand Magazine* No. 23 – David Stuart Davies

- "The Mystery at Kerritt's Rood" *Sherlock Holmes: Tangled Skeins* – David Marcum
- "The Devil of the Deverills", *Sherlock Holmes: Before Baker Street* – S.F. Bennett
- "The Case of the Devil's Voice", *The Curious Adventures of Sherlock Holmes in Japan* – Dale Furutani
- "The Adventure of the Haunted Hotel", *The Untold Adventures of Sherlock Holmes* – Luke Benjamen Kuhns
- "The Death Fetch", *The Game is Afoot* – Darrell Schweitzer
- "The Yellow Star of Cairo", *The MX Book of New Sherlock Holmes Stories – Part XIII: 2019 Annual (1881-1890)* – Tim Gambrell
- "The Adventure of the Devil's Father", *The Great Detective: His Further Adventures* – Morris Hershman
- "The Horned God", *The MX Book of New Sherlock Holmes Stories – Part X: 2018 Annual (1896-1916)* – Kelvin Jones
- "The Dowser's Discovery", *The Strand Magazine* No. 58 – David Marcum
- "The Phantom Gunhorse", *Sherlock Holmes: The Soldier's Daughter* – Malcolm Knott
- "The Adventure of the Winterhall Monster", *The MX Book of New Sherlock Holmes Stories – Part XIII: 2019 Annual (1881-1890)* – Tracy Revels
- "The Case of Hodgson's Ghost", *The Oriental Casebook of Sherlock Holmes* – Ted Riccardi
- "The Case of the Haunted Chateau", *The MX Book of New Sherlock Holmes Stories – Part XV: 2019 Annual (1898-1917)* – Leslie Charteris and Denis Green
- "A Ballad of the White Plague", *The Confidential Casebook of Sherlock Holmes* – P.C. Hodgel
- "The Adventure of the Dark Tower", *The MX Book of New Sherlock Holmes Stories – Part III: 1896-1929* – Peter K. Andersson
- "The Adventure of the Field Theorems", *Sherlock Holmes In Orbit* – Vonda N. McIntyre
- "The Adventure of Urquhart Manse", *The MX Book of New Sherlock Holmes Stories – Part I: 1881-1889* – Will Thomas
- "The Haunting of Sutton House", *The Papers of Sherlock Holmes Vol. I* – David Marcum

- "The Stolen Relic", *The MX Book of New Sherlock Holmes Stories – Part V: Christmas Adventures* – David Marcum
- "The Chamber of Sorrow Mystery", *The Outstanding Mysteries of Sherlock Holmes* – Gerard Kelly
- The Case of the Vampire's Mark", *Murder in Baker Street* – Bill Crider
- "The Case of the Phantom Chambermaid", *The Execution of Sherlock Holmes* – Donald Thomas
- "The Ululation of Wolves", *The MX Book of New Sherlock Holmes Stories – Part I: 1881-1889* – Steve Mountain
- "The Night in the Elizabethan Concert Hall in the Very Heart of London" *Traveling With Sherlock Holmes and Dr. Watson* – Herman Anthony Litzinger
- "The Adventure of the Phantom Coachman", *The MX Book of New Sherlock Holmes Stories – Part IV: 2016 Annual* – Arthur Hall
- "The Strange Case of the Voodoo Priestess", *Sherlock Holmes: The Hidden Years* – Carole Buggé
- "A Dormitory Haunting", *The Associates of Sherlock Holmes* – Jaine Fenn
- "The Night In The Burial Vault Under The Sanitarium At Soames Meadow", *Traveling With Sherlock Holmes and Dr. Watson* – Herman Anthony Litzinger
- "The Witch of Greenwich", *My Sherlock Holmes* – Gerald Dole
- "The Adventure of Jackthorn Circle", *Sherlock Holmes: Mysteries of the Victorian Era* – Rock DiLisio
- "The Phantom of the Barbary Coast", *Sherlock Holmes in Orbit* – Frank M. Robinson
- "Sherlock Holmes, Dragon Slayer", *Resurrected Holmes* – Darrell Schweitzer
- "The Adventure of the Towne Manor Haunting", *Sherlock Holmes, Consulting Detective: Volume III* – Andrew Salmon
- "The Mysterious Mr. Rim", *The MX Book of New Sherlock Holmes Stories – Part XV: 2019 Annual (1898-1917)* – Maurice Barkley
- "The Haunted House", *The Singular Adventures of Mr. Sherlock Holmes* – Alan Stockwell,
- "The Dorset Witch", *Sherlock Holmes: The Soldier's Daughter* – Malcolm Knott

12

- "The Devil's Painting", *The MX Book of New Sherlock Holmes Stories – Part XV: 2019 Annual (1898-1917)* – Kelvin I. Jones
- "The Adventure of the Phantom Coachman", *The MX Book of New Sherlock Holmes Stories – Part IV: 2016 Annual* – Arthur Hall

In the spring of 2018, it was time once again to start planning for the 2019 MX anthologies, and again while I was mowing – in pretty much the same spot, so there must be something buried there that radiates some kind of beneficial mind-influencing waves – I had the idea for these current books. If *Eliminate the Impossible* had been so successful, why not do it again? And what else could it be called but a variation from the same Holmesian maxim?

The three companion volumes that make up *Whatever Remains . . . Must Be the Truth*, like those in *Eliminate the Impossible*, contain stories where Holmes faces ghosts and mythological creatures, impossible circumstances and curses, possessions and prophecies, Some begin with the impossible element defined from the beginning, while others progress for quite a while as "normal" cases before the twist is revealed. Some are overt encounters with supposed monsters or phantoms, while others are more subtle, pondering the nature of existence and the vast patterns around us that we cannot perceive. As with all Holmes adventures, this collection represents one of the great enjoyments of reading about The Great Detective – the reader never knows where each tale will lead. And while each of the adventures in these volumes is categorized by Holmes *eliminating* the impossible to obtain, however improbable, the truth, the various impossibilities contained within these covers are presented in an incredibly varied and exciting manner. I'm certain that you will enjoy all of them.

As always, I want to thank with all my heart my patient and wonderful wife of thirty-one years (as of this writing,) Rebecca, and our amazing son and my friend, Dan. I love you both, and you are everything to me!

Also, I can't ever express enough gratitude for all of the contributors who have donated their time and royalties to this ongoing project. I'm constantly amazed at the incredible stories that you send, and I'm so glad to have gotten to know all of you through this process. It's an undeniable fact that Sherlock Holmes authors are the *best* people!

The contributors of these stories have donated their royalties for this project to support the Stepping Stones School for special needs children, located at Undershaw, one of Sir Arthur Conan Doyle's former homes. As

13

of this writing, these MX anthologies have raised over $50,000 for the school, and of even more importance, they have helped raise awareness about the school all over the world. These books are making a real difference to the school, and the participation of both contributors and purchasers is most appreciated.

Next is that group that exchanges emails with me when we have the time – and time is a valuable commodity these days! I don't get to write as often as I'd like, but I really enjoy catching up when we get the chance: Derrick Belanger, Bob Byrne, Mark Mower, Denis Smith, Tom Turley, Dan Victor, and Marcia Wilson.

A special shout-out to Tracy Revels, Arthur Hall, and Kelvin Jones, who joined me in writing multiple stories for these volumes. When the submission deadline was fast approaching, I wrote to Tracy, who had written one story at that time for this set, and asked if she'd be interested in writing others to appear in the companion volumes. She took it as a challenge and wrote two more amazing tales in just a week or so. Arthur consistently pulls great tales from The Tin Dispatch Box, and I'm glad that they end up here. And I was a fan of Kelvin's work back in the 1980's, so I'm very happy that he's a part of these books.

There is a group of special people who have stepped up and supported this and a number of other projects over and over again with a lot of contributions. They are the best and I can't express how valued they are: Larry Albert, Hugh Ashton, Derrick Belanger, Deanna Baran, S.F. Bennett, Nick Cardillo, Jayantika Ganguly, Paul Gilbert, Dick Gillman, Arthur Hall, Stephen Herczeg, Mike Hogan, Craig Janacek, Will Murray, Tracy Revels, Roger Riccard, Geri Schear, Robert Stapleton, Subbu Subramanian, Tim Symonds, Kevin Thornton, and Marcy Wilson.

I also want to thank the people who wrote forewords to the books:

- Kareem Abdul-Jabbar – Along with your fame as a sportsman, you are a necessary, noted, and effective voice for improving society. And on top of that, you're a Sherlockian too! Thank you for helping to round out our understanding of Mycroft Holmes, and for participating in these books as well!
- Roger Johnson – It seems like a lifetime ago when I sent a copy of my first book to Roger, because it really mattered to me that he review it. He had never heard of me, but he was most gracious, and we began to email one another. I've been incredibly fortunate to have since met him and his wonderful wife, Jean Upton, several times in person during my three Holmes Pilgrimages to England. Roger always takes time to answer my questions and to

participate in and promote various projects, and he and Jean were very gracious to host me for several days during part of my second Holmes Pilgrimage to England in 2015. In so many ways, Roger, I can't thank you enough, and I can't imagine these books without you.

- Steve Emecz is always positive, and he is always supportive of every idea that I pitch. It's been my great good fortune to cross your path – it changed my life, and let me play in this Sherlockian Sandbox in a way that would have never happened otherwise. Thank you for every opportunity!

- Brian Belanger – Just a few days before I wrote this, I received a series of new cover designs from Brian for a forthcoming three-volume set that I edited, *The Further Adventures of Sherlock Holmes – The Complete Jim French Imagination Theatre Scripts*. What Brian sent was typical – excellent, brilliant, and with a great understanding of what needed to be conveyed. He's very talented, and very willing to work to get it right, instead of simply knocking something out or insisting that it be *his* vision. I'm very glad that he's the cover designer for these and other projects that we assembled together.

And last but certainly *not* least, **Sir Arthur Conan Doyle**: Author, doctor, adventurer, and the Founder of the Sherlockian Feast. Present in spirit, and honored by all of us here.

As always, this collection has been a labor of love by both the participants and myself. As I've explained before, once again everyone did their sincerest best to produce an anthology that truly represents why Holmes and Watson have been so popular for so long. These are just more tiny threads woven into the ongoing Great Holmes Tapestry, continuing to grow and grow, for there can *never* be enough stories about the man whom Watson described as *"the best and wisest . . . whom I have ever known."*

David Marcum
*August 7th, 2019*
*The 167th Birthday of Dr. John H. Watson*

*Questions, comments, or story submissions*
*may be addressed to David Marcum at*
*thepapersofsherlockholmes@gmail.com*

15

# Sherlock, Mycroft, and Me
## by Kareem Abdul-Jabbar

If you're reading this, there's nothing new that I can tell you about being passionate about Sherlock Holmes. You wouldn't have bought this book unless you shared that passion. It is a robust passion shared by hundreds of millions of fans around the world. There are over two-hundred-and-fifty international societies dedicated to the Holmes legacy. It is a testament to fans' loyalty that they persist in gobbling up new Holmes stories by literary interlopers such as myself, despite Sir Conan Doyle's own dismissive attitude toward Holmes, even to the point of killing him off in "The Final Problem". Explained Doyle: "*I have had such an overdose of him that I feel towards him as I do towards* paté de foie gras, *of which I once ate too much, so that the name of it gives me a sickly feeling to this day.*"

Fortunately, we don't share that feeling.

For eight years, Doyle fought against public outrage at Holmes' "death" and intense pressure to produce another story. And ever since he brought Holmes back, the character has become immortal. I am delighted to be one of the many authors who have contributed to his immortality through my three novels and graphic novel featuring Mycroft Holmes, Sherlock's smarter brother.

My love of the genre was inspired by watching Basil Rathbone and Nigel Bruce playing Holmes and Watson in the movies when I was a child. Later, when I was traveling so much as a professional basketball player, I read all the Holmes stories on the long plane flights. This in turn led me reading other mystery writers, which I continue to do today.

Why then did I choose to write about Mycroft rather than Sherlock? Part of the reason is that the stories barely mention Mycroft, except to say that he was smarter and less disciplined than Sherlock. This gave me leeway to create from practically nothing the character I wanted to write about. One of the things I like about mysteries is that they are, at their core, morality tales in which characters must grapple with choices of right and wrong. The best mystery writers offer layered detectives who struggle and who try to restore justice and order to the chaos created by murder. For me, that chaos was symbolic of the endemic injustice in society, so I wanted a detective who was willing to face those injustices head-on with courage and intelligence.

Sherlock is a bit of an anomaly in that he uses his remarkable abilities to quench his own intellectual thirst. If someone else benefits, that's just a happy byproduct. Mycroft, on the other hand, uses his abilities to further justice and to benefit society. Sherlock is more like the amoral Sam Spade in Hammett's *The Maltese Falcon*, whose motivation for solving the case is that it would be "bad for business" not to. Mycroft is more like Marlowe in Raymond Chandler's novels or Ross Macdonald's Lew Archer. They also doggedly pursue the truth, but they do so out of a commitment to justice. Although I am entertained by brilliant loners like Holmes and Spade, I admire characters like Mycroft and Marlowe who want to better their communities.

In both my novels and graphic novel, I write about the young Mycroft. Basically, it's a superhero origin story about how he came to hone his skills and why he chose to use them to make the world a better place for everyone. Maybe it's my own origin story: Honing my basketball skills and using my fame as a platform to better society. And when the basketball days were done, honing my writing skills to tell stories about a young genius who time and time again faces moral crossroads – and each time chooses the right path.

It's not just that he chooses the right path, but that he uses rational thinking to do so. We are in an Age of De-enlightenment, when politicians openly lie because they know their followers don't care about the truth. We have smart phones, the most powerful educational tool in the history of the human race, and we use it send photos of our food rather than fact-check our leaders who control our economic and social futures. The Holmes brothers represent logic, rational thinking, keen observation – all the tools people need to seize control of their lives and improve their communities and country. They represent us at our intellectual best and present a benchmark that we should all strive toward.

More important, they're entertaining and exciting.

We all have our personal reasons for loving the stories of Sherlock Holmes. Whatever yours are, Dear Reader, you need only to turn the page with giddy anticipation because on the other side, the game will be afoot.

Kareem Abdul-Jabbar
*June 2019*

# All Supernatural or Preternatural Agencies are Ruled Out As a Matter of Course
## by Roger Johnson

In his preface to the 1928 anthology *Best Detective Stories of the Year* (London: Faber & Faber), Mgr. Ronald A. Knox wrote:

> *I laid down long ago certain main rules, which I reproduce here with a certain amount of commentary; not all critics will be agreed as to their universality or as to their general importance, but I think most detective "fans" will recognize that these principles, or something like them, are necessary to the full enjoyment of a detective story. I say "the full enjoyment"; we cannot expect complete conformity from all writers, and indeed some of the stories selected in this very volume transgress the rules noticeably. Let them stand for what they are worth.*

The second rule – "All supernatural or preternatural agencies are ruled out as a matter of course" – seems obvious, though it had already been successfully broken by William Hope Hodgson in his tales of *Carnacki the Ghost-Finder,* who applies proper detective methods to determine whether a supposed haunting is genuine or not. [1] The rule would be broken again, of course, most notably, perhaps, by John Dickson Carr in some excellent short stories and an outstanding novel, *The Burning Court.*

Knox's commentary on this particular rule reads in full:

> *All supernatural or praeternatural agencies are ruled out as a matter of course. To solve a detective problem by such means would be like winning a race on the river by the use of a concealed motor-engine. And here I venture to think there is a limitation about Mr. Chesterton's Father Brown stories. He nearly always tries to put us off the scent by suggesting that the crime must have been done by magic; and we know that he is too good a sportsman to fall back upon such a solution. Consequently, although we seldom guess the answer*

18

*to his riddles, we usually miss the thrill of having suspected the wrong person."*

That dig at G.K. Chesterton's most famous contribution to the genre is rather curious. It suggests that the identification of the culprit is the only point of a detective story. Mgr. Knox may have believed it,[2] and the term "whodunnit" unfortunately perpetuates that blinkered idea, but it ignores character, atmosphere and two of the essential puzzles posed by Chesterton and solved by Father Brown. To the question of *"Who?"* we should add *"Why?"* and – most important in this context, though dismissed by Knox as mere riddles to be guessed – *"How?"*

Like Sherlock Holmes in at least three indisputable Canonical exploits, the little priest is faced with situations that appear to be impossible and therefore the work of unearthly powers. But he knows, and we know, that magic has no place here: A human, or at least a natural, agency is at work. Despite Knox's censure, we are not deprived of *"the thrill of having suspected the wrong person", and* we have the additional excitement of trying to work out how the apparently impossible was achieved.

We know too that Sherlock Holmes was there before Father Brown. The tradition established by Arthur Conan Doyle in *The Hound of the Baskervilles*, "The Devil's Foot", and "The Sussex Vampire" lives and flourishes, as this collection proves!

Roger Johnson, BSI, ASH
Editor: *The Sherlock Holmes Journal*
*August 2019*

## NOTES

1 – One of Carnacki's investigations, a very neat little detective story called "The Find", doesn't even hint at the supernatural.

2 – His own mystery novels are rarely read these days, unlike the Father Brown stories.

# Stories, Stepping Stones,
# and the Conan Doyle Legacy
## by Steve Emecz

Undershaw
*Circa 1900*

The MX Book of New Sherlock Holmes Stories has now raised over $50,000 for Stepping Stones School for children with learning disabilities and is by far the largest Sherlock Holmes collection in the world - by several measures, stories, authors, pages and positive reviews from the critics. *Publishers Weekly* has been reviewing since Volume VI and we have had a record ten straight great reviews. Here are some of their best comments:

> *"This is more catnip for fans of stories faithful to Conan Doyle's originals"* (Part XIII)

> *"This is an essential volume for Sherlock Holmes fans"* (Part XI)

*"The imagination of the contributors in coming up with variations on the volume's theme is matched by their ingenious resolutions"* (Part VIII)

MX Publishing is a social enterprise – all the staff, including me, are volunteers with day jobs. The collection would not be possible without the creator and editor, David Marcum, who is rightly cited multiple times by *Publishers Weekly* and others as probably the most accomplished Sherlockian editor ever.

In addition to Stepping Stones School, our main program that we support is the Happy Life Children's Home in Kenya. My wife Sharon and I are on our way in December for our seventh Christmas in a row at Happy Life. It's a wonderful project that has saved the lives of over 600 babies. You can read all about the project in the second edition of the book *The Happy Life Story.*

Our support of both of these projects is possible through the publishing of Sherlock Holmes books, which we have now been doing for a decade. You can find out more information about the Stepping Stones School at:

You can find out more information
about the Stepping Stones School at:

*www.steppingstones.org.uk*

and Happy Life at:

*www.happylifechildrenshomes.com*

You can find out more about MX Publishing
and reach out to us through our website at:

*www.mxpublishing.com*

Steve Emecz
*August 2019*
Twitter: *@steveemecz*
LinkedIn: *https://www.linkedin.com/in/emecz/*

**Undershaw**
*September 9, 2016*
*Grand Opening of the Stepping Stones School*
*(Photograph courtesy of Roger Johnson)*

The Doyle Room at Stepping Stones, Undershaw
*Partially funded through royalties from*
The MX Book of New Sherlock Holmes Stories

23

**Sherlock Holmes** (1854-1957) was born in Yorkshire, England, on 6 January, 1854. In the mid-1870's, he moved to 24 Montague Street, London, where he established himself as the world's first Consulting Detective. After meeting Dr. John H. Watson in early 1881, he and Watson moved to rooms at 221b Baker Street, where his reputation as the world's greatest detective grew for several decades. He was presumed to have died battling noted criminal Professor James Moriarty on 4 May, 1891, but he returned to London on 5 April, 1894, resuming his consulting practice in Baker Street. Retiring to the Sussex coast near Beachy Head in October 1903, he continued to be associated in various private and government investigations while giving the impression of being a reclusive apiarist. He was very involved in the events encompassing World War I, and to a lesser degree those of World War II. He passed away peacefully upon the cliffs above his Sussex home on his 103rd birthday, 6 January, 1957.

**Dr. John Hamish Watson** (1852-1929) was born in Stranraer, Scotland on 7 August, 1852. In 1878, he took his Doctor of Medicine Degree from the University of London, and later joined the army as a surgeon. Wounded at the Battle of Maiwand in Afghanistan (27 July, 1880), he returned to London late that same year. On New Year's Day, 1881, he was introduced to Sherlock Holmes in the chemical laboratory at Barts. Agreeing to share rooms with Holmes in Baker Street, Watson became invaluable to Holmes's consulting detective practice. Watson was married and widowed three times, and from the late 1880's onward, in addition to his participation in Holmes's investigations and his medical practice, he chronicled Holmes's adventures, with the assistance of his literary agent, Sir Arthur Conan Doyle, in a series of popular narratives, most of which were first published in *The Strand* magazine. Watson's later years were spent preparing a vast number of his notes of Holmes's cases for future publication. Following a final important investigation with Holmes, Watson contracted pneumonia and passed away on 24 July, 1929.

*Photos of Sherlock Holmes and Dr. John H. Watson courtesy of Roger Johnson*

# The MX Book
## of
## New Sherlock Holmes Stories
## Part XVIII:
## Whatever Remains . . .
## Must Be the Truth
## (1899-1925)

# The Adventure of the Lighthouse on the Moor
## by Christopher James

It rose up through the mist
like a raised finger, hushing the wind,
its light like the glint of a wedding ring.
Holmes pushed open the door,
which gave easily to the dark.
Inside, there were two grey ulsters,
a dog lead, and a Davy lamp.
We spiralled up and found a room
with a fire already lit, a fresh loaf,
two hammocks, and a pan of soup,
miraculously hot. The pair of us
drank greedily. We found wine,
a store of a thousand candles,
and enough tobacco to last a year.
Through the window, we watched
the moor spool into nothing.
We saw spook-lights, hell-hounds,
and corpse-candles, the ghosts
of legionnaires, and lead miners
stumbling through the heather.
Turning in, we found a copy of
*The Lighthouse Keeper's Handbook*
and a note in the flap which read:
*Welcome. You are the keepers now.*
*The door only opens from the outside.*

# The Witch of Ellenby
## by Thomas A. Burns, Jr.

"**I** am afraid, Watson, that I shall have to go."

"Go, Holmes? Go where?"

"To Cumberland. To the Lakes."

I have said previously that my friend Sherlock Holmes was remarkably unappreciative of the beauties of nature, preferring instead entrenchment in London, vigilant as a spider in its web, anticipating the slightest vibration along its strands. Neither did he believe in the venerable English tradition of holidays, because going on holiday meant absconding from one's work, and for Holmes, to work was to live.

The morning of May 1, 1899 had dawned gloriously in London – the slight predawn chill in the air was rapidly expunged by the rising sun, giving promise to the notion that the severities of the English winter were but a memory at last. It was the perfect time to turn one's thoughts to the countryside, and where to better than the Lake District, which quite possibly harbours the most stunningly beautiful landscape in all of England. However, knowing Holmes as I did, I strongly suspected that this proposed excursion had a more sombre purpose than mere tourism.

"See what you make of this, Watson," Holmes said, tossing me an envelope that had arrived in the first morning post.

In the early days of my association with Holmes, I would have immediately removed the letter from the envelope and begun reading, but now, I took time for scrutiny. The envelope was of rich parchment, ecru in colour. A high rag content was indicated by the strands I could see when I held it to the window. If further proof of the high station of the sender was necessary, it was provided by the coat-of-arms embossed in the upper left-hand corner – gules, a pale *Or* with three *torteaux*. As I am not a trained herald, I would need *Burke's* to identify the owner, or I could simply look at the sender's name. The envelope was addressed in black ink (a woman's hand) to *Sherlock Holmes, Esq., 221b Baker Street, NW1*.

I removed and unfolded the several sheets of paper inside. The top sheet was written in strong male copperplate hand. I read:

*35, George's Street, Hanover Square, May 1, 1899*

*Re: Witchcraft*

*My Dear Mr. Holmes:*

*This letter is to assure you that you may rely absolutely upon the account which accompanies it, written by our governess Rachael Hodgson, as factual. Miss Hodgson has been in my employ for the last two years and has proven herself capable, level-headed, and not given to flights of fancy. I trust her implicitly, as evidenced by the fact that I have entrusted her with the care of our children. I do hope that you will be able to help her with her present difficulties. Do not concern yourself with your fee, as I will guarantee payment of any reasonable charges.*

*I am, sir, yours sincerely,*

*The Rt. Hon. The Viscount Porter, GCVO*

A second letter inside was neatly written in a simpler round-hand script, the same female hand as on the envelope.

*April 30, 1899*

*My Dear Mr. Holmes,*

*I am Rachael Hodgson, late of the village of Ellenby in the Lake District, now governess for the family of Lord Porter in London. I am taking the extraordinary step of writing to engage you to assist me with a matter involving my aunt, Miss Griselda Hodgson.*

*Auntie G is a spinster who lives in our ancestral home in Ellenby. She has supported her frugal lifestyle for many years by selling herbal medicines, which she brews herself from foraged materials. She has always been a bit simple-minded, but capable of fulfilling her own meagre requirements for life and well-being. I try to visit her once or twice a year to ensure that she is getting on.*

*Auntie G has a querulous disposition and has had sporadic altercations with some townspeople, but never anything serious. Lately she has become embroiled in a feud with Mrs. Adele Pennington, the wife of Squire Rayner Pennington, because one of Auntie's tinctures provoked an adverse reaction in the lady. Auntie is reported to have laid a*

34

*curse on Mrs. Pennington. Such behaviour is unfortunately typical and would usually be discounted by those who knew Auntie, except that shortly thereafter, Mrs. Pennington fell ill. Her symptoms progressed until, at present, her very life is feared for. The town doctor, who has had some problems with alcohol, could find no medical explanation for her condition.*

*The town gossip holds Auntie responsible for Mrs. Pennington's illness, saying she cast an "evil eye" on the lady, and the word witchcraft is being bandied about. Because I fear for Auntie G's safety, I have gone home to Ellenby to be with her.*

*I realise you are not a doctor, Mr. Holmes, but I would be grateful if you could come up to Ellenby and provide a mundane explanation for the decline of the Squire's wife. I greatly fear what might befall my aunt if you cannot.*

*Yr. obd't servant,*

*Rachael Hodgson*

"I am not familiar with Ellenby, but a glance at my *Baedeker* should set that aright," said Holmes, retrieving the weighty volume from the shelf and paging through it. "Ah! Here 'tis. No wonder I do not know it. Ellenby is a small village of some three-hundred souls on the shores of Mereswater. It is accessible from the town of Windermere, which in turn may be reached by a branch of the London and Northwestern line. Mr. Bradshaw will provide us specific directions and departure times." He turned to me. "Watson, there is little time for delay. Pack your bags for an extended excursion."

I have long ago ceased to take umbrage at such peremptory demands, knowing how much Holmes has come to rely on my assistance. So I retired to my room and before long, my Gladstone and portmanteau were packed with enough clothes for a week. I donned my Harris tweed flat cap, draped my Norfolk jacket over my arm, and felt prepared for any vagaries of weather that the Cumberland climate might offer. Returning to the sitting room with my luggage, I tucked a copy of *Swallow*, by that excellent storyteller Henry Rider Haggard, into the commodious pocket of my Norfolk. Holmes had two bags as well, along with his Inverness and beloved deerstalker. To accommodate our luggage, he had ordered a four-wheeler for our trip to Euston Station.

It was scarcely a mile to the depot along Marylebone and Euston Roads. We had little time to enjoy the splendid spring weather before we were passing beneath the great Doric arch that guards the terminal. Holmes summoned a porter for our bags, and then we descended the grand staircase into the concourse to purchase tickets. The atmosphere inside was close with tobacco and coal smoke, as well as the miasma of humanity, so I was grateful we had only a short wait before boarding.

"Surely the Viscount will not object to a first-class accommodation for so long a journey," said Holmes as we entered our compartment. It was not long before the train lurched, then settled down to a smooth glide along the rails.

The trip to our first point of embarkation, Oxenholme near Kendal, consumed nearly six hours because of numerous stops along the way. We passed through Hertfordshire, Buckinghamshire, Northamptonshire, Warwickshire, Staffordshire, and Cheshire, before arriving at the northern industrial city of Manchester for a protracted layover. Holmes had lapsed into one of those deep brown studies to which he was prone. I amused myself in turn with Haggard's rousing story of the Boer Trek of 1836, and enjoyment of the ever-changing panoply of the English countryside.

The train lurched again and we were off northward, this time for a much shorter ride to Oxenholme, a hamlet that comprised a railway station and a few scattered houses. We changed trains for the last leg of our passage to Windermere village, on the banks of the lake of the same name. Windermere is the largest lake in England, a so-called "ribbon lake" because it curls between the bosom of the surrounding hills, its banks handsomely forested and draped with a necklace of rustic villas.

While not yet dusk when we arrived at Windermere Station, it was so late in the day that no more coaches were scheduled to travel to Mereswater. Instead, we took an omnibus to the nearest hotel and hired a dogcart to carry us to Ellenby. I rode in front with the driver while Holmes lounged in back with the luggage. Our route took us along the banks of Windermere, then through the charming village of Ambleside, before entering a pristine forest, where we passed burbling becks that fed the mighty lake from the north. The trees gradually disappeared as we ascended the fells, giving way to open country and affording spectacular views of the glistening lake twisting amongst the emerald fields and the budding copses.

"By Jove, Holmes, isn't this absolutely grand?" I said, and receiving no answer, I glanced in back to find my companion slumbering peacefully, his head propped on a bag.

Topping a col, we descended back into the woods, dimmer and more foreboding than before – ruddy beams of light filtered through the branches overhead, signalling the proximity of dusk, and a damp, cool hand lay upon the land. The setting sun had painted the sky a deep crimson by the time we rolled up in front of The Fells, the sole inn and public house in Ellenby. It was a two-story stone building swathed in strands of ivy, the largest in the square. Because of the lateness of the hour, we decided to secure lodging first, then send word to Miss Hodgson, advising her of our presence and inquiring whether a visit tonight or in the morning would suit her.

After signing the register, we stepped back outside, where we had noticed several boys skylarking. Holmes hailed one of them: "Halloa, you lad! Do you know the Hodgson house?"

The youths froze, staring at us with wide eyes, then scattered to the winds as one.

"That bodes ill indeed," I said.

We returned to the public room, its round wooden tables filled with taciturn provincials who regarded us with accusatory eyes. Holmes addressed the innkeeper, who was plying a cloth on the shiny wooden bar, doing his best to ignore us.

"My name is Sherlock Holmes. I would like to send a message to Miss Rachael Hodgson, informing her of my presence here."

The innkeeper turned to us with a look bordering on hostility. "Ah canna stop tha'," he said with a thick northern accent, looking Holmes up and down. "But they'll be nobbut a place 'ere fer aw what's 'ankled up wi' witches."

Without a word, Holmes turned on his heel and returned to the reception area, where we had left our bags. I followed.

"It seems we must find other accommodation," he said. "Perhaps Miss Hodgson can provide it."

"But how shall we locate her?" I said. "The villagers seem disinclined to aid us."

"You know my methods, Watson. Apply them."

We took up our luggage and exited back to the square. Darkness was rapidly encroaching, and our dogcart had departed to return to Windermere. I foresaw a vile evening ahead indeed if we had to sleep rough.

Holmes looked about, then said, "Perhaps the local constabulary can aid us." He set out across the square at a lope. We approached another two-story building of roughcast grey stone, its bright green wooden door papered with ragged handbills and bars securing the windows on the upper floor. Holmes worked the latch and entered.

We found ourselves in a lamplit room with unfinished stone walls and a crude plank floor. A tall wooden counter with a gate at the far end divided the chamber into a narrow walkway that ended in a casement window and a much larger area containing a desk, filing cabinets, an over-stuffed sofa, easy chairs, and a compact kitchen. Waves of heat rolled from a stove, and the odour of coal fumes was nearly overpowering.

A flight of stairs in the far corner led upward. A female voice filtered down. "You cannot do this, Weed! Auntie has done nothing wrong. You cannot lock her up like a common criminal!"

Repairing down the walkway and entering the office area through the gate, we ascended. We entered a large room that comprised the entire second floor, yellow with light from a lantern hanging from the ceiling. One side seemed dedicated to storage, filled with barrels, sacks, crates, and various pieces of furniture thrown higgledy-piggledy on top. A wall of iron bars divided the other side into four cells. A man and a woman stood in front of one, in which an older woman was imprisoned.

The man was a most singular individual. He was of impressive height and girth – he must have been nearly seven feet tall and twenty-five stone – I wondered how he had been able to negotiate the narrow staircase. His heavy blue woollen uniform marked him as the village constable. He was saying to the woman, "Ah'm tellin' thee, Rache, ah'm doon it fer 'er own guid." He noticed us and turned our way "Guid evenin', gennleman! Ah'm Constable Weedon Trelawney. 'Ow kin ah aid thee?"

"Good evening, Constable. My name is Sherlock Holmes." He addressed the young woman. "Miss Hodgson, we have come in response to your letter. I wish to offer you my humble assistance."

Rachael Hodgson had shoulder-length sandy hair and looked much too young to be entrusted as governess to a noble family, although I was to learn later that she was twenty-five years of age. She had an amiable, round face and bright blue eyes – she would have been a comely lass except for her agitated state, evidenced by her flushed complexion and wild hair. I could see a resemblance between her and the incarcerated woman – the same rotund facial features – but her aunt's were drawn and haggard, doubtless due to stress.

"Mr. Holmes!" she cried. "Can you not make him see reason? He has locked Auntie up in a cell!"

"Aye, a ruffian, 'e is!" screeched the old woman. "Ah'll gi'e thoo the evil eye, Weedon Trelawney, and t'cleppets'll shri'el up lak a wether's!" I did not know what the old woman said, but Rachel brought a fist to her open mouth and looked at her aunt with horror.

"Constable, can you explain yourself?" asked Holmes.

Trelawney glowered at us, but acquiesced. "They's bin threats made against Missus 'Odgson," he said. "Ah canna protect her and Rache if they's in their 'ouse."

"Perhaps the constable is correct, Miss Hodgson," I said in a conciliatory tone. Her face contorted and tears began as her aunt shrieked unintelligibly. Suddenly angry, I began, "Constable, I must say that this is deplorable . . . ."

Holmes cut me off. "No, Watson. As you said, it may be for the best. Please conduct Miss Hodgson downstairs."

I did as Holmes asked. He and the constable followed, the harridan squawking curses in our wake.

Holmes addressed our client, "Perhaps we should see you home, Miss Hodgson, and hear your account. We can see about getting your Auntie out tomorrow. By the way, the innkeeper seems unwilling to accept our custom. Could we prevail upon you to put us up for the duration of our stay?"

"I am sorry to tell you, Mr. Holmes, Auntie's cottage is very tiny. There would be no room for two gentlemen to stay there with a lady."

As my heart sunk to the floorboards, the constable spoke up. "Wot's that? Jackie Lad would nae 'av thine custom? Ah'll mak talk wi' 'im. Thoo'll 'ae beds fer the nacht! Thoo gan yam, Rache. We'll mak talk in da mornin'."

Given the constable's assurances, we left our luggage with him and accompanied Miss Hodgson home.

The Hodgson cottage was miniscule indeed, a lime-washed white clay building with a thatched roof, known as a "dabbin" by the locals. It had one room on the ground floor, with a ladder though an opening in the ceiling leading to a loft. After Miss Hodgson had gone round lighting oil lamps and candles, we could see that the downstairs room was as tidy and compactly arranged as any ship's galley, with a diminutive kitchen in one corner. A glass-fronted cabinet against a kitchen wall contained a myriad of labelled jars and bottles, and an assortment of various sized cauldrons and a balance reposed on top. A sitting area near the front door was furnished with a padded rocking chair and an overstuffed sofa – a pillow and rumpled bedclothes on the latter indicated that Miss Hodgson slept there. Heat was provided by a coal-fired cooking stove in the kitchen, which imbued the cottage with a heavy atmosphere.

Miss Hodgson waved us to a pub table covered with a green checked cloth. "Can I make you some tea, gentlemen, or perhaps something stronger? Auntie G brews her own damson wine." She considered a moment, then thought to ask. "Have you eaten this evening?"

"Tea will be fine, Miss Hodgson," said Holmes. "And no, we have had nothing since luncheon on the train, hours ago."

"That will never do," Miss Hodgson said as she placed a kettle on the stove. In short order, the table was replete with a meat pie, a coil of cooked sausages, a wedge of cheese, and a loaf of bread. A bowl of mustard and a jar of pickles completed the feast.

39

"Now Miss Hodgson, please state your case," said Holmes as he began filling a plate. "Omit no detail, however unimportant it may seem to you."

"My mother died birthing me, gentlemen, and my da' had long since skedaddled," she began. "I was raised by Auntie G in this very cottage. She was not always like she is now. Oh, always a bit odd, to be sure, but it is only in the last few years that she has claimed to have magical powers."

"What kind of powers?" I asked.

"She has always made her living as the village midwife, as well as by brewing tinctures and extracts to treat the villagers' minor ailments. But some years ago, she went off on one of her forays into the country to collect plants, mushrooms, and other things that she needed to craft her little potions. She was gone for nearly a week, and everyone was worried that she had tumbled from a fell. Weed – that is, Constable Trelawney – organised search parties, but no one could find her. Then she suddenly reappeared, bruised, covered in muck, her clothes in tatters, babbling nonsense. She – "

Holmes interrupted. "What do you mean, babbling nonsense?"

"She spoke of bright lights and strange beings who had taken her, and subjected her to unspeakable things, then released her back into the wild. Weed said that she had probably taken a fall, hit her head, and become delirious. In time, she recovered physically, but she was never right mentally afterwards. When I was in my teens, she began to claim to have arcane powers." She paused for a sip of her tea, then went on. "It was also around then that her spats with some of the villagers began to escalate."

"What was the nature of these spats?" asked Holmes.

"Have you ever lived in a small village, Mr. Holmes?" Holmes nodded. "Then you know that from time to time, people in such close quarters can antagonise each other. Little things can set it off – a chance remark on the street, a jostle in the marketplace, and before long, a real row is ensuing. Some in town thought Auntie was going soft – 'nick't at t'heid', as they say round here – because she professed supernatural abilities. Many tended to treat her as if she were a child, which she greatly resented. She would usually respond to such slights with threats to bring all sorts of evil down on the offender. Most folk realised that this was simply a result of her injures, and that she was harmless."

"So what transpired with the squire's wife?" Holmes inquired.

"You must understand that I got this second-hand, from Weed. Apparently, the good lady was feeling puny, and came to Auntie seeking a remedy for her ills. That was unusual, because Auntie and the Squire have not been attuned for years."

"Could Mrs. Pennington not have consulted the doctor?" I asked.

"Apparently she did, but whatever he prescribed was of no help. Auntie gave her something but she continued to get worse, publicly laying the blame for her decline at Auntie's door. The two of them had a right barney at the market, complete with slapping and hair-pulling. Auntie was heard to threaten Mrs. Pennington – 'A curse be t' thee and thine!' she said. When the lady became ill enough that she had to take to her bed several days later, rumours began circulating that Auntie had given her the evil eye."

"And how did you learn of this in London?" asked Holmes.

"I had a wire from Weed informing me. He said that I should try to come home and see if I could smooth things over."

"I don't suppose you know what your aunt prescribed for the squire's wife?" Holmes asked. Miss Hodgson shook her head.

"How was it that you came to find employment in London?" I asked. "Is that not unusual for a young woman raised in these parts?" Holmes gave me a baleful glare for changing the subject, but I had long since grown used to his ways and did not care.

"It was a teacher, Dr. Watson, Miss Deborah Jones, who thought I deserved better than to settle down in Ellenby as a farmer's wife. She worked with me since I was a little girl to cure me of the Lakeland manner of speaking and taught me things that would make me attractive as a governess – literature, history, music, and the like. It is well that she did, because after her accident, Auntie couldn't earn as much as previously. It is my salary that keeps her comfortable here in her old age."

Holmes brought her back to her narrative. "What did you do after arriving in Ellenby?"

"I went to visit Squire Pennington, with whom I'd always had a good relationship when I lived here. He assured me that he did not blame Auntie for his wife's illness, but other than saying so in public, he was powerless to control any gossip that might be spread."

Having finished his repast, Holmes reached into his pocket for his briar and tobacco, and then asked, "May I smoke?"

"By all means."

He glanced at the ceiling pensively as he tamped shag into his pipe with his thumb, then he struck a Vesta and applied the flame to the bowl. When it was drawing to his satisfaction, he asked, "Do you know the nature of the ailment for which the Squire's wife sought treatment?"

"No, Mr. Holmes. We did not discuss it."

"And what does your Aunt have to say about all of this?"

Miss Hodgson smiled ruefully. "Although she claims that the medicine she dispensed was efficacious, Auntie is only too happy to credit Mrs. Pennington's present state to her magic."

Holmes asked, "Will you give me leave to look round?" On Miss Hodgson's nod, he went to the kitchen cabinet and examined the containers within. Removing one, he carefully inspected the label. He replaced it and turned away with a grim expression.

He asked, "How long ago was it that Mrs. Pennington consulted your aunt?"

"I am not entirely sure. Perhaps the beginning of last week?"

"Do you know if she has had any other clients since?"

"I do not, Mr. Holmes."

"Well, Watson," Holmes said abruptly, "I think it is time to take our leave, and hope that the constable has had his chat with the innkeeper. Miss Hodgson, thank you very much for feeding two hungry travellers."

Miss Hodgson nodded, and we quit the stuffy cottage for the cool of the evening.

I had been associated with Holmes long enough that I knew when something was troubling him. "What is it?"

"My perusal of Auntie G's medicaments revealed that she has many dangerous elixirs. Many of them might be responsible for Mrs. Pennington's condition."

"Do you think Miss Hodgson's aunt deliberately poisoned the Squire's wife?"

"How many times must I tell you that it is a cardinal error to theorize without data? I merely mention it as a possibility, and one that would make Miss Hodgson sorry indeed that she engaged us, should it be true."

No one was in the reception area when we returned to The Fells, so we entered the public room, which was even more crowded than earlier. The bustle of conversation immediately ceased at our entry.

"Weed tells me ah mus' gi'e t' a bed," said the innkeeper. "Thoo'll find 'un upstairs."

He turned back to his perpetual bar cleaning.

It was apparent the churl was going to obey the letter of the law and that we would get no assistance with our bags. Returning to the reception area, we saw that upper floor at the top of the stairs was unlit, so we appropriated a couple of candles before ascending.

I spent a restless night. Although there was a fireplace in the room I had chosen, there was no fire, and I was not going downstairs and ask the landlord for one. The bed was lumpy, the coverings musty, and a draft that penetrated the window casing managed to make that Jezail bullet throb just as it had when it first became part of my anatomy. I reckoned it was

42

about five in the morning when the first light peeped through the glass. The sun rose soon afterwards. A jug and wash bowl stood on a stand at the end of the bed, but I had no delusions that hot water would be provided for my morning ablutions. My father's watch informed me that it was nearly seven a.m. I gave up the hope of any more sleep.

Holmes was already in the public room when I descended, attacking a plate of cold sausages, hard bread, and cheese. The innkeeper sullenly provided the same for me, but grunted negatively when I inquired about coffee.

"If thoo wan' suthin' t'wash it doon wi', thoo can 'ae a tippenny ale."

I am ashamed to say I took him up on it.

After Holmes had lighted his post-prandial pipe, he said, "I fancy a visit to the Squire is in order, Watson. Perhaps we will have a better reception there."

The square was empty when we exited the inn, and Holmes immediately stuck off down the road toward the lake at a fast pace, causing me to hurry after him.

"How do you know that the Squire's house is this way?" I asked.

"We did not pass it on the way into town," he said, and I felt like an ass.

A cool breeze blustered down from the fells as we walked, but the rapidly ascending sun gave promise of a fine mellow day. Most of the buildings surrounding the square were stone with slate roofs, giving way to more plebeian thatched clay dabbins as we approached the village perimeter. Rounding a bend, we were confronted by a stone wall, which we followed until we arrived at black cast iron gate. A bronze plaque adjacent to the gate announced that this was Mereswater House. Holmes lifted the latch and we entered. Closing it behind us, we proceeded up a gravel drive through a copse until we came upon a fine old farm house in a clearing. The house had stepped gables and a wing on either side, all constructed of local stone and slate rubble. Holmes strode confidently up to the front door and rapped sharply on the jamb with the head of his stick. A moment later a woman in a striped grey dress, white lace apron, and cap opened the door.

Holmes extended his card. "Sherlock Holmes and Dr. Watson to see Squire Pennington, if you please."

She took it in a white-gloved hand. "Come in and wait in the parlour, gennlemen, and I'll see if the Squire is takin' callers."

As I followed her through the foyer, Holmes, behind me, shouted, "Watson, stop!" It was well that I obeyed, for a feathered shaft flew in front of me, arcing to the floor and skittering into the wall. I turned to see a boy of seven or eight standing in a doorway with a bow in his hand, busily nocking another arrow. As I glared at him, he said, "Hold, varlet! I am Robin of Locksley, and I do not gi'e thee leave to pass!"

"Gan wi' thoo, Ray, or ah'll tell thy da!" the maid admonished him. He smirked and disappeared into the room behind him.

She conducted us into a room in the east wing, furnished with chintz-covered chairs and a daybed flanking a stone fireplace. French doors afforded a fine view of the garden outside and the sparkling Mereswater beyond. An easel next to the doors held a covered canvas.

"I'll tell the Squire you're 'ere," said the maid.

I began to examine the framed photographs adorning the walls – family pictures and views of the lakes. Holmes had thrown back the sheet on the painting.

"The Squire's wife is a handsome woman," he said. "Of course, a tactful artist will always flatter his subject."

I turned to view a partially completed, full-length portrait. Holmes was correct – Mrs. Pennington was a striking lady with long auburn hair curled round her bosom, accentuated by a brilliant green, floor-length gown. The painting of her figure looked to be nearly complete, with only the background, apparently the parlour doors and the garden, unfinished.

A cultured voice spoke from behind us. "I'd rather that not be viewed until it can be unveiled for my wife when she's well."

Holmes let the cover drop, then we turned to greet Squire Pennington.

He was a tall, thin, austere-looking chap with sharp angular features, dressed in mismatched tweeds and a black-and-white houndstooth vest. Piercing blue eyes glared at us from under a mane of unruly, light-brown hair. Even though I knew I'd never seen him before, his face was eerily familiar. He seemed less than delighted to welcome us into his home.

"Pardon me if I have intruded," said Holmes. "I was merely trying to while away the time as we waited."

"Well, I am here now," the Squire said. "Kindly state your business."

"This portrait is very good, you know," Holmes went on as if he had not heard. "That is a singular green gown. Who was the artist?"

"A local woman. Deborah Jones. Please state your business."

"We have come to inquire about the health of Mrs. Pennington," said Holmes.

Apparently, the news of our arrival and our purpose had travelled rapidly throughout the small town. "You can tell the elder Miss Hodgson that Adele is very ill, and that I intend to hold her responsible after I have seen to my wife's recovery," the Squire replied.

Holmes frowned. "Miss Rachael Hodgson is under the impression that you do not blame her aunt for your wife's condition. Did you change your mind?"

"I did indeed, Mr. Holmes, as Adele's condition worsened and that horrible old termagant prattled about the village that she accomplished the deed with her black magic."

"Surely an educated man like yourself does not believe that," I said.

"Perhaps not," rejoined the Squire, "but the old witch could have certainly given my wife some hellish potion to make her sick."

"Dr. Watson is well-regarded among London physicians. Perhaps he might discover something your local doctor has overlooked."

"That will not be necessary," said the Squire. "I have the utmost confidence in Dr. Phillip."

I could not resist. "Even though he has a drinking problem?"

Pennington spitted me with that aquiline glare of his. "If you repeat that canard outside of this house, I shall advise Dr. Phillip to sue you for slander." He turned his back in dismissal. "Billie will see you out."

It is slander only if untrue was on the tip of my tongue, but before I could get it out, Holmes said, "Quite. Come, Watson. If Squire Pennington is satisfied with the care that his wife is receiving, it is not our place to interfere. Good day, Squire. We can see ourselves out."

Holmes opened the French doors and we exited to the garden. As we walked into the woods, approaching Mereswater, I sputtered to Holmes, "How could you let that insufferable ass speak to us that way?"

"It is his home, Watson. In it, I am sure that he can speak to us in any way that he likes." He hesitated, then, "Just as sure as I am that he is poisoning his wife. It is vital that we get back into that house so you can examine the lady."

"Poisoning his wife! How do you – "

"I thought we would walk back to the village along the lakeshore," Holmes said. "It will provide a nice change of scenery."

So it was going to be that way, was it?

"I have said previously that the English countryside is more conducive to hellish cruelty and hidden wickedness than the meanest of London's streets," Holmes continued as we walked along the trail. "The utter remoteness and isolation of a village such as Ellenby can act as the accomplices of the murderer, the abuser, and the thief. Add to that the power and prestige of a man of a prominent social class, and you have a dire situation indeed. Hello! What have we here?"

We had encountered a singular construct. Someone had hammered two wooden posts made from rough-cut logs waist-high into the ground about two feet apart, a yard from the water, then lashed a crosspiece between them with a hempen rope. I could conceive of no earthly use for such a structure.

45

"Those logs were recently cut from yon felled tree," said Holmes, pointing to a prone sapling nearly thirty feet long, which lay in the weeds to the side of the path, "and the project seemed to require the assistance of five men, at least," he continued after scrutinising the ground.

He resumed his examination of the forest, then turned round, giving his attention to the shore and the water beyond. "I wonder . . . ." he said. Then "Watson, we must hurry. There is bad business afoot."

We quick-marched back to the public house. Upon entering, we heard raised voices from the barroom.

"We're nae gonna suffer a witch in our village, eh?" The speaker was a stout man with brown, curly hair whom I hadn't seen before, in his thirties and wearing a blacksmith's apron. He had climbed up on a large, carved armchair the public room, and was addressing a crowd of perhaps a dozen townsmen.

"Shut yer mush, Joss Ferrier!" Constable Weed spoke up from the back of the room where he towered over the throng. "Missus 'Odgson ma' be bak yam, but she's still under ma care. Thoo'll nae 'urt her! Now be off wi' thoo afore ah clap thoo in irons." The crowd grumbled as the erstwhile rabble rouser glared at the policeman, but he showed the inestimable good sense to get down from the chair and quit the common room.

Holmes and I took a table and were able to prevail upon the publican to serve us a ploughman's lunch, largely a duplicate of breakfast. As I was about to tuck in, Holmes nudged me with his foot and surreptitiously pointed towards the bar. Billie, Squire Pennington's maid, was handing a pitcher to Jackie Lad, presumably to be filled with ale.

Holmes raised his voice. "Oh, Billie! Might I have a word?"

The woman glanced our way, indecision rife on her face. Few of her class could resist Holmes's commanding manner, though, so she guardedly approached us.

"Sit down, Billie."

"I don't know as I should, sir. The Squire'll be cross wi' me."

"You do love your mistress, do you not, Billie?" Holmes asked in a low voice. She nodded her assent. "Then please sit down, if you would see her well again." Elbows on the table, she clasped her white-gloved hands before her like a supplicant. "Now Billie, to save your mistress, it is vital that Dr. Watson and I get in to see her without the Squire's knowledge. Do you care for her sufficiently to make that possible?"

Her mouth popped open and her eyes became wide. "I don't know, sir! I 'eard the Squire forbid it! I could lose my position . . . ."

"Your mistress will likely perish if you refuse us, Billie," Holmes snapped. "Is that what you want?" Her lips became a thin white line and tears ran down her cheeks. She shook her head. "Good. Now, when does Squire Pennington retire for the evening?"

"He generally goes to 'is chamber after 'is cigar and brandy," she said.

"Can you show a light, and let us in by the parlour doors after he does so tonight?" Another hesitant nod. "Excellent! We shall await your signal in the forest behind Mereswater House." Holmes reached forward and took her hand, and when she withdrew it, he held on to her glove, peeling it from her hand. The livid flesh beneath was mottled with dark, crusty lesions. "Dreadfully sorry!" he said. "How clumsy of me." Appalled, she leapt up from the table and dashed out of the pub, leaving behind a full pitcher of ale on the bar.

I stared at my companion, aghast. "Holmes! Those were arsenical lesions!"

"Yes, Watson. They were."

After luncheon, Holmes informed me that he had to do some investigating that would not accommodate a companion, so he was going to leave me on my own for a while. "Perhaps you can walk about and meet some townspeople, and see if you can extract any helpful information." Having served as Holmes's amanuensis as long as I had done, I was used to such treatment. I readily assented.

Ellenby was really not much of a village. It did not even have a church, so it was technically a hamlet. Most of the activity was in the town square, which contained, in addition to The Fells and the constabulary, a bakery, a greengrocer, and a general merchandise market. Several roads, lined with private residences, led from the square. Due to our hasty departure from London, I found that I was running low on tobacco, so I decided to visit the market and try to replenish my supply. I knew a custom blend would likely not be available, but a tin of commercial shag or Navy cut would fill the bill nicely.

The market was in a small stone building two doors away from the inn. A little bell tinkled as I opened the door, announcing my arrival. There were only two people inside – the proprietress, a stout woman in an apron and cap who stood behind the wooden counter, waiting on another lady. Both looked my way at the sound of the bell, and I must confess that the beauty of the customer nearly took my breath away.

She wore a simple grey dress and a hooded cape, but it draped her Rubenesque form like a gown on a noblewoman. Her red hair, blazing like a mountain sunset, poured over her shoulders in a fiery cascade. Vivacious jade eyes, over a pert nose and a full mouth with dazzling white teeth, regarded me questioningly, imploring me to introduce myself.

"Good afternoon, Miss, I am, err . . . ." Those green eyes bored into mine, her vibrant smile leaving me as nonplussed as a schoolboy on the carpet in front of a favourite teacher.

"Oh, I know who you are," she said.

"You do?"

"Of course! Ellenby is a small village. There are no secrets here. You are Sherlock Holmes, the great detective!"

She smiled ravishingly as my heart tumbled from my chest and bounced across the hardwood floor.

"Err, not exactly, Miss. I am Doctor John Watson, Mr. Holmes's associate."

Her face fell. "Oh. I am so sorry, Doctor, that I mistook you for your famous partner."

"Quite all right," I muttered. "Happens all the time."

"I am Miss Deborah Jones," she said.

"Oh! Rachel Hodgson's teacher!"

"Not anymore. Miss Hodgson has found employment in London. But I remain the village schoolmistress."

I studied her elegant features, and could barely detect a hint that she might have tutored Rachel Hodgson. She hid her age admirably.

She continued, "So you must tell me all about what has brought you and Mr. Holmes to Ellenby."

"Quite so!" I replied. I spied the familiar green can of Skipper's Navy Cut behind the counter. "I will just purchase some tobacco, and then we can talk."

The doorbell tinkled as the clerk handed me the can. I turned to see Squire Pennington entering the shop.

Miss Jones brightened. "Hello, Rayner," she said.

"Deborah." He turned his glance to me. "And Dr. Watson."

I turned back to the counter and gave the clerk a shilling. After receiving my change, I again regarded the pair.

The Squire had an evil look about him. "Oh, do as you will," he snarled at Miss Jones, then stalked outside, slamming the door in his wake. I raised an eyebrow.

"Rayner invited me to walk with him, but I told him that I was already taken."

I held the door open so she could precede me. "I hope I didn't interrupt a previous appointment."

"His wife's illness has been difficult for him," she said. "Sometimes it helps him to just talk. But we mustn't neglect visitors to our humble village. I'll see him later."

"Where would you like to go?" I asked her. "The public house?"

"I hardly think that would be appropriate," she said. "If you'd care for a short walk, I can show you an overlook with a fine view of the dale and the surrounding fells."

I assented, so she led me off at a brisk pace to a path that climbed the pike behind the village. She had neither stick nor staff, but she ran up that twisty, narrow track like a mountain goat. I, on the other hand, had a difficult time remaining upright, even with the aid of my stick, because a treacherous coating of roundish gravel covered the trail and threatened to take my shoes from beneath me. Mostly, I kept my eyes on the path at my feet, but once I glanced up to see the craggy peak towering so far above me, and my heart sank – my wounds were already paining me. How would I be able to follow this lissom wench to the top? However, I rounded a bend to find her sitting on a rocky shelf. She smiled at me and patted the stone.

"This is as far as we need to go," she said. "Come and sit beside me."

I sat and then began to apologise for my poor physical condition, but she schussed me by placing a finger on my lips, then indicated the expanse of the valley below with a wave of her arm. "Feast your eyes on the Lakes, Doctor. Have you ever seen such a sight?"

I could scarcely breathe as I beheld the vista that stretched before me. The afternoon sun shone over the peak behind us, bathing the scattered groves that dotted the emerald valley in a soft buttery light, the cottages of Ellenby nestled comfortably in their verdant bosom. The argent expanse of Mereswater glimmered beyond, winding amongst the knolls like a silvery cord. I turned my glance to the achingly beautiful woman sitting beside me and, for the first time in ages, my heart ached for my Mary, cruelly taken from me so many years ago. I longed to put an arm around Miss Jones and draw her close, but that was sheer foolishness – we had just met and she would surely be repulsed by such an imposition. She must have felt my gaze though, because she turned her grass-coloured eyes to mine, and before I realised what she intended, she leaned forward and placed a soft kiss on my lips.

I sat there like an idiot, stunned by her rashness. Her expression transformed from one of affection to disappointment. "I am sorry, Doctor," she said. "I shouldn't have done that. Perhaps we should go."

I said to her, "Not at all."

She was silent for a moment, then, "It's lonely for a spinster in such a small village."

"Then why remain?"

"For the children," she smiled. "I came here originally because they had no one to teach them."

"It was a fine thing that you did for Miss Hodgson."

49

"She was a delightfully bright child. I couldn't bear to see her wasting away in a backwater like this, as a brood mare for some illiterate bumpkin."

"I say!" I ejaculated, again taken aback by her frankness. I hesitantly contradicted my earlier statement. "Perhaps we should be getting back to the village? Holmes may require my assistance."

Thankfully, she ignored my suggestion. "What has he discovered about Mrs. Pennington's condition? Does he actually think that Griselda Hodgson cast a spell on her?"

"No," Abruptly, I realised that she might be pumping me for information, and that anything I said might become the talk of the town. "I really shouldn't discuss Holmes's investigation . . . ."

Her face fell, and my heart with it. Why did I so desperately want to please this woman? "Well, if you can't tell me . . . ." she continued.

"I really should not," I said.

Miss Jones and I walked back down the mountain in silence, holding hands a good part of the way to steady each other on the slippery path. When we reached the outskirts of town, she took both of my hands in hers and looked deeply into my eyes with those mesmerizing, verdant orbs.

"I must say, John, that I had a most enjoyable afternoon. Please do call on me again before you go back to London. And if you find it in your heart to let me assist you and Mr. Holmes . . . ."

"I will speak with him about it," I said, and she smiled. "I must go."

That entrancing smile remained in my head all the way back to The Fells.

I found Holmes in the public room, smoking his briar and nursing a pint. He looked up at me and said, "Did you learn anything of note from Miss Jones?"

I was d-----d if I was going to ask him how he had perceived that. For all I knew, he may have been following the two of us until we started up the mountain path. "Possibly," I answered him. I gave him a brief account of my afternoon's adventures, *sans* my personal feelings.

"Very interesting," was his comment when I had finished. He hesitated, then said, "I know that you did not say anything to that woman about our surmises, Watson, and I thank you. There are deep waters here, and I do not mean Mereswater."

This time I had to ask. "How do you know she questioned me about our activities?"

Holmes smiled. "Watson, your eyes have been a window to your gentle soul all the years I have known you." After a moment of silence he

50

continued, "We should have an early dinner and get ready. I want to be in the woods behind Mereswater House at dusk."

So it was that we found ourselves crouched behind some bushes in the rain, as the rubicund sky slowly faded to deep purple. The lights of Mereswater House beckoned me, because I knew warmth and dryness could be found within. The French doors of the parlour, however, remained dark. We would have no welcome from the owner there.

I pulled the collar of my Norfolk jacket more tightly about my neck. Holmes, in his cape and deerstalker, was more appropriately dressed for the weather. "I hope Billie has not lost her courage," I said. Holmes did not reply.

Good British wool is an amazing material. Because of its lanolin content, it requires hours to become saturated, even in a downpour, and it confers warmth even when soaked. But wet wool is hardly comfortable and its smell is truly odious. I had experienced enough of these nocturnal vigils with Holmes so that I knew better than to say anything about the discomfort – while quiet conversation might help me pass the time, it would simply irritate him. Thus, it was a great relief when, at last, we saw the light of a candle flickering in the parlour.

Billie had the French doors opened when we arrived. In a low voice, Holmes commanded, "Take us to your mistress at once!"

We followed her out into the lamp-lit foyer and up the curved staircase. She turned and held a finger to her lips, then led us down a hallway with closed doors on either side to a room at the end. She ushered us inside, where the sweet smell of a woman's boudoir mingled with the sour scent of sickness that I knew so well.

Billie lit a lamp on a round table next to the canopied bed, then whispered, "The old 'un's chamber is right through that door," indicating a portal on the other side of the room. "I'll leave tha' now."

Holmes took the candle holder from her before she could leave with it. After the door to the corridor had closed, he motioned towards the bed. "See to the lady, Watson," he whispered, "while I look around."

I parted the curtains enclosing the bed and beheld a pitiable sight indeed. The woman lying there bore little resemblance to the green-gowned lady in the portrait downstairs. Her face was pale, wizened, covered with crusty half-healed lesions, and her auburn hair was thin and faded. Her eyes were closed and she was still, scarcely breathing. I reached down and pressed two fingers to the side of her neck, finding a barely perceptible pulse.

Meanwhile, Holmes was searching the armoire and the chests of drawers. "It isn't here," he muttered. "What has the fiend done with it?"

Suddenly, Adele Pennington's eyes snapped open and here features transformed into a mask of dread. She began breathing rapidly and shallowly, and her already mottled skin took on a bluish tint. Then her gaze became fixed and she gave a long, rattling exhalation that I had heard too many times before on the battlefield.

"There is nothing more to see to, Holmes," I said angrily, in a normal voice. "Mrs. Pennington is dead."

Holmes immediately appeared at my side. "Hush!" he whispered, indicating the door to the Squire's room, behind which a clatter arose. He glanced quickly about, then grabbing the bed curtain, he ripped it and removed a ragged piece about three inches square. This he soaked in the dregs of a cup on the bedtable, before stuffing the scrap into an envelope taken from a pocket. He dashed over to the window and tore it open. "Hurry, Watson! The devil has heard us!" He put a leg over the sill to step on the sloping roof beyond.

With my wounds from Afghanistan already throbbing from hours in the cold and damp, I realised there was no way that I was going to escape from this house by sliding down a roof and jumping to the ground, so I resolved to remain and do my best to see that Holmes could flee with his evidence. As he vanished outside, I extinguished the bedside lamp. I did not have long to wait before the door to the hallway burst open and Squire Pennington confronted me, his dark form backlit from the lighted corridor, aiming a fowling piece at my midsection. If he fired at this distance, it would surely tear me in half! I steeled myself to meet my God.

Several hours later, I found myself occupying the elder Miss Hodgson's former quarters in the Ellenby Constabulary. Because the Squire Pennington had to hold me at gunpoint while Billie went for the constable, he could not pursue Holmes.

"Thoo'll be gan t' Carlisle in a day or two t' gae t' th' dock fer burglary, Dr. Watson," Constable Trelawney was saying. "And wi' most of the gadgees in Ellenby huntin 'im, thy Mr. 'Olmes won't be free for lang."

I trusted that Holmes would be able to evade most of the men of Ellenby for as long as he wanted to. But I knew that I was in serious trouble. Billie had refused to say that she had admitted us to Mereswater House, implicating us as burglars, which carried a sentence of years of hard labour.

I spent a wretched night in that small stony cell, my clothes drying slowly on my back. Very little heat from the coal stove downstairs was able to penetrate up there, so I shivered miserably until dawn. Other than to bring me a breakfast very similar to the one I had in the public house and a pot of hellishly strong tea, I saw nothing of the constable after he locked me away. Lunch was more of the same.

The afternoon seemed interminable. It was warm now – indeed, the attic had become almost uncomfortably hot when I heard a noise on the stairs. Then Miss Jones appeared, carrying a covered basket.

"My poor John!" Even in my present wretched state, a thrill passed through me at the sight of her. "What have they done to you? Burglary, indeed," she snorted, tossing her fine head like a spirited mare. She turned to regard Constable Trelawney, whose great bulk was emerging from the staircase. "Constable, please open this cell so I can give Dr. Watson the victuals I prepared for him."

"You shouldn't have . . . ." I began.

"Bosh and nonsense!" She cut me off. "You shouldn't be in here so I had to." She cast an evil glare at the constable once more.

He obediently unlocked the cell to allow her to pass the basket inside. She contrived to stroke my hand as she did so, sending a line of fire up my arm.

Trelawney relocked the door, saying "Miss Jones, ah 'av other business . . . ."

"So attend to it, Constable," she snapped. "Do you think I'm going to rip these bars off and fly away with him?"

"I'll gi'e thoo ten minutes." The constable returned downstairs.

She stared at me earnestly with those green, green eyes. "Mr. Holmes came to me last night," she said. "He's at my cottage now. He wants me to tell you to be strong – he's going to Carlisle to get the sample from the bedroom tested. He hopes to be back in a few days to have you freed."

My effort last night was not in vain, then. "Thank you for telling me. It will make my imprisonment easier."

We spent the rest of her time simply chatting. I placed my hand on a bar and she covered it with hers, stroking my knuckles with her thumb to comfort me. By the time Trelawney returned for her, she had me totally bewitched.

I nibbled from her basket to while away the time as the sun sank slowly outside my barred window. The constable returned just before nightfall to light the overhead lantern so I should not have to sit in the dark, and I thanked him for his kindness.

Night had fully embraced the land when I heard another hubbub on the stairs. I was shocked to see Sherlock Holmes appear and hurry towards my cell.

"Up, Watson, up! There is deviltry afoot!"

Holmes unlocked my cell and threw open the door, then wheeled back to the stairs.

"What?"

"A mob has descended on Miss Hodgson's house," he said over his shoulder. "They have taken her! To be tried as a witch!"

My wounds were still paining me. I struggled to keep up with him as we hurried below.

Standing at a gun rack, Holmes removed a rifle and tossed it to me, followed by a box of ammunition.

"Load quickly," Holmes said. "The constable has gone ahead, but there may be too many for him."

"Where did he go?" I asked.

"To the banks of Mereswater."

I followed him as best I could out into the square and down the road toward the Squire's house. Before we had gone that far, he veered off into the woods. I lost sight of him for a moment, and was worried that I'd be left behind, but then I saw his shadowy form rushing towards the orangey glow of a fire ahead. A threatening growl of angry men throbbed through the dark.

I burst into a smoky clearing on the lakeshore where a bonfire begot shadowy fingers that waved over the massed crowd. Something whirled above me and I heard a woman scream, then I spied a long, thick pole with a chair on the end, a struggling figure within it. It reeled above the lake, then descended into the icy waters with a splash.

The crack of a rifle split the air.

"Back, you rabble!" shouted Holmes. "Back, or my next bullet will find the body of a man!"

The crowd turned as one in Holmes's direction. I could see that three farmers held Trelawney fast – he must have unwisely rushed into the throng. I brought my rifle to my shoulder and added my voice. "Release the constable, or I will shoot!" My eye caught motion and I saw someone raising a rifle at Holmes. I shifted targets and squeezed off a round. The fellow went down. "Hold, I say! I have no wish to injure anyone else."

The pair seizing the constable let him go. "Thoo gadgees gae' Miss 'Odgson outta t'lake!" he shouted in his stentorian voice. "Now!"

A half-dozen men jumped up and grabbed the end of the long pole suspended in the air, its centre resting on the curious structure that we had discovered the other morning, which acted as a fulcrum. It was an old-fashioned dunking chair! They hauled downwards and the end erupted from the lake, the sodden, unmoving body of the victim still tied into the chair, as the water cascaded to whence it came. They pushed the shaft sideways and swung the woman's body over the bank, and then they lowered her to the ground.

My shot had cooled the ardour of the crowd considerably, so I was happy to drop my weapon and return to my nobler calling. I rushed over to examine Miss Hodgson. She wasn't breathing!

"Get me a knife! We must free her from this chair!"

We soon had her face first on the ground. I straddled her, placed my hands on her shoulder blades, and began pumping for all I was worth, to expel the lake water from her lungs. After a few minutes hard labour, I was rewarded when she began gasping and coughing.

Meantime, Holmes had taken centre stage in front of the fire. "You lot have nearly perpetrated a grievous injustice," he declaimed. "Miss Griselda Hodgson is no witch!"

A voice from the crowd shouted, "She murdered the Squire's wife w" her evil eye!"

"She did nothing of the kind," said Holmes. "Squire Pennington murdered his wife! He poisoned her with arsenic!"

The Squire emerged from the crowd, his rage causing him to lapse into his childhood vernacular. "Gan then, tha' lyin' dog! I'll sue thee for slander!"

Holmes reached inside his Inverness and produced a mass of cloth, its brilliant green folds sparkling in the firelight. He shook it in the Squire's face. "You murdered her, I say, with this noxious garment! You made her wear it daily under the guise of sitting for her anniversary portrait. The results of a Marsh Test in the police laboratory at Carlisle will be sufficient to send you to the gallows."

The look of horror on the Squire's livid face as he stared at the garment in Holmes's hands attested to his guilt.

A few days later, we were again ensconced in Baker Street, Holmes in his mouse-grey dressing gown and me with a towel over my head, trousers rolled up to my knees, and my feet immersed in a steaming basin of Epsom salts provided by Mrs. Hudson. I had not escaped unscathed from that rainy night in the woods and my subsequent incarceration in a chilly jail cell.

He tossed a telegram he was holding onto the table. "The Marsh Test of the dress and the contents of the cup in Adele Pennington's bedchamber both came back positive," he said. "As I said before, the Squire will hang."

"Good," I sniffed. "Perfidious dog, murdering the mother of his son. But how did he ever poison her with a dress?"

"Some years ago, these emerald ball gowns became all the rage on the Continent," Holmes said. "No one had seen their like before – until that time, such a brilliant green hue in an article of clothing could simply not be attained. But then the clothing manufactures happened on a dye that had been synthesised in the eighteenth century by the German chemist Carl Wilhelm Scheele, which gave gratifying results. Unfortunately, it was a compound of cupric hydrogen arsenite.

"Of course, there were incidents among women who wore such gowns, skin rashes mostly. The workers who manufactured the clothes suffered more greatly because of prolonged contact with the raw dye, and there were even some deaths."

"How in the world could they allow such clothing to be sold?"

"The law is still *caveat emptor*, Watson. But word of mouth was sufficient to at least limit the damage from the toxic garments. And, truth be told, the effects were generally not catastrophic if a gown was worn only for a few hours at a ball.

"Now, our man the Squire set up an entirely different situation. Using the pretext of the portrait sitting, he had his wife wear the gown for hours a day, day after day. She would become hot and sweaty posing in the sun in front of the parlour window, more and more poison leaching from the cloth, solubilising in her perspiration, facilitating its entry into her system. He could monitor the progress of his scheme by watching her get sicker and sicker."

Holmes rose and went to the mantel for his pipe and the Persian slipper. "Her deteriorating condition drove Adele Pennington to consult Griselda. My examination of the medicament cabinet in her dabbin that first night suggested that she had prescribed oil of pennyroyal, a treatment for nausea and an upset stomach, but also associated with deleterious systemic effects. Regardless of Mrs. Pennington's later opinion, I think that Griselda had tried to do her best by her patient. But she could not resist gaining a reputation for infamy when the Squire's wife labelled her as a witch."

Holmes had his pipe going to his satisfaction, so he went back to his chair. "When we arrived on the scene inquiring about his wife's health, the Squire contrived to hurry her along to Paradise by adding a tot of rat poison to her bedtime cup of milk. Once he knew I had seen the unfinished painting, he also took the precaution of getting rid of the green dress.

"The Squire was an evil, evil man, Watson. Not only did he murder his wife, but I also believe that he was responsible for Griselda's present condition."

"How do you mean?"

"Surely you have noticed the resemblance between the Squire and our client."

I digested that for a moment, then realised what must have happened to Griselda on that ill-fated foraging trip so many years ago. "Did you inform Rachael?"

"No. Some truths are best left untold."

I came back to another point that had been bothering me. "The green dress, Holmes. Wherever did you find it?"

My friend regarded me with a sympathetic expression. "Watson, I must ask you to brace yourself. I have to tell you that the true perpetrator of this crime has escaped justice, at least for now."

I was suddenly wary. "What do you mean?"

"I have not yet discussed the Squire's motive for the murder of his wife. I am afraid he shared it with a Hebrew king."

"What do you mean?" I said again, fearful this time.

"The Squire was engaged in an adulterous affair. With Miss Jones."

"With Miss Jones? That is not possible!"

"I am afraid it is, old fellow. I found the arsenical dress in her hope chest."

I sat there as if poleaxed. It could not be! I thought she was like my Mary . . . .

"I am so sorry, Watson," Holmes said softly.

I took a moment to compose myself. I would not have my voice break when addressing Holmes. When I was ready, I asked, "How did you know?"

"I suspected when you told me of the meeting between Miss Jones and the Squire in the market. You told me they addressed each other by their first names. Now that is not uncommon in Ellenby among childhood friends, but everyone addressed Pennington as "Squire", and moreover, Miss Jones was not a village native. So, their informality likely meant only one thing.

"I took a chance and went to her after I left you at Mereswater House. I gambled that she would not betray me to Trelawney until after she discovered how much I knew. Naturally, I feigned ignorance of her involvement. I prevailed upon her to take a specious message to you, and then searched her cottage after she left and found the dress. Apparently she realized it was missing while we were rescuing the elder Miss Hodgson, and lost no time in decamping."

I had received a note from Miss Jones the day after Griselda Hodgson was rescued from the mob, telling me that she was upset by the affair and had gone to spend some time with her mother in Cardiff. I'd no reason to question it. Now it was apparent that she knew that Holmes had found her out.

"So for the second time in my illustrious career, I find myself bested by a woman," Holmes said. "I would not be surprised if the entire nefarious scheme was hers. Miss Deborah Jones was truly the Witch of Ellenby."

# The Tollington Ghost
## by Roger Silverwood

It was in the freezing cold winter of 1899 that Holmes and I were summoned to Carlisle by our old ally and occasional adversary, Inspector Lestrade. In his telegram he stated that he'd appreciate our assistance with a most unusual case that was baffling the local police. Scotland Yard had been called in to investigate the mysterious death of a guest of Lord Tollington. We arrived late in the afternoon absolutely chilled to the bone.

Lestrade was at the door to greet us. "Ah, there you are, Mr. Holmes. So good of you to come. And Doctor Watson."

"Yes, Inspector," Holmes said. "What is it that makes you need my services so urgently this stark winter's day in the middle of nowhere?"

Lestrade led us over to the warm fire in the great hall and said, "What I have to tell you, Mr. Holmes, is impossible! I must say I can't make head nor tail of it."

Holmes looked down his nose and said, "Please try, for all our sakes."

"Well, yes. The facts unfold like this . . . For his entertainment, Lord Tollington had a houseful of guests over Christmas and during the jollifications, there was talk about the ghost that haunts the house. You will probably have heard of it, the Tollington Ghost – probably the most famous ghost in the world!"

Holmes looked into the man's eyes and said, "My agency is founded on rationality, Lestrade."

I had to intervene. "I wouldn't be so dismissive, Holmes. I've heard of it. It is well documented."

"Remember my motto, Watson," Holmes said. "'No ghosts need apply at 221b'. Please continue, Lestrade."

"Well, for a bet, a man well-known for his eccentricities, Wellington Pinchbeck by name, declared that he didn't believe that ghosts existed and to prove it, he bet his Lordship a hundred guineas that, not only would he spend the night in the room where the ghost is supposed to appear, but that, if he could find a corpse, any corpse, he would do it in the company of that corpse in an open coffin."

I was utterly astonished at the idea. Holmes raised his eyebrows and waited for Lestrade to continue.

"Mr. Pinchbeck was quite a one for his outrageous eccentricities. I had known him slightly. I've been in his company several times at the

58

giant August Bank Holiday parties for police orphans he supported in Hyde Park these past few years."

"From your use of the past tense, I take it all did not end well for Mr. Pinchbeck. Please go on, Lestrade. You have my full attention."

"Well, by private arrangement with the local undertaker, the body of a local vagrant, who was to have been buried the following day, was delivered into the room in an open coffin. Then Wellington Pinchbeck, apparently with much hilarity, was locked in the room at ten o'clock that night. Some of the guests took it in turns to stay outside the door and make sure he didn't attempt to pick the lock or find another way of escape. Then at nine o'clock the following morning, his Lordship, the undertaker, and his Lordship's butler unlocked the room in company with many of the guests to discover that the corpse of the vagrant had disappeared, and in the coffin in its place was the dead body of Wellington Pinchbeck!"

I am afraid that I found it most grotesque. Holmes, in his most businesslike manner, said, "Well, Lestrade, our first step is clear: We must see the room."

"Indeed," Lestrade said. "His Lordship has given me possession of the key. Please follow me, gentlemen."

The entrance to the room was by the front door of the hall and only twenty yards away from where we had been standing.

Lestrade inserted the key in the lock and turned it. The solid oak door opened noisily. Lestrade led the way. It was a large room with only one door and one huge window. Our footsteps clattered noisily on the marble-like floor. There was not much in the way of comfort and I immediately noticed how cold it was. Our breath showed up white, like steam from a kettle.

Holmes's eyes were everywhere, although there was very little to see. Just a make-shift bed, a chair, a table, and two trestles on which the coffin had rested.

Lestrade said, "You'll note, gentlemen, that the trestles were positioned next to the bed. A great joker was Wellington Pinchbeck!"

Beyond the primitive furniture were twelve stone statues like pillars purporting to hold up the roof. "Who are these fellows, Lestrade?" I asked.

"Figures of all the previous Lord Tollingtons. The present holder of the title is the thirteenth."

"The thirteenth!" I said. "Huh. An ominous number."

Holmes said, "Only to the superstitious, Watson. And I credit you with more sense than that." He turned to Lestrade. "Who made the discovery in the morning?"

"First at the door were Lord Tollington, the butler, Cramphorn – an entirely dependable man if you ask me – and the undertaker, Josiah Deep.

But they were also in company with many of the other guests. Cramphorn had a breakfast tray for Mr. Pinchbeck, and was prepared to assist Josiah Deep to remove the coffin containing the vagrant to the hearse, which was waiting to go straight to the church for the funeral."

"I see," Holmes said. "They searched this room, of course?"

I looked around, and thought that there really wasn't anywhere to search.

"They found nothing," Lestrade said, "so his Lordship summoned the Carlisle police. They came immediately, but they also found nothing."

"And has the vagrant's body turned up anywhere?"

"No. That's the mystery. That, and who killed Wellington Pinchbeck. And why."

"And *how*," Holmes added. He pursed his lips briefly. "And where is Pinchbeck's body now?"

"In Josiah Deep's funeral parlour."

Holmes looked up. "We need dally here no longer. We must visit Deep's funeral parlour immediately."

I was pleased to leave that cold hall and return to the main hall and the comforting fire. We waited there until his Lordship's carriage arrived at the front door and then made our way to it and suffered the two-mile journey to a somber-looking building on the perimeter of Tollington village. It chilled me even more to read the sign fixed to the entrance of the yard: "*Josiah Deep and Son. Funeral Parlour – Coffin Maker to the Gentry*".

We stepped down from the carriage to see a man coming out of the door. He saw us and walked our way. It was clear from his apparel that he was a man of the cloth.

"Good evening, gentlemen," he said.

"Good evening, Rector," Holmes replied.

The man briefly removed his hat and said, "Not yet rector. Just a humble curate, I fear, in the service of the Lord. Excuse me, gentlemen, I haven't seen you around these parts. Have you recently moved here? Should I be calling on you and welcoming you and your families to the parish of Little Tollington, and hopefully counting you among my congregation at The Church of Saint Peter?"

Holmes said, "I think not, Curate. But thank you. We are guests of Lord Tollington, staying for a day or two at Tollington Hall."

"Oh? Ah yes, you must be the policemen investigating the death of the unfortunate Mr. Wellington Pinchbeck. Strange business. Hmm," he said and shook his bowed head. Then he said, "My name is Striker. I wonder if you could assist me? I am trying to construct an appropriate service of burial for the poor man. I have chosen the *Psalms*. The Twenty-

Third . . . '*The Lord is my shepherd I shall not want*', is always appropriate, and perhaps The Hundred-and-Fifty-Fourth . . . '*Let them come forth with cymbal, drum and fife*'. Hymns are easier to choose. I let Mr. Moffat the organist have the last word there. But the mourners will expect a eulogy, and I don't know the first thing about the poor man."

"I should speak with Lord Tollington," Holmes said. "What he doesn't know about Wellington Pinchbeck, I am sure he would be able to glean from Pinchbeck's acquaintances."

"A good idea, Mr. Holmes," the rector said. "I will contact him forthwith. Thank you."

"Please excuse us. We must press on."

"Delighted to have met you, gentlemen. Good night."

He made for the yard gate and disappeared into the darkness.

Lestrade stepped up to the undertaker's front door. "Let's hope Josiah Deep hasn't retired to bed."

"Funeral Directors are expected to keep odd hours, Lestrade," Holmes said. "People often choose the most inconvenient times to die."

Before Lestrade could lower the knocker, the door was snatched open and a tall, thin man stared out at him and said, "Ah! Josiah Deep at your service, gentlemen. What can I do for ye? Are ye looking for a coffin? Have ye need of a funeral? I am very sorry about your sad loss."

Lestrade introduced himself, then Holmes and myself.

Deep stared at my friend and said, "Not *the* Sherlock Holmes?"

"The very one," I said.

"And *the* Doctor Watson," Holmes added.

"Come in, come in," Deep said busily and led us into a dark workshop illuminated by two candles on a stand.

"Mr. Deep," Holmes said. "I understand that you delivered a corpse to Tollington Hall for an overnight stay, intending to collect it the following morning."

The undertaker's eyes shone reflecting the candlelight. They looked as if they were illuminated from behind.

"Aye, that is correct," Deep said. "It's not against the law, is it? He was a vagrant. He was to have been buried on the parish. It was a charity case. The cost would have been borne by the ratepayers of Lower Tollington if Lord Tollington had not offered – out of the goodness of his heart – to pay for a brand new shroud, a secondhand coffin with four reconditioned brass handles with sixteen brass screws, a sprig of holly, the hire of two horses with re-fluffed plumes, the hire and washing and polishing and use of my brand new glass sided hearse recently imported from Bohemia – "

Lestrade said, "Losing a body is a serious offence."

"With respect, Inspector," Deep said. "I didn't lose him. You must talk to his Lordship about that."

"Where is the body now?" Holmes said.

"I don't know," Deep replied. "Nobody knows. All that I know is that I delivered the body in a pine coffin to Tollington Hall at nine o'clock that evening and when I came the following morning, prepared to take the vagrant straight to the church for the curate to bury him, the body in the coffin was not him at all, but that of the gentleman, Wellington Pinchbeck."

"Well, where are the last remains of Wellington Pinchbeck now?" Holmes said.

Deep pointed to a coffin leaning against the wall. "He's there. Behind the Good Doctor."

I moved swiftly to one side.

Holmes said, "Calm yourself, Watson. He cannot harm you."

Holmes never missed an opportunity to poke fun at me. "I've seen many a corpse," I replied.

"Aye," Deep said. "He stands in there. In one of our finest caskets. The fine inlaid gold lettering in copper-plate on the lid was engraved by my own fair hand. Aye."

Lestrade picked up the candlestick, took it to the coffin and read the brass plaque. "'*Wellington Pinchbeck, 1842 to 1899. R.I.P.*'"

Deep looked at Lestrade and said, "It's a work of art, isn't it?"

Lestrade didn't know what to answer. I came to his rescue.

"Mr. Deep," I said. "I would very much like to see the corpse."

"Of course, of course," he said, and he came over to the coffin and removed the lid. He turned back for the candlestick and said, "He looks quite respectable now."

I was the nearest and so I peered in at the body. The eyes were closed and the face was pale. It was in a white shroud in a neat white silk-lined coffin and in every way appeared normal.

Lestrade came forward and so did Holmes.

Holmes said, "Lestrade, you knew Wellington Pinchbeck? Would you say that that is his body?"

"Without doubt, Mr. Holmes. Without any doubt at all. That's Wellington Pinchbeck all right."

"Mr. Deep," Holmes said. "Do you have the death certificate?"

"Indeed I do," Deep said, blowing wood dust and shavings off it.

"Would you be good enough to let Doctor Watson peruse it?"

"Of course," Deep said and he passed it to me.

I went to the candlestick and read it quickly.

"What does it say, Watson?"

I finished reading every word for my own benefit, then I read aloud the pertinent words: "'*Wellington Pinchbeck . . . December 28th 1899 . . . Heart failure . . . Broncho pneumonia . . .*' Signed by Septimus Flynn, D.M. Dubin, 112 London Road."

Holmes sniffed and then said, "Are you satisfied, Watson?"

"Looks all right to me, Holmes," I said passing the certificate back to Josiah Deep.

"Well, what would cause heart failure?"

"Almost anything. If he already had a weak heart, almost anything. I'm not surprised he caught pneumonia. These last few nights, in that room without heating, it would be perishingly cold at night."

"Watson, are you saying he died of natural causes?"

"I'm saying it's possible, Holmes. Only possible."

"Very well. If it were so, who removed the vagrant's body from the coffin?"

"Good question, Mr. Holmes," Lestrade said.

"In the middle of the night, did the dead vagrant obligingly remove himself from it and assist Wellington Pinchbeck to take his place? And then disappear into thin air? I think not."

Holmes then took one look round the candlelit undertaker's workroom and said, "Come along, gentlemen. Our work is finished here. Goodnight, Mr. Deep."

We left the undertaker's premises and took the carriage back to Tollington Hall. I was tired, cold, and hungry. Holmes was irritable. He was always like that when he had a difficult case. He enjoyed the challenge, but he could be somewhat tetchy when he was making no progress. As for me, I couldn't make any sense of the case at all.

Lestrade introduced us to Lord Tollington and then took his leave, as he had been called back to London on some other urgent business. Lord Tollington was very kindly providing us with rooms in Tollington Hall, and what was even more welcome, he had invited Holmes and me to have dinner with him, just the three of us, and soon we were enjoying the most delightful roast pheasant with parsnips and potatoes in the big dining room.

"You are both most welcome," Tollington said. "I have your company to enjoy, and if you can solve the mystery, I shall be obliged to you."

He turned to his butler, Cramphorn, and said, "A bottle of the "84, and put another two on ice."

"Very good, my Lord," replied the butler, and he left the room.

"This a grand meal, your Lordship," I remarked. "I give you thanks."

Holmes held up his glass and said, "Hear, hear."

Tollington smiled.

Holmes said, "Watson has been telling me about the Tollington Ghost. How long have you been aware of its presence?"

"It has always been here," his Lordship said. "Even before I was born, my father spoke of it. It appears from the porter's pantry by the front door. That's why we always keep the room locked. I don't know if you can stop a ghost by locking a door, but anyway . . . It is the ghost of a Scottish piper, a friend of the fourth lord, who was passing through Carlisle on his way to Glasgow and was invited to stay the night. However, during the early hours, the night porter caught the man searching through his belongings in the pantry.

"Assuming he was an intruder, he hit him on the head with a lantern stand. The blow killed the soldier, and it subsequently turned out that he was searching through his own trunk looking possibly for some clothes, bagpipes, or some whisky, for those were the sole contents of his luggage. I've never seen the ghost myself, but I have seen things move in response to its antics. And I've heard it traversing the hall and I have heard the pipes. You can sometimes most unexpectedly hear them played in the grounds, from the island in the loch or even further away than that."

"Most interesting," Holmes said, chewing thoughtfully.

"Ah, good," Tollington said. "Cramphorn is back with the wine."

There was the pop of a cork and the welcome sound of champagne fizzing in the glasses.

"Tell me, your Lordship," Holmes said. "Was this man, Wellington Pinchbeck, a friend of yours?"

"I didn't know him at all, but I had heard he was excellent company, so I invited him to lighten our Christmas and entertain us, as we hoped to entertain each other. I didn't expect him to push me into making a silly wager of a hundred guineas – which I couldn't get out of – that he would spend the night in the porter's pantry, as he did.

I tasted the champagne. It was delightful. I held up my glass to his Lordship and to Holmes and took a sip. They nodded and joined me.

"Ah," I said. It was both enjoyable and refreshing. "The '84 is unmistakeable."

Holmes resumed the questioning of his Lordship.

"And what can you tell us about the poor vagrant, whose remains have so mysteriously vanished?"

"Nothing, Mr. Holmes. Absolutely nothing. Josiah Deep was given the task of providing Wellington Pinchbeck with a corpse and that he did. I saw the remains of the poor man in a shroud in the coffin, on its arrival at about nine o'clock that night. I haven't seen anything of the corpse since."

"Nor has anybody else. When I have finished this entirely delightful repast, your Lordship, I will retire to the porter's pantry. I will lock myself in, and I will take my pipe. I will need to beg a full box of matches from you, Watson."

The idea filled me with horror. "Oh no, Holmes," I said. "No."

Tollington's face went pale. "I would strongly advise against it, Mr. Holmes," he said, "considering what happened to Wellington Pinchbeck. It could be very dangerous."

"Dangerous or not," Holmes said. "It will have to be done if we are to make any progress at all in solving this mystery."

Well, of course, despite my objections, Holmes got his own way. I was mightily apprehensive about the whole business, spending the night or even part of the night in that cold inhospitable chamber on his own. I offered to join him, but he wouldn't hear of it. He went in with his pipe, tobacco pouch, and a full box of matches, just before midnight.

I couldn't leave him and retire to bed. Cramphorn furnished me with a blanket, a storm lantern, and a glass of port, and though very tired, I settled down in the hall porter's chair facing the door. I was very apprehensive. I was determined to be on hand in case he required assistance. I was prepared, as much as I could be, should the Tollington Ghost decide to show itself.

The next thing I remember I was being gently squeezed at the shoulder. It took me a few moments to realise where I was and what was happening. "Are you all right, Doctor?" Cramphorn was saying. "Are you all right, Doctor Watson? You must have fallen asleep, sir."

My first thought was of Holmes. "What's happening? Where's Holmes?" I asked.

"I've brought you a pot of tea, Doctor," Cramphorn said. "It's eight o'clock. I thought you would want to be wakened."

"Oh! What time? Eight o'clock? Oh yes. Thank you. Where's Mr. Holmes?"

"I haven't seen him this morning, Doctor."

I looked across at the big brown door facing me "Oh my goodness, he's . . . he must still be in there," I said.

"Where, sir?" Cramphorn said.

"In there. The porter's pantry. I must go in. Holmes said he only intended being in there for a couple of hours or so. Bring that lantern, will you?"

Cramphorn's face turned white. "I don't think we should go in there, sir. It's still dark."

I whisked away the blanket, jumped up, and said, "Never mind, Cramphorn. I'll go in alone."

Then I noticed the key was in the lock. That was strange. I tried the door. It was locked, so I turned the key. It made a heavy clunking sound,

"I'm right behind you, Doctor," Cramphorn said,

He must have had a change of heart. I have to admit, I was glad of his support,

"The door was locked," I said. "Who could have locked Holmes inside? I've been out here all night."

"You must have slept all though it, sir."

"But Holmes had the key . . . took it in with him. So . . . who . . . ?"

I opened the door. The hinges squeaked. I ventured inside. It felt a perishing ten degrees cooler. "Holmes! Holmes! Are you here?" I said. "Hold up the light, Cramphorn, my dear fellow."

"Right, sir," he replied in a small voice.

I noticed that even a whisper echoed round the chamber.

"Nobody here," I said. We stepped further into the chamber.

"Hmm. I'll just take a look behind all these statues. Can't think what the devil has happened to him. Holmes, where are you?"

We went around the pillars.

Cramphorn said, "There's nobody here, sir."

It was indeed so, and so very cold. "Let's get out of here," I said.

I was pleased to return to the comparative warmth and electrical illumination of the main hall, but was highly concerned about the disappearance of my friend. I wondered if he had found a trapdoor or other means of access to the pantry and had had an accident, and was at that very moment at the mercy of some fiend, or was sick and suffering from the cold.

Cramphorn said, "I'll lock the door, sir."

"By all means," I said. "I wonder where he could have got to?"

"Oh look, Doctor," Cramphorn said. "He's coming down the staircase now. He looks in fine form."

My heart warmed. "Ah, so he is. Well I'm blessed."

"Excuse me, Doctor Watson. I have to attend to his Lordship," Cramphorn said and rushed away.

"Thank you," I said, but he had gone.

Holmes came up to me as bright as a new pin. "Good morning, Watson. I trust you had a comfortable night?"

He was teasing me. I could tell by his eyes and general demeanour that he had not only had a good night, but he had also made some momentous progress in the case.

"Holmes, you had me worried. Where on earth have you been?"

"Where every sober, and intelligent Englishman should be, of course, when the sun is set. In bed."

"Lucky you. I waited for you and – "

"Yes, but when I came out of the porter's pantry, you were propped up in the chair fast asleep and you looked too comfortable to disturb. So I bid you a passing goodnight and went up to my room."

"Never heard a thing. What time was that, pray?"

"It was eight minutes past two."

"So you were in there for over two hours. Did you see the ghost? Was there an appearance?"

"I did not. I experienced nothing ethereal whatsoever."

"Oh. Well, did you discover anything?"

"I did, Watson. I did indeed."

"You found out where the dead body was hidden, and who dressed Wellington Pinchbeck in a shroud and put him in the coffin?"

"No. I didn't discover how that came about."

"Well, come along , Holmes, don't tease me. What did you find?"

"I went to look for a concealed cavity, nook, room, or passageway, or any place where a body could have been hidden or removed."

"Ah yes," I said. We were getting to the crux of it at last.

"I knew that the temperature in such a secret place, if one existed, would inevitably be different and would have caused a flow of air, even though it might have been very slight. There, utilising the smoke from my pipe, I checked on all the seams and joints in the panelling, the floor, and the décor of the room.

"Yes?" I said quickly.

"And I can say categorically that there are positively no secret places where a body could have been concealed or transported."

"Really?" I said. "Ah. The window? Access must have been made via the window."

"I'll wager that window hasn't been opened since Queen Victoria visited the Hall in 1849."

"So what do you deduce from all that?"

"It's obvious, my dear Watson. We have been misled."

"Misled? Misled by whom?"

"Of that I am still in doubt. But the certainty that a body was not hidden or traversed through concealed places raises other trains of thought. Hmm. Watson, I must make a telephone call. I suggest that you join his Lordship in the breakfast room. I must find the telephone."

Holmes dashed off in the direction of the library while I wandered down the corridors, following the smell of fried bacon to where his Lordship was taking breakfast.

Courtesies were exchanged and Cramphorn assisted me to liberal helpings of fried bacon, tea, and toast.

67

Holmes appeared a few minutes later and joined his Lordship and me at the breakfast table.

Lord Tollington said, "Ah, Holmes. Cramphorn will attend you."

Holmes was soon served and then the butler departed.

"Any nearer the truth, Mr. Holmes?" his Lordship said.

"Yes, my Lord. But I cannot help but wonder what happened to your last valet. I trust he must have left your employ at very short notice?"

Tollington's eyebrows shot up. "My valet? You are quite right, Mr. Holmes. But how could you possibly have known anything about my valet?"

"And your butler, Cramphorn is filling his place – willingly, nay, conscientiously, but not as efficiently?"

Tollington stared at Holmes, utterly bemused. "That's absolutely right, Mr. Holmes. Absolutely correct. But how could you possibly know that?

"Last night, my Lord, your trousers, if you will forgive me, had two parallel creases in them, when by common agreement among the Knightsbridge fashion gurus of the day, that is one too many."

"Really? I didn't notice. But how did you know Cramphorn had executed the pressing?"

"Well, whom else could it be? It was very likely, wasn't it? The fact that his eyesight is so weak tended to confirm it."

It was both pleasing and amusing to see that his Lordship was impressed by Holmes's revelations.

"What? Well, yes. True, I knew he was having some difficulty with his eyes and recently seen an optician, but how did you know that?"

"Yes," I said. "Do explain."

"The champagne that we had at supper last night was not John de la Vére, 1884, but *1887*. You asked Cramphorn for the '84. I took it that the reason for the error was Cramphorn's struggle with a dusty champagne label, a candle, and his weak eyesight in a dark cellar. I could conceive of no other explanation."

"Remarkable!" Tollington said. "I must say, I wouldn't have known."

"Well done," I said. Then I turned to his Lordship. "Well, my Lord, what did happen to the valet?"

Holmes answered quickly: "I'll tell you what happened to him, Watson. He was dismissed by his Lordship for stealing."

Tollington smiled broadly. "By Jove, that's right, Mr. Holmes. How did you know that?"

Holmes said, "And his name was Striker."

"And how did you know that, Mr. Holmes?"

"Last night we met a confidence trickster of that name, posing as a curate, coming out of Josiah Deep's funeral parlour."

"You didn't tell me he was a confidence trickster, Holmes. How did you find that out?"

"For one thing, he proposed to include Psalm Number One-Hundred-and-Fifty-Four at Wellington Pinchbeck's funeral.

"And what is that wrong with that?" I asked.

"Watson! Every self-respecting clergyman knows that there are only one-hundred-and-fifty Psalms in the book!"

I felt a little foolish, but I soon recovered.

Tollington said, "You never cease to amaze me, Mr. Holmes."

"His dress as a curate was no doubt intended as a disguise. He called me 'Mr. Holmes', even though he didn't know who we were. He was quizzing us to see how much we knew! A man who dressed up as a curate, with the aid of crude cosmetics and his brother-in-law's assistance, could just as easily dress up as a corpse."

"That's right," Tollington said. "He is Josiah Deep's brother-in-law."

"A corpse," I said. "Oh really, Holmes. I think it is dashed unsporting of you to keep that back."

"Watson, my good friend! I didn't know for certain – not until five minutes ago, when, on the telephone, I accused Josiah Deep and he admitted the whole thing."

"Well hadn't we better send the police off to arrest Striker, before he gets away?"

"There is no need," Holmes said. "There is no crime."

"No crime, Mr. Holmes?" Tollington said. "The man's dead."

"Natural causes," Holmes said. "Heart failure, no doubt aggravated by the intake of alcohol followed by pneumonia. It would be recorded as 'accidental death'."

Holmes was correct. "Yes," I said. "That is so."

Tollington ran his hand through his hair. "What happened then, Mr. Holmes?"

"After I had assured myself that there were no places to hide in the porter's pantry, I realised that there never was a dead vagrant. It would have to have been someone living, posing as the dead man. The only person who knew the identity of the corpse was Josiah Deep. So I telephoned him five minutes ago. I told him that he would never bury another soul in England, Scotland, or Wales if he didn't admit that it was his brother-in-law, Striker, your ex-valet, who had been posing as the corpse of a vagrant in the coffin.

"Wellington Pinchbeck boasted that he would spend the night in the porter's pantry in company with a corpse. Josiah Deep was approached to

69

supply a dead body. His brother-in-law, Striker heard of this, and, out of revenge – saw a golden opportunity to make mischief and get back at his Lordship. He knew a substantial wager had been made. So Striker put himself up to be the corpse. Deep made him up to look the part and duly delivered him here in the coffin.

"During the night, Striker tapped on the coffin or sat up in it or performed some other manifestations and frightened poor Wellington Pinchbeck out of his skin. The shock killed him. Striker was in a predicament. The prank had turned to tragedy. He got out of the coffin, exchanged his shroud for the dead man's clothes, and put Pinchbeck in the coffin and waited until morning. When he heard the door opening, he hid behind one of the statues. All the attention would be on the dead man in the coffin. Striker was thus able to make his way out of the room, while his brother-in-law, Josiah Deep, realising what had happened, held the guests' attention as Striker sneaked his way out of the house and away."

I could hardly believe it.

"You've done it again," I said. "You've solved the unsolvable."

"Mr. Holmes," Tollington said, "I am truly amazed."

Holmes smiled and stood up to leave.

"But what about the ghost then?" asked our host. "Is there really a Tollington ghost?"

Holmes looked from me to his Lordship and said, "Who knows? There are things in this world that we cannot know. Only time itself will reveal to us the absolute truth."

# You Only Live Thrice
## by Robert Stapleton

The streets of Guildford felt cold and depressing. The chill January wind cut through even my corpulent frame, whilst the strident voices of newspaper vendors broadcast news of Queen Victoria's latest illness.

The moment I reached the comparative warmth of the Surrey County Police Headquarters that morning, the Superintendent called me in to his office.

"How do you like this weather, Baynes?" he asked me, as he sat back in the luxury of his upholstered leather chair.

I contemplated the smart new calendar for 1901, standing between us on the desk. "I shall be much happier when the summer comes, sir."

"In that case, how would a trip to the West Indies suit you?" He smiled as he watched my expression brighten.

I knew from years of experience that far more lay behind that question than initially met the ear. I replied cautiously, "It would be a refreshing change, sir. Where exactly do you have in mind?"

"Barbados," he replied. "I understand the climate there can be more agreeable than even Guildford at this time of the year."

"I should hope so, sir." I wondered what was coming next.

"You are to go there and arrest a man going by the name of Jason Fairworthy-Smith. Though what his real name might be is beyond both myself and Scotland Yard."

"Fairworthy-Smith, the swindler?" I replied. "That fellow from the village of Greenford Steeple, who makes himself out to be a gentleman? The last time I came across him, he was making a fortune out of selling shares in some bogus Australian goldmine – amongst other dubious projects."

The Superintendent nodded. "He targeted mostly rich people, but some other investors lost everything they owned. In his determination to make himself a rich man, Fairworthy-Smith also made a number of powerful enemies among the criminal underworld."

"No wonder he wanted to make himself scarce," I added, "and head to sunnier climes."

My superior consulted a paper lying before him. "Mr. Sherlock Holmes has recommended you for this particular job." He looked up at me again. "You have had dealings with this gentleman on a previous occasion, I believe."

"But that was several years ago now, sir," I replied, taken aback by this unexpected revelation. "I have no idea why he might have considered me suitable for such an assignment."

"Nevertheless, his recommendation is good enough for me," said the Super, looking me squarely in the face. "You are to travel by Royal Mail steamer to Bridgetown, secure Fairworthy-Smith's arrest, and return with him as soon as possible. And remember, Baynes, this is constabulary business, and not some holiday jaunt for indolent police officers."

"I shall try to remember that, sir."

"Fairworthy-Smith absconded before we could complete our case against him. But the documentation is now prepared." The Super pushed a bundle of papers across the desk. "Your ship leaves on Friday."

I picked up the documents, and examined the travel warrant and arrest authorization.

"That gives you three days to prepare."

I hesitated. "It occurs to me, sir, that if our man is desperate enough to travel so far away in order to avoid apprehension, he might turn out to be particularly dangerous when threatened with arrest."

The Superintendent pondered the matter. "You have a good point, Baynes. In that case, you'd better take your revolver with you."

The voyage to Bridgetown lasted a week, much of which time I spent in utter misery, as *mâl de mer* seized me with a grip of iron, and confined me to my cabin.

On the morning I was feeling better, I descended to the saloon for breakfast.

I collected my choice of food, approached an empty table, and sat down.

As I picked up my knife and fork, another man approached. He had dark hair, a sallow complexion, and was wearing a brown suit over a thin but wiry frame.

"Do you mind if I join you?" he asked.

Not wishing to appear rude, and in need of some company for a change, I replied that I had no objection.

The man sat down.

"My name is Mordred Scarrington," he began, fixing me with his steely gaze.

I wondered if I had heard the name somewhere before.

"And I am Inspector Baynes," I replied plainly, not feeling in the mood to play games of guess-what-I-am.

"A policeman," observed Scarrington. He seemed taken aback by this revelation.

"On police business."

"Metropolitan Force?"

"Surrey County Constabulary."

He relaxed somewhat. "With business in Barbados?"

"Indeed. And yourself?"

"I am also traveling to the island on business," replied Scarrington. "On behalf of an important client in London."

Being a naturally suspicious policeman, I wondered if perhaps we were both after the same man. "I understand Barbados is a small island."

"Then perhaps our paths might cross again."

The remaining days of that transatlantic voyage were distinguished by only two notable events. One evening, as the weather was becoming warmer, I ventured out on deck. The sea was calmer than it had been farther north, and the clear air made the stars shine with a brilliance I had rarely seen in Surrey.

As I stood beside the safety rail, smoking my final cigarette of the day, I had the distinct impression that somebody was approaching me from behind.

I stepped adroitly to one side, and turned to face whoever was there. A shadowy figure, with hands outstretched toward me, immediately turned and slipped away into the shadows, leaving me with the unpleasant impression that I had escaped death by only a few seconds. I also had the impression that the figure I had seen was my recent acquaintance, Scarrington.

The second occasion was the night before we were due to arrive at Bridgetown. I was lying on my bunk, trying in vain to remain cool, when I heard the door to my cabin unlock and open. The sound was slight, but distinctive. In the darkness, I became aware of another presence in my cabin. Moonlight, filtering in through the porthole, glinted on a fragment of steel. A knife. That was enough for me. I stood up, shouted my defiance, and threw one of my boots at the approaching figure. Instead of leaving, the intruder drew closer. It was at times such as this that I cursed by bulky size. I had no wish to make a fight of it, since I would be at a disadvantage on almost every count: Fat, slow, middle-aged, and, at that moment, unarmed. But my size and muscular strength gave me one advantage in the darkness. I threw myself at the intruder, knocking him off balance. Then I grasped the hand holding the knife, and twisted it until the weapon clattered to the floor. Now disarmed, the figure cursed me, turned, and fled.

Having secured the cabin door with a chair against the handle, I slept fitfully for the rest of the night, and awoke in the morning, alert to the fact that the ship had stopped moving, and the engines were no longer running.

I looked outside, and saw land.

*Barbados.*

After a hurried breakfast, during which time I noticed that Scarrington was keeping his distance from me, with his right wrist strapped up and resting in a sling, I ventured out on deck, and looked around. The steamer was now moored to a buoy, stationary in a turquoise sea. Across the water, beyond a flotilla of other harbored vessels, the island looked magnificent in the light of the early dawn. The shore was lined with trees, behind which houses with whitewashed walls and red tiled roofs lay partially hidden, as though nervous of too impulsive an encounter with their foreign visitors. A gentle off-shore breeze carried the smell of earth and humanity. Above the horizon, beyond flat farmland and green rolling moors, the rays of the rising sun reached up into a blue sky, promising a warm and glorious day.

One of the ship's officers approached me.

"Is this your first time in the West Indies, sir?" he asked.

"It is indeed," I replied. "I assume we have now reached our destination."

"Quite correct. We are now lying in Carlisle Bay, awaiting transfer to the dockside at Bridgetown. It shouldn't be long now, sir. You will find Barbados a delightful place. I hope you have an enjoyable stay."

I hoped so too.

The moment I set foot on the quayside, I was greeted by a young man, dressed in a khaki uniform, and displaying a distinctly military bearing. He gave me a broad grin, white teeth lighting up his dark face. "Good morning, sir," he said. "You must be Inspector Baynes."

I took out a handkerchief, mopped my brow, and nodded.

"I am Sergeant McAdam, sir, of the Royal Barbados Police Force, Central Station Guard. I have been sent to welcome you to Bridgetown, and to take you to meet the officer in charge."

"I also need to check in to my hotel," I told him.

"You have no need to worry about that, sir. I have already arranged for your luggage to be taken there directly."

"Very well, Sergeant. Lead the way."

He took me through the city center, past sellers of yams and sweet potatoes, to the impressive Police Headquarters building. I was looking forward to meeting the man in charge, hoping that he might exert his utmost effort in helping me complete my mission to the island.

74

The officer in charge, an Englishman with a cut-glass accent, greeted me warmly and invited me to sit down in a wicker chair. After a few polite enquiries about the voyage, he clasped his hands together, and leaned over his mahogany desk. "News has come through from England, via the miracle of undersea telegraphy, that Her Majesty the Queen has sadly passed away. She died on the twenty-second, surrounded by her family."

"That is very sad new, sir, even if it was to be expected," I replied. "Long live King Edward."

"Indeed. *God Save the King!* I am sure that we now stand on the very brink of a new era, as well as a new century."

I nodded.

"Now, to the reason for your visit here, Baynes. This business of yours shouldn't take very long to complete. I should think that you'll be on your way home by the very next steamer."

"I hope so, sir," I replied. "I am here with the single purpose of arresting that fellow, Fairworthy-Smith. I only need to know where I can find him, and then I can prepare to be on my way."

"Yes, we know about Fairworthy-Smith," he replied guardedly. "A slippery customer. If we'd had the paperwork earlier, we might have had him arrested before you arrived."

"Of course, sir." I passed across to him the documents concerning the case, which I had been given in Guildford.

He glanced at them, nodded, and put them to one side. "I can safely leave you in the capable hands of Sergeant McAdam."

"Thank you, sir. He seems a keen and personable young fellow."

"He will be able to supply you with anything else you might require."

"I am sure he will prove to be a most useful companion, sir."

"Splendid. Well, don't let me delay you."

I left, feeling slightly disappointed by my interview, and found Sergeant McAdam waiting for me outside, standing beside a horse and trap. The animal seemed as anxious to be on its way as did the policeman.

I climbed aboard. "What do you have planned for me, McAdam?"

A broad grin once more lit up his face. "If it's all right with you, sir, I shall give you a guided tour of the city, show you the sights, and then drop you off at your hotel, in time for your midday meal."

"That sounds extremely civilized," I told him. "Then I shall need you to find out for me as much as you can about the present whereabouts of our fugitive, Jason Fairworthy-Smith."

As promised, McAdam made sure I reached my hotel room around midday, allowing me time to change out of my traveling clothes before luncheon.

75

The moment I stepped through the door of my hotel room, I had a feeling that I was not alone there.

I was trying to remember where I had left my revolver, when a man stepped out of the shadows. "Hello, Mr. Baynes," said a voice I remembered from another time and another place.

I looked the man over. His hair was a rich ginger color, as was his thin moustache. His appearance was further distinguished by a monocle which he wore in his right eye. I recognized the fellow at once. "Hello, Smith," I growled. "I am here to take you home. You are to stand trial for fraud."

Fairworthy-Smith gave a mirthless chuckle. "Most of those people had done nothing to deserve their money, you know. Some had inherited it from their parents, whilst others had themselves swindled it from the poor and innocent. I have never shed a tear over taking their money, and I doubt that many of them will have lost much sleep over it either."

"Except those you left impoverished."

"They only have themselves to blame."

"But that does not excuse your crimes."

"And you are merely carrying out your duty. Yes, I know. I was warned that you were on your way, Inspector."

"Warned? By whom?"

"By a friend."

"Then I hope you will surrender yourself to my custody without further ado."

Fairworthy-Smith stood erect and defiant. "I can assure you, Inspector, that you will never take me back to England. I have powerful enemies at home, and if I go back to stand trial, they will take their revenge by seeing me dead within the week."

"We can offer you protection."

"Can you protect me from the assassin they've already sent here to kill me?"

"Assassin?"

"He arrived on the same ship that brought you."

It took me only a moment to remember. "Scarrington?"

"I don't know *who* he is, but I do know *what* he is. And if he suspects that you are here to arrest me, then your own life could well be in danger."

"He already tried to kill me on two occasions."

"Then the matter is indeed serious."

"But you can hardly evade both of us. At least with me, you will stand a chance of surviving a little longer."

"There are other ways to survive, Inspector."

"Maybe, but my immediate business if to arrest you." I glared back at him. "Jason Fairworthy-Smith, I have a warrant for your detention, and I am now placing you under arrest on suspicion of committing crimes of fraud. You will accompany me to the Police Headquarters, where the formal charge will be made. Then I shall take you back to stand trial in England."

"I really don't think you will, Inspector," replied Fairworthy-Smith. "I fear that your journey here has been a total waste of valuable time, which you could have used for more profitable purposes. As I told you, I shall never go back to England."

"Now you are guilty of the additional offence of resisting arrest."

Fairworthy-Smith gave me a sour look, made all the more poisonous by the monocle. He then pushed past me, and stomped away down the corridor.

I slumped into the bedroom chair, and contemplated this turn of events. I had found my man, but taking my prisoner back to stand trial would prove to be a more demanding task than I had imagined.

After luncheon in the restaurant downstairs, I sat in the lounge, sipping a fruit juice, and feeling sorry for myself in the unfamiliar heat.

I was nodding off to sleep when Sergeant McAdam arrived.

"Good afternoon, Inspector."

"Oh, hello, McAdam. Please take a seat."

"Thank you, sir." He sat down on another easy chair, and looked at me, expectantly.

"Well, have you discovered anything about our friend, Fairworthy-Smith?"

"Yes, sir."

"Then first allow me to tell you that I found him before you did."

The sergeant's face showed great surprise. "You found him?"

"Yes. He was already in my room, waiting for me. The fellow then left whilst resisting my arrest."

McAdam stood up in alarm. "Then we must lose no time in apprehending the man."

"That might not prove an easy job, now that he knows that I am here. But first sit down, and tell me all you know."

"Mr. Jason Fairworthy-Smith arrived in Barbados in September of last year, sir. He deposited a large quantity of cash at the Central Bank, arranged to hire a small villa on the edge of town, and since then has kept himself very much to himself."

"In that case, we need to begin by visiting the villa. Although I suspect that will be the very last place we will find him."

I returned to my hotel room, slipped my revolver into my pocket, and grasped my straw hat. A few minutes later, we were traveling in convoy along the city streets. Myself and McAdam in the front four-wheeler, and a bevy of constables in a police-wagon behind. We passed along white roads, between avenues of palm and banyan trees, to the attractive city suburbs, resplendent with the rich colors of hibiscus and bougainvillea.

We turned in through an entrance guarded by a pair of stone gateposts and made our way along a gravel driveway. We stopped in the turning circle in front of a whitewashed front entrance and climbed out.

"Here we are, Inspector," said McAdam. "This is the place Fairworthy-Smith has been renting."

I strode up to the front door and tugged on the bell-pull. A large woman answered by opening the door and glaring out at us. Her face carried a look of intense suspicion.

"Yes? How may I help you?"

I showed her my police accreditation, and replied, "I am Inspector Baynes from Surrey, England, now working in cooperation with the Barbadian Police. I am here to see Mr. Fairworthy-Smith. Is he home?"

"Mr. Fairworthy-Smith has not been here for a couple of days now," replied the lady, in a slow drawl. "I am his housekeeper, so I ought to know."

"Do you know when he will return?"

"He didn't tell me."

"May we come inside?"

As the constables gathered around the entrance, the housekeeper scowled and stepped reluctantly aside.

I found the cool shade an immense relief after the heat of the afternoon sunshine. Sergeant McAdam accompanied me as I searched through the rooms, but we stopped the moment we reached the dining room. There we found ourselves confronted by a man reclining a wicker chair, with his feet resting on a footstool.

Not Fairworthy-Smith.

"Scarrington."

"Good afternoon, Inspector," said my erstwhile traveling companion. "You were right when you told me we would meet again. It seems we both have business with the same man."

I indicated the sling he was still wearing. "I hope your wrist will soon be better."

Scarrington glowered back at me.

His presence there confirmed my suspicions, and his attempts on my life now made sense. This man was here to kill Fairworthy-Smith, and my presence would only complicate matters for him, if not bring failure to his entire enterprise.

"I am here to arrest Fairworthy-Smith and return him safely to England to stand trial in a court of law," I told Scarrington. "But your business is surely to kill him."

"But our man has disappeared. That makes us confederates in our search for him."

"I am no confederate of yours," I replied coldly.

"And yet, I am in a better position to find him than you are," said Scarrington. "I have arranged to lodge here, in the house that Fairworthy-Smith has been renting – enjoying his hospitality, so to speak, until he shows his face again."

"If you kill him, I shall make sure you stand trial for murder."

"I am a professional, Inspector." Scarrington picked up a lighted cigar from its ashtray at his elbow, drew deeply upon it, and filled the room with its aromatic scent. "You will never find enough evidence to convict me. Even if you live long enough to see me accused. Which in doubtful."

"I wouldn't be so sure about that. I too am a professional."

Scarrington laughed, and gave a dismissive wave of the hand. "Kindly close the door on your way out."

This was enough for my first day on the island, and without any new leads to go on, I decided to retire early for the night. I dismissed Sergeant McAdam, ate a hearty supper, which contained slightly too much spice for my preference, and retired to my bed, with the mosquito netting firmly in place.

The following morning, McAdam turned up as I was concluding my breakfast, and met me in the entrance hall.

"Now, Sergeant," I greeted him. "Do you have any new leads on our disappearing confidence trickster?"

"Not yet, sir," said McAdam. "But it seems Mr. Scarrington is offering a reward to be given to anyone who can find Fairworthy-Smith for him."

I chuckled. "Why didn't I think of that?"

McAdam appeared shocked. "We must do things the proper way, Inspector."

"I suppose you're right. But we could do with a fresh lead in this case."

Another uniformed man appeared in the doorway, and addressed McAdam. "Excuse me, Sergeant."

"Yes?"

"Dr. Monteith has been called to a death, and he wonders if you and the inspector would care to accompany him to the scene."

I looked out into the street, and saw a man sitting patiently in a four-wheeler parked at the roadside. He was dressed in dark formal clothing, and was clutching a black medical bag.

McAdam looked to me for confirmation.

I nodded. Why not?

I found Dr. Samuel Monteith to be a traditional man of medicine, of the old school, with plenty of experience of life in the tropics.

"I have lived on this island for the last fifteen years, Inspector," he told me, "and I never fail to be amazed at the variety of ways people can find to die in places like this place."

I watched the landscape slip past the window as the four-wheeler left the city and drew up beside a wooden cabin at the head of a small, white-sanded bay. I followed McAdam out of the vehicle and looked around. I noticed a small army of large land crabs, warning us of their presence by the scratching noise they made as they walked along – enough to make the skin crawl.

As I followed the doctor to a small hut, I studied the grove of trees around me. They had a red-gray bark, serrated leaves and bore small, green, apple-like fruits.

"Please do not even touch those fruits, Inspector," McAdam warned me. "They are the fruit of the Manchineel tree."

"Are they dangerous?"

"Extremely poisonous."

I shuddered. "There seems to be an abundance of horrors in this place."

The hut was dark and was haunted by the smell of decaying fish. It had clearly been used in the recent past by the local fishermen as a place for storage.

I watched the doctor approach a makeshift bed, on which lay a man I recognized as Jason Fairworthy-Smith. The man's monocle lay beside him on the straw-filled paillasse.

"He is certainly dead, Doctor," came a woman's croaking voice from the far corner of the room.

I looked across the room, and saw what looked like an elderly woman, sitting quietly in the shadows, watching us with snake-like eyes. She was small, and wore a large, variously colored dress, with beads hanging down beneath a hydra's head of oiled dreadlocks.

Sergeant McAdam leaned closer to me, and whispered, "That is Mama Moon."

"Tell me more."

"She is a local voodoo priestess."

Alarmed, I looked at her with curious respect, and she returned my look with an enigmatic smile.

Dr. Monteith put down his bag, and examined the body. "It seems you are right, Mama Moon."

"He was a stranger to this island," explained Mama Moon, "and he didn't know what was bad for him. He consumed too many Manchineel apples." The priestess pointed to the floor, where the remains of several of the apple-like fruits lay scattered. "The poor man asked me for protection, because he believed that somebody was coming here to kill him. But I was powerless to save his life today."

"If he believed his life was in danger, then he was quite right," I added.

"Ah, yes. Inspector Baynes." She looked directly at me.

"Indeed."

"He considered you to be his enemy as well."

"My intention was only to return him to face justice," I replied defensively. "And now he is dead."

The doctor finished his cursory examination of the body, and began to write out a death certificate. "Cause of death: Manchineel poisoning. Time of death?" he looked at the priestess.

"Not long ago. Say an hour."

"Would you mind letting me have a copy of the death certificate, Doctor?" I asked him. "I came here to arrest this man, so if I am unable to take him back with me, then at least I need proof that he is dead."

"Of course."

As the doctor gathered his equipment together, I looked around the scene. First I examined the body and found no sign that *rigor mortis* had yet set in. Then I observed his face. In the gloom, I noticed unusual markings around the mouth and nose. Interesting. I viewed his body, and noticed a puncture mark where a hypodermic needle had been inserted into the left forearm. Not prominent, but certainly present. I surveyed the floor, and discovered, almost hidden in the darkness, a small piece of gravel. I picked it up and put it away in an inside pocket of my jacket.

All eyes were watching me as I finally stood up, turned to McAdam, and nodded. I was ready to leave. Then I noticed the old woman holding in her lap what looked like chicken wing feathers. Three of them.

"How many times do you think a man should be given a fresh chance in life, Inspector?" the priestess asked me.

"What do you mean by that?"

"Once? We all have one chance, Inspector." She held up one feather. "Twice? Some people are given a second chance." She held up two feathers. "Thrice? Very rarely are we given the chance to live a third time." She held up all three feathers, and looked me in the eye.

"I am not here to play mind games," I replied. "What will happen to the body now?"

"It will be taken back to the hospital, until this evening," said the priestess. "Then it will be cremated. On the beach. Tonight."

I raised my eyebrows in surprise. "Why so soon?"

"There is no need to delay. Particularly in the tropics. We have the death certificate, so obtaining special permission to cremate the body will present no problem. It was Mr. Fairworthy-Smith's expressed wish to be cremated, and his ashes consigned to the deep."

"Am I permitted to attend the cremation?" I asked her.

"I would expect you to be there, Inspector," she replied, "so you can report back to England that all has been done in order, and that your mission here is at an end."

That evening, as the light began to fade, I stood on a slight rise in the ground, looking down at a gathered of people on the white sands of a bay just outside Bridgetown. At the center of the assembly stood a pile of wood with something like a corpse, wrapped in white cloth, resting upon the top. I watched as one of the men lit a flame and applied it to the base of the pyre. The dry wood rapidly caught alight, and flames rapidly licked up around the swathed body.

As I stood watching this ritual, I became aware of somebody beside me. I turned and found Scarrington observing the scene as intently as I was.

"Well, Inspector," said he, "there you have your man. His body consigned to the flames."

I continued standing there until darkness had fallen, the flames had been extinguished by the incoming waves, and the remains finally swept out to sea.

When I returned to my room that evening, I found something lying on my pillow. A single chicken feather. Somebody, apart from the regular hotel staff, had been in my room. I recalled Mama Moon, and the feathers I had seen her holding. He she been here?

I retired to bed a troubled man. I had witnessed the death of the man I had been sent to arrest. I had seen his body burned and his ashes claimed by the sea. And yet, I was not convinced. Fairworthy-Smith was a professional confidence trickster who had deceived dozens of people over the years, all to his own profit, and now I was expected to believe that all I had witnessed here was real. But no – something was wrong. My intuition told me that I had been watching an illusion. A conjuring trick. Was

Fairworthy-Smith really dead? Or was he still alive? I had seen it, but I still did not believe.

A few days later, Sergeant McAdam called for me shortly after breakfast. "With your case now closed, sir," said he, "you will be making plans to leave Barbados by the next steamer."

"Perhaps."

"Before you do leave, sir, I have an outing planned for you."

"That is very thoughtful of you, Sergeant. Where do you plan to take me?"

"I have an open invitation for you to visit Codrington College. You might even meet the principal there."

Thirteen miles away, across the center of the island, Codrington College was set in magnificent grounds of colored foliage and avenues of tall palms. With the gentle breeze of the trade wind blowing in from the east, it was very different from the dusty roads we had traveled to reach it, and from the bustle of the west coast city we had left. The principal welcomed me with a friendly smile and a firm handshake, but he was too busy to linger in conversation. Instead, he allocated me a guide, who took me to explore the magnificent college chapel, introduced me to some of the students, and finally took me to visit a small museum.

For several minutes, I examined the exhibits on display there. Each had its own tale to tell. Some were documents relating to the history of the island. Others were fetters employed at one time to shackle the slaves who had labored on the sugar plantations. I also spent a few moments looking up at a pair of spears fixed to the wall above one of the display cases. A label read, "*Arawak spears*".

I turned to McAdam. "Arawak?"

"A race of people who, along with the Caribs, once inhabited parts of South America and the islands of the Caribbean."

"They must have been a warlike race."

"In such a dangerous world, they had to be, sir."

That night, I began to plan my return to England. The steamer would be leaving for home in a few days' time, and I had a copy of Fairworthy-Smith's death certificate with me. But I was reluctant to depart with doubts still haunting my mind.

In the pre-dawn darkness, I was awakened by the sound of shouting in the street outside. I looked out of the window and noticed men and women running. With purpose and direction. I dressed and joined them in the street. There I met McAdam.

"What's happening, Sergeant?"

"It seems that one of Scarrington's men has found Fairworthy-Smith hiding in one of the workers' houses on the edge of town."

"Alive?"

"Apparently so. The whole of Bridgetown is gathering there."

We made our way, as fast as I could manage, in the wake of the crowd, until we stood facing a simple wooden house. The building was surrounded by people, many of whom held blazing torches.

I heard Scarrington's voice. "I know you're in there, Smith. We have the place surrounded, so come out and show yourself."

Neither answer nor any sign of life came from the house.

Scarrington shouted an order, and two men in the crowd threw their blazing torches in through open windows on opposite sides of the house.

"You'd better call in the firefighters," I told McAdam.

"They are already on their way, sir. I had a feeling we might need them."

The fire rapidly took hold, and before long the wooden house had become a blazing inferno. I tried to push my way inside, but the flames forced me back. I imagined Fairworthy-Smith burning to death inside, and watched the firefighters as they cleared a way through the crowd, and tackled the burning building.

After a couple of hours, morning light found the city shrouded beneath a mixture of acrid smoke and gathering mist.

In the gloom, I joined members of the Guard, and the Firefighters, as they sifted through the remains of the wooden house. It was now nothing more than a burned-out shell. A scene of utter devastation. But, of Fairworthy-Smith, we could find not a trace.

I wandered wearily back to my hotel and was greeted by the man at the reception desk, who informed me that he had a message for me. I took the envelope, opened it, and removed a small sheet of paper. It read, *"Meet me at Prospect, at 11.00 a.m."* It was unsigned.

When McAdam turned up an hour later, I showed him the letter. "It has to be from Fairworthy-Smith," I told him. "Can you get me to Prospect in time to meet him, Sergeant?"

"Of course, sir."

I took the precaution of pushing my revolver into the right hand pocket of my jacket.

The place called Prospect lay to the north of the city and overlooked the ocean, but the views which justified the name were mostly hidden at that moment by mist. However, I was not there to admire the vista.

With McAdam remaining a few yards behind me, I stood on a high point of the land, and looked around.

Then I noticed him. A man in a white shirt and white cotton trousers, sitting on a rock beneath a stand of trees, holding a revolver in his hand.

"Smith," I called out to him. "How does it feel to be a dead man?"

"Better than I imagined."

"Are you ready now to surrender yourself to the law?"

"I would prefer to remain a free man, Mr. Baynes." The man stepped closer. "So, I propose to finish this business here and now."

I watched him stop about twenty feet away, and raise his gun. I was too shocked to respond quickly enough.

"No!" shouted McAdam, hurrying forward.

But he was too late. Above the sound of the waves crashing against unseen coral rocks, I heard the sound of a gunshot cut through the air.

I felt myself thrust back, so that I fell heavily to the ground. A throbbing pain in my left shoulder brought me back to my senses. I realized he had shot me.

Fairworthy-Smith stepped closer and again raised his gun, making as though to finish me off. Instead, I slipped my right hand into the pocket of my jacket, and took out my own revolver. As I struggled against the pain, I lifted the gun in my shaking hand, and fired directly into the middle of the man's chest. Fairworthy-Smith collapsed to the ground. Before I passed out, I watched a drop of blood ooze from the corner of his mouth, and a red stain grow in the center of his chest. This time, he really did look dead.

I awakened to find myself lying in a hospital bed. My left shoulder still throbbed, and I felt weak through loss of blood. I recalled that Fairworthy-Smith had shot me, and that I had replied by shooting him dead.

I also remembered other things. I had a vague impression of having a mask placed over my face before anaesthetic gas was given to me. That memory jogged another recollection into my mind: The marks on the face of the man I had taken for dead in the small shoreline hut. Clearly, Fairworthy-Smith had been drugged in order to simulate his death.

Sergeant McAdam came to visit me.

"Well, Sergeant," I began. "If Fairworthy-Smith wasn't dead before, then he certainly is now."

McAdam remained painfully silent.

I leaned on my elbow, to look up at him, but collapsed back onto my bed in agony. "What's the matter, Sergeant?"

"When I went back to collect the body," said McAdam, "I could find no trace of him, sir."

"No trace?"

85

"Not a sign."

"How can that be?" I gasped. "I shot the man dead."

"As a matter of police procedure, we examined your gun, sir."

"And?"

"By chance, we discovered that it had been loaded with blank cartridges."

Even half-drugged against the pain, I felt stunned. "So I didn't kill Fairworthy-Smith."

"That's the way it seems, sir."

"And he is not dead."

"We can only conclude that the entire incident was deliberately fabricated in order to convince the world that Fairworthy-Smith really was dead. For a second time."

"The fellow is well known as a confidence trickster," I replied. "That is the very reason I came to Barbados. To take him back to stand trial for his nefarious dealings."

I lay back, thinking hard, whilst the sergeant stood patiently at my bedside. The entire situation had slipped out of my control. Things were happening that I failed to understand. I needed a second opinion. I also needed to report back to Guildford.

"McAdam."

"Yes, Inspector?"

"When does the next Royal Mail steamer leave for England?"

"Tomorrow, I think."

"That soon? Then we must move quickly. I need to send a couple of letters. Would you kindly bring me writing-paper, ink, pen, and an envelope? And find me a table and a hard chair."

Fighting against the pain in my shoulder and the weakness in my body, I managed to write down an account of my progress in the case so far. A task I had to endure twice. As the last of my energy ebbed away, I left the price of two stamps on the table, and sealed the letters inside their envelopes. One I addressed to my superior in Guildford. The other, together with a request for professional advice, I addressed to, Mr. Sherlock Holmes, 221b Baker Street, London.

I then collapsed back onto the hospital bed, and knew nothing for the next two days.

At the end of a couple of weeks, with my arm no longer in a sling, I moved away from the hospital, and took up residence at the home of Sergeant McAdam and his family. Their house was small but comfortable, and they treated me with great kindness as I continued to make my steady recovery. The sergeant kept me informed of life on the island and allowed me to make the occasional foray into the city to take the sun and to strengthen my muscles.

I counted off the days until the return date for the Royal Mail steamer, and on the morning of its arrival, I accompanied Sergeant McAdam down to the Post Office, to enquire after any correspondence addressed to myself.

The man behind the counter handed me one letter. It was from my Superintendent in Guildford, reminding me not return home without the man I had been sent to arrest.

"I was expecting another letter as well," I told the man.

"I'm sorry, sir," he replied. "There is nothing else."

"Nor is there any need for it," came a voice from behind me. I turned, and found Sergeant McAdam standing beside a man dressed in a light suit. It took me only a moment to recognize the searching eyes and aquiline features. Mr. Sherlock Holmes.

"Mr. Holmes," I exclaimed. "It is indeed wonderful to see you here."

"It is good to see you too, Baynes."

"When I wrote, I never imagined you would come all this way yourself."

"I am here merely on holiday," replied Holmes, nonchalantly. "A private consulting detective does require time off sometimes."

"Certainly."

"My physician approved of a sea voyage and a few days in the Caribbean sunshine. He said it would do me good. Following the Queen's funeral, I had no pressing engagements, so, with a mystery to be solved, there was no way anybody could prevent me from coming here. Besides, I respect your judgement. When you call for my assistance, I know it is something important."

"We have arranged for Mr. Holmes to stay in the same hotel room that you occupied," said McAdam.

I nodded. "A comfortable room."

"You are feeling stronger," observed Holmes. "But you are staying with Sergeant McAdam for the moment."

"Indeed. He and his family are delightful company."

"Splendid. Then I suggest we repair to their home to discuss our business further."

A few minutes later, Holmes was seated opposite me. "I read your letter with the greatest interest. You have done well. But tell me, have there been any further developments since you wrote it?"

"Very few," I replied. "Jason Fairworthy-Smith seems to have vanished from the face of the earth."

"From what you told me, I imagine he is lying low somewhere. Perhaps not far away from here."

"And Mordred Scarrington is taking out his frustration on everyone else," I told him. "He has organized several criminal activities on the island, and has stirred up a great deal of conflict in Bridgetown, giving the police a particularly difficult time."

"In that case, we must deal with this matter as soon as possible," said Holmes, decisively.

"What should be our next move then, Mr. Holmes?" I asked.

Sherlock Holmes leaned closer and fixed me with his piercing eyes. "We need to have a meeting with the voodoo priestess. Mama Moon."

I felt my blood run cold. "I remember our previous encounter with voodoo practices," I told him, "so I have little wish to look further into that matter."

"Nevertheless, she lies at the very heart of this business," replied Holmes. "After considering the matter carefully for the whole of my voyage out here, I am convinced that we have no choice but to interview her at the earliest opportunity."

I looked round at McAdam, who had been standing beside the door all this time, listening to our conversation. "Can you arrange for us to visit Mama Moon, Sergeant?"

"Of course, sir. When would you like to meet her?"

I glanced at Holmes. "Today?"

"Capital!" declared Holmes.

We found Mama Moon in her small and humble home on the edge of the city. As we entered the room where she was sitting, I could smell something in the air akin to incense. Following McAdam's lead, Holmes and I sat down on the carpet spread out across the earthen floor. I was the one who struggled the most to sit down with any dignity.

The priestess was seated upon a cushion, with her keen eyes studying the three of us carefully. I had a distinct impression that Holmes was studying her every bit as closely.

"Welcome, gentlemen," said the priestess.

I began. "Thank you for agreeing to see us, Mama Moon. We have already met. I am Inspector Baynes of the Surrey County Constabulary. You know Sergeant McAdam. And this is Mr. Sherlock Holmes, a private consulting detective from England."

"The man from my dreams," she said mysteriously, and then burst into strident laughter, as though to cover her embarrassment. "I am always happy to help the police with their investigations."

"But I am here purely on holiday," Holmes pointed out.

"Either way, you are here."

Holmes watched the priestess like a hawk. "I see from your hands that you are not as ancient as you pretend."

Mama Moon smiled, intrigued by the man in front of her.

"You appeared here," he continued, "as if out of the blue, but long enough ago for the people to have come to accept and revere you. Your gown is one object that you brought with you. It is worn, and almost threadbare, but it is still important to you."

The priestess nodded slowly.

"From the snake-decorated charm around your neck," continued Holmes, "I would suggest that you came originally from Haiti."

She chuckled.

Holmes hadn't finished yet. "I see from your bare feet, Mama Moon, that you value your connection with the earth."

"Many people here go barefooted."

"But with you it is deliberate. You are particularly aware of everything that happens in Bridgetown."

"I like this man," said Mama Moon, her broad grin showing that his reading of her had been close to the truth. "We could learn a great deal from each other, Mr. Holmes."

Holmes shrugged. "I merely observe what others fail to notice."

"But you seem to know a great deal about my business."

"Baynes and I once worked together on an investigation which involved voodoo."

I nodded. "No doubt the very reason that Mr. Holmes recommended me for this particular case."

"Since then," continued Holmes, "I have made a study of its beliefs and practices."

Mama Moon turned her piercing black eyes onto me. "This is all very interesting, but how exactly may I help you, Inspector?"

"Tell us where we can find Jason Fairworthy-Smith."

The priestess sat back and laughed. "And you think I know where he is?"

"I know you do."

"We have other matters to discuss first." Mama Moon leaned over a small, low table standing between us and lifted the covering cloth.

Now revealed on the table in front of us, I saw a scattering of flower petals, a garlic clove, and four wax dolls, each approximately the size of a man's hand. The sight made me shudder.

Looking at me, the priestess pointed to the first one. "Who is this?"

I looked more closely. The figure was slightly plumper than the others, and wore a very small hat, made out of woven grasses. I gasped. "That must be me."

"And how do you feel about that figure?"

"Sympathetic."

"And your wishes for this person?"

"I hope he returns home safely."

The priestess pointed to the next doll in line. This was longer and thinner than the others, and had a small button sewn to the middle of its chest. "And this one?"

"I can only imagine it to be Mr. Holmes," said I, looking up at her. "Does that button have anything to do with him?"

"Indeed, it does," interposed Holmes. "A man pushed past me in the crowd on the waterfront, and I realized a moment later that one of my buttons was missing. The man had apparently cut it off with a knife – obviously, a man in our hostess's employ. This has clearly all been planned."

"And how do you feel about this figure?" Mama Moon asked me.

"I have great respect for him, as a wise and extremely competent detective."

"And your wishes for him?"

"That he also returns home safely."

The priestess nodded, and pointed to the next figure. This one had a few strands of ginger hair adhering to its face, like a stylized moustache, and a tiny simulation of a monocle.

"Without a doubt, that has to be Jason Fairworthy-Smith."

"And how do you feel about Mr. Fairworthy-Smith?"

"Nothing personal, apart from the pain he put me through when he shot me."

"And your wishes for him?"

"That he accompanies me back to England to stand trial. He is a crook and a fraudster, and he needs to answer for his crimes."

"One way or another?"

"Perhaps."

The painful silence which followed was broken when Holmes interjected, "The tale is only half-told, Mama Moon. Pray continue."

The priestess pointed to the fourth wax figure. It wore a tiny brown jacket. "And this man?"

"That has to be Mordred Scarrington. A dangerous man."

"And how do you feel about him?"

"I have no love for the man. He tried to kill me twice while we were on the boat. And Fairworthy-Smith believes he has come to Barbados in order to kill him."

"And your wishes for him?"

"I wish he would leave us all in peace."

Mama Moon sat back, and looked around at us with wise and knowing eyes. "Permit me to explain. Mr. Fairworthy-Smith came to this island during the second half of last year. Without giving any details, he told me he was on the run, and he asked me to afford him my personal protection. I agreed. Then, at the turn of the year, I offered a sacrifice on behalf of Fairworthy-Smith. The gods told me that two men were coming to the island in order to find Fairworthy-Smith. One was coming to kill him. The other to take him away. The actions of both men would result in his death."

I replied, "As I told you, I have no personal hatred for the man. It is simply my job to take him back to stand trial."

"When you both arrived in Bridgetown, I arranged for Mr. Fairworthy-Smith to fake his own death. Poisoned, as though by ingesting Manchineel fruit. I used a combination of medical gas, and the injection of a combination of drugs found in nature, in order to simulate death. Which was good enough to convince Dr. Monteith to issue a death certificate."

"I already had my doubts," I told her. "I could find no sign of *rigor mortis* on the body, but I did notice marks on his face which I later identified as having been made by an anaesthetist's mask. I also noticed the puncture mark made by that needle in his arm. At the same time, I found a piece of gravel on the floor, which had most likely come from the pathway outside the hospital. That suggested some equipment had been brought to the site from the surgical department. It must have been an extremely risky business."

"There was no risk to him whatsoever," said the priestess. "We took him back to the hospital, and brought about a rapid and safe return to life."

"Then came the cremation on the beach," I continued. "We never saw the body, but I now believe it to have been a freshly slaughtered pig."

"It also failed to convince Scarrington," said Mama Moon. "Hence his attempt to flush Fairworthy-Smith out by burning down the house where he had taken refuge."

"And that meeting at Prospect?"

"Once again, we had to convince both you and Scarrington that he was dead."

"So, he shot me, and I fired directly into his chest. I thought he was dead that time, but then I discovered I had been using black cartridges."

"It was easy enough for me to slip into your room and exchange them for your real bullets."

"And the blood that soaked his chest?"

"A bag of pig's blood, which he could burst easily enough to simulate a gunshot wound."

"And you placed the chicken feather on my pillow."

"That as well."

Holmes had been listening intently. "Now, with Jason Fairworthy-Smith hiding in fear of his life," said he, "and with Mordred Scarrington running riot in Bridgetown, we need to bring this matter to a rapid conclusion."

"The matter is in hand, Mr. Holmes," said the priestess.

"I have no doubts that it is," replied Holmes, "but we need to find Fairworthy-Smith. Am I correct in believing that he is hiding here is this building?"

She nodded. "I promised to keep him safe, and this has to be the safest place on the island. Scarrington has been uttering threats against my life, but none of his cronies dare raise a hand to threaten my safety, nor that of anyone in my household. They are all too fearful of the powers they believe I possess."

Holmes stood up, and call out, "Jason Fairworthy-Smith, come out of there, and face us like a man."

The curtain behind the priestess parted, and Fairworthy-Smith himself stepped into the room. He appeared a mere shadow of the man I had first met in my hotel room. His face had grown thin, his monocle making him look even more pitiable, and his skin appeared almost transparent. "You are two very clever men," he told us. "But I can assure you, once again, that I shall never return to England."

"Perhaps," replied Holmes. "But we shall see."

Mama Moon had the final word. As we turned to go, leaving Fairworthy-Smith in the care of the priestess, we heard her say, "All four of you gentlemen, remember: You only live thrice."

"But you have miscounted," I told her. "Including the fire, Fairworthy-Smith has already died three times, so to speak."

"Not at all," she told me. "They burned down the wrong house."

"Superstitious nonsense," I opined as we made our way outside.

"Agreed," replied Holmes. "But the power of superstition lies in the fact that people believe it."

That evening, Holmes and I enjoyed a meal of local foods, and retired to bed early. During the night, I was roused by the sound of a loud and blood-curdling shriek coming from somewhere outside.

The rays of the early morning sun revealed the dead body of Mordred Scarrington lying in the market place. He had a spear protruding from the center of his chest.

"I recognize that spear," I told Holmes, as we joined the growing crowd gathered around that gruesome spectacle. "It looks like one of the ancient Arawak spears I saw in the museum at Codrington College. I am sure they will confirm it as one of theirs."

Holmes knelt down and examined the body, still soaked with the man's life-blood. "Hello, what have we here?" he asked, carefully removing something clutched in the man's hand.

"It looks like one of those wax figures Mama Moon showed us."

"The one you identified as representing Scarrington himself. The one you had strong feelings against. The man who now lies dead before us."

I looked more carefully at the figure and felt shaken by the implications of my expressed feelings. "Do you think I was responsible for his death?"

"In view of the bitterness he has been stirring up here in Bridgetown, I should have thought Scarrington was entirely responsible for his own demise," said Holmes.

"The police will have to deal with this."

"Quite. But forces are at work here which are beyond the reach or reason of even the island's police force."

When the police arrived, we told them all we knew about the incident, and left them to secure the scene. The time had come for us to reconsider our own situation.

"We still have to arrest Fairworthy-Smith," I reminded Holmes.

"True, but I suggest you forget about him for the time being," he replied. "Our man is as secure now as he would be in any prison. However, I believe his villa is now vacant once more. Perhaps we could use that as a base for exploring the many delights of the island."

The short break improved the health of both of us, but the day of our departure quickly arrived, and, with our berths booked on the next steamer back to England, we made our farewells.

"What about Fairworthy-Smith?" I again asked Holmes. "I still need to secure his arrest."

"That matter is in hand," said Holmes. "Just make sure you board the steamer as planned. With Scarrington dead, Fairworthy-Smith will find it impossible to resist the temptation to venture outside and watch you depart."

"And yourself?"

"I have arranged for the ship's captain to heave-to a few miles along the coast. I shall accompany Sergeant McAdam and his men as they arrest Fairworthy-Smith, and bring him on board the steamer. By force if necessary."

As things turned out, far from resisting arrest, Fairworthy-Smith surrendered without a struggle, finally resigning himself to the inevitable. I bade farewell to my Barbadian sergeant and placed my prisoner in a locked cabin, with a member of the steamer's staff alternating with me on guard outside. Throughout the voyage, I made sure Fairworthy-Smith had all he needed, apart from his freedom.

Our voyage was uneventful, until we reached the Western Approaches and entered the English Channel. I wanted to make sure my prisoner was ready for disembarkation, but when I unlocked the door, I found the cabin empty. Fairworthy-Smith had certainly been there when I checked on him the night before. But since then, nobody had seen him, and even the man on guard outside the door was astounded to learn that his charge had gone missing.

"Everyone on board has been interviewed," I reported to Holmes, "and a search has been made of the entire ship. The crew discovered nothing unusual. No blood. Nobody who ought not to be here. But there is still no trace of our missing man. He has simply disappeared. Along with his monocle."

Whilst I was distraught at losing my prisoner, Sherlock Holmes had no strong feelings about the matter. "Fairworthy-Smith knew he was coming home to face death at the hands of those who had lost money through his fraudulent schemes. They would be eager to finish off the job that Scarrington so evidently failed to accomplish."

"Perhaps his enemies reached out to him even before he landed."

"Or possibly it was his fear of them," said Holmes. "Indeed, the question of what happened here offers a vast scope for speculation. But the only plausible explanation has to be the most simple."

"That somebody released him during the night, and allowed him to leap overboard to his certain death in the ocean."

"Exactly," replied Holmes.

"Thank you, Mr. Holmes. We appear to have reached the solution that I can report to my Superintendent."

"At least you have the man's death certificate."

I gave a wry smile. "Even if it is for the wrong death."

I stood with Holmes one final time in Fairworthy-Smith's untouched and vacant cabin. Although I could see nothing to occupy my attention, Holmes was smoking his pipe, deep in contemplation of the scene before him.

After a few moments, he crouched down, and drew closer to the pillow still neatly occupying the head-end of the bunk. In an instant, Holmes whipped the pillow from its place.

"A-ha!" he declared, as he indicated two objects hidden beneath.

I approached the bunk. "What have you found, Mr. Holmes?"

"A wax figure," declared my companion. "I believe it to be another of those we saw when we visited the priestess. It bears a crude resemblance to our missing prisoner."

"But who left it here? Smith, or somebody else?"

"That hardly matters now," replied Holmes mysteriously. He passed me an envelope. "And this is for you."

I noticed it bore my name, so I opened the envelope, and tipped out the contents into the palm of my hand.

Holmes watched me. "I believe this spells the conclusion to our case, Baynes. Maybe not to our complete satisfaction, but neat enough all the same."

The words of Mama Moon echoed in my mind. *"Remember, you only live thrice."*

It now seemed clear to me that, however he had met his end, Fairworthy-Smith had used up his allotted number of lives. In my hand, I now looked down at the priestess's parting gift to me: Three chicken feathers.

# The Adventure of the Fair Lad

## by Craig Janacek

Throughout my long and intimate acquaintance with Mr. Sherlock Holmes, I had never known him to consider taking a holiday from the relentless pressure induced by the exertions of detection. While I often yearned for the glades of the New Forest or the shingle of Southsea, Holmes was content to wallow unceasingly in the grime and squalor of London. It was simply not within his nature to take part in an aimless holiday. Certainly, before he went into active practice, he once accepted Trevor's hospitality at Donnithorpe for the span of a month. Moreover, there were several examples of times when his iron constitution broke down and he was forced by his physicians to surrender himself to complete rest in locales as diverse as Reigate and Cornwall. Nevertheless, even in these instances, he managed to discover a crime which engaged his attention. It will therefore come as little surprise if I inform my readers that our trip to Ireland was no different.

In the middle of the year 1901, Holmes had been persuaded to travel to Dublin to deal with a forgery case that had besmirched the good name of a prominent Member of Parliament. [1] After the successful conclusion of this incident, I noted a few signs of the same strain that had previously laid him low in Lyons, and had once forced us to take the airs of the westernmost point of England. Therefore, with some diplomacy, I eventually managed to convince him to take a cottage in the little town of Fethard with the promise that he could occupy his mind with a study of the medieval charters held nearby in the old library at the Rock of Cashel.

Once we settled in, I found it a lovely spot, filled with sweet valleys, low hills, and green meadows, as different from the alleyways of London as chalk and cheese. Holmes busied himself with reading through masses of illuminated manuscripts, while I took in the countryside via a series of long walks. It was on one of these jaunts where I made the acquaintance of the local curate, Mr. Vitus-Grey, who was something of an amateur antiquarian. He was an elderly man, rail-thin, but gregarious and lively. He soon proved to be a fount of knowledge regarding the local areas of historic interest.

As Holmes seemed to be recuperating nicely while sequestered in the Cashel Library, I met Stewart Vitus-Grey every morning for a constitutional amble. In the early hours of the day, the night-mists still

96

hung low upon the land, while the sun struggled to gain supremacy in the sky. On one such excursion, the curate pointed out a series of strange rock formations, including one known as the "wishing chair". Sitting in this and gazing out over the stunning scenery was reckoned to provide the supplicant with a granted wish, and though Vitus-Grey urged me to try it, I felt rather foolish doing so. The local area was dominated by the wooded green slopes of the mountain called Slievenamon. In the region, there was also a small stone circle and a massive dolmen, their origins lost to the passage of centuries. All in all, it seemed an idyllic place, out of time with the rapid industrialization which befouled so many other parts of Great Britain. If I closed my eyes, I could almost imagine myself back in the Middle Ages.

Besides the curate, our other neighbours were mainly farmers, and Mr. Vitus-Grey warned me that the occupant of the nearest manor house, the Earl of Moyglass, was not a very sociable individual. It was therefore a great surprise when – as Holmes and I were smoking together one afternoon in our sitting room – an invitation to tea arrived from the local peer.

Holmes initially declared that he was not interested.

"Well, if you will not go, Holmes, at least I will perform the usual social niceties and pay the Earl a visit."

Holmes waved his hand. "If you will, Watson."

However, the Earl's footman cleared his throat. "I apologize, Doctor, but the invitation is only for Mr. Holmes," said the man.

At this pronouncement, Holmes's eyebrows climbed and I could see his ire had been raised. "Very well. I shall go." He rose to his feet. "Come, Watson. The Earl is waiting."

"But the invitation is only for you, Holmes," said I, motioning to the footman.

Holmes shook his head. "I am afraid that the Earl of Moyglass shall have to learn that I am lost without my Boswell."

The footman seemed uncertain of the proper reaction to such a suggestion, but Holmes's attitude brooked no discussion.

The footman had brought round a comfortable Stanhope gig, in which we rode the several miles through narrow country lanes to the Earl's residence. The avenue ran through a splendid park and ended at a large circular drive. Although there were some signs of attempts towards modernization, by and large it appeared that Moyglass Hall was little-changed from the days when these small castles were all which stood between safety and pillaging bands of invaders. Its mullioned windows were narrow, and the embattled parapet was punctuated by machicolations. A bridge ran over the remnants of a moat towards a massive iron-banded door.

Inside, we were promptly shown into the presence of the Earl. He was a tall and dignified person, meticulously dressed, with a drawn face, an eagle-hooked nose, and thinning dark-coloured hair. His eyes were a brilliant blue, but curiously unfocused, as if he was staring off into the future. He struck me as a man who was rather inaccessible to ordinary emotions.

After the usual introductions, the Earl cleared his throat. "I am not much for entertaining, gentlemen. You will understand, Mr. Holmes, that I asked you around on a professional matter."

If Holmes was put out by this slight, he hid it well. "And how exactly may I be of service, Lord Moyglass?"

"I wish for you to investigate some strange matters involving my son, Liam."

"Of course. Pray tell what these matters entail."

"He reports that he was walking down a lane by Slievenamon, between green hedges, when he saw seated in one of the privet hedges a little green man, perfectly well made, who looked at him with his beady black eyes."

"How little a man?"

"According to Liam, he was about a foot, or perhaps fifteen inches, high. He was so frightened that he ran home."

Holmes frowned. "I fail to see the nature of the crime, Lord Moyglass."

"Make-believe is all well and good, sir, but this has gone much too far," said the man, huffily. "I believe my son's imagination has become rather twisted."

"And what would you have me do about it?"

"I want you, Mr. Holmes, to figure out from where he is hearing these absurd fairy tales. Some of it is from books, I reckon. I found several such tomes in his room and confiscated them." He waved his hand in the direction of a stack of volumes, amongst which I noted works by Spenser, McDonald, Le Fanu, and Yeats. [2] "But where he got them is beyond me. A boy his age should be engaged in riding and shooting, not shut away with books all day."

Holmes rose and inclined his chin slightly. "I fear, sir, that I am too busy to assist you in this matter. I regret exceedingly that I have wasted your time."

He then strode out of Moyglass Hall, impervious to the protestations of the Earl.

As we made our way back to our temporary home, Holmes shook his head. "Imagine the temerity, Watson. I am a detective, not a nursemaid."

"So you do not think that there is anything amiss at Moyglass Hall?"

"No. Not unless you count the possibility that the Earl may be half-way to madness. Perhaps that is where the boy inherited his rather overactive imagination."

Holmes would say no more on the matter, but I could tell that his not-inconsiderable pride had been wounded by the haughty attitude of the Earl. When Holmes was just setting out in his chosen profession, he may have been content to perform small services for people who were in trouble about various things and in want of a little enlightening. However, he had since moved onto weightier matters, and I thought it probable that Holmes considered the over-active fancy of a young boy to be rather lacking in the peculiar details that he required in order to prevent his brain from stagnating.

However, not three days later, we learned that Holmes had been terribly wrong. For Liam, the Earl's son, had vanished. We were informed of this calamity from my new acquaintance, Mr. Vitus-Grey. Just as I was taking my morning cocoa, he appeared at our cottage in an extremely agitated state.

After I calmed his nerves with a small glass of brandy, the curate explained what had transpired.

"Liam went out yesterday for a ride at dusk," said the curate. "When the chambermaid went into his room this morning, it was noted that his bed had never been slept in. The Earl questioned the stable boy, who admitted that he hadn't seen Liam return from his ride. The stable boy had gone round to the village to visit a lass, and when he returned, the horse Liam had been riding was back in its stall. It had not been rubbed down and still wore its saddle, but the boy thought that Liam has simply neglected to perform this task."

"So it is possible that the horse made its way home without its rider," concluded Holmes.

"Precisely, Mr. Holmes!" exclaimed the curate. "Upon further questioning of the staff, it appears that no one had seen Liam since he left for his ride."

"Surely, that is unusual?" said I. "How could no one have noticed his absence last night?"

Mr. Vitus-Grey shook his head. "Liam is known to conceal himself in the various nooks and crannies of the manor for hours at a time, so no one made anything of it when he did not appear for dinner."

"What of the Earl?"

"He is now frantic with worry that the boy has been abducted."

"And Liam's mother?"

"Lady Ailin?" The curate paused, as if to consider his words. "She is away. In Dublin, I believe."

"Surely she must be notified at once?" I asked.

"Of course, Doctor. It is just . . . ." His words trailed off.

"What is it?" barked Holmes.

"I hate to spread rumours . . . ."

"It is hardly the time for such niceties, Mr. Vitus-Grey. If you wish me to help find the lad, there can be no secrets here."

"Yes, well, when you put it that way," said the man, nodding. "You see, Mr. Holmes, Lady Ailin has never been close to her son. Her pregnancy was a difficult one, and she went to town, where she had a much longer confinement than is typical. It is said that she almost died, and that she cannot have another child. Perhaps that is the explanation for her coldness to Liam, which is not a secret, I suppose. It is plain to all who have come into contact with them."

Holmes's eyes gleamed with interest. "Although I confess to little understanding the nature of it, there is no doubt that the maternal instinct is a universally strong force. When it is absent, I find that it is rather unnatural."

The curate nodded slowly. "'Unnatural' is a good word for it, Mr. Holmes."

"How so?"

"Truth be told, the villagers round here are all certain that young Liam is a changeling."

"A what?" I exclaimed.

"A fairy child that was left in place of a human child, which had been stolen by the fair folk."

"Why would they think that?" asked Holmes.

"Well, Liam came early and has always been a sickly and small boy. But he is unusually bright for his age, with a great talent for the flute. However, mostly it is because he little resembles either of his parents. You have met the Earl, and his wife – who is his cousin on his mother's side – is much the same dark colour. On the other hand, you see, Mr. Holmes, young Liam has light hair and eyes."

Holmes stood. "Enough of superstitions, Mr. Vitus-Grey. If we wish to find the boy, I will need to inspect the grounds from which he vanished."

We set off at once in the curate's trap, which he expertly directed towards Moyglass Hall. Along the way, Holmes inquired more about the boy's family.

"What do we know of the Earl, Mr. Vitus-Grey?"

100

"What do you mean?"

"Is there someone who would wish him harm?"

The man shook his head. "Not that I can think of. The Earl is hardly a warm individual, but he is a fair man to his tenants and generous enough at holiday time."

"So he is wealthy?"

The vicar shrugged. "Not overly. Moyglass Hall is expensive to keep up, especially as he refuses to close off the older sections. I am hardly privy to the Earl's finances, but I suspect that he recently has been forced to engage some creditors."

"And yet he maintains a townhouse in Dublin for his wife?"

"It is expected, of course," said the vicar, weakly.

"Then who inherits the estate should Liam vanish? Does the Earl have a younger brother?"

"No, Dermot himself is the younger brother. He is the second son of the seventh Earl and inherited the title after the concurrent death of his father and brother in a tragic boating accident off Wexford. Prior to that, he had served in the 18th Regiment of Foot under Macdonell. After he resigned his commission, Dermot had been leading the life of a *bon vivant* in London. But he gave all of that up when he received the news regarding the deaths of his father and brother."

Holmes eyes narrowed at this news and turned to look at me. "Then who, Watson, stands to gain?"

I assumed that this was a rhetorical question, as we were now pulling into the drive in front of Moyglass Hall. The Earl soon appeared, his face haggard, as if he had not slept all night.

"I accept your apology, Mr. Holmes," said he.

Holmes's eyebrows rose. "Excuse me?"

"You may not have believed me three days ago, when I informed you that something was amiss with Liam. However, I am now proven correct. You must find him at once, and determine who has taken him."

I noted a strain of tension appear in Holmes's grey eyes, so attempted to forestall him from making an injudicious reply. "Of course, your Lordship," said I. "Can you show us from where Liam vanished?"

He shook his head. "Not I. I am not overly familiar with all of the paths through the woods. But my game-keeper, Seamus, knows this land like the back of his hand. He can guide you."

Seamus proved to be a taciturn man of roughly fifty with a deeply lined face and balding pate. His green eyes were hooded by bushy brows, and his clothes were well worn. He carried a stout blackthorn shillelagh in his left hand. After listening respectfully to the Earl's orders, Seamus nodded his head brusquely.

"Follow me, gentlemen. If I know the young master, he would have taken the north loop."

"Why do you say that?" asked Holmes, as we strode after the man.

"He was riding at dusk, weren't he? Only one reason to do that. Last night, the moon rose over Slievenamon. The best view of that is from the ridge along the north loop."

Seamus led the way along a path through the woods. Sunlight streamed in through the breaks, but the forest was otherwise still. Many hoof-prints were evident in the ground, but I could make nothing of them. Was Liam's the only horse that passed along here, one day after the other, or was this a sign that others had ridden after him?

Holmes, for his part, was silent, his eyes trained on the ground along both sides of the track. We had gone about a mile from the manor when Holmes called out for the man to stop.

"We ain't at the ridge yet, sir."

"No matter, Mr. Seamus. Look, Watson," said Holmes, pointing to some faint indentations in the ground. "The boy dismounted from his horse here. He made his way deeper into the trees. I see no other recent prints, so he was alone. Let us see where he was headed."

Holmes pushed his way through the branches, Seamus and I close on his heels. As we moved further from the path, the sunlight struggled to find a way to the ground through the thickening overgrowth. Finally, we broke into a small, perfectly circular clearing. In its centre sat a low grass-covered mound. It was as if the trees refused to grow any closer to this rise in the earth.

Holmes was more than half way through the glade when he suddenly stopped.

"What is it?" I asked.

"The tracks stop right at the edge of the mound."

"Did he climb it?"

He shook his head. "No, there is no sign of that."

"I wonder what he wanted in this place?"

Holmes turned to me with a puzzled look. "That is hardly the question, Watson."

"What do you mean?"

"The critical question is, 'Where did he go?'"

I shrugged. "Well, let's follow his tracks out of here and find out."

"That is the problem. There are no tracks out of here."

I was rocked back upon my heels by this statement. "How could that be possible?"

"I do not know," said he, quietly.

I considered the problem. "What if he simply retraced his steps, walking backwards?"

Holmes sniffed sardonically. "I trust, Watson, that you give me more credit than that. First, it would take a great deal of care to step back precisely into each footprint. Second, even if the lad was capable of such a deception, the prints would be twice the depth of those in which he stepped only once. The only way that I could fail to observe that is if he maintained this method all of the way back to his horse. I deem such an effort to be highly improbable. I doubt that even I could perfectly accomplish such a thing."

"Then what are you proposing? Where did he go?"

"I don't know," said he, slowly. He looked over at the groundskeeper. "What is this place?"

The man looked terrified. "That be a *sidhe* – a fairy mound. Can't you see, sir," he said, a hint of hysteria entering his voice, "that the boy has been taken away to *Tir na nog*?"

"What is *Tir na nog*?" I asked.

Seamus turned to me with wonder in his eyes. "The land of eternal youth. The home of the fairies."

The game-keeper proved to be of little further use, for he was plainly frightened of the place. Holmes waved him away, and the man retreated to the path, his club clenched tightly before him, as if it were the only thing which prevented him from being carried off to the otherworld.

"What do you make of it, Holmes?" I asked.

He was slowly pacing the length and breadth of the glade, a puzzled look upon his face. "I'm not certain. I know that Liam entered this glade under his own power. However, I cannot determine how he possibly left."

"Then how are we to proceed?"

"That much is clear. Someone wishes us to believe that Liam was abducted into a fairy realm. Do not forget, Watson, that Liam himself was recently reading books about these creatures. His father wished to know from where he obtained such books, and now we have good reason to learn the answer to this question."

We re-traced our steps to the hall, where Holmes reassured the Earl that he would soon locate Liam. Considering that he had no idea how the lad had vanished, I thought that perhaps his promises were a shade overblown. Holmes was not infallible. He had been beaten a handful of times by human foes. And if our adversary hailed from beyond this world, what possible hopes did Holmes and I have of beating it?

We rode in silence back to Fethard. However, as we drew nearer to our cottage, Holmes stirred from his thoughts and waved at the curate. "If you don't mind, Mr. Vitus-Grey," said he, "I would trouble you for some additional information. May we retire to your home for a few minutes?"

The man looked surprised, but rapidly nodded his head. "Certainly, Mr. Holmes." He flicked his wrist and directed the horse to pass by our cottage until it came to a tidy house in the centre of town. Holmes and I settled into a pair of comfortable armchairs in the curate's library and the man poured us each a steaming mug of tea, before sitting down across from us.

"What more do you wish to know, Mr. Holmes?"

"Watson tells me that you are a veritable repository of the local area's history."

"Indeed! I could tell you all about the first Earl. How he fought for the Kilkenny Confederation against the rapacious invasion of Cromwell, or how – "

"No," said Holmes, holding up his hand. "I am interested in another topic altogether. When we were in the woods with the game-keeper, we passed a glade which was distinguished by something called a fairy mound."

"A *sidhe*?" said the man, his brows rising with interest. "I was unaware that there was one located on the Earl's estate. I have categorized forty-two of them throughout the area." He turned and began to reach for a leather-bound journal.

"Yes, I see you have quite the collection, Mr. Vitus-Grey," said Holmes, waving his hand to the overflowing shelves. "Do you lend out your books?"

The man shook his head. "Very rarely. You see, many of these are quite rare, and if truth be told, most of my small income has been spent on them. While I may cherish my fellow men, Mr. Holmes, I am afraid that most of them have little appreciation for the care that must be taken with a fine volume. I once made the mistake of loaning out my copy of Moore's *Melodies* to the postman Donal, and it came back in such a state – " [3]

"Yes, I understand," interrupted Holmes. "And are there other sites nearby which are connected to the fairy world?"

"Of course! This is a very magical part of Ireland, Mr. Holmes. Slievenamon is one of the sacred hills, which guard the centres of living force that link the past to the future of the land of Erin. The mountain is steeped in folklore, and they say that on its summit lies a portal to the Otherworld. Through it passed Fion mac Cumhaill to the halls of the *Tuatha-de-Danann*."

Holmes shook his head. "Your parishioners may know these tales, Mr. Vitus-Grey, but I assure you that Watson and I are in the dark."

104

"Fion – or Finn MacCool as it is often transcribed in English – was the great warrior of the Irish age of mist, Mr. Holmes, from the days before our history was transcribed into books. The *Tuatha-de-Danaan* are the fair folk, the ancient inhabitants of the land, who have retreated to their realm after the coming of man. But at times such as this, when midsummer is high, the fabric between the realms is thinned."

"Legends," said Holmes, with a dismissive wave of his hand. "The stuff of playwrights."

"Shakespeare did not invent Puck and the court of Oberon, Mr. Holmes. They are much older than the Elizabethan Age."

"But still the stuff of fiction."

"You think so? Not according to the great painter, William Blake. Cunningham reports that Blake once told of how in his garden he had seen a fairy funeral. A procession of creatures of the size and colour of green and grey grasshoppers bore a body laid out on a rose-leaf, which they buried with songs, and then disappeared. [4] What do you say to that?"

"As I understand it, sir, Blake had many such visions. There is no doubt that the poor man was quite mad. Inspired, perhaps, but mad."

"And do I appear mad to you, Mr. Holmes? Should I be shut up in Bedlam?"

Holmes's eyes narrowed. "You can never really know another man, Mr. Vitus-Grey, but at first glance, I would say that you appear in full possession of your senses."

"What if I told you that I too have seen the wee folk with my own eyes?"

"Pray go on."

"In the year 1818," said he, "when I was a small boy of four years old, we were driving to Waterford on a hot summer day over a long straight road that traversed a pebble and rubble-strewn plain, on which grew nothing save a few aromatic herbs. I was sitting on the box with my father when, to my great surprise, I saw legions of dwarfs of about two feet high running along beside the horses. Some sat laughing on the pole, while others were scrambling up the harness to get on the backs of the horses. When I remarked to my father what I has seen, he abruptly stopped the carriage and put me inside beside my mother. There, the conveyance being closed, I was out of the sun. The effect was that, little by little, the host of imps diminished in number till they disappeared altogether."

"Heatstroke," said Holmes, simply.

"You may scoff, Mr. Holmes, but I am hardly the only person to think that the existence of the Fair Folk is a distinct possibility. [5] I speak not only of the shepherds on the South Downs who, to this day, will throw a bit of their bread and cheese over their shoulders at dinnertime for the little folks to consume. All over the United Kingdom, and especially in Wales and here in Ireland, the belief is strongly held among those folks who are nearest to Nature. Perhaps there is more gravity to the accounts that our ancestors gave of these creatures? However fanciful they may be in parts, they may have some core of truth."

Holmes shook his head. "The truth is that there is a scientific explanation for such things. Take the fairy rings, which are so often seen in meadow or marshland, and are proposed to be caused by the beat of tiny fairy feet. It is certainly untenable, as they unquestionably come from fungi, such as *Agaricus gambosus* or *Marasmius oreades*, which grow from a centre, continually deserting the exhausted ground and spreading to that which is fresh. In this way a complete circle is formed, which may be up to a twelve-foot diameter. These circles appear just as often in woods from the same cause, but are, smothered over by the decayed leaves among which the fungi grow."

The curate smiled. "Perhaps you are correct, Mr. Holmes. But even if the fairies do not produce the rings, it might be asserted, and could not be denied, that the rings once formed, whatever their cause, would offer a very charming course for a circular ring-a-ring dance. Certainly, from all time these circles have been associated with the gambols of the little people?"

"Myths do not equal truth, sir."

"Very well, you are a man of science, are you not, Mr. Holmes? Perhaps there is a scientific explanation for the existence of these creatures?"

"Such as?"

"Victorian science would leave the world hard and clean and bare, like a landscape in the moon. However, this science is, in truth, but a little light in the darkness, and outside that limited circle of definite knowledge, we see the loom and shadow of gigantic and fantastic possibilities around us, throwing themselves continually across our consciousness in such ways that it is difficult to ignore them. It is hard for the mind to grasp, Mr. Holmes, what the ultimate results may be if we were actually to prove the existence upon the surface of this planet of a population that may be as numerous as the human race – one which pursues its own strange life in its own strange way, and which is only separated from ourselves by some difference of vibrations."

"What sort of vibrations?" asked Holmes, sceptically.

"Sure you will admit, Mr. Holmes, that we see objects within the limits that make up our colour spectrum, with infinite vibrations, unused by us, on either side of them? Yes? Well, if we could conceive a race of beings, which were constructed in material that threw out shorter or longer vibrations, they would be invisible unless we could tune ourselves up or tune them down. It is exactly this power of tuning up and adapting itself to other vibrations that constitutes a clairvoyant, and there is nothing scientifically impossible – so far as I can see – in some people seeing that which is invisible to others. If the objects are indeed there, and if the inventive power of the human brain is turned upon the problem, it is likely that some sort of psychic spectacles, inconceivable to us at the moment, will be invented, and that we shall all be able to adapt ourselves to the new conditions."

"That seems unlikely."

"So said the doubters to Michael Faraday. But if a mechanical contrivance, keyed to other uses, can convert high-tension electricity into a lower tension then it is hard to see why something analogous might not occur with the vibrations of ether and the waves of light."

Holmes smiled. "That is quite the hypothesis, sir. I shall take it into consideration." He rose and shook the curate's hand.

The man appeared confused by this sudden end to the conversation. "Why do you ask, Mr. Holmes? What does this have to do with the disappearance of Liam?"

"Perhaps nothing," said Holmes with a shrug. "However, I assume that you would be aware of whether the Earl's ancestors have done anything which would have brought down the wrath of the fair folk? Any terrible legends associated with the family?"

The curate shook his head. "No, not to my knowledge."

"Thank you, Mr. Vitus-Grey. Good afternoon," said he, before turning to depart.

When we reached our own cottage, the sun was setting behind the western woods. I looked at my friend. "Do you believe Mr. Vitus-Grey's theories as to the fairies?"

He gazed out over the gloaming countryside. "I believe that Mr. Vitus-Grey is almost certainly convinced of their existence. However, that does not make them any more real than Sir Hugo's hound. No, this is nothing more than an elaborate and ingenious hoax."

"A hoax?" I exclaimed. "Come now, Holmes! A boy is missing! How do you explain that?"

"I have a mental file cabinet in which I list things as proven, probable, possible, improbable, and impossible. Fairies fall firmly in the latter category."

"What then? Is this a kidnapping? Shall we expect a ransom demand?"

He nodded slowly. "That is possible, even probable. We shall see what tomorrow brings."

But Holmes was wrong again. For another day passed, with no word of the boy. Of course, Holmes had not been idle during this time. In the morning, I accompanied him in making the rounds about the village. There we were subjected to a great deal of gossip, and a plethora of tales about other families who had run afoul of the fair folk. Holmes appeared mostly uninterested by the majority of these conversations, as if he could tell that the speaker had no useful information before they had completed their first sentence. Only an old widow named Bridget O'Beara seemed to spark his interest.

She lived in a little cottage on the far end of the village from us. By the wrinkles on her face, and her snowy hair, I judged Mrs. O'Beara to be nearing eighty years of age. She spent most of her time confined to a rocking chair, and her eyes were covered with dark glasses. Her cottage was kept tidy, free of even a smote of dust. As to be expected of a woman of failing sight, it contained few decorations, and the one small bookstand stood empty except for a *Bradshaw's*.

Due to her advanced years, Mrs. O'Beara kept a young dark-haired serving girl about her cottage. Siobhan didn't pause to talk with us, as she was much occupied with the hanging of the day's wash, but Mrs. O'Beara seemed pleased to have visitors, for they represented someone new with whom to speak.

"Siobhan is very useful, Mr. Holmes," said she, "but hardly much of a conversationalist. And with my failing eyes, I have little else to do but talk with people."

"Have you heard about the disappearance of Liam MacMorrow?"

"Of course! It is the only thing being talked about in town. It's not every day when the local nobleman's son is abducted."

"And what is your view on the matter?"

"Do you mean to ask if I believe that he has stepped into *Tir na nog*?"

Holmes smiled. "Indeed."

The old woman shrugged. "Perhaps. I should tell you, Mr. Holmes, that I have lived a long life and seen many strange things, some of them unexplainable by modern science."

"I see. Well, as one who has resided in Fethard for so long, you must know whether anyone has a grudge against the Earl."

She shook her head. "I am afraid that I cannot help you, Mr. Holmes. I only moved here about a year ago."

Holmes's eyebrows rose. "Surely that is unusual?"

"You would not think so if you had met my daughter-in-law. There was not room in Glenties for both of us. So my son moved me here, as far from her as I could get. I had an old aunt who once lived in the area, and I had fond memories of childhood visits to her home."

"I see. Have you met the Earl then?"

"I have not had the privilege. But then, why would his Lordship interest himself in me?"

"And what about Liam?"

"Oh, yes," said she. "He came round once. He had somehow formed the notion that I might be a witch, and as such I could assist him with his task."

"Which was?"

"He didn't tell me straight out, Mr. Holmes. But I gathered that he was interested in determining which of the local springs might be the most likely candidate to grant him a wish."

"A wish?" I exclaimed. "For what?"

"Well, of course, he didn't tell me, Doctor. That would abrogate the effect of the ritual," said she, before her lips curled in a smile. "Should you believe in such things."

Holmes laughed and we made our farewells to the old woman. But his face was grim as we made our way back to the cottage.

"Well, Holmes," said I, "a morning wasted. What now?"

He pursed his lips. "I intend to return to the woods where Liam vanished. I must have missed something."

He indicated that my company on this trip was not required, so I instead joined the local constable, Thomas O'Connell, and his men in beating the countryside. O'Connell appeared grave, as if he little expected to locate Liam with any life left in his body. I noted that his men all carried iron truncheons as we made our rounds.

As soon as he had heard about Liam's disappearance, the constable had posted men at the train station, as well as at each of the major roads. There were only so many places where a boy could be kept hidden in the local area. We inspected every home with a cellar, as well as each barn and hut, no matter how distant. But it was all for naught, for there was no sign of the lad. As the light failed, we finally turned our steps back to Fethard for a late supper when a man raced up with news for O'Connell. I matched my steps in order to overhear their conversation.

"A note came in to the post office, sir," said the man. "For the Earl. It demands a ransom for Liam's return."

"What?" roared the constable. "Where is it?"

The man shook his head. "Donal took it up to the Earl straightaways."

"Without inspecting it?"

"You know how Donal is, sir. He said nothing would interfere with his duty."

109

"But we need to see it!"

"Well, sir, I did inform Donal that – given the circumstances – we were obliged to open all letters coming in for the Earl. That's how we knew it was a ransom demand. I can tell you this much. It was postmarked from Dublin, and Donal swore that it was written by a man."

"Well, of course it was written by a man, you dunderhead!" cried O'Connell. "How many women kidnappers do you know? Let's get over to Moyglass right away before the Earl does something foolish."

Full of this vital information, I quickened my stride and hurried back to our cottage, where I found Holmes perched, cross-legged, in front of the fireplace. Two ounces of shag tobacco and a box of matches lay before him, and his oily black pipe was clenched between his lips. His eyes were directed generally towards the crackling flame, but the distant gaze told me that his mind was far away. I hesitated for a moment to speak, as Holmes was never pleased when one of his meditation sessions was interrupted, and his acerbic temperament could, on occasion, turn rather vitriolic. But I decided that he needed to hear about the ransom note, for it changed everything about the case.

"Holmes!" I cried. "There has been a development!"

He did not stir for the span of a minute. However, I saw the light return to his eyes, and he soon pulled the pipe from his mouth. "I highly doubt that, Watson," he sighed. "Unless you can tell me that you have located Liam?"

"Well, not precisely, but he is likely in Dublin."

Holmes shook his head. "He is not in Dublin."

"How can you say that, Holmes?" I paused. "Unless you know where he is?"

He nodded slowly. "I have a fair notion."

"How is that possible? I thought you were going to visit the fairy glade?"

"Indeed I did."

"And it proved informative?"

"Oh, yes. You see, I missed a critical clue upon our first visit."

"And it has allowed you to solve the case?"

"Not on its own. But a visit to the train station and the post office has supplied other points of interest, which I think form a reasonable tableau of what transpired."

"Ah, so you saw the ransom note then? It seems that you were correct."

He shook his head. "On the contrary. I can assure you that this case has nothing to do with a ransom."

I stared at him in surprise. "Whatever are you talking about? The note is plain."

"Not at all. It is a fake."

"A fake?" I cried. "That's preposterous! Who would do such a thing? Do you mean to say that someone is trying to extort money from the Earl when they don't even have Liam? That is terrible? Moreover, if that is true, then who took the lad?"

He frowned. "I thought that was obvious, Watson. He was taken by a fairy."

I stared at him in astonishment, but he had already replaced the pipe and would say no more.

I spent the next few hours pacing back and forth in the road before our cottage. What could Holmes have possibly meant? Surely, he hadn't reversed his opinion on the supernatural? After dismissing hell hounds, vampires, and ghosts, was he now actually prepared to admit the possibility of the *sidhe*?

Finally, at almost eleven o'clock, Holmes stirred from his spot before the fire. When he looked in my direction, I noted a glimmer in his eyes.

"Do you have the solution?"

"Indeed."

"What is it? Where is Liam?"

But he only shook his head. "All in good time, my friend. First, we must gather the players in this most lamentable comedy. If you would be so good as to go round to Moyglass Manor and rouse the Earl. Make certain that the game-keeper Seamus accompanies him."

"To where?"

"The fairy glade, of course."

"And what are you going to do?"

"I will call upon Mr. Vitus-Grey. I am certain that he will wish to be present at the final act of this performance."

I hurried off to follow Holmes's orders. Shortly after I arrived at the manor, the Earl appeared, wrapped in a green dressing-gown. He immediately demanded to know what had happened.

Unfortunately, I could only shake my head. "I know not, your Lordship. But, I believe that Holmes has determined the location of Liam."

"Then let us lose no time." He hurriedly returned upstairs to change and was soon ready to depart, a lantern clenched in his hand.

However, the game-keeper proved more difficult, as he initially refused to stir from his cottage. We had found the man huddled near an iron stove, an oily pipe clenched between his lips.

"I am sorry, my Lord," said Seamus. "But, 'tis bad fortune to venture into the woods on a night like this. The fair folk don't take kindly to those who intrude upon their *rades* and frolics." [6]

The Earl was hardly in a mood to negotiate. Therefore with some not-so-veiled threats about his employment, Seamus finally sighed heavily and got to his feet. He reached out and picked up a stout walking stick, banded round with iron.

As we walked, Seamus explained that the stick was carved from a rowan tree branch. "With one of these, it is possible that a man might safely witness the fairies, Doctor. And the cold iron helps repel them if they get too close."

The Earl simply shook his head at such foolishness, and I noted that his lips were tightly compressed with strain.

The three of us made our way through the woods, which took on a very different appearance than it had during the sharp light of day. The moonbeams barely pierced the overhanging branches and the thickets appeared to swallow the feeble light cast by the Earl's lantern. Although in my youth I had spent considerable time outdoors, the years of living in the world's greatest city had made such a forest an unfamiliar place. I am not too proud to admit that I was startled by several noises, and I was reminded of the time when Holmes and I had pushed our way through the park grounds of Stoke Moran. However, where the terrors on that night were nothing more ominous than a baboon and cheetah, who could say what unnatural creatures lurked in the shadows of Moyglass Woods? Even if I had thought to bring my service revolver, what good would it possibly do against a creature made of something beyond flesh and bones?

When we finally arrived at the glade, I was surprised to find that two others had accompanied Holmes and the curate, the old woman Bridget O'Beara and her serving girl, Siobhan. The four of them were bathed in the thin light of Holmes's lantern.

The Earl's eyes narrowed dangerously at the sight of the large gathering. "What is the meaning of this, Mr. Holmes?"

"You wish the return of your son, do you not? I assure you, your Lordship, that everyone here has a role to play in his successful reappearance."

"Go on."

"At first, the vanishing of Liam seemed to be something past the wit of man."

"Of course!" exclaimed Seamus. "The poor lad is in *Tir na nog*. He went through a door in the *sidhe*." The groundskeeper waved to the mound.

"Perhaps," said Holmes, nodding slowly. "Perhaps this is indeed the threshold to another world. But a portal can serve as both an ingress and an egress. If Liam entered through it, surely he can be brought forth again."

The Earl's brow darkened. "What foolishness is this?" he cried. "My son was not taken by any supernatural beings! We have the ransom note! He has been taken to Dublin!"

Holmes's mouth curled up in a sardonic smile. "Ah, yes, the note. That was an interesting touch. It certainly distracted the local constabulary, which was its intention. You are correct, Lord Moyglass, that the *note* was mailed from Dublin. But what makes you think that *Liam* is in Dublin?"

"Well," the man spluttered, "he must be. The kidnappers plainly took him away before the constabulary could set up their cordon."

"It is a logical conclusion, your Lordship, but an inaccurate one. Liam never went to Dublin. In fact, Liam never left the vicinity of Slievenamon."

"That's impossible. Every home in the area has been searched. Unless you are accusing Constable O'Connell of incompetence?"

"Not at all. I trust that Constable O'Connell and his men were exceptionally thorough in their search."

"Do you suggest, Mr. Holmes," interjected the curate, "that Liam is actually in *Tir na nog*? Surely, the great mountain Slievenamon exists on both sides of the door."

Holmes shook his head. "No, Mr. Vitus-Grey, I have a rather simpler explanation. You see, while this farce was something past the wit of man, I am no ordinary man. I first asked myself where in this area a boy like Liam could be hidden against his will." He turned to me. "Well, Watson, do you know the answer?"

I considered this for a moment. "Perhaps some secret cellar? Something long forgotten and recently rediscovered?"

"No, no, Watson, there is no need to invoke lost caves or secret crevices. The answer is far less obscure than that. There is, in fact, no place around here to hide a boy against his will. Not for long, at least, and not in the face of Constable O'Connell's hunt."

"I am afraid that I don't follow you, Mr. Holmes," said the curate.

"If there is no place to hide Liam against his will, then we must conclude that Liam is not being held involuntarily."

"Aye," interjected Seamus. "The food and drink of the fair folk makes you forgot all notions of time. The poor lad probably thinks he has been in there for mere minutes."

I knew that was not the meaning of Holmes's comment. "You think Liam went willingly with his kidnapper?" I asked.

"I do indeed, Watson."

"That's ridiculous!" cried Lord Moyglass. "Why ever would he do such a thing?"

"You may ask him that yourself, your Lordship."

"What! When?"

"When I produce him. However, in order to do so, I must ask you to extinguish your lantern."

"Don't do it, your Lordship," exclaimed Seamus, his voice rising with fear. "The fairies love the dark. They might take you too."

"I grow tired of this foolishness, Mr. Holmes," said the Earl.

"Very well, your Lordship," said Holmes. "If you do not wish to see Liam again, you are free to return to your home. However, I warn you that this may be your last chance to summon him back from the world which he has entered."

A wave of conflicting emotions flickered across the man's face. "Very well." He opened the door of the lantern and blew it out. The light in the glade immediately dropped in half. "Now then, where is my son?"

"He is here," said Holmes. Then he extinguished his lantern.

We were immediately thrown into darkness. As the voices of my companions were raised in surprise and fear, I felt the lantern being thrust into my hands. I heard Holmes whisper in my ear to relight it. I fumbled about in my pocket for some matches, and after a minute, I succeeded in doing so. As I raised the lantern above my head, I was astounded by the scene before me.

Mr. Vitus-Grey seemed frozen in place. Seamus had retreated back to the very edge of the glade, a look of absolute terror on his face. Bridget O'Beara had sunk to her knees and buried her head in her hands. The girl Siobhan had vanished. Lord Moyglass stared at Holmes, a look of utter astonishment upon his face. For my friend stood a few feet from his original position, his hand clasped upon the shoulder of a young boy.

"Liam!" exclaimed the Earl. He staggered forward a couple of steps, and then stopped. As he mastered his emotions, his face grew cool. "What is the meaning of this, Mr. Holmes?"

"He's returned from *Tir na nog*!" cried Seamus.

"Surely that is obvious, your Lordship?" said Holmes, ignoring the groundskeeper. "Ever since his supposedly supernatural disappearance, Liam has been masquerading as the serving girl, Siobhan."

Mr. Vitus-Grey shook his head. "That's impossible. Siobhan has been living with Mrs. O'Beara for over a year. Liam cannot possibly have been Siobhan all of that time."

"He was not," said Holmes. "Only the last few days. The real Siobhan took a train to Dublin a week ago. I confirmed this fact with the station master today."

114

"But why did he not say anything about this to Constable O'Connell?" asked the vicar.

"Why would he?" said Holmes, with a shrug. "Who would ever connect an old woman sending her serving girl off to Dublin for some shopping with the later disappearance of the Earl's son? Especially when Liam's vanishing was so clearly a supernatural act. Similarly, there was nothing remarkable about Siobhan's return to Mrs. O'Beara's cottage. Nothing – that is – except that no one can recall witnessing her ever disembarking from one of the return trains. Still, such a thing would have been easily missed in the hullabaloo surrounding Liam's disappearance, and hardly something noteworthy. Meanwhile, the real Siobhan was carrying out her final instructions . . . posting the ransom note."

"What possibly could have been her motive?" I asked.

"To draw away the cordon from the station and the roads, of course. Once the constabulary suspected that Liam was in Dublin, what further reason would there be to watch for people leaving Fethard? The coast would be clear for Liam and Mrs. O'Beara to depart to Waterford or Cork."

As Holmes spoke, it was clear from the expression on his face that the Earl was stunned by this deception. He looked at his son. "Liam, why would you do this? What hold does this woman have over you?"

The boy merely stared at the ground, so Holmes answered for him. "She is his mother."

The Earl of Moyglass staggered backwards. "What did you say?"

At this, Bridget O'Beara looked up, her face streaked with tears. "You are correct, Mr. Holmes." Slowly, she rose to her feet, and lifted her hands to her head. With a deft motion, she swept off a wig, revealing a wave of blond curls. "I am Annabel Shorrock, and Liam is my son."

The Earl was mute with shock, but the vicar recovered his voice.

"How is this possible?" cried the vicar.

"You told me yourself, Mr. Vitus-Grey, that Lord Moyglass had a rather wild youth, and that he was never expected to inherit the estate. His marriage to his cousin was a rushed one. Shortly afterwards, I expect that he received a letter from a young lady of his acquaintance – an actress at the Allegro – with whom he had been on a rather friendly footing for some years during his days in London. She informed him that she was carrying his child. I can only speculate about the sequence of events which led to his ultimate decision, but the nature of it was plain. Lord Moyglass took in Liam, and Lady Ailin pretended that she had birthed him, so that Liam would be considered the legitimate heir to the earldom."

"That is why Liam doesn't take after his parents, and why Lady Ailin is so cold to him!" I cried.

"Of course, Watson. Surely that is a more logical explanation than him being a changeling? Miss Shorrock will have to tell us why she originally agreed to this plan, and what has caused her to now change her mind."

"Who wouldn't have agreed to Dermot's plan, Mr. Holmes? You must know what life there is for a child born out of wedlock. No mother would see such a thing, when instead he could one day become an earl. But that was my brain speaking. My heart said something else. Eventually, I became desperate to see him," cried Miss Shorrock. "At first, I took the cottage just so I could be close to him. I would watch him ride through the woods, and I was content to be proud of the little man that he had become. But then he stopped to speak to me. We became friends, and eventually I learned how unhappy he was. So, I forced him to come away with me."

"That's not true!" cried Liam, finally opening his lips. "I want to be with you! I want a mother who loves me."

"But no father?" asked the Earl, quietly, his expression full of hope.

"Better no father than one who is constantly disappointed in me," said the boy, bitterly.

The Earl's face fell and he struggled to speak.

"He was not always so cold and aloof, Mr. Holmes," said Miss Shorrock, her voice choked with emotion. "Once upon a time, Dermot was a dangerous suitor, with his glib Irish tongue, and his pretty, coaxing ways. There was about him also that glamour of experience and of mystery that attracts a woman's interest, and finally her love. I suspect that his loveless marriage has poisoned his soul."

"And now, Lord Moyglass has a choice to make," said Holmes. "Will he reveal all to Constable O'Connell, and have the mother of his child locked away, as surely the law insists he must? Or will he share Liam with her?"

"How?" croaked the Earl.

"Liam might spend his winters with you here, dutifully attending school and learning how he will one day become the Earl of Moyglass. But in the summer, let him travel with his mother. You may put it about that she is his governess."

"Like a modern Oisin, he would live in two worlds," said Mr. Vitus-Grey, his voice warm. [7] "It is an elegant solution, Mr. Holmes."

All eyes turned to the Earl, as he struggled with his decision. Finally, he nodded his head. "Very well. If all here will swear themselves to secrecy, so that Liam's parentage is never called into question, I will do as you suggest, Mr. Holmes. [8] Constable O'Connell will be told that Liam was merely lost in the woods all of this time."

116

"The constable may accept that explanation," said Mr. Vitus-Grey. "But I hardly think the general populace of the area will do so. They will be convinced that Liam has returned from *Tir na nog*."

"Let them think that," said Lord Moyglass. "As long as they accept that he is my legitimate heir, they are free to believe what they will about his adventures over the last four days."

With the safe return of Liam to Moyglass Hall, it was clear that Holmes had recovered from the strain that had originally brought us to this quiet corner of the Emerald Isle. We took passage on a mail boat departing Waterford to Bristol. We stood on deck as it steamed out of the harbour, not knowing when we might return to the shores of old Hibernia. Once we settled into our seats, I took the opportunity to clarify a few points.

"I still don't understand how Liam vanished from the glade."

"Ah, that was the key question, Watson!" said Holmes, with a smile. "Once I determined the method of his disappearance, the rest fell easily into place."

"How so?"

"I first began with the hypothesis that there must be a non-supernatural explanation of how a boy's tracks might suddenly vanish from a forest glade. I had already established that Liam could not have simply retraced his steps by walking backwards. Nor did he jump some remarkable distance over the fairy mount. So, if he did not go forward or backwards, and discounting the possibility of a mystical doorway to another world, there is only one potential direction – *upwards*."

I shook my head. "That is impossible, Holmes. There were no tree trunks within a dozen feet of where he vanished."

"No, but there were overhanging tree branches, Watson. If someone rigged these branches with a clever rope-and-pulley system, a boy might clip these into a harness-like system and be suddenly whisked away."

"I have never heard of such a thing."

"Hardly surprising, for it is very new. It is known as a 'Kirby Pendulum Wire'. The inventor, George Kirby, intended it for flying performers about a stage. [9] I was forced to climb several trees until I could find evidence that such a system had been installed in the branches. Fortunately, the marks in the oak's soft bark were unmistakeable. Once I had this proof, my thoughts naturally turned to the London theatre scene, and I made the connection to Lord Moyglass' wayward youth. From there, it was a rather simple feat to wire to White's Club in London – that was the purpose of my visit to the Post Office. Langdale Pike obligingly provided the name Annabel Shorrock as that of an actress who was once rumoured to have kept close company with the Earl. He even noted that she was a flaxen-haired beauty. Strangely enough, Miss Shorrock has been absent from London for the past year. She had put it about that she was joining a travelling company headed to New York. However, I noted that the timeline matched closely with when Bridget O'Beara moved into her cottage. From there, it was a simple deduction from Liam's fair complexion and artistic temperament to establish that Miss Shorrock was the boy's real mother. Why else would the lad choose to run away with her?"

Taking all of this in, I shook my head. "I cannot believe that I was convinced this was the work of fairies," said I, bitterly.

"If it soothes your feelings, Watson, rest assured that you are hardly the first person to be so fooled. In fact, in your eager willingness to accept the possibility of the supernatural, despite a complete dearth of supporting evidence for such beings, you are joined by the vast number of our fellow men. The compulsion to invent reasons for the unexplained is so strong, that one might call it a universal sentiment. Frazer is good on the matter. [10] It takes a mighty will to resist these mystical temptations in favour of the light of pure science and reason."

"A will such as you possess?"

Holmes's lips curled up in a sardonic grin. "But of course, Watson."

I shook my head. "'Tis a hard philosophy, Holmes."

He gazed at me for a moment. "Ah, don't be cross with me, Watson. Give me your hands if we be friends, and Sherlock shall restore amends." [11]

# NOTES

1 – Though the details of this case have been lost, the modern reader should recall that Ireland was fully part of the United Kingdom until 1922.

2 – Presumably, Spenser's *Faerie Queene* (1590), George McDonald's *Princess and the Goblin* (1872), Sheridan Le Fanu's *The Child That Went with the Fairies* (1870), and W.B. Yeat's *Song of the Fairies* (1885).

3 – Properly, *Irish Melodies* (1859) by the poet Thomas Moore (1779-1852).

4 – This anecdote is related in *Lives of Eminent British Painters, Sculptors, and Architects* (1833) by Allan Cunningham.

5 – Perhaps the most famous person fooled by the possibility of the mystical was Watson's first literary editor, Sir Arthur Conan Doyle. Conan Doyle's fascination with the paranormal has always been a source of puzzlement, given his interest in the firmly flat-footed Holmes. It is postulated that the many deaths during World War I, especially that of his son Kingsley, drove Conan Doyle into the false solace of Spiritualism. The low-light of this period was his book *The Coming of the Fairies* (1922), in which Conan Doyle was hoodwinked by the perpetrators of the Cottingley Fairies hoax. Some of Vitus-Grey's later words echo those of Conan Doyle.

6 – A fairy *rade* is a mounted procession held each year at the onset of summer.

7 – The warrior-poet Oisin was the son of Fionn mac Cumhaill in Irish mythology. He marries the fairy woman Niamh, and they lived together in *Tir na nog*. Although Mr. Vitus-Grey surely knew the old tales, the average Victorian reader would have been familiar with Oisin's story from James Macpherson's *The Works of Ossian* (1765) and W.B. Yeats' epic poem *The Wanderings of Oisin* (1889).

8 – Now we understand why Watson never published this case. Even after Lord Moyglass' death, to do so would potentially invalidate Liam's succession to the estate. He must have written it up in hopes that a harmless opportunity would someday arise, which never happened.

9 – Invented in 1898, the Kirby wire was most famously used in the J.M. Barrie's 1904 play *Peter Pan, or The Boy Who Wouldn't Grow Up*, which featured the fairy Tinkerbell. Barrie was a great friend of Sir Arthur Conan Doyle, and wrote three parodies about Sherlock Holmes from 1891-1893.

10 – Presumably a reference to James George Frazer (1854-1941) whose work *The Golden Bough* (1890) posited that human belief has progressed through

three stages: Primitive magic, which was then largely replaced by religion, which in turn has been replaced by science.

11 – A paraphrase of the final lines of *A Midsummer's Night Dream*.

# The Adventure of the Voodoo Curse
## by Gareth Tilley

T*his script has never been published in text form, and was initially performed as a radio drama on June 22, 2003. The broadcast was Episode No. 38 of* The Further Adventures of Sherlock Holmes, *one of the recurring series featured on the nationally syndicated* Imagination Theatre. *Founded by Jim French, the company produced over one-thousand multi-series episodes, including one-hundred-twenty-eight Sherlock Holmes pastiches – along with later "bonus" episodes. In addition, Imagination Theatre also recorded the entire Holmes Canon, featured as* The Classic Adventures of Sherlock Holmes, *the only version with all episodes to have been written by the same writer, Matthew J. Elliott, and with the same two actors, John Patrick Lowrie and Lawrence Albert, portraying Holmes and Watson, respectively.*

This script is protected by copyright.

CHARACTERS
- Sherlock Holmes
- Dr. John H. Watson
- Niles Seymour
- Professor Tarrington
- Professor Sebastian Collingwood

SOUND EFFECT: OPENING SEQUENCE: BIG BEN, STREET SOUNDS

ANNOUNCER: *The Further Adventures of Sherlock Holmes.*

MUSIC: *DANSE MACABRE* UP AND UNDER. FADE TO

WATSON: My name is Doctor John H. Watson. The story I'm about to relate occurred in the summer of 1901. It was a curious case from beginning to end, one which bore no similarity to anything Sherlock Holmes had investigated before. It began on a quiet morning in our lodgings at 221b. I was enjoying some diverting reading when Holmes

121

returned after being out since an early hour, on a case involving the notorious missing son of Lady Evelyn Chadwick.

MUSIC: (OUT)

SOUND EFFECT: DOOR OPENS, STEPS IN, DOOR CLOSES

HOLMES: (OFF-MICROPHONE) Hello, Watson.

WATSON: Ah. Did you find the young lord?

HOLMES: (ON-MICROPHONE) Oh yes, a trifling affair. He was in Limehouse. Tried to stow away on a ship bound for South Africa. He had a romantic notion about joining in the Boer War.

WATSON: Humph. Romantic notion. I've had my taste of war and there's nothing romantic about it.

HOLMES: Indeed. The idea was put in his head by those cheap penny novels, of which I found several in his room . . . And what's that you're reading? No doubt something intellectually stimulating?

WATSON: It's called *Haiti, or The Black Republic*. All about voodoo, witch doctors, and black magic.

HOLMES: Really, Watson! Black magic? I expected more of you.

WATSON: Yes, well, I found it on *your* bookshelf!

HOLMES: Ah, you did? There are times when I find it prudent to be in possession of arcane knowledge. One should be aware of the myths and legends people cling to.

WATSON: But this voodoo business – just superstition. Pure mumbo-jumbo. Ah – I almost forgot! A telegram came for you first thing this morning! Sorry . . . .

SOUND EFFECT: FOOTSTEPS

WATSON: Here it is.

HOLMES: (PAUSE) Upon my word! Have you read this, Watson?

WATSON: Of course not. It's addressed to you.

HOLMES: You don't know what this wire is about?

WATSON: No.

HOLMES: Listen to this: (READS) "*Urgently need your help. Two Oxford professors suffering voodoo curse. Believe foul play involved. Doctors no help. Awaiting reply at Oxfordshire telegraph.*" Signed "*Miles Seymour*".

WATSON: A voodoo curse? Let me see that . . . .

SOUND EFFECT: TELEGRAM HANDLED

WATSON: This is amazing! I've been reading about voodoo curses and there sat that telegram.

HOLMES: Makes one wonder, doesn't it?

WATSON: You'll ignore it, of course.

HOLMES: Ignore it? Do you think I should ignore it?

WATSON: Well: It's summer, classes are out at Oxford, and the scholars are restless. They're having some sport with you. Too much time on their hands.

HOLMES: Let's find out, shall we?

SOUND EFFECT: HE STALKS TO THE DOOR AND OPENS IT

HOLMES: (OFF-MICROPHONE, SHOUTS) Mrs. Hudson!

SOUND EFFECT: INTERIOR, TRAIN RUNNING

WATSON: I'll be glad for a holiday from London, and Oxfordshire will be pleasant, but be reasonable, Holmes. You certainly don't think there's a case here?

HOLMES: There is something here. You saw his reply.

WATSON: Yes, especially the part about not having funds to pay you.

HOLMES: Then we'll chalk up our efforts to experience. You did bring that book you were reading?

WATSON: *Haiti, or The Black Republic*? Yes. And I also packed my pistol.

HOLMES: Good man. Now let's open our lunch basket and see what Mrs. Hudson's given us.

SOUND EFFECT: TRAIN UP PULLS INTO STATION (UNDER)

WATSON: (NARRATING) We rode beside the Thames through unspoilt country dozing in the golden summer afternoon. At last, the train stopped at a station in the Cotswold Hills, and as we got off, a young man hurried up to us anxiously.

SEYMOUR: (EXTERIOR) Excuse me. Would you be Mr. Holmes and Doctor Watson?

HOLMES: Indeed. And you would be Mr. Seymour.

SEYMOUR: Yes. Niles Seymour. Thank you both for coming. I know you think this is madness, and frankly, so do I, but I've been a student of these two professors and I've come to think highly of them, and to see this happening to them . . . to men of such intelligence . . . I could only think of one thing: Sherlock Holmes could get to the bottom of this! Please, come this way. I have a trap waiting.

SOUND EFFECT: THREE MEN WALKING (UNDER DIALOGUE)

HOLMES: Do they know you've sent for us?

SEYMOUR: It was my idea, but yes, they know. Professor Tarrington – he's the senior of the two – is terribly depressed. When I told him I'd

124

wired you, he shrugged and said that his fate couldn't be changed by a detective. And Professor Collingwood feels the same. He's convinced nothing can cure his withered hand.

WATSON: Oh? He has a withered hand'?

SEYMOUR: It started coming on him during the voyage back from Port-au-Prince, at the same time Professor Tarrington began to feel ill. Now, you must understand, these are intelligent, learned men, Mr. Holmes. They're not gullible people, but you can see at a glance that they're . . . ah, here's the trap. Let me help you up.

SOUND EFFECT: STEPS STOP. MEN CLIMB INTO THE CART

SEYMOUR: All right, we're off. It's not far.

SOUND EFFECT: (UNDER) HORSE PULLING WAGON ON DIRT

HOLMES: You must tell me all you can about these men. You said you were a student of theirs?

SEYMOUR: Yes. Professor Tarrington has been head of Anthropology at Oxford for years and years. I took my degree under him. Mr. Collingwood is younger – been teaching there somewhat less time. In fact, he was also a student under the professor. Top of his class, so I'm told.

HOLMES: And now you're employed by Professor Tarrington?

SEYMOUR: Yes. The professor was kind enough to ask me to take the place of his regular man when he took ill last year. I want to teach, but jobs are scarce. I've heard of work in Australia, but I'd prefer to live here, so I've stayed on. I've become a sort of jack-of-all-trades, you might say.

HOLMES: I see. Does the professor live on campus?

SEYMOUR: Oh no, he lives where we're going – his estate. Well, it's not an estate any more. He has only about two acres left – a comfortable old cottage, a stable, and a small garden. His holdings were much larger at one time, but over the years the professor found it necessary to sell off portions of it.

125

HOLMES: And where do you live?

SEYMOUR: There are rooms over the stable.

WATSON: I believe your wire mentioned the men had seen a doctor about these symptoms of theirs?

SEYMOUR: Yes. As soon as they got off the boat from Haiti. Professor Tarrington was given some pills for anemia, but Professor Collingwood was diagnosed as having acute joint inflammation or something like it, and they couldn't give him anything. If you ask me, the doctor thought they were malingering.

SOUND EFFECT: CART FADES

WATSON: We found Seymour to be a pleasant young man, quite open and forthcoming. We learned that Mr. Collingwood had given up his rental in Oxford proper and was living in a spare bedroom in Tarrington's cottage. The two men did their own cooking, and shared the other chores, while Seymour worked outside looking after the garden and tending the chickens and rabbits and three horses, and he took his meals with the professors. An informal but practical living arrangement. (PAUSE) Shortly, we turned into a break in the hedgerow, and pulled to a stop in front of a thatched-roof cottage, and in we went.

SOUND EFFECT: DOOR OPENS, MEN WALKING IN (UNDER)

WATSON: In the study sat a white-haired man. He had several days' stubble of beard, a shawl round his shoulders, and both of his bony hands grasped the handle of a cane on which he leaned forward, anxiously.

SEYMOUR: Professor Tarrington, our guests have arrived. Mr. Holmes and Dr. Watson.

HOLMES: Professor Tarrington?

PROFESSOR: Welcome to my home, such as it is.

126

HOLMES: I am Sherlock Holmes, and this is my colleague, Doctor John H. Watson.

WATSON: How do you do, Professor?

PROFESSOR: Heh. How do I do? Not well, not well at all. You're a doctor, you say? What do you know about voodoo, Doctor?

WATSON: I've only read about it. Frankly, I doubt its existence.

PROFESSOR: Oh, it exists! I'm the living proof of it . . . or the *dying* proof! Your question should be, "Does voodoo really have power?" and I am very much afraid that it does, although, like you, I never used to believe that, and I don't want to believe it now! How much has Seymour told you?

SEYMOUR: I've told him everything I knew.

HOLMES: What is your present condition, Professor? How do you feel?

PROFESSOR: I am suffering from a disorder that robs me of my energy, and it gets worse every day. A weakness of the blood. I cut myself by accident Monday and the wound bled all day. My blood's getting as thin as water.

HOLMES: And what makes you think this has something to do with a curse?

PROFESSOR: Because until I went to Haiti, the only thing that's ever been wrong with me was a slight murmur of the heart.

HOLMES: And what happened in Haiti?

PROFESSOR: My associate and I were cursed by a voodoo witch doctor! Ah, here comes Sebastian . . . .

SOUND EFFECT: (OFF-MICROPHONE) MAN WALKS IN AND STOPS (UNDER)

PROFESSOR: Sebastian Collingwood, meet Mr. Holmes and Dr. Watson.

HOLMES: Mr. Collingwood.

127

SEBASTIAN: (OFF-MICROPHONE) Yes, gentlemen. Good of you to come. (ON-MICROPHONE) Please pardon my left hand. The right one is no good any longer.

WATSON: Excuse me, Mr. Collingwood. Do you mind if I have a look at it?

SEBASTIAN: Look all you want.

WATSON: (PAUSE) How long have your fingers been curled like this?

SEBASTIAN: It started on the ship.

PROFESSOR: The ship back from Haiti.

SEBASTIAN: Actually, the first night out. When we got our first letter.

PROFESSOR: The letter "*M*". The first of the four fatal letters. That was when my energy began to leave me, as well.

WATSON: If I try to gently bend your fingers back to normal –

SEBASTIAN: Ah! No, no! Don't do that! They're paralyzed!

WATSON: Sorry –

SEBASTIAN: The joints are frozen! And they get worse every day!

WATSON: Like arthritis. But arthritis comes on gradually. I've never heard of it striking all at once.

SEBASTIAN: No, this began a minute after we got the first letter!

HOLMES: Now, if I'm to be of any help, you must tell us everything that happened, in the order that it happened, and leave out no detail, however unimportant it may seem.

SEBASTIAN: Beginning when?

HOLMES: Beginning with your first experience with voodoo.

SEBASTIAN: You begin, Tarrington.

PROFESSOR: Very well. Professor Collingwood and I were collaborating on a paper exploring the various religions stemming from Africa, from the Egyptians right through to the present day. And so early this summer, we sailed to Haiti and landed in Port-au-Prince.

SEBASTIAN: As you may know, Haiti is officially Roman Catholic, but we found Voodooism being practiced rather widely . . . .

PROFESSOR: A mixture of certain Catholic practices blended with pagan rituals – rituals involving things such as that mask you see there on my desk.

WATSON: I've been looking at it. Gruesome thing.

SEBASTIAN: Yes, it represents the *chien noir*, or "black dog".

PROFESSOR: And the natives are terrified of it. Well, how we obtained it was . . . we hired a native guide. There was no doubt that he was an outcast from the voodoo cult. He promised to take us to a voodoo ceremony, but days went by and he had one excuse after another –

SEBASTIAN: He took us round to meet some voodoo cult members, but they didn't tell us much at all.

PROFESSOR: So we demanded that he take us to one of their voodoo rituals.

SEBASTIAN: I said, do what we're hiring you to do, or you won't see another penny! So the next night, just at midnight, he took us into the forest, and that's what sealed his fate.

PROFESSOR: And our own.

HOLMES: What do you mean?

PROFESSOR: He took us to where we could hide and watch what took place round a fire in a clearing. We had no sooner taken up our positions when the witch doctor himself spotted us, and the entire group of natives set upon us! I've never run so fast in my life! I thought my heart would burst!

129

SEBASTIAN: But we managed to get back to town. But the guide wasn't so fortunate. The next day they found his body . . . with a note pinned to it! A note meant for us! We have it here. Do either of you read French?

PROFESSOR: Never mind, I'll read it. Roughly translated, it says, "*For crimes against the* chien noir, *you are cursed. You will be visited by the devil himself, who will deliver to you the letters from the word* mort. *Each letter will weaken you, and when you have received the last letter, you shall die.*"

SEBASTIAN: *Mort* is the French word for death.

HOLMES: Yes. And how did you come to see this note?

SEBASTIAN: The police brought it to us. Questioned us for some time.

WATSON: Did they know how the guide died?

SEBASTIAN: By a curse!

WATSON: No, I mean, with a weapon?

SEBASTIAN: No! His life was simply taken!

PROFESSOR: It's nothing new to the authorities in Haiti. Happens all the time!

HOLMES: I see. What did you do after that?

PROFESSOR: Since we could do no more research, we booked passage home on the first available ship, but the next ship out of Port-au-Prince was nearly two weeks off, so we stayed in our hotel room.

HOLMES: The entire time?

PROFESSOR: Yes. Living like prisoners.

HOLMES: And did anything happen to you after that?

SEBASTIAN: Nothing until the first night we were on the ship. That's when we received the letter "*M*".

PROFESSOR: It was brought to our table on a serviette. The serviette was folded over and when we unfolded it, there was the letter "*M*", drawn in blood.

HOLMES: Who brought it to your table?

SEBASTIAN: The waiter. He said a native fellow gave it to him and told him to give it to us. We asked him who, he was but he said he'd never seen him before, and he didn't belong in first class anyway.

PROFESSOR: We complained to the captain, and he had the purser search the entire ship, to no avail.

SEBASTIAN: But we knew they wouldn't find him – because, well, you see . . . (PAUSE) *he wasn't of this earth*!

HOLMES: Come, come, Mr. Sebastian.

PROFESSOR: I'm afraid he's right. We were in the middle of the ocean. The man appeared, delivered his message, and disappeared. Voodoo priests can leave their bodies through their *ti bon ange* — their "little guardian angel" – and travel through the spirit world to . . . wherever they like.

WATSON: You don't actually believe such things, do you, Professor?

PROFESSOR: I know that before we finished our dinner, I was getting ill. I had nausea. Heart palpitations.

SEBASTIAN: And my fingers started going stiff.

PROFESSOR: And the symptoms were still with us until the second letter appeared . . . and then they got worse!

MUSIC: VIOLIN BRIDGE (UNDER)

WATSON: Holmes and I sat in the gloomy study of Professor Tarrington's house in Oxfordshire as he and Professor Collingwood

131

related the events that convinced them that they'd been struck with a voodoo curse.

<u>MUSIC: (OUT)</u>

HOLMES: Now, the warning note from the witch doctor said you would receive an added curse for each of the four letters in the French word for death, *mort*. Have you received any more since the first one?

SEBASTIAN: Oh, yes indeed. After we docked and we got into a carriage at Tilbury, there on the inside of the door was marked a letter "*O*", six inches in diameter!

HOLMES: Marked how?

SEBASTIAN: Chalk. Wouldn't you say?

PROFESSOR: Yes, chalk. Fresh, as if it had just been done.

HOLMES: Did either of you ask the driver about it?

PROFESSOR: He didn't know a thing.

HOLMES: And how did that discovery make you feel?

PROFESSOR: For a moment I couldn't breathe! My head swam!

SEBASTIAN: And my fingers ached so ferociously I wanted to slam the door on them!

HOLMES: Has the third curse happened?

SEBASTIAN: Indeed it has! And we all saw it! Including Seymour!

HOLMES: What was it?

SEBASTIAN: Yesterday, I made a pot of tea. I made it in the usual way, pouring scalding water over the leaves. I let it steep, then I set out the cups and poured the tea. We sat about, having our tea and biscuits, and then I went back to the kitchen to bring in the teapot, and I saw it! On the sink, right beside the stove, the letter "*R*" had been spelled out in tea leaves . . . a huge letter "*R*"!

132

SEYMOUR: It's true. I did see it.

HOLMES: Who'd been in the kitchen while you were having your tea?

SEBASTIAN: No one!

PROFESSOR: No one . . . *living.*

HOLMES: What did you do with it?

SEBASTIAN: I wiped it away as fast as I could!

PROFESSOR: But the moment I saw it, I had to come in here and sit down, my heart was hammering so. I've barely stirred from this chair since then, except for the necessities. I'm ashamed to admit it, Mr. Holmes, but I'm afraid to go to sleep, for fear of what I may dream!

HOLMES: Have there been any further warnings since then?

SEBASTIAN: No, but we're on tenterhooks, waiting for the letter '*T*' to appear! And when it does . . . .

HOLMES: (PAUSE) Gentlemen, may I speak frankly?

SEBASTIAN: Certainly.

PROFESSOR: I know what you're going to say. "It's all in our minds."

HOLMES: Precisely.

PROFESSOR: Then how do you explain the death of our guide? That was not in our minds, sir. That happened to a man who defied the voodoo curse, and it cost him his life! And what about the letters of death? On the serviette! The door! The sink! We saw them!

HOLMES: If . . . *if* these events are caused by a spirit and not by man, I can do nothing. Sherlock Holmes has met his master at last.

PROFESSOR: Of course, we know that. Seymour shouldn't have wired you. We shouldn't be wasting your time. We're beyond mortal help. Sebastian, I – I should have gone to Haiti alone! I shouldn't have led

133

you into this. I'm old, I've lived my life. But . . . you're still a young man —

SEBASTIAN: Stop it, man, stop it! (PAUSE, SOBERLY) Working beside you has been the acme of my ambition! If I must die, well —

HOLMES: Gentlemen, before you resign yourselves to the devil and his works, I have one last idea.

PROFESSOR: What?

HOLMES: Is there an inn nearby?

SEYMOUR: Yes, sir, there is. The Flaming Oak, just the other side of the railway crossing. It's not too expensive, and they set a good table.

HOLMES: That's fine. Then Professor Collingwood, may I impose upon you to take a room there tonight?

SEBASTIAN: Me? Why do you want me to leave here?

HOLMES: Because I want to separate you and Professor Tarrington. From what you've told us, all three of these voodoo warnings have occurred when the two of you were together.

SEBASTIAN: That's true, but I —

HOLMES: I will be at your side at the inn until you retire for the night, and Doctor Watson will be here, watching over Professor Tarrington.

SEYMOUR: And where do you want me to be, Mr. Holmes?

HOLMES: You are obviously not a target, Mr. Seymour, so you may spend the night in your quarters above the stable.

SEYMOUR: I'll be glad to help in any way I can.

HOLMES: We will need you to drive us to the inn. Now, Professor Collingwood, if you will please pack for an overnight stay.

SEBASTIAN: Well, you know, there may not be any vacancies at the inn this time of year, what with the summer holidays . . . .

SEYMOUR: Oh, but there's the Prince Michael Inn, just a mile farther down the road.

PROFESSOR: Now Mr. Holmes, you want me to stay here?

HOLMES: Yes, you'll stay right here in your own house.

PROFESSOR: Well, that's a relief!

HOLMES: And Doctor Watson will stay here with you. A better doctor and a braver man, I've never known, and he is armed. Now, while you pack, Professor Collingwood, I have some instructions for Watson. Step outside with me for a minute, will you, Watson?

WATSON: Certainly.

SOUND EFFECT: TWO MEN WALK TO DOOR. OPEN IT, THEN CLOSE IT. COUNTRY EXTERIOR

HOLMES: I don't expect trouble tonight, but be very, very watchful.

WATSON: It's Seymour, isn't it?

HOLMES: Nothing is certain. We'll both have to be prepared. Here is what I want you to do: I want you to prepare the professor's supper for him. Make his food. Brew his tea. If he wants wine, open a new bottle. Observe him as a physician. I'll be doing the same with Collingwood. This house has no telephone, so you'll be on your own.

WATSON: Leave it to me, Holmes.

HOLMES: I shall, old friend. I shall.

SOUND EFFECT: EXTERIOR EFFECTS FADE

WATSON: (NARRATES) Seymour brought the trap round to the front and Holmes and Collingwood got in and drove off. I went back inside. Professor Tarrington rose from his chair and took my arm. His hand was shaking.

135

PROFESSOR: It's a comfort to have you here, Doctor — whatever my fate is to be.

WATSON: I'm sure there is a logical explanation for the things that have happened to you, and Holmes will find it.

PROFESSOR: I hope you're right. Now, if you'll excuse me, it's time for my pills.

WATSON: Which pills are those?

PROFESSOR: My regular medicine. For my heart and my nerves.

WATSON: Have you taken them a long time?

PROFESSOR: Years.

WATSON: Ah.

PROFESSOR: I suppose you're wondering if I'm being drugged, if that's what's making me tremble. No, the tremors began just after the first of the voodoo warnings came.

WATSON: In your hotel in Port-au-Prince.

PROFESSOR: Yes.

WATSON: How long did they last?

PROFESSOR: They – they haven't left me since then!

WATSON: May I get them for you?

PROFESSOR: Oh, no, I'll get them. I keep them in the night stand beside my bed.

WATSON: Why don't I get them? You stay here and relax.

PROFESSOR: Oh, all right. (MOVING OFF-MICROPHONE) The top drawer, in the white envelope. I'll get a glass of water.

SOUND EFFECT: HE WALKS QUIETLY UNDER NARRATION

WATSON: (NARRATES) I walked into the professor's bedroom. Like the other rooms, it was small and filled with old-fashioned furniture. There was the nightstand.

SOUND EFFECT: STEPS STOP. WOODEN DRAWER SLIDES OPEN

WATSON: The drawer was filled with miscellany. Pencils, scraps of paper, pairs of spectacles, and on top, a pharmacist's envelope, three-by-four inches, with "*Heart Medicine*" written on its face.

SOUND EFFECT: TINY ENVELOPE OPENED

WATSON: I opened the envelope and shook a few of the tablets into my hand. They were a grayish blue in colour, a quarter-inch in diameter and half that in thickness. I took one and crushed it into powder between my thumbnails, then licked the powder. It had a distinctive bitter taste.

SOUND EFFECT: DRAWER CLOSED FIRMLY. STEPS WALK BACK TO PARLOUR

WATSON: Professor Torrington! Where did you get these tablets?

PROFESSOR: My doctor prescribed them.

WATSON: What did he say they would do?

PROFESSOR: Slow my heartbeat. Make me calmer.

WATSON: And you took them with you on your trip to Haiti?

PROFESSOR: Of course. I have to take them every day.

WATSON: And did they do you any good?

PROFESSOR: Oh, they used to. But . . . I think I was so scared when the voodoo curse was cast –

WATSON: Oh, blast it, man, forget the curse! There was no curse! *There is no curse*!

137

PROFESSOR: Now just a minute, Doctor! You weren't there with me in Haiti! A man was killed! His killer left a note! The note was for me! For me and Collingwood! My heart turned over in my breast when I read it! I felt faint!

WATSON: And you took a pill to calm yourself!

PROFESSOR: Yes!

WATSON: But immediately you felt worse!

PROFESSOR: Yes!

WATSON: And you've been nervous and aware of your fast heartbeat ever since!

PROFESSOR: Yes! What are you telling me?

WATSON: I'm telling you that these pills are meant to do exactly the opposite from what you want them to! They're a compound made from the purple foxglove plant. It's called Digitalis! Too much of it can kill you!

MUSIC: VIOLIN *AGITATO* (UNDER)

SOUND EFFECT: COUNTRY MORNING. HORSE AND WAGON APPROACH AND STOP

HOLMES: (EXTERIOR, OFF-MICROPHONE) Good morning, Watson! And good morning, Professor Tarrington. Did you sleep well?

SOUND EFFECT: (UNDER) TWO MEN STEP DOWN FROM WAGON

PROFESSOR: (EXTERIOR) Good morning, Mr. Holmes! And Seymour! Lovely morning!

SEYMOUR: (EXTERIOR, OFF-MICROPHONE) That it is, Professor! Why, you're looking very well this morning!

PROFESSOR: Yes, I'm feeling much better. Where's Collingwood?

HOLMES: Professor Collingwood decided to go back to his digs at Oxford. He had a rather poor night.

PROFESSOR: A poor night? What do you mean?

SEYMOUR: (EXTERIOR, OFF-MICROPHONE) I'll put the horse away and be right back.

HOLMES: No, Mr. Seymour, we'll be needing you to drive us back to the railway station immediately to catch the train for London.

PROFESSOR: What about Collingwood?

HOLMES: Well, last night his crippled hand was cured. It became perfectly normal, and has been ever since.

PROFESSOR: No! Not really?

HOLMES: Oh, yes.

PROFESSOR: But you said he had a poor night! What happened?

HOLMES: Oh, I think he'll want to tell you about it himself. Let's pack, Watson.

SOUND EFFECT: SEGUE TO TRAIN INTERIOR

WATSON: . . . And so, I convinced Tarrington that someone was trying to make him ill . . . perhaps even trying to kill him! And that was when he realised that one person had a good reason to want him out of the way –

HOLMES: – Collingwood –

WATSON: Yes, Collingwood stands to take over as head of the Anthropology Department. But I don't think Tarrington quite believes Collingwood plotted this whole charade.

139

HOLMES: A constable should be coming round to show him the supply of Digitalis he found this morning in Collingwood's shaving kit. Then Tarrington can decide whether to press charges or let him go.

WATSON: But how did you find out Collingwood was pretending to be cursed?

HOLMES: Oh, I waited until he was fast asleep and then I walked into his room – there are no locks on the doors at that inn – and simply looked at his right hand.

WATSON: And it wasn't clenched.

HOLMES: No. It was resting in peaceful repose on the blanket, just like his left one. Of course, I woke him and told him the game was up and asked him to explain about the death of the guide, which never happened, and the bloody "*M*" on the serviette, and the "*O*" on the carriage door. He agreed to tell me how he arranged those tricks, in return for my not calling the authorities. And of course he didn't even know yet that you'd found out he'd been drugging Professor Tarrington.

MUSIC: *DANSE MACABRE* IN AND UNDER

WATSON: This is Doctor John H. Watson again. I've shared many more adventures with Sherlock Holmes over the years, and I'll be happy to tell you another one . . . *when next we meet*!

# The Cassandra of Providence Place
## by Paul Hiscock

$W$e received many distressed men and women in our rooms at Baker Street during my years living with Mr. Sherlock Holmes. While there are some that I barely remember, others made a more lasting impression. One notable visitor was Miss Margaret Croft of Providence Place, possibly the youngest client ever to come seeking our assistance.

The summer of 1901 was particularly hot and, in an attempt to cool ourselves, we had flung open all the windows. It made little difference to the temperature, but it did mean that we were able to hear clearly when Mrs. Hudson began arguing with someone outside our front door.

"Get out of here. We have nothing else for you."

Holmes walked over to the window and looked down.

"What is the problem, Mrs. Hudson?"

"Oh, Mr. Holmes, this child won't leave. I even gave her a piece of bread, but see, she just sits there on the doorstep crying."

"Mrs. Hudson, I think you will find that she is hoping to speak to me."

"She isn't one of your 'Irregulars' is she, Mr. Holmes? I thought we'd agreed that they must always call at the rear entrance."

"Nothing of the sort. I believe this young lady is a client. Would you please send her up and, if it isn't too much trouble, provide us with some cooling refreshments."

Holmes sat back down. I was eager to ask about our visitor, but I could tell that Holmes wasn't going to answer any of my questions until she was present, so we waited in companionable silence.

Mrs. Hudson took slightly longer than usual to show the client upstairs. However, during that brief delay she managed to find a jug of lemonade, which she placed on the table between us. I would have preferred a refreshing glass of ale, but anything was welcome on such a hot day. She poured out three glasses and then left us to our business.

The girl had stopped crying now, but the tracks of her tears could still clearly be seen in the grimy streaks they had left on her dirty face. I handed her a pocket handkerchief. I'm not sure it made much difference, but the small kindness made her smile slightly.

It wouldn't have been fair to describe her as dirty, for that would have suggested that she had no care for her appearance. Rather, she was grubby

141

from too much time spent in the dusty streets. She couldn't have been more than six or seven years old, and she wore a short brown smock that hung shapelessly over her skinny body and didn't cover her knees. I thought that it had been made from calico, but even though the coarse material should have been hard-wearing, it had been patched multiple times. There were also places that were almost completely worn through and would have benefitted from similar attention. Her long brown hair had that greasy appearance when it hasn't been washed for some time, but she had tied it back with a blue ribbon in an effort to make it look nice. The ribbon was cleaner than any other part of her, and it was obviously a prized possession of which she took especial care.

It was a sad sight, but I couldn't see anything that distinguished her from the hundreds of other children roaming the streets of London, and certainly nothing that indicated that she was in need of the services of Sherlock Holmes.

Holmes gestured to the visitor's chair. "Please sit down, Miss . . . ?"

"Peg, Mr. Holmes. My name is Peg."

She climbed into the chair. It was too high for her and her feet dangled in the air once she was seated. They were bare, and I noticed for the first time that they were bleeding. I immediately reached for my medical bag and then knelt in front of her to tend her wounds.

"Very good, Watson," said Holmes. "While you work, maybe Peg can explain what has brought her all the way to Baker Street, and in such a hurry?"

Peg seemed intimidated and reluctant to reply, squirming backwards in the chair to put more distance between herself and Holmes.

"Let me start then," said Holmes. "I saw how you were still breathing heavily when you were speaking to Mrs. Hudson in the street. You have obviously exerted yourself greatly to get here today, and travelled some distance. It must be a matter of grave importance to make you run in such a heat and to make you endure such injuries."

I finished cleaning Peg's wounds. They were superficial and had already stopped bleeding. I could tell from the hardened scar tissue that covered her soles that she often injured herself in this fashion, as one must inevitably if one walks around the city in bare feet.

Still she said nothing and Holmes continued. "My condolences to you on the loss of your mother. It must be hard, now that it's just you and your father. He is clearly a man of variable temperament, but you obviously love him greatly to have gone to such lengths on his behalf."

As he spoke, Peg sat up straighter in her chair and smiled for the first time since her arrival. It was clear that Holmes's words had excited her greatly.

142

"You have the sight, like me," she said. "I knew I was right to come to you for help."

"The sight?" I asked. "Do you mean some form of psychic powers?"

"Of course. How else could he know all that about me? Ma died last winter, and now there's just me and Da, and soon he'll be gone too." Her excitement faded back into sadness as she said this.

With any other client, Holmes would have been scathing of her belief in the supernatural. However, in this instance, no doubt in deference to her tender years, his rebuke was gentler than usual.

"I am sorry to disappoint you, but I possess no magical 'sight'. The observations of my own eyes told me everything that I needed to know. In the past, your dress has been carefully patched, presumably by your mother, but more recent damage has gone unrepaired, suggesting that she is no longer with you. Sadly, the most logical assumption is that she died. However, the ribbon in your hair is newer and tied by your father – Watson you will observe the mark on one end, clearly a man's thumb print. It was probably a gift from him."

Peg nodded, clearly awestruck by Holmes's deductions.

"The bruise-marks on your arm, made by the same hand, tell the rest of the story of your relationship. Yet you suggest that you are afraid for his life, not your own, and I assume this is why you have sought our assistance."

Peg started crying. "It's all true, but if you don't believe in the sight, you won't believe me."

"There, there," I said. "Just tell us everything and we will do what we can."

"I *do* have the sight, I *do*, and last night I had a vision. My Da is going to be murdered."

Once again Holmes confounded my expectations. He was not dismissive, but took this statement as seriously as that of any witness we had questioned in the past.

"Tell me everything that you saw. Any small detail could be important."

"There was so much blood. I don't want to remember. I just want to be wrong this time."

"Please, Peg," I said. "You have come all this way. Let us try to help you now."

She blew her nose loudly on my handkerchief and then, after a moment, she started again.

"I saw a knife, stones . . . gravestones, and my Da. He was so angry, and then they hit him, and there was blood, so much . . . ."

Then she stopped, unable to hold in the tears any longer.

"That's enough Holmes," I said. "We should not press her further."

"Wait, Watson. There is one more thing I must know. Peg, where do and your father live?"

"Pro . . . Providence Place."

"Excellent," said Holmes and rushed out, leaving me to comfort the girl alone.

By the time that Holmes returned, Peg had calmed down slightly. We went to the other side of the room to speak privately, leaving her sipping a glass of lemonade.

"I have sent word to the police," said Holmes, "telling them to look for her father's body in the graveyard at All Saints' Church Poplar. It is very close to Providence Place."

"You think there is some truth to her story then? Surely you are not saying that she really had a vision?"

"Of course not. I fear this young girl actually saw her father's body, possibly even the murder itself. Imagining that it is a vision and that it might yet be prevented is her way of coping. It goes against all my instincts but, in this case, it may be better to indulge her fantasies than to confront her with the truth, at least until we are certain of all the facts."

We went back over to our chairs and sat down next to Peg.

"Are you going to help my Da?" she asked.

"Mr. Holmes has already sent a message to the police. They are looking for him as we speak," I said. I chose my words carefully so that I didn't lie. Nevertheless, I felt guilty for deceiving her.

"Oh, but they won't listen. They've never believed any of my visions, not even when the robberies happened."

"Robberies?" asked Holmes, his interest piqued by the mention of criminal activity.

"Oh, there's been lots recently. All the shopkeepers have been worried. I saw some with my sight and tried to tell, but people never want to hear the bad stuff. All they want to hear is: 'You'll fall in love', 'You'll get some money', or 'You'll live a long time'. I think Mr. White at the baker's might have listened though because, the day after he was robbed, he thanked me for telling him and gave me a penny. Isn't that strange?"

"Nevertheless, I am sure the police will listen now," I said. "They take the word of Sherlock Holmes very seriously."

"I hope they find him soon. I tried to tell him to stay at home today where he would be safe, but he wouldn't listen."

"You told him this morning?" Holmes leaned forward, an expression of worry on his face.

144

"Of course, as soon as I woke up. Then I told Mrs. March, but she wouldn't listen either, and it was her who first told everyone I had the gift."

"But if she spoke to her father *after* seeing her vision . . . ." I started to say.

"Then I was premature in passing judgement. Let that be a lesson, Watson. Gather all the facts before you draw your conclusions."

He leapt up from his chair. "We must leave at once."

"Where are we going?" I asked.

"Why, to gather those facts, of course! There is something more going on here that I do not yet see, but hopefully the residents of Providence Place will have the answers we seek."

The cab journey to Stepney was uneventful, yet Peg seemed to find it terribly exciting. She sat between us and the first time we went over a bump in the road she squealed with a mixture of fear and joy and clutched my hand. I realised that this was probably the first time that she had travelled in any sort of vehicle.

After that first shock, Peg seemed less scared by the bouncing of the carriage, although she did squeeze my hand a little harder during the larger jolts. As we travelled, I also realised how far and fast she must have run to get to us. The journey to her home from Baker Street was long enough by cab, and it was no wonder that her feet had been bleeding at the end of her journey.

When we reached our destination, Peg jumped down from the cab quickly and ran off shouting for her father. I prayed that she found him and that this proved to be a waste of our time.

I paused consider our surroundings rather than chasing after her. I couldn't remember having visited this particular corner of the city before. There was obviously a major railway line nearby, as the noise in the background from the trains passing by was almost constant. One could sense it in the air as well, which felt thick with coal dust and hard to breathe.

"The graveyard is over there," said Holmes, pointing north. "We should send someone to call off the police, now that we know that it was all in her imagination."

"You do not believe her then?"

"That she had a vision? Surely, Watson, you know me better than that. Yet she was scared enough to come to us, and that bears further investigation."

Just as we were about to turn into Providence Place, following the route Peg had taken, a boy ran out into the road. Holmes put his fingers in

145

his mouth and let out a loud whistle. The boy stopped in his tracks and turned to face us.

"Do you know the graveyard?" asked Holmes.

The boy nodded. Holmes took a notepad from his pocket and scratched out a short note.

"Take this to the policemen you will find there, and tell the man in charge that he will find us at Providence Place."

Holmes held out the paper with a penny and, quick as a flash, both were snatched from his hand and the boy was running up the street.

We turned the corner into Providence Place, and the first thing to strike me was the smell. It was the inevitable stench of too many people living too close together, magnified to oppressive levels by the heat of the summer. I had smelt it before in other slums around London.

"I'd hoped to have seen the last of places like this when they tore down Old Nichol," I said to Holmes, but he just grunted by way of reply.

The conditions seemed terrible to me, but the people living there seemed happy enough. All the way down the cul-de-sac, groups of women stood together, doing their chores while they talked. Children ran between the groups, hiding behind skirts and then shrieking with laughter as their friends found them before scampering off to hide again.

Then the women began to notice our presence and, one by one, the groups ceased their conversations. The children noticed something was amiss too and stopped to stare at us. I felt incredibly self-conscious, but Holmes seemed unfazed and walked down the middle of the street as though he owned the place.

Then there was a shout from above us.

"He's not here."

I looked up and saw Peg leaning out of a first floor window at the end of the row.

"Margaret Croft, what trouble are you causing now?" shouted one of the women. "Get down here at once."

Peg disappeared from the window, emerging on to the street a minute later. She ran up to the woman who had shouted.

"Mrs. Marsh, Mrs. Marsh, these men have come to help my Da."

"What do you mean, help your Da? These don't look like preachers who might wean him off the bottle, and that's the only cure that might help him."

"I told you, I had a vision. Why don't you believe me this time?"

"Margaret, usually your visions are a bit of harmless fun, but we don't joke about death. It's unlucky. Don't you understand?"

Holmes walked up to her.

"Madam, am I correct in believing that you know something about this girl's visions?"

"She's the one I told you about," said Peg. "I had a vision that she was going to have a baby and look, I was right."

Mrs. Marsh flushed with embarrassment, but there was no denying what Peg had said. She was heavily pregnant, and looked as though she might give birth any day.

"Yes, that's right, Margaret, but these gentlemen don't want to hear about that. You shouldn't go around shouting about other people's business. I'll be having words with your father."

"But they are going to kill him!" Peg shouted at her and ran back into the building, crying.

"I'm sorry, gents," said Mrs. Marsh. "She's been a bit funny ever since her mum died, but everyone here is very fond of her."

"She told you this morning that someone was going to kill her father," asked Holmes.

"Yes, that was queer. I mean, we're all used to her little announcements, but nothing like that. Jimmy, her dad, he didn't like it one bit. I thought he was going to hit her, right here in the middle of the street, but luckily for her he was sober. She'd be best off avoiding him when he gets home tonight though, 'specially if he sees she's dragged you gentlemen down here."

I was about to ask more about Peg's visions when someone spoke up behind us.

"Mr. Holmes, Doctor Watson. I was told I should find you here."

We turned around and saw that a man had entered Providence Place behind us. He was obviously no more a resident than we were. His suit might have been shabby, but it was far smarter than any of these people could afford.

"Inspector Pride at your service, gentlemen. We received your message, and I've had my men searching the graveyard, as per your instructions."

"I am sorry, Inspector, to have wasted your time like this," said Holmes.

"So you said in your note, but that's the thing. We have found a body, just like you said. Back of his head cracked open. Blood everywhere. It really is a terrible mess. You should come look for yourselves."

"Oh my God!" cried Mrs. Marsh, who had overheard our conversation. "I didn't believe her, and now . . . ."

"Calm yourself, please," said Holmes. "Take care of the girl and keep her away while we get to the truth of this matter."

147

We followed Inspector Pride and found the body, just as Peg had described it. A couple of police constables stood nearby and with them was a man wearing a cassock.

"The rector here has identified the deceased as one James Croft," said the inspector. "Is that the man you were expecting us to find?"

"Yes, that's the man we were looking for," said Holmes. "He was a member of your congregation?" he asked the rector.

"After a fashion. He wasn't a regular churchgoer, not the type, but I remember when his wife died, not so long ago."

"And did you know anything about his daughter's visions?"

"Visions? That was his daughter? That sweet little girl?" The rector's face contorted in horror. "I'd heard rumours of some heathen fortune teller nearby, tricking people into paying for messages from the devil. I thought it was some travelling trickster, not a member of my own congregation. Truly Satan is among us, and now God is punishing the wicked for their sins."

"Superstitious nonsense," muttered the inspector. "It was a regular human being who did for this poor chap."

"Could it have been an accident?" I asked. "You can see blood on the top of this gravestone. Maybe the poor man fell rather than being attacked?"

"You called us here about a murder and here we have the man you told us about, dead. Now I'm not a fancy detective like you, Mr. Holmes. I'm a straightforward man and I don't believe in coincidences, so I will be treating this as a murder."

"And so you should," said Holmes. "I do not believe in coincidences either, and finding this man dead so soon after his daughter's prediction is far too unlikely to be happenstance."

"Prediction? What are you talking about?"

We briefly explained how we had come upon this case and, with every word we said, Inspector Pride's expression became grimmer.

"A very unpleasant situation, no doubt about it. I will need to interview the man's neighbours. You may come along, if you wish."

Then without waiting for a reply, he set off back towards Providence Place.

By the time we caught up with the inspector, he was already interviewing a group of women. I had thought that Holmes would stay and listen, but instead he made his way into the building. He seemed unconcerned by the alarming creaks that came from the stairs as he ascended, but I followed cautiously, fearful that they might collapse beneath me at any moment.

When we reached the top, we searched until I saw Peg sitting on a thin mattress in the furthest corner of the building. We navigated a winding path across the room, through all the other sleeping places, until we reached her.

"I am sorry, Peg," I said. "Your father is dead. We were not in time to save him."

"I know. I heard the mums talking below." She looked up at me and the anguish on her face was heartbreaking. "Why didn't he listen to me?" she wailed. Then she threw herself at my chest and hugged me tight.

For a moment I wasn't sure how to react, but then I wrapped my arms around her and muttered, "There, there," gently until I felt her relax. After a while she let go and sat up straight again.

"This is your bed?" asked Holmes.

"It's ours. We share it. Unless he's had a bad night, then I try to find another space if I can. People are usually kind, and I'm only small."

"I am afraid Inspector Pride is going to want to talk to you," I said. "Do you think you can do that?"

"Of course," she replied and I saw a flash of the determination that had brought her to Baker Street in the first place. "I want to help him any way I can."

She stood up and we escorted her downstairs to join the other residents in the street.

"So you claim to have known that your father was going to be murdered," said Inspector Pride. "I don't suppose your 'vision' showed you by whom?"

"It isn't like that. I can't control what I see."

"Yet I've been told that people come to you to hear their fortunes. If you don't control you visions, how do you answer their questions?"

Holmes nodded in appreciation. Inspector Pride was brusque, but he was not unintelligent, and making a credible effort to investigate.

Peg looked at the ground and shuffled her feet nervously. "I just do, sir."

It was obviously a lie and I could see the inspector was getting impatient. I squatted down beside her.

"Tell the inspector the truth, Peg. You will not get in trouble, but we need to know everything if we are going to establish what happened to your father."

"He made me to do it."

"Who, your father?" I asked.

"Yes. After all the fuss over Mrs. Marsh's baby, he told me to charge for fortunes. He told me some things to say. 'You'll have some good luck.' 'You'll find something lost.' Things like that."

Inspector Pride snorted in disgust. "As I suspected, a simple trick. There is no such thing as the supernatural."

"But I do have real visions, sir. I just had to keep my Da happy."

"Or he would hit you? Isn't that right? Don't look surprised. I've been talking to your neighbours. They heard you fighting."

"He drinks too much sometimes, but he loves . . . loved me." Once again Peg started crying.

"Surely that is enough, Inspector. We can all see how things were. You are just upsetting the girl."

"Not quite, Doctor Watson. The witnesses report hearing Mr. Croft arguing with his daughter this morning and that she said he was going to be murdered."

"This is hardly news, Inspector. We told you this ourselves."

"Indeed you did, Doctor Watson. I don't know what she hoped to accomplish by involving you and Mr. Holmes, but once you discount her false visions there is only one possible conclusion. She knew her father was going to be murdered because she planned to do it herself."

"No!" Peg screamed and she tried to run away, but Inspector Pride had stationed a constable nearby and he grabbed her before she could escape.

All around me there were gasps of horror. None of the residents of Providence Place could believe that this sweet young child could be a murderer, yet the inspector had laid out a compelling argument.

"Inspector, please reconsider. Surely you can see that a young girl like this could not possibly have committed such a violent crime."

"Doctor Watson, you said it yourself. The blow to his head might have been an accident. Perhaps he fell down because she poisoned him, or maybe she had an accomplice. We'll establish the truth soon enough, but I'm confident this is the only logical answer."

Holmes had remained silent throughout, but now he spoke.

"A valiant effort Inspector, but you are wrong. We must not discount Miss Croft's visions so swiftly. They remain the key to this case."

Inspector Pride scoffed. "You cannot be telling me that the great Sherlock Holmes believes in visions and prophecies? I thought you were a man of science, not superstition."

"I assure you that my logical faculties are sound and far superior to yours in every way. In the morning, I will prove Miss Croft's innocence."

Then he strode off without another word. I looked at Peg and she was obviously terrified.

"Don't worry," I said. "Just go with the inspector and we will see you soon."

Then I hurried after Holmes, unable to stand her pitiful gaze a moment longer.

I caught up with him on the road where the cab had first dropped us.

"We can't leave Peg there alone with Inspector Pride," I said. "Surely she needs our help."

"We are helping her, by finding the truth. The inspector is an honest man, albeit with a regrettably limited imagination. She will be perfectly safe with him for now."

"You really believe her visions were true?" I asked, incredulous at the very idea.

"I believe there is truth to them."

We had continued walking as we spoke, and as we travelled, Holmes kept sniffing at the air. I took a deep inhalation myself, only to start coughing as I breathed in too much of the over-ripe scent of the city at the height of summer.

"There it is," exclaimed Holmes as we rounded a corner. "I knew that it couldn't be far." Then he hurried into the bakery that he had just spotted.

I don't know how Holmes detected the bakery from so far away, but I have learnt never to underestimate his olfactory prowess. Still, once we were inside the shop, the scent of fresh bread and cakes was unmistakable, and a pleasant antidote to the smell of the streets.

"Can I help you gentlemen?" said the man standing behind the counter. It took no great deductive skills to conclude that he was the baker. Flour clung to his apron, and his rolled-up sleeves revealed muscles made powerful through the kneading of so many loaves. Unlike Peg, I could easily see this man bludgeoning someone to death with little or no effort.

"Is he the murderer?" I whispered to Holmes. It made some sense. Peg had mentioned his kindness to her in the past. Perhaps he had stepped in to save her from her father's abuse.

"Of course not," he said. Then he addressed the baker. "Sir, I have heard that recently there was a robbery at this establishment. Would you be so good as to tell us what happened?"

"There's nothing much to say, sir. They broke in overnight and cleaned out my safe, just like they've done at a dozen other shops around here in the last few months. Are you from the police? You need to do something about it. Hard enough for a man to make an honest living already without this kind of thing."

151

"No, we aren't with the police," said Holmes, "and I don't think you are entirely honest."

The baker blanched at this, turning as white as his flour.

"You're with the insurance, aren't you? Look, I'm sorry. Really, truly I was robbed. It's just that I emptied the safe that night before they came. This girl came and told me she'd had a dream that I was going to be robbed next. I was going to ignore her, but my wife said she'd heard of the child. Some sort of local fortune teller or something. So I thought, why not take precautions? Then, that night, they came, just like she said. Look, they smashed the glass to get in." He pointed to a boarded-up section of window. "I didn't make it up. I just exaggerated a little."

"Thank you," said Holmes. "That is all we needed to know." Then he walked out, leaving the baker nervously wringing his large hands.

"Should we tell the insurance company about his little trick?" I asked when we were outside.

"Let them work it out for themselves and earn their money," said Holmes.

Our investigations continued in that vein for the rest of the day. Holmes seemed particularly concerned about the robberies. Some of the other shopkeepers had also been told about Peg's visions, but none seem to have acted on them.

"They probably thought that she was trying to take advantage of these crimes," said Holmes, and I was inclined to agree. It was certainly easier to believe than that a girl would receive visions of the future, and yet the evidence of her powers was growing in a way that I could not ignore.

Eventually, towards dusk, we made our way back to Providence Place.

"Maybe we should go home and get some rest," I said. "If we leave now, we might still persuade Mrs. Hudson to prepare a light supper for us before she retires for the night."

"I'm afraid that we will be going hungry this evening. It is my intention that we should spend the night here."

I groaned. "Are you sure that is really necessary? Do you think that the killer might return tonight?"

"No, I simply wish to spend the night in the company of Miss Croft's neighbours."

"Do you think we are some sort of show for your entertainment?"

I turned to see who had spoken and saw Mrs. Marsh standing in the doorway.

152

"I thank you for trying to help Margaret, but we don't need gentlemen coming here pretending to be poor and indulging whatever 'fancies' they might have."

"I assure you, madam, we are not here for anything of the sort. Are we, Holmes?"

He ignored my question and instead asked, "The vision about your child was the first, was it not?"

"I suppose it was," Mrs. Marsh replied. "At least the first that I can remember."

"You said you believed her and started her down this path?"

"I did. I had to."

She stood there, staring down Holmes and defying him to continue his deduction.

"Your husband works away from home. We are near the docks, so on a ship maybe."

She nodded grimly.

"And he returned home just in time to hear this announcement."

"That same day."

"He believed Miss Croft's vision too?"

"Not at first, but I convinced him. The baby convinced him."

"Then you are a very lucky woman and I wish your family every happiness for the future. Now, if you have no further objections, we will spend the night in Miss Croft's corner of the house, since neither she nor her father will be needing the space."

Mrs. Marsh stepped aside and let us enter the building.

"I'm sorry," she whispered to me as I passed. "Please help Peg if you can."

"We will do our very best," I assured her, and then I followed her upstairs.

We made our way to the back corner of the upper floor, where we had found Peg earlier, and sat down next to each other on the mattress.

"So all this started because a woman was unfaithful to her husband and was afraid that she might be caught out," I said. "But why did people believe her?"

"I'm not sure they did. They chose not to upset matters. After all, a child needs its parents, and it should have ended there. Only then Miss Croft had more visions that came true, and people began to wonder if they had really believed in her all along. They chose the easy answer, however improbable it might have been, rather than digging further to reach the truth."

"Like the inspector."

153

"And us earlier today. We are all attracted to tidy solutions."

"So if we do not believe in visions and we do not think Peg killed her father, what is left?"

Holmes smiled. "I hope all will become clear after a good night's sleep."

I sighed and looked down at the mattress we were sitting on. It was thin, dirty, and probably crawling with bed bugs. I had no intention of lying down there.

Clearly Holmes didn't either. He just pulled his hat down over his eyes and no longer answered when I spoke to him. After a while I followed his example and tried to rest.

I had not expected to sleep in those squalid conditions. Yet clearly I must have done, as I woke with a jolt when something warm dropped into my lap.

"Here, Watson, this will help fill that rumbling stomach. Freshly baked this morning."

I lifted my hat and looked down to see half-a-loaf of bread in my lap. Holmes was standing over me nibbling at the other half. I tore into the bread without hesitation. It would have been better with butter and a nice spoonful of jam. Still, it was fresh enough to be tasty on its own, and I was hungry enough to not to care.

I had swallowed a few mouthfuls when a memory sprung to the forefront of my mind.

"Holmes, the thieves are going to strike again," I cried. "They are planning to rob the church."

"How do you know that, Watson? Are you having visions now too?"

He laughed and I suddenly felt embarrassed. How did I come to know this?

"It is not a vision. It is more like the words just floated into my mind."

"That would be a fair enough description of what happened. You did hear it, while you slept, and if you had stayed awake you might have learnt more. There is no private business in the slums. The accounts of Mr. Croft's arguments with his daughter, which have proved so damning, should have taught you that."

"So the visions were just conversations Peg heard while she slept, nothing more?"

"Nothing more. Another simple explanation, but this time supported by all the facts."

I thought about it for a moment. It made perfect sense, but still something bothered me.

"Why was Peg the only one to hear these conversations? Surely other people must have heard them too, like I did last night."

"Look at where you are sitting, Watson. You are leaning against one of the outer walls of this building. The wall is thicker here, but not so thick that you cannot hear what transpires in the neighbouring building, if you are close enough."

"That's amazing," I said. "Should we investigate the building behind us now?"

"No need. I sent a message to Inspector Pride before I purchased our breakfast. He should be raiding the thieves' den at any moment."

He sat down next to me and we both leant back against the wall. Sure enough, after a few minutes we clearly heard crashing sounds coming from next door. A cacophony of shouts, banging, and police whistles followed, but soon it became quiet once again.

Holmes stood up.

"Shall we go and see what Inspector Pride has caught for us today?"

In order to reach the other building, we had to leave Providence Place and make our way around the block. As we walked, a troubling thought entered my mind. I had become so caught up in the excitement of finding the solution Peg's visions that I had completely overlooked that we still had not proven her innocent.

I was about to mention my concerns to Holmes when we arrived at a warehouse guarded by two police constables. One of them recognised me from the graveyard the day before and waved us through.

Inside, Inspector Pride was waiting. He pointed to three men sitting on wooden crates. Their arms had been secured behind them and one had a nasty cut above his left eye.

"They gave us a bit of trouble," said the inspector, "but we caught them off-guard thanks to your tip. My men are searching the building now for their loot, and then it will be off to lock-up for the lot of them."

One of the men smiled, a rat-faced little man with a thin moustache. "Inspector, I keep telling you there is nothing to find. We are law-abiding citizens, falsely accused and attacked by your brutish constables."

"Shut your mouth," said Inspector Pride. "I know you are responsible for the thefts around here, and it's only a matter of time before we find the evidence." However, he looked worried.

"You won't find anything here, Inspector," said Holmes. "They were too clever for that."

The rat-faced man smirked.

"However, not so clever so as not to talk where they could be heard. If you send your men to the graveyard, you will find their haul in a recently filled grave, probably not far from where we met yesterday."

The inspector called over a couple of the constables and sent them off to search based on Holmes's instructions.

"Now tell me, Mr. Holmes. How did you come to overhear the plans of these ruffians?"

We explained our experiences during the night in Providence Place, with Holmes filling in some of the details of the conversation that I had slept through.

"That explains the girl's visions," said the inspector when we had finished, "but it still doesn't explain her father."

Holmes pulled out a small cloth sack and tipped out the contents on to the top of a barrel. I looked and saw a small collection of coins and banknotes, and something else – a small cameo like the ones women sometimes wore.

"This is distinctive," I said.

The inspector took a look and nodded in agreement. "That is one of the items reported missing, although it was meant to be on a blue ribbon."

"I found this beneath Mr. Croft's mattress last night," said Holmes. "It clearly ties him to these men. I think Miss Croft was not the only one to hear them planning but, while she tried to warn people, we know that her father's first instinct was to try to turn a profit. These are the proceeds of his blackmail, but he clearly grew too greedy, and that is when Miss Croft overheard them planning to kill him."

Inspector Pride nodded. "It is a logical solution, and these men are far more likely murderers than a little girl. I'll send word that Margaret Croft should be released and returned home immediately."

"We should return home too," said Holmes. "It has been a long night, and we would both appreciate the comforts of home."

"Should we stay and wait for Peg?" I asked Holmes as we left.

"I am sure her neighbours will take care of her," he replied. "Besides she'll get by well enough on what her father put aside for her, at least for a while."

"I hardly think a ribbon in her hair will keep her fed."

"No, but the rest of the money he had hidden might help. Blackmail is an ugly business, but it pays far better than prophecies."

# The Adventure of the House Abandoned
## by Arthur Hall

In examining the contents of my dispatch box, temporarily retrieved from the vaults of Cox and Company, I have discovered my notes concerning a case that I had almost forgotten, and that I cannot remember my friend Mr. Sherlock Holmes mentioning since its conclusion. However, since he has indicated no restriction on my placing the account before my readers, I now do so to the best of my recollection.

Holmes was, for once, in an uncharacteristically light frame of mind because of the favourable development of several cases which he had watched closely. He had remarked that, although he was at present unoccupied, he had high hopes for the seeds he had sown in penetrating four impending criminal enterprises to bear fruit before long.

"It appears then, that you expect to be extremely busy in the weeks to come," I replied, lowering my morning edition of *The Standard*.

"I would consider that extremely likely. Adrian Tynan seeks to escape the rope after cruelly disposing of his mother-in-law, and that scoundrel Jake Meredith believes that his plans for robbing the mail train on the night of the forthcoming gold shipment are known only to himself and his lieutenants. Both, I think, will be disappointed. I have informed Lestrade as to my findings, and will accompany the official force at their capture. I would greatly appreciate your company on those occasions, Watson, if you are free."

I took out my pipe. "When you specify the dates, Holmes, I will make arrangements. As always, I will be pleased to be with you,"

"Excellent!" He leaned forward abruptly in his chair, listening. "But I do believe that Mrs. Hudson is at the front door speaking in urgent tones to someone. It may be that we are to receive a new client."

I replaced my pipe unused in its pouch and stood up expectantly. A moment later we heard footsteps ascending the stairs, as well as those of our landlady which were familiar to us.

"A lady," my friend deduced from the tread, "and, from the tone of her voice, rather confused."

Mrs. Hudson admitted a young woman of average height whom I would have thought to be about twenty-five years of age. Her hair was very dark, but her facial features, although not unattractive, struck me as rather sharp. I was sorry to see that she appeared to be in a highly nervous state.

"Miss Laura Willis to see you, Mr. Holmes," Mrs. Hudson announced, and was about to withdraw when Holmes called for tea.

"I must apologise for having no appointment," Miss Willis began in a muffled voice. "I hoped that you would see me regardless. It is kind of you to do so."

I saw at once that my friend's interest was aroused by her stiff movements and indistinct speech.

"But I see that you are ill. Come, be seated near the fire and rest yourself, and then, after you have taken tea, tell us what brings you to us." He paused until she was settled. "I am Sherlock Holmes and this is my friend and colleague, Doctor John Watson. You have my assurance that his discretion is equal to my own."

Mrs. Hudson reappeared with the tea tray after a few minutes had passed and I poured for the three of us. I noticed that Holmes's eyes never left our client, as he studied her closely. We replaced our empty cups and she hesitated. Then anxious words poured from her mouth before either of us could prompt her.

"Mr. Holmes, I saw mention of you in a newspaper. Is it true that you investigate strange situations, such as are sometimes dismissed by the official police?"

"There have been many occasions of that sort over the years," he replied. "Tell me, pray, is your reason for consulting me connected with the bruising that I now see as you turn your face to the light?"

For an instant, she dropped her gaze to the carpet. "It is directly connected."

"Who has treated you so?" said I, but Holmes dismissed my question with an impatient glance.

"Take a moment to consider," he advised, "and then tell us all at your leisure. There is no need to hurry."

Miss Willis nodded, her gaze taking in both of us in turn. "Thank you, gentlemen. The marks on my face and, indeed, on my body, are the result of a whipping I received at the hands of an unknown man. I do not know why he treated me so, nor am I aware of his identity, and that is why, in my confusion, I have sought your help."

"Any man who would treat a lady in this manner is an absolute scoundrel!" I retorted.

"Relate all that occurred," Holmes asked quietly. "From the beginning, I beg of you."

"I am employed as a seamstress at Beales and Welford, of Lewisham," she said in a soft voice. "Three days ago, I completed my

158

work for the day and left the premises at six o'clock, as is my usual practice. My lodgings are not far away, no more than a ten-minute walk, and I was about halfway there when I suddenly realised that I had been otherwise alone in the street since leaving the main thoroughfare, and that a man walked persistently behind me."

"Were you able to take note of his appearance?" Holmes enquired.

"As soon as I suspected his pursuit, I glanced quickly behind me. I saw a man who was tall and thin with a short, pointed beard."

"Did he speak to you?"

"Not until later. A coach came to rest just ahead of me, and the man who followed quickly closed in. I felt his strong grip on my shoulder, and had no time to scream before a piece of cloth or muslin was pressed against my face. I can dimly recall a smell such as is present in hospitals or doctors' surgeries, before being carried into the coach."

"Chloroform," said I.

"Undoubtedly," Holmes agreed.

"I remember nothing more," our client resumed, "until I awoke in a well-furnished sitting room. For an instant, I believed myself to have fainted or been taken ill and brought there, perhaps while a doctor was summoned. I looked around me at the tasteful decorations and furniture and suddenly realised that I was tied hand and foot to a stiff-backed chair."

"Were your abductors present, then?"

"Indeed they were, Mr. Holmes, and they immediately began to question me. Repeatedly they shouted 'Where is it?' or 'What have you done with it?' until I could stand it no more. I screamed at them and shouted that I knew not to what they were referring, and that was when the whipping began."

I felt a surge of outraged anger but said nothing. Holmes leaned towards her and spoke in his gentlest tone.

"I see that they have used you most cruelly. Did these men then specify what it was that they believed you to have hidden?"

"They did, but it meant nothing to me. I was accused of stealing documents – the plans of something called '*The Thunderer*'."

"And you are completely unaware of their meaning?"

"I swear that I have never heard such a title."

Holmes closed his eyes briefly, in contemplation. "Pray continue. Your narrative grows more interesting."

"I was struck several more times, as you see. Then their assaults suddenly ceased when the second man, a short bald individual whom I presumed to have driven the coach, left the room. The bearded man sat on the sofa drinking brandy, and I believe that I fainted."

"That is not surprising." I remarked.

She nodded. "I came to myself feeling weak and ill, just as the short man returned. He spoke quickly to the other and they both stared at me. I think they discussed for some minutes whether to kill me. Then the bearded man shrugged and said that I could not harm them, and that I would probably starve to death before I was discovered. They did nothing more, but turned their backs on me and left. I saw nothing more of them."

"Do you know why they left so abruptly?"

"I cannot be certain, but the short man returned in a state of excitement. Possibly they had received urgent news that made their presence necessary elsewhere."

"That may be. How, then, did you free yourself?" Holmes enquired.

"When I felt able, and I do not know how much time had passed by then, I began to struggle against my bonds. At first it seemed hopeless, but after a while I came to realise that the chair was old and that some of its joints were loose. Although now hungry and thirsty, I redoubled my efforts and loosened them further, and it was by doing this that the chair turned around and I saw the short flight of steps leading down to another chamber. I moved the chair across the room and hesitated at the top of the steps, unwilling to suffer further injuries. Then, with no other course open to me, I tipped myself forward so that the chair was beneath me. The fall was of course painful and I screamed once more, even weeping as I came to rest at the bottom of the steps. When the pain had passed I thought that my efforts had been futile, until I found that the back of the chair had shattered and one of my arms was now free."

"I commend you on your endurance and bravery," Holmes said, and I concurred.

"Thank you, gentlemen, for listening to my experience and for your patience," she said with relief in her voice. "There is not much more to tell. I sat in one of the armchairs until my senses returned to me. I found some bread in the other room, which I discovered to be a kitchen, and drank some brandy from the decanter that the men had used. When I finally gained the strength to leave the house, I found to my amazement that I was no more than a few streets away from my own lodgings! I forced myself to walk, my unsteadiness attracting many curious glances until I came upon the Lewisham police station, where my account was received with some incredulity. I believe that the desk sergeant smelled the brandy on my breath, and rather than accept that it had been taken as a restorative, chose to believe that I had spent time in a tavern. But I persisted, and eventually a constable was despatched to accompany me back to the house. The street was composed of numerous shops, a small factory, and many dwellings and, as I have said, was not far away. Inside the place of my confinement, I was appalled to discover that the broken chair and the ropes that had bound me had disappeared, as had the decanter and all signs that the room had been inhabited. My first thought was that I had somehow brought the constable to the wrong house completely, but a moment of consideration told me that this could not possibly be, especially as the mirror near the entrance and the full-length portrait of a lady who could have been my sister were as I remembered."

"Do you, in fact, have such a sister?"

"Not at all. My only relative is an elderly uncle who lives in Northumberland."

My friend nodded slowly. "And what did the constable make of this?"

Miss Willis' face reddened visibly. "He was most impolite. He made remarks to the effect that I should give up drinking if I could not hold my spirits. I think those were his words. He also swore rudely as he left."

"I am not surprised to hear it," said Holmes. "Most of the official force are confounded at the first suggestion of the unusual, and shrink from it." He then said nothing for a few moments before he straightened his posture. "It is apparent, then, that you have been mistaken for another person. The resemblance of the picture near the entrance to yourself reveals this immediately. Thus is explained your being held in an unfamiliar room where you were assumed to have hidden an item, of which you have no knowledge. As to the nature of that item, we have no means of identification, although I have a high expectancy of my investigation revealing it before long. Are you now quite recovered from your ordeal?"

"I returned to my lodgings yesterday afternoon, and slept long and heavily after consuming food and drink. When I awoke I felt sore, but sufficiently recovered to come here today."

"Capital! If you will give Doctor Watson the address of this house, we will pay a visit there after luncheon. Is there anything else you wish us to know of this?"

Miss Willis shook her head. "No, Mr. Holmes, I think . . . But wait! I believe I failed to mention that my captors spoke with foreign accents."

"Thank you," Holmes said after a pause. "I had suspected that. If you will allow the Good Doctor to show you out, I think I can confidently say that you will hear from us quite soon."

After depositing Miss Willis in a cab, I climbed the stairs to our rooms with a question in my mind. "Holmes, why do you suppose that the two men returned to the house, after Miss Willis had escaped?"

He looked up from the volume of his index that lay open on his lap. "I imagine that they had reconsidered, and decided that to let her live was dangerous to them. On returning and finding her gone, they did what they could to erase all traces of the incident, making detection by the official force more difficult." He considered for a moment. "A possible alternative theory is that they observed Miss Willis leaving the house and, knowing that to attempt her murder in the street would probably attract the attention of passers-by at that time of day, they decided to remove what evidence they could to make the accuracy of her story seem unlikely."

"Who are these blackguards, Holmes?"

"I am not yet certain, but already I have my suspicions. Nevertheless, this afternoon our first action must be to visit that house ourselves, in the hope that the constable has not entirely destroyed all valuable indications by his blundering. I take it that you are with me?"

"As ever," I smiled.

"Capital! But I hear Mrs. Hudson on the stairs, so doubtless lunch is imminent. The moment we have fortified ourselves sufficiently, we will set out on the trail of these men who ill-treat helpless women."

It was not yet mid-afternoon as we watched the hansom out of sight. We found ourselves in a street that was very much as Miss Willis had described, a long line of Georgian houses with many shops and a factory which manufactured replacement teeth.

"Is this the address, Watson?"

I took out my notebook. "Miss Willis stated the address as 41 Ordmond Place. There is no number on the door, but counting from the nearby houses brings us to here. Also, the windows are dusty and the front garden has received no attention for some little time, and from our client's indications, it seems obvious that the owner was absent."

A fleeting smile crossed my friend's face, and I could not tell whether it was in approval of my small deductions or as mockery of them. On reaching the front door, he rapped upon it twice with his cane, before producing his pick-lock to gain admittance.

We stood in a carpeted hallway. There were no sounds. Holmes saw at once the picture that Miss Willis had described, hanging opposite a full-length mirror.

"There is indeed a close resemblance," he observed, "but no one with whom she was familiar would mistake Miss Willis for this lady."

"No, indeed," said I. "Her abductors may have acted upon a description by a third person, or perhaps they had a poor likeness from which to work."

He nodded. "Both are possibilities. Now, let us examine this room and the kitchen, which I presume is behind that door ahead. The entire space is carpeted, which indicates that the owner, whomever she may be, is quite wealthy, but it also hampers my investigation. You have seen me reconstruct events from marks on a dusty floor before now."

This was true, but not applicable here. Nevertheless, I stood against one wall while Holmes kneeled to examine the carpet through his lens. He eventually came upon the short flight of stairs that our client had described.

"Ha! If we needed substantiation of Miss Willis' account, Watson, we have it here. Her abductors clearly took considerable trouble to leave no trace, but these splinters from the shattered chair eluded them. Also, the tiny fragments of ash dropped upon the carpet are of a tobacco mixture not usually found in England, as I had come to expect. My studies that enabled me to write a monograph on the subject have not been in vain."

"Has the kitchen given up any clues?"

"Only the fact that there are fresh water traces in the pitcher. They did not taste stale, and the vessel was therefore used recently, probably to dilute the men's drinks. I think we have learned all that we can here, however, so we will progress to the next stage of our enquiry."

"And what is that to be?"

He rose to his full height. "As we arrived, I noticed that we were under observation from the house opposite. A woman, I think, with long dark hair. If it is her habit to be so inquisitive, she may have seen something that can be useful to us."

We left the house shortly afterwards, re-locking it after Holmes had satisfied himself that all was as it had been on our arrival. After crossing the street, we approached the residence that he had specified, a house almost identical to that we had just left, with a tiny front garden beset with weeds. He rang the doorbell without response, and was about to rap upon the door with his cane when we heard faint footsteps from within. A moment later, the door swung open to reveal a tall thin woman with long dark hair. She wore a garment quite unlike usual female apparel, a long piece of cloth wrapped around her body somewhat resembling the Indian sari, but with the most intricate and fantastic designs along its length. The overall impression, I thought, was something like a gypsy fortune-teller at a travelling fair or circus.

She scrutinized us from beneath long eyelashes, her gaze passing from Holmes to me. Her slow smile encompassed us, and she spoke unhurriedly, in a husky, almost masculine voice.

"Forgive me gentlemen, for not answering your summons immediately. At this time of day I commune with the spirits, and one cannot leave that far-off plane hurriedly."

Holmes and I glanced at each other, trying to conceal our surprise.

163

"We apologise for disturbing you," my friend said with a straight face, "but we are anxious to speak to the occupant of the house opposite. It is a lady who lives alone, we are told."

A faint shadow of suspicion clouded her expression for a moment. "And who are you gentlemen, may I enquire?"

"My name is Sherlock Holmes, and this is my colleague, Doctor John Watson. We are here in connection with a private matter."

"Your names I have heard somewhere, but I cannot bring their significance to mind." Her eyes settled on us again, and her smile returned. "I am Tanith le Grande, a servant of departed spirits. What is it that I can tell you?"

"To begin with," Holmes said after a moment of hesitation, "we would like to know when she was last seen here. Her home is empty and shows no sign of recent habitation."

"Her home is a house abandoned. Miss Stayforth has not lived there for the past few weeks. I fear that she has passed to another realm."

"Why do you believe such a thing?" I asked.

Miss le Grande stared at me as if I had asked a preposterous question. "The spirits told me, of course."

Holmes ignored this. "Do you know of any recent activity in her house, since Miss Stayforth left?"

"Recently I saw two gentlemen visit the premises. With them was a woman who bore some resemblance to Miss Stayforth, probably a relative. She appeared to have difficulty with her movements, and it struck me that she was either unwell or drunk. Sometime later the men left without the woman. If she is no longer there then she must have left during the night, or while I spoke with the departed."

"And you are quite sure that Miss Stayforth is no longer alive?"

"Of course, though I cannot tell what has befallen her. No, we will not . . . ." Her voice changed, suddenly becoming deeper still. Her eyes glazed, as if she peered into the far distance. "But yes, I am hearing their voices. They are telling me that you, Doctor Watson, will see her again. You alone will see her again!"

I gaped at her in surprise, startled as much by the risen note of her speech as by the content of it. "What is your meaning, Miss le Grande? Either Miss Stayforth has passed on, or she has not. How am I concerned with this?"

"You will shortly discover . . . ." But the glazed look had faded, and her tone changed to its former level. She covered her eyes with her hands and I saw a great shudder pass through her body. "Gentlemen," she said breathlessly, "I must apologise most profusely. It is unusual for the spirits to come upon me in the presence of others, except during a séance, when

164

we strive to seek them out. I regret that I must rest now, for I am near to exhaustion."

"If I can be of any assistance . . . ."

"No, I will be restored if I have sufficient sleep to regain my strength. Goodbye, gentlemen."

She retreated, closing the door before we could say anything more. We turned away, and struck out in the direction of the end of the road.

"I noticed several hansoms passing here during our conversation," Holmes said. "We should have no trouble procuring one quickly."

"You surprised me, Holmes, with so little comment on Miss le Grande's apparent seizure."

He laughed harshly. "I cannot believe that you were deceived for an instant. That was a contrived performance to speed our departure and confuse us, nothing more."

"I can see that she would appear convincing to a believer."

"I noticed immediately her reluctance to admit us, probably because the contraptions she uses to conduct her séances were not concealed at this time of day, or were dismantled. Also, the aroma of raw opium followed her as she came out to us which, I suspect, is the source of any 'genuine' trances she may experience. As for her sudden seizure, it was no more than common play-acting. I find it difficult to see how you are to encounter Miss Tayforth if, as the spirits are supposed to have revealed to Miss le Grande, she has already passed away. Perhaps you, too, will have a vision."

"I am not quite as dismissive of the supernatural as you, Holmes. You will recall a strange incident which I wrote of as 'The Moonlit Shadow', which was never satisfactorily explained."

"Much can be imagined from tricks of light and shade, and the effect of an uncertain atmosphere in a strange place contributes to such an illusion."

"You are right, I am sure." I conceded after a moment of thought.

"That woman is a charlatan, but she at least confirmed some of Miss Willis' account."

"It is a strange name she has," I observed.

"Not her real one, I'll be bound, but another invention meant to support her manufactured aura of mystery. She shares it with the Phoenician goddess of the moon."

A cab emerged from a side street, and came to a halt as Holmes signalled with his stick.

"Back to Baker Street, then?"

"Not at all. I think we must seek an audience with Mycroft."

Less than an hour later, we found ourselves sitting in an anonymous waiting room in Whitehall. We had listened to the closing of doors and echoing of footsteps in the corridor for too long, for Holmes was beginning to show signs of impatience. Then the door opened and the uniformed lackey who had met us on arrival and conducted us in here reappeared, to inform us that my friend's brother was now able to spare us a little of his valuable time. We were escorted further into the building until a row of doors at the end of a silent passage confronted us. Our guide rapped upon the first of these, waited for permission to enter, and announced us. He withdrew as we stepped into a thickly-carpeted chamber, wood-panelled and rather dark. Mycroft rose to his feet behind a massive desk of oak.

"Sherlock, and Doctor Watson! A pleasant surprise indeed. Pray be seated. You will find the chairs to your left to be the most comfortable."

When we were settled, he asked if we would like tea. We both thanked him but declined. He sat with his arms folded across his ample frame and studied us for a few moments. Then, his conclusions doubtlessly formed, he spoke in a quiet voice.

"I see that you are both perturbed about something. This will certainly be the reason for your presence here today." He scrutinized Holmes carefully, before allowing his gaze to fall upon me. He stared briefly at the blotting-pad before him, then his eyes met ours. "Very well then, how can I assist you?"

"We are attempting to discover the whereabouts of a missing woman," Holmes began. "It is likely that she is pursued also by those who wish her harm. In addition, there is the possibility that these are foreign agents who seek to extract information from her and so, Mycroft, as I have no means of recognising such people, I am forced to request your help."

The elder Holmes had begun to frown as my friend spoke, and his expression deepened with every word.

"Have you been able to discover where this lady normally resides, Sherlock?"

"We have, and we have visited the house to little avail. The address is 41 Ordmond Place, Lewisham."

At this, Mycroft's face went blank. "No doubt," he said after a moment, "the lady in question is Miss Iris Stayforth."

I must have betrayed my surprise, but Holmes stared at his brother impassively.

"She is one of your people, then?"

"It is imperative that you divulge to me the identity of your client, if there is one. I must know who else is concerned with this."

166

Holmes reflected briefly, and then must have concluded that there could be no harm in confiding in his brother, though complete confidentiality was his usual practice.

"The lady who approached me is Miss Laura Willis. She did so because she was abducted, taken to the address in Lewisham, and mistreated, with the object of forcing her to give up plans of which she knows nothing."

"Plans for what, pray, and why did these foreigners choose Miss Willis?"

"She apparently resembles Miss Stayforth, who lives not far away. They were probably watching the area, and abducted the wrong woman."

Mycroft nodded. "If they were working from a photographic portrait, that is quite possible. The two women are not actually related?"

"Not at all. The resemblance is close, but far from identical."

"I see." Mycroft's eyes narrowed. "I would be grateful if you would explain how you became aware of this, since by your own implication, you have never seen Miss Stayforth."

A shadow of a smile crossed Holmes's face. "I have already disclosed that we have visited the house. A full-length portrait of the lady graces the hallway."

"Of course," the elder Holmes said. "And the plans that seem to be the cause of this? You were about to tell me, moments ago."

"Miss Willis mentioned a name. It was, as I recall, '*The Thunderer*'."

Again there was a heavy silence. For what seemed like an age, no one spoke or moved. When Mycroft looked up again, his face was solemn.

"I am very glad that I can take for granted the absolute discretion of you gentlemen."

A bird flew past the single tall window, twittering alarmingly. When that momentary distraction had passed, Holmes said coldly, "You can indeed, Mycroft. I had thought we had demonstrated that sufficiently on past occasions."

"Of course, of course. I was merely emphasising the importance of what I am about to tell you. At once you will realise the enormity of this affair."

"Pray proceed." Holmes and I leaned forward together.

Mycroft hesitated, and I formed the impression that the words to come were torn from his conscience. He struggled to overcome his reluctance, as if he feared to betray a trust.

"Your conclusion that foreign agents are involved is correct. There have also been persistent reports that, although not imminent, war may not be many years away. For some time now, word has reached us from our people in Imperial Germany that a huge gun, a cannon with a range far exceeding any in use until now, has been invented, tested, and constructed."

"'*The Thunderer*'," I ventured.

"Indeed. You can imagine the devastating effect such a weapon would have on opposing forces with field guns of a lesser range. Experience had taught us that German assurances of continued peace cannot be trusted, leaving us with no choice but to maintain the development of our arms at least to a standard equal with theirs. To this end, arrangements were made for a considerable sum to be paid to someone closely concerned with the design of this gun, in exchange for a duplicate set of plans. Our agent charged with the task of bringing them to London was unfortunately discovered and pursued into the capital. Realising this, she hid the documents – or at least that is what we believe."

"Our agent being Iris Stayforth," Holmes concluded.

"Indeed. She is highly skilled in the art of deception. In Germany, she became the confidante of a high official in the Imperial Court. Naturally, with foreign spies in such close pursuit, on her return to England she could not present herself at Whitehall or at any connected government department. We know that she arrived at her home, but she has since disappeared."

"But surely, it is unlikely that German agents disposed of her, since they would not do so until the hiding-place was revealed. Also, in that event the abduction of Miss Willis would never have taken place, much less her torture."

"Quite so, Sherlock. The only explanation is that she has met with some sort of accident, an event unknown to us, or more likely that Count von Schell has caught up with her."

"What part does he play in this?" my friend asked.

"He is the official I mentioned, who Miss Stayforth found it necessary to become close to in the course of her work. Of course she was known by a German name, and had succeeded in falsely establishing herself as a member of an old Prussian family. As I said, she is a highly skilled agent. Apparently the Count had great affection for her and proposed marriage on several occasions. Finally, because at that time she was very near to obtaining the plans and it was imperative that her position was maintained, she agreed. Later, when her true purpose became known, Count von Schell swore that he would cause her to be hunted down and killed – to avenge the slur on his family name, as he put it. I fear that the man does not take disappointment well."

"So there is more than one hostile agency concerned here," said I.

Mycroft shrugged. "Not necessarily. If the Count's people have murdered Miss Stayforth, they will have returned to Germany, for they have no interest in the plans. He is said to be a young man of impulsive and erratic nature so, even if aware of the situation regarding them, he would spare it no consideration."

"If they have done so," Holmes observed, "the other group does not know of it. Hence their mistakenly turning their intentions to Miss Willis."

"The indications are that they are working independently and unbeknown to each other."

Holmes spent a few minutes in contemplation, his head upon his chest. I was about to turn to him to speak, when he looked directly at his brother expectantly.

"You have identified one possibility that explains Miss Stayforth's disappearance, Mycroft. Are you now prepared to tell us the name of the two German agents who abducted Miss Willis?"

Again the elder Holmes was hesitant, and I reflected that he must be fighting an inner battle against the habit and official restrictions of a lifetime.

"To the best of our knowledge until now, there are but two German spies of any note working in the capital. One of those has been arrested and is currently being investigated concerning a different matter. So we are left with Herman Baumann, a contemporary of Oberstein, whom you may remember has crossed your path and mine in the past. Baumann is thought to be a ruthless and intelligent man, obsessed, as his masters are, with the concept of his country eventually ruling all of Europe. While I consider that to be unrealistically ambitious, it does not bode well for the years to come. Should you chance to discover the plans in the course of your enquiries, Sherlock, you will of course convey them to me immediately?"

Holmes nodded. "Your trust in us is not misplaced, Mycroft. Pray be good enough to tell us where Baumann is to be found."

"He is in the habit of changing his place of residence often," Mycroft said, "probably because he suspects that he is being watched – which he is. I think, gentlemen, that sooner or later he will return to Ordmond Place, since the plans still have not been discovered. Your best course of action may be to lie in wait for him there."

We returned to Baker Street in time for a cigar before dinner. The conversation during the meal was interrupted by frequent silences, and I knew that this was because Holmes was considering how to proceed.

"We will return to Ordmond Place when it is fully dark, Watson," he said as he pushed away his plate. There are but two remaining problems: First we must devise a way to induce Baumann to join us tonight. We clearly cannot conduct a vigil indefinitely, awaiting his convenience. Then we must ourselves attempt to discover the hiding-place of the plans. Knowing how long Miss Stayforth spent in her home before departing once more would be of immense assistance, but such information is not available to us."

"Such a pity. If we could make it appear that the plans are in danger of being lost or destroyed, perhaps it would attract Baumann quickly."

Holmes smiled briefly. "Sometimes I could believe that it is you who can read my mind, Watson. I have already begun such a course of action, but I am doubtful if it will take effect tonight. That is why I mentioned two remaining problems."

"You refer, I think, to the telegram you despatched, during our return from Whitehall."

"Indeed. I wired Fleet Street, hoping for an insertion in the late editions. If this is in time to be seen by Baumann, we can be sure of his company tonight."

"What was the message?" I enquired.

"Simply that the owners of 41 Ordmond Place (for Miss Stayforth is merely a tenant) have discovered instability in the foundations. They have therefore resolved to commit the place to demolition, without delay."

"That would certainly attract Baumann's immediate attention," I agreed, "and the severe disapproval of the owners. This will cause them considerable difficulty, if they wish to re-let in the event of her not returning."

He waved away my objection. "I will of course publish a retraction."

Darkness had fallen some time earlier. Holmes and I watched the lights of the departing hansom grow fainter, and finally disappear.

"Ordmond Place is quiet tonight," Holmes observed. "I will enter Number 41 alone, Watson, while you conceal yourself among these bushes. Although they form the boundary of a garden, you should not be disturbed, since there are no lights showing in any windows hereabouts. You are armed, of course?"

"My service revolver is loaded and in my pocket."

"Capital! Remain concealed until you observe someone else entering, then follow with your weapon drawn. If our trap is not sprung in two hours or so, we may assume that Baumann has not seen the newspapers, or else he has not been deceived."

And so he entered and my vigil began. I crouched uncomfortably, with my face rubbing against twigs and leaves which rustled as a faint breeze sprang up. After a while a landau appeared, and deposited its passengers much further along the street. Two hansoms came and went in

170

succession, and a solitary man, unsteady on his feet, ambled by from the other direction.

Just as I began to feel cramped, a four-wheeler arrived and two men alighted. I heard harsh remarks in guttural German as the conveyance left and the smaller of the two set off away from the house. The other man, in a cape and top hat, stood listening for some little time before, apparently satisfied that he was unobserved, advanced towards Number 14 and picked the lock as Holmes had done. The door closed behind him softly.

I waited for no more than a minute or two, before rising with some relief and feeling the reassuring weight of my revolver in my hand. As I crossed the street, I ensured that I was alone and resolved to wait near the entrance until Baumann, if it was he, reappeared. He would then be confronted by me while Holmes stood guard at his back. Nevertheless, it seemed prudent to ascertain whether the door had been re-locked, and to my surprise it had not. I entered stealthily, momentarily startled by my reflection in the mirror in the hallway.

I saw a faint light ahead, and as I advanced a solitary oil lamp became visible near the hearth.

"You know me then?" Holmes said to the man whose question I had not heard, and who now held him at gunpoint.

"Oh yes, Mr. Holmes," came the thickly-accented reply. "Our communications here are excellent. We are aware of your prowess at detection, and so it is most fortuitous that I should find you here, for who else is more capable at finding something that is lost? I would be obliged if you would conduct a search of this room and, if necessary, the others, until the missing document is discovered. I am aware also that you know of its contents, or else you would not be here, so you will have realised its importance to my country from which it was stolen."

"What has happened to the lady who lives here?" Holmes asked.

"Ah, a most intriguing woman, I am told. I had orders to dispose of her after she relinquished the document to me, but news has reached me that she has been dealt with elsewhere. This leaves me in a difficult position, but I have every confidence that you will discover its hiding-place, sparing me the effort. You will begin searching at once."

I stood in the shadows. Holmes's adversary appeared formidable. His iron-grey moustache and whiskers seemed to bristle as he spoke, and his voice held the authority of the parade-ground. My friend had not moved, as I stepped forward with my weapon levelled.

"Good evening, Herr Baumann."

He whipped round to face me, enabling Holmes to grip him from behind and wrest the gun from his fingers.

"Who are you, sir? What right do you have here?"

171

"At least as much as you, I think." I answered.

"Excellent, Watson," said my friend. "Now all that remains is to convey this beauty to the official force, before we set about our own search."

"I suggest you begin at once. Let go your weapons go and unhand my comrade."

We all turned at this new voice, to see the indistinct figure of the other man I had seen earlier. I realised then, the terrible mistake I had made. This man had acted as a look-out, until he was certain that Baumann would be undisturbed. That was why he had left his comrade on arrival, to position himself nearby. It was for his return that the door had been left unlocked, enabling me to enter before him. He was the second man that Miss Willis had described. Inwardly I sighed, because I felt I had failed Holmes. Our discarded revolvers struck the carpet with a muffled impact.

"A timely entrance, Gruber." Baumann said in relieved tone. "If you will begin, Mr. Holmes, we have not much time."

Holmes moved towards a cabinet where an assortment of porcelain was displayed. He paused and took out his pocket watch.

"Take care, Mr. Holmes," warned Gruber, made wary by the gesture as he walked into the light.

"If you would be so good as to hurry," Baumann pointed to the cabinet with his retrieved gun.

My friend seemed to pause in his search, every few moments, and I formed the impression that he listened for some new sound.

He slammed a drawer noisily as if in impatience, but I realised that this was a signal as it was immediately followed by a rushing of heavy footfalls and three figures emerged from the gloom.

"It seems you were right, Mr. Holmes," said Lestrade from near the door. "All right you two. These constables and I have you in our sights. Drop your pistols to the floor at once."

Baumann complied, but Gruber raised his weapon.

"*Nein!*" Baumann slapped his comrade's hand and the gun went spinning across the room.

"That was very sensible," said the inspector. He turned to the tallest constable. "Put the cuffs on them, Charlesworth,"

Baumann mumbled something in German, probably curses or regrets. Holmes smiled briefly as they were led away.

"I will see you at Scotland Yard in the morning, Lestrade," my friend assured the inspector.

"Evidently you telegraphed Scotland Yard, in addition to Fleet Street," I remarked when we were again alone.

"It seemed an appropriate precaution. Lestrade was to come here if he had not heard from me by ten o'clock."

"Are we to leave the finding of the plans to the official force, then? Or perhaps to your brother's people?"

"Very much to the contrary, Watson. I had deduced the hiding place before Baumann's arrival, and the plans will be on Mycroft's desk before we visit Lestrade in the morning."

He approached a tall bookcase and pulled out a volume. Within it was a flat bundle of paper, secured by string.

"But how did you know which book concealed it, even if you identified the hiding-place?"

Holmes placed the papers in his pocket. "It was a simple observation, depending at first on the length of time that Miss Stayforth spent in this house before fleeing the agents of Count von Schell, who she knew were closing in. Obviously, the less time she had, the less intricate the place of concealment would be, and I quickly noticed the disturbance to the fine layer of dust that had accumulated on these bookshelves in her absence. Thus the particular book she had chosen was evident, and my attempt to remove it from between its companions proved difficult because of its increased thickness after the insertion of the plans. As soon as I became aware of Baumann's presence, I wiped away the dust with the sleeve of my coat so as to leave no indication, and began the search he ordered elsewhere. It really was quite uncomplicated, old fellow."

He made to leave and I turned down the wick of the oil lamp and followed in the darkness. As I neared the door I became very still, because I had seen something for a fleeting instant that took away my breath and made movement impossible.

There before me stood a young woman, she of the picture on the nearby wall. She raised a hand in greeting and smiled, and my heart raced as I realised that she was as transparent as glass, Holmes being clearly visible beyond her. Almost immediately she faded from my sight, but I recalled at once the prediction of Tanith le Grande, of which my friend had been so contemptuous.

I felt a cold chill envelop me, though the image, or apparition, had not appeared to be hostile. Holmes paused in his departure and turned to look back at me, no doubt warned by the strange sense he sometimes displays when there is sudden alteration in my emotional state. I realised that he had seen the alarm in my face, and drawn his conclusions at once.

"It was the reflection of the picture in the mirror, nothing more," he assured me. "A glass of port on our return to Baker Street will steady your nerves."

I told myself that he was undoubtedly correct. That Tanith le Grande was a charlatan, like all those who made use of the supposed supernatural for their own profit. Holmes was usually right, in most things.

But I have never been sure.

# The Winterbourne Phantom
## by M.J. Elliott

$T$*his script has never been published in text form, and was initially performed as a radio drama on April 24, 2005. The broadcast was Episode No. 60 of* The Further Adventures of Sherlock Holmes, *one of the recurring series featured on the nationally syndicated* Imagination Theatre. *Founded by Jim French, the company produced over one-thousand multi-series episodes, including one-hundred-twenty-eight Sherlock Holmes pastiches – along with later "bonus" episodes. In addition, Imagination Theatre also recorded the entire Holmes Canon, featured as* The Classic Adventures of Sherlock Holmes, *the only version with all episodes to have been written by the same writer, Matthew J. Elliott, and with the same two actors, John Patrick Lowrie and Lawrence Albert, portraying Holmes and Watson, respectively.*

CHARACTERS:

- SHERLOCK HOLMES
- DR. JOHN H. WATSON
- INSPECTOR LESTRADE
- NATHAN WINTERBOURNE – Fifties, Upper-Class English, Bad-tempered
- DUDLEY CROSS – Twenties, Middle-Class English, Softly spoken
- CECILIA WINTERBOURNE – Early sixties, Terrifyingly jolly
- LINUS DOGBERRY – Forties, Working class, Very Nasal

SOUND EFFECT: OPENING SEQUENCE: BIG BEN, STREET SOUNDS

ANNOUNCER: *The Further Adventures of Sherlock Holmes.*

MUSIC: *DANSE MACABRE* UP AND UNDER. FADE TO

SOUND EFFECT: WINTERBOURNE IS COMING DOWNSTAIRS

175

NATHAN: Morning, Dudley.

CROSS: Good morning, Mr. Winterbourne. No post yet, I'm afraid. You've had a call from Ronson in London. Padbury has been dismissed, as per your instructions.

NATHAN: (DISTRACTED) Very good. Snow's finally let up, I see.

CROSS: Are you going out, sir?

NATHAN: (UNCONVINCING) Not far, Dudley, not far. I just feel like stretching my legs. Paget's Glade and back, perhaps.

CROSS: If you're sure, sir. It's still terribly cold out.

NATHAN: I'll be sure to wrap up. I'll be back in about . . . . (HE DOESN'T KNOW) I'll be back soon.

SOUND EFFECT: WINTERBOURNE TRUDGES THROUGH THE SNOW, BEFORE COMING TO A HALT

NATHAN: (CALLING OUT, ANGRILY) Well, I'm here, as you asked. Now where the devil are you? Show yourself, damn you. This better not be some sort of hoax! Pentecost, if you're behind this, I'll destroy you! You know I will! (PAUSE. THEN, TO HIMSELF) This is ridiculous. You must be getting old, Nathan.

SOUND EFFECT: HE STARTS TO TRUDGE BACK, BUT IS STOPPED SHORT BY THE HORRIBLE SOUND OF A KNIFE ENTERING HIS BODY

NATHAN: (A GROAN OF PAIN AND SHOCK)

SOUND EFFECT: HE FALLS TO THE GROUND, DEAD

MUSIC: *DANSE MACABRE* UP AND UNDER

WATSON: My name is Doctor John H. Watson, and it was my privilege to share the adventures of Sherlock Holmes. In the November of 1901, we were summoned to the Yorkshire village of Overdale by our old ally and occasional adversary, Inspector Lestrade. In his

176

telegram, he stated that he'd appreciate our assistance with a most unusual case. The famous industrialist Nathan Winterbourne had been found dead in the middle of a field near his home. But as to whether or not he had been murdered . . . .

LESTRADE: My first thought was that the killer might have hidden behind that tree, then run out and stabbed Winterbourne before he knew what was happening.

WATSON: Except there are no footprints in the snow. Only those of the victim.

HOLMES: And those of the person who discovered the body. I suggest we view his testimony with the utmost suspicion.

LESTRADE: I'm sorry to hear you say that, Mr. Holmes. You see, I was the one who discovered him.

HOLMES: Oh?

LESTRADE: I received information that a group of coiners had set up their operations in this area – remember Dr. Lysander Stark's gang?

WATSON: Only too well.

LESTRADE: The whole thing was a wild goose chase, and I was just about to make my way back to London, when Winterbourne's secretary – young fellow named Dudley Cross – comes into the station and says his employer hasn't returned from his stroll. I joined in the search, and – well . . . .

HOLMES: A grisly discovery, Lestrade.

LESTRADE: And that's when I sent a message to you, Mr. Holmes. I don't know that it's a mystery as such, but it's mighty peculiar. There must be easier ways to kill yourself than by walking out into the middle of a field and then stabbing yourself. And it can't be murder – there's no sign of a struggle.

WATSON: No sign of anything, in fact.

LESTRADE: So if it isn't suicide and it isn't murder . . . .

HOLMES: Please don't tell me that you're going over to the supernaturalists, Lestrade?

LESTRADE: Find me a more plausible explanation, Mr. Holmes, and I'll embrace it. Hard to put handcuffs on a phantom, in any case.

HOLMES: Has Mr. Winterbourne's home been searched?

LESTRADE: I wanted to wait until you were here, Mr. Holmes.

HOLMES: You anticipate my every need, Inspector. Perhaps you would be so good as to describe the household.

LESTRADE: Handful of servants – all in Winterbourne's employ for years, all loyal and trusted.

WATSON: You mentioned a secretary.

LESTRADE: Dudley Cross. Young fellow, about twenty-five, I'd say. Deals with – *dealt* with Winterbourne's correspondence, handled his overseas interests. Apparently, his employer couldn't speak a word of any other language. The only other member of the household is Cecilia Winterbourne.

HOLMES: His wife?

LESTRADE: His elder sister. Sixty years old if she's a day.

WATSON: The poor woman! She must be distraught.

LESTRADE: You'd think so, wouldn't you?

SOUND EFFECT: (OUT)

CECILIA: Oh, it's simply too too delicious!

178

HOLMES: Delicious?

CECILIA: Nathan's murder, Mr. Holmes! All this excitement! First a Scotland Yard Inspector, and now Sherlock Holmes and Dr. Watson! Bliss!

HOLMES: I hope you won't think me impertinent, Miss Winterbourne –

CECILIA: Ask me, Mr. Holmes! Ask me whatever you wish!

HOLMES: From the time your brother left the house until the time his body – until the time he was discovered – where were you?

CECILIA: I prefer the term "*corpse*" to "*body*", don't you? So much more vibrant. Well, I'm afraid it's terribly careless of me, but you know, I simply have no idea where I was or what I was doing.

LESTRADE: You told me that you fell asleep while knitting, and that Mr. Cross woke you later to tell you that your brother was dead.

CECILIA: Oh, Inspector! Why did you have to give it all away? I was looking forward to being a suspect for a while.

WATSON: Do you find knitting enjoyable, Miss Winterbourne?

CECILIA: No, extremely boring – that's why I fell asleep.

HOLMES: And when Mr. Cross broke the news to you – what was your reaction?

CECILIA: Oh, I took it very well, I think. I mean, we've all fantasized from time to time about our loved ones being murdered, haven't we?

WATSON: (TO SELF) Have we?

HOLMES: Hush, Watson.

CECILIA: But an impossible murder, with no footprints and no clues – Why, this is more than I could have dreamed of! It's the next best thing to Nathan being killed in a locked room! I tell you, it's simply too delicious!

179

SOUND EFFECT: CROSS, HOLMES, WATSON AND LESTRADE ARE DESCENDING A FLIGHT OF STEPS INTO A CELLAR. THERE'S A SLIGHT ECHO ON THEIR VOICES.

CROSS: All of Mr. Winterbourne's papers are filed away down here, gentlemen. Mind your head, Inspector.

SOUND EFFECT: LESTRADE HITS HIS HEAD

LESTRADE: Oof!

CROSS: May I ask what it is you hope to find?

LESTRADE: We won't know 'til we find it, Mr. Cross.

CROSS: Suit yourself. This is as good a place to start as any.

SOUND EFFECT: HE OPENS A DRAWER

LESTRADE: I'll decide where we start, if you don't mind.

SOUND EFFECT: LESTRADE OPENS A DIFFERENT DRAWER

CROSS: As you wish, Inspector.

WATSON: Mr. Cross, I was wondering. Your employer was a very successful businessman . . . I'm surprised to find that he conducted his affairs from the country rather than in London – at the heart of things, so to say.

CROSS: Mr. Winterbourne had no time for London life. Once he'd made his fortune – his first fortune – he moved to Overdale and continued to prosper. It can all be done by wire or telephone nowadays – "Buy this, sell that, employ him, sack him." His businesses more or less ran themselves.

WATSON: He saw no-one, then?

CROSS: Very infrequently, Doctor. And nobody's been to the house in weeks.

HOLMES: You have been Mr. Winterbourne's secretary for how long?

CROSS: About five years. He was a very generous employer. I doubt I'll find another like him.

HOLMES: Is that your way of telling us you have no motive for murdering your employer?

CROSS: I've too much to lose, Mr. Holmes; and now it's all lost. Besides, if what Inspector Lestrade says is true, in order to have killed Mr. Winterbourne, I'd have to know how to fly. And that's a trick I've never learned.

HOLMES: Additionally, I understand Nathan Winterbourne was killed by a downward stroke of the knife. His killer would have to have been the same size or taller.

CROSS: And I am considerably shorter. I didn't know that – about how he died, I mean.

HOLMES: Lestrade, I suggest that you and Mr. Cross make a start here.

LESTRADE: Where will you be?

HOLMES: A private study is the ideal place for discovering the facets of a man's character – you will find us there. Come along, Watson!

MUSIC: SHORT BRIDGE

SOUND EFFECT: HOLMES IN CONDUCTING AN INTENSIVE SEARCH

WATSON: What exactly are we looking for?

HOLMES: To quote the good inspector, we won't know until we find it. But it seems perfectly obvious that Winterbourne didn't walk into that field for the good of his health.

WATSON: Quite the opposite, I'd say.

HOLMES: He was there for a purpose. Now, if he had arranged to meet someone . . . .

181

WATSON: Surely it can't be someone in the house. They could have spoken to him at any time. And Cross says Winterbourne hadn't had any visitors for days.

HOLMES: Correct. Therefore . . . ?

WATSON: A letter!

HOLMES: Really, Watson, you excel yourself! Now, there is no trace of the missive among his papers, current or discarded.

WATSON: Holmes, in the Baskerville case, I found a fragment of a letter in the grate, and that letter led us to one of the key witnesses. If we can't find it in any of the obvious places . . . .

HOLMES: Hope springs eternal, Watson. Fortunately, the fire hasn't been lit since the master's death. Pass me that poker, would you?

SOUND EFFECT: HOLMES POKES THE ASHES

WATSON: Anything?

HOLMES: It appears not . . . Wait! Yes, there *is* something here!

WATSON: Be careful with it.

SOUND EFFECT: HOLMES REMOVES THE PAPER FROM THE GRATE

HOLMES: Got it!

SOUND EFFECT: LESTRADE ENTERS

LESTRADE: Gentlemen, we've just found something rather unusual!

HOLMES: As have we, Inspector.

LESTRADE: (DEFLATED) Oh. Well, you go first.

HOLMES: It appears to be the latter half of a brief note arranging a meeting. (READING) " – *at Paget's Glade tomorrow morning at ten to discuss the Pentecost Scandal*". It's signed "*Poena*".

LESTRADE: *Poena*? What sort of a name is that? Sounds Italian.

WATSON: I think it's Latin.

HOLMES: Well done, Watson. The English translation would be "*penalty*".

WATSON: Penalty? Or punishment? I think the meaning would have been lost on Winterbourne. Didn't you say he spoke no other languages?

LESTRADE: Punishment, eh? So just what was he being punished for?

HOLMES: Once we discover that, Lestrade, we'll be a step closer to knowing the identity of the murderer.

MUSIC: UNDERCURRENT

WATSON: We adjourned to the dining room for tea and biscuits, served by the gleeful Miss Cecilia Winterbourne. I was troubled by the mention of the Pentecost Scandal on the fragment of paper we had just recovered. The phrase seemed somehow familiar to me, but I couldn't recall where I had heard it before.

MUSIC: (OUT)

SOUND EFFECT: GENERAL TEA CONSUMPTION NOISES THROUGHOUT THIS SCENE

CECILIA: Sugar, Inspector?

LESTRADE: Two, please, Miss Winterbourne.

SOUND EFFECT: SHE ADDS SUGAR

CECILIA: I say, wouldn't it be marvellous if one of us were to suddenly drop dead at the table? Potassium of cyanide in someone's tea, perhaps?

LESTRADE: (GROANS)

SOUND EFFECT: LESTRADE PUSHES THE CUP AWAY

CECLIA: Something wrong, Inspector?

LESTRADE: Just waiting for it to cool.

HOLMES: Lestrade, you said that you and Mr. Cross discovered something in the late Mr. Winterbourne's correspondence.

LESTRADE: Oh yes. Well, there's a lot more to go through yet. Winterbourne must have kept every letter ever sent to him. All kinds of stuff – business proposals, requests for investments, just plain begging letters. Even found something from some Professor – says he's discovered an area of the South American jungle where dinosaurs still exist, and wants Winterbourne to fund an expedition.

HOLMES: And did your employer respond to every letter, Mr. Cross?

CROSS: He judged every case on its individual merits – or lack of merit. Professor Challenger received a polite but firm refusal.

WATSON: What precisely have you found, Lestrade?

LESTRADE: This.

SOUND EFFECT: LESTRADE UNFURLS A POSTER

WATSON: A poster advertisement! (READING) *"Cruciare's Circus – Clowns, tumblers, novelty acts . . . Final Appearance of Vittoria the Circus Belle . . . Henry the Horse Dances the Waltz!"* Hmm, something for everyone.

HOLMES: *"For one week only on Hampstead Heath"* – June, 1899.

CECILIA: And what does it mean, Inspector, now that you've found it?

LESTRADE: Well, I don't know. But it seems strange that there's no letter, just the poster.

HOLMES: Any deviation from Mr. Winterbourne's usual pattern is certainly interesting. Mr. Cross, you were in his employ in 1899, were you not? Do you recall any correspondence regarding this circus?

CROSS: I think it might have been just another request for funds, Mr. Holmes. A struggling enterprise. The owner probably looked to Mr. Winterbourne to bail him out.

WATSON: And did he?

CROSS: I'm afraid I don't recall, Doctor.

CECILIA: I do. I remember Nathan saying something about it – turned them down flat. Found the whole thing quite amusing, as I recall. But then, he always did have an appalling sense of humour.

HOLMES: Inspector Lestrade has a point – why do you suppose the accompanying letter is not in the files?

CROSS: I've really no idea. Perhaps it was simply mis-filed and we haven't come across it yet.

LESTRADE: Well, we've still got your clue, gentlemen – the Pentecost Scandal. But what, or where, is Pentecost?

WATSON: Not what, Inspector – *Who!* I've just remembered where I know the name: Darwin Pentecost, the owner of the Pentecost Shipping Line. I read something about "The Pentecost Scandal" in *Fact*.

LESTRADE: *Fact?*

WATSON: It was a short-lived publication dedicated to uncovering evidence of corrupt business practices – particularly between those attending the same Masonic Lodge.

LESTRADE: So Winterbourne was "on the square", then?

WATSON: Well, I don't know about that, but the editor of *Fact* had quite a bee in his bonnet about the Brotherhood, I recall.

185

HOLMES: My search of the house turned up none of the accoutrements associated with Masonic membership – arc-and-compass breastpin, ring, apron . . . .

CECILIA: If he was a Mason, he kept it from me. But then, we lost touch some years ago.

LESTRADE: Lost touch? You lived in the same house!

CECILIA: Your point being?

LESTRADE: (SIGHS) All right, Doctor, what was the Pentecost Scandal, if it wasn't connected with the Masons?

WATSON: (A LITTLE ASHAMED) I'm afraid I don't recall, Lestrade. *Fact* ceased publication some years ago after losing a legal action against Dan Brigstock, the society moneylender.

CROSS: Perhaps the files will give some indication.

LESTRADE: Surely your employer won't have kept anything incriminating.

CROSS: Mr. Winterbourne never threw anything away.

HOLMES: Except, it seems, a letter from the owner of Cruciare's Circus.

CECILIA: And I doubt Nathan would ever have expected a Scotland Yard Inspector to go through his papers.

LESTRADE: So it's back to the cellar again. Mr. Holmes, I don't suppose you'd be interested in taking over?

HOLMES: You're doing so well, Lestrade, it would be a crime to stop you now. Might I suggest that you hold the fort here, while Watson and I return to London and try to locate the former editor of *Fact*. It's entirely possible that he holds the key to this mystery.

SOUND EFFECT: TEA CONSUMPTION OUT. FADE TO TRAIN CARRIAGE (BACKGROUND)

WATSON: I thought I was the literary half of the partnership! What are you writing, Holmes?

HOLMES: Telegram, Watson. It just so happens that I have need of Shinwell Johnson's services on this case. We'll stop in at a telegraph office when we arrive in London.

WATSON: Isn't it anything we could deal with while we're here?

HOLMES: Perhaps, but I wouldn't want to leave Lestrade to Miss Winterbourne's tender mercies for longer than necessary.

SOUND EFFECT: (OUT)

MUSIC: UNDERCURRENT

WATSON: Later that day, we were back in London, visiting the disreputable Carlisle Street offices of Mr. Linus Dogberry, the editor of the now-defunct *Fact Magazine*. The tiny room was filled with tottering piles of documents, the results of his ongoing investigations – like pillars in a temple dedicated to the worship of scandal.

MUSIC: (OUT)

SOUND EFFECT: DOGBERRY IS CONSTANTLY SHIFTING PILES OF PAPER AROUND

DOGBERRY: Mr. Holmes! I can't tell you how proud I am that you're taking an interest in my little enterprise.

HOLMES: I was under the impression, Mr. Dogberry, that *Fact* is no longer an active concern.

DOGBERRY: At present, Mr. Holmes, at present. But so long as there's corruption in politics and industry, there must also be someone to shine a light upon those misdeeds. Once I've raised the requisite funds, I can resume my crusade. I don't suppose I could press you gentlemen for a donation?

WATSON: What we're interested in at present, Mr. Dogberry, is the so-called Pentecost Scandal.

187

DOGBERRY: Ah, one of my favourites! 1893, I think it was. Yes, regrettably I was never able to print too much about it. Now where's the file? Touchy business. Some innocent people would have been hurt – ah, here we are – 1893! (HE STARTS TO TUG AT THE FILE) And I am not in . . . the business of hurting innocent people!

SOUND EFFECT: THE WHOLE PILE COLLAPSES

DOGBERRY: Leave them where they are, please, Doctor. I know what order they go in. Now then, Darwin Pentecost . . . * Owner of Pentecost Shipping, prosperous little firm. Just the thing old Nathan Winterbourne needed for his overseas dealings. Rather than pay Pentecost for the privilege of using his vessels, he decided to buy him out. At the lowest price imaginable, of course.

SOUND EFFECT: * HE BEGINS FLIPPING THROUGH THE FILE

HOLMES: Blackmail.

DOGBERRY: It's such an ugly word, isn't it? But an appropriate one. Yes, Winterbourne found out something that Darwin Pentecost would give a lot for his wife and children never to learn.

WATSON: Had a taste for younger women, eh?

DOGBERRY: Not younger women, Doctor.

WATSON: Ah.

DOGBERRY: Of course, this was a couple of years before Mr. Wilde's little difficulty, but even so, the importance of – shall we say "discretion"? – was clear to Pentecost. After all, he had a great deal to lose. Family, business . . . In the end, he lost the one to keep the other.

HOLMES: So Winterbourne forced Pentecost to sell the shipping business at a bargain price in return for his silence.

DOGBERRY: That was the rumour. And that's why I never printed too much about it – it was only a rumour.

HOLMES: Perhaps a chat with Darwin Pentecost would confirm or refute that rumour.

DOGBERRY: You'll have a long way to go, gentlemen. After the sale of Pentecost Shipping, the family relocated to Provence. So I heard.

SOUND EFFECT: LONDON STREET (BACKGROUND)

HOLMES: It seems I may have misjudged *Fact* and its proprietor, Watson. Mr. Dogberry is quite a fund of valuable information. Perhaps I should add him to my list of minions.

WATSON: Along with The Baker Street Irregulars, Langdale Pike, and Shinwell Johnson, you mean.

HOLMES: I wonder how Johnson's getting on. Perhaps we'll hear something upon our return to Overdale.

SOUND EFFECT: (OUT)

LESTRADE: Well, that settles that, then! It seems obvious that Darwin Pentecost came to England, killed Nathan Winterbourne, and then returned to France. Your Mr. Dogberry's story certainly ties in with these rather graphic photographs we discovered in the victim's files.

HOLMES: Tell me, Lestrade, just how did Pentecost manage to stab Winterbourne without leaving any tracks?

LESTRADE: We can ask him that when we have him under arrest. By the way, Mr. Holmes, this telegram arrived about a quarter-of-an-hour ago.

HOLMES: Excellent!

SOUND EFFECT: HOLMES RIPS OPEN THE ENVELOPE

WATSON: But if the blackmail occurred some eight years ago, why did Pentecost wait 'til now to murder Winterbourne?

LESTRADE: Didn't Bismarck say, "Revenge is a dish best served cold"?

HOLMES: He did, but an Italian said it first. However, I understand what you are trying to say, Lestrade, and there is certainly some merit in it.

LESTRADE: Right! I'll arrange for Inspector Hopkins to go over to France with a warrant.

WATSON: A few days in Provence doesn't appeal to you, Inspector?

LESTRADE: (SHEEPISH) Uh . . . like our Mr. Winterbourne, I don't have much skill with languages. But Hopkins is a bright lad. I'm sure he'll be able to manage.

HOLMES: What an excellent notion!

LESTRADE: (SARCASTIC) Oh, I'm glad you approve.

HOLMES: Forgive me, Lestrade, I was just thinking . . . I would be very surprised if the victim's lack of linguistic ability didn't turn out to have a vital bearing on this case.

WATSON: Holmes, it's just occurred to me: "*Poena*" is Latin for "*Penalty*", yes? Well, "*Penalty*" and "*Pentecost*" both begin with the same three letters!

HOLMES: Proving what, precisely?

WATSON: Uh . . . I don't know. I just thought it was interesting.

HOLMES: It isn't. I wonder, Inspector, do you think you could round up Miss Winterbourne and Mr. Cross? I feel like a chat.

LESTRADE: Does that telegram tell you who killed Nathan Winterbourne, then?

HOLMES: Of course not. Surely there was never any doubt about that?

MUSIC: SHORT BRIDGE

CECILIA: Isn't this wonderful, Dudley? It's beyond my wildest dreams! You know, I really think he's going to say I killed Nathan!

190

DUDLEY: I sincerely hope not, Miss Winterbourne.

CECILIA: Well, Mr. Holmes? Are you going to tell us who did it?

HOLMES: Not only *who*, Miss Winterbourne, but *how*. How did someone stab your brother without leaving any footprints in the snow round about?

DUDLEY: Suicide!

HOLMES: The letter from the mysterious *"Poena"* seems to rule that out, Mr. Cross.

CECILIA: You're not suggesting, Mr. Holmes, that the knife simply flew into his chest?

HOLMES: On the contrary, Miss Winterbourne, that is precisely what I am suggesting. Lestrade, you said that the knife entered the victim's body at a downward angle.

WATSON: Holmes, please! Miss Winterbourne!

CECILIA: Oh, it's quite alright, Doctor, I haven't enjoyed myself this much since father fell off the roof while he was repairing the weather vane.

LESTRADE: That's right, Mr. Holmes. But there was no sign of a struggle. No sign of anything, as the doctor says.

HOLMES: You said, I recall, that you imagined the killer had hidden behind a nearby tree.

LESTRADE: I toyed with the idea, yes, but we keep coming back to the absence of footprints.

HOLMES: But what if that is because the killer never came face-to-face with his target?

LESTRADE: I don't understand you, Mr. Holmes.

HOLMES: What if he was perched in the branches of that tree, and *threw* the knife, tied to a string, into Winterbourne's chest, and then pulled it back?

CECILIA: I hardly think so, Mr. Holmes!

HOLMES: Oh?

CECILIA: For someone to make an accurate throw like that, they'd have to have the skill of –

HOLMES: A professional knife-thrower?

WATSON: Holmes, the circus poster! Cruciare's Circus!

HOLMES: Mr. Shinwell Johnson conducted a few enquiries on my behalf. It seems that the circus did indeed founder without Winterbourne's financial assistance. The owner and his wife were ruined.

WATSON: And they, or someone else from the circus, exacted their revenge?

HOLMES: I think it extremely likely.

LESTRADE: It's going to be a difficult task, tracking down circus folk. They don't put down roots as a rule. Our murderer might not even be in the country any more.

HOLMES: I believe our murderer is closer than you might imagine, Lestrade. You were puzzled as to why Winterbourne retained all other requests for money, but not the letter from the Cruciare, the circus owner. Did you or Mr. Cross find it, by any chance?

CROSS: I'm afraid not. But there must have been one.

HOLMES: Unless the request was a verbal one.

CROSS: I don't believe so, Mr. Holmes. Now I come to think of it, there was a letter, I'm certain of it.

HOLMES: Your employer had no grasp of languages, I believe?

CROSS: That's right.

HOLMES: Would you include Latin in that category? The name of his mysterious correspondent – "*Poena*" – is Latin for "*Penalty*".

CROSS: I don't think Mr. Winterbourne had any Latin, no.

HOLMES: You see, I believe that in choosing that name, and knowing that Winterbourne could never decipher it, the killer was laughing at his prey before ending his life.

LESTRADE: You've lost me, Mr. Holmes.

HOLMES: Then let us consider Cruciare's Circus for a moment. "*Cruciare*" is the Latin for "*Torture*". It is from "*Cruciare*" that the word "*Crucifix*" is derived.

WATSON: Crucifix – or *Cross*!

HOLMES: Well, Mr. Cross?

CROSS: I haven't the faintest idea what you're talking about!

HOLMES: Shinwell Johnson is a very thorough investigator. He discovered that Cruciare had one son, Dudley. A young man of about your age, in fact. He even furnished me with a description – your description. You are Cruciare's son, are you not? Growing up in the circus environment, you no doubt learned a variety of skills – including knife throwing.

WATSON: You approached your employer, begging for his assistance, and gave him the poster advertising the circus in hopes that it would pique his interest.

CROSS: Sheer nonsense! I've never even been to the circus!

WATSON: But he refused to help. Your parents were ruined, and you blamed him.

CROSS: No!

HOLMES: You are *Poena*. You sent the letter, taunting Winterbourne with hints about his improprieties during the Pentecost affair.

CROSS: How would I know anything about that? I wasn't even employed by him then!

LESTRADE: No, but you had access to his papers, didn't you? It would've been easy enough for you to dig up proof of something illegal in his past.

HOLMES: Come, Mr. Cross, it would be best to make a clean breast of it here and now. Would you rather I examined your shoes and clothing for splinters of bark from the tree in which you hid? Or perhaps you would like Inspector Lestrade to make enquiries into your background?

CROSS: No . . . no, there's no need. You know, when I told him about the circus . . . about my parents . . . he just laughed at me. Said he found it impossible to believe that someone of my intelligence could hail from such a background. From that moment, he couldn't respect me any longer. And I couldn't respect him. I know that doesn't excuse what I did – nothing could – but I want you to understand how I felt.

HOLMES: For what little it is worth, Mr. Cross, I believe I do understand. Did you know, by any chance, that some scholars refer to English as *la lingua pura*?

CROSS: Because there are no Latin corruptions. Yes, as a matter of fact, I did know, Mr. Holmes. (PAUSE) I've been too clever by half, haven't I?

LESTRADE: Too clever by two- or three-and-a-half.

HOLMES: I only wish you could have put your skills to a less destructive purpose.

MUSIC: *DANSE MACABRE*

# The Murderous Mercedes
## by Harry DeMaio

*Of all the traits that characterize Sherlock Holmes, my friend, associate, and sometime fellow lodger, his ability to totally concentrate his entire being on a perplexing problem is probably the most distinctive. No matter the time or effort required, once he is on the trail of an answer, bizarre though it may be, he can reduce all else to extraneous noise. I have known him to go without eating or sleeping for extended periods once he is caught up in the resolution process. His tenacious zeal for facts, data and the truth is boundless. This story is one such example.*

### Chapter I

On a snowy Sunday morning in January 1902, London had slowed to a crawl. So had the inhabitants of 221b Baker Street. Mrs. Hudson had served Holmes and me another wonderful and elaborate breakfast. He was now catching up on reading the news from the last several days and I was fighting off a serious case of postprandial lethargy. Suddenly, we heard movement on the stairs. The tread was familiar. We stared at each other and then simultaneously groaned, "Lestrade!" A rapid knock on the door and Holmes shouted, "Come in, Inspector, come in!"

"Good morning, Mr. Holmes! I won't ask how you knew it was me at your door. Your reputation for clairvoyance is known far and wide. In fact, that's the reason I'm here. Good morning, Doctor!"

He removed his hat and, unbidden, took a seat.

"Would you care for a coffee or something stronger to take away the chill?" I asked.

"Thank you, Doctor. Coffee would sit very well, if you please."

While I rose to call Mrs. Hudson, Holmes suggested that Lestrade remove his coat. "Now what major catastrophe has you out in this godforsaken weather on a Sunday morning?"

"As you well know, Mr. Holmes, Sunday morning is when the police pick up the wreckage of the wild Saturday nights. In spite of the snow, today is no exception. We have several rather peculiar deaths that need accounting for. Three in all."

"Peculiar, how?" I asked.

"Early this morning, a constable trudging his beat in this dreadful weather came upon a luxurious closed-body limousine leaning at a

195

precarious angle against a street lamp with the engine still running. Thinking that the Mercedes may have skidded in the snow and ice causing injuries, he approached it to offer assistance. He discovered three people, two men and a woman, dressed in evening clothes, lying in the passenger seats. There was no driver. All three appeared to be lifeless. He immediately called his station and Scotland Yard was alerted. That is to say, *I* was alerted. I, in turn, called the police surgeon who, once he arrived, determined that the subjects were indeed deceased. The bodies have been removed to the morgue and the auto has been impounded."

Holmes interrupted. "Have the victims been identified?"

"From their papers, the men are believed to be Lord Godfrey Pruitt, Viscount Harting, and his son Ewen. The woman had no credentials or proof of identity. She is not Lady Harting. The car is usually housed at the Harting mansion in Park Lane."

"And the cause of death?"

"That is the peculiar part. There were no signs of violence. The skin of each victim was flushed. The surgeon suspects they died of carbon monoxide poisoning induced by the running engine of the auto, but that is hardly a certainty."

"Was the car sealed?"

"The constable claims it was not. But we don't know whether it had been closed earlier or how long the victims were in the vehicle. There is also the question of the driver's whereabouts. I am leaving for the Harting mansion. I don't suppose you and the doctor would care to accompany me."

"Well," said Holmes, "you have piqued my curiosity to the point that I am willing to face this terrible weather. Do you have a police vehicle?"

"Yes, and a skilled driver who is waiting downstairs."

"Excellent. However, I would like to stop at the morgue first. Will that fit your plans? I assume you will have someone examining the automobile."

"We will have a Mercedes technician on hand tomorrow at the start of business to examine it. It's practically brand new, built just last year. As for visiting the morgue first, we can delay our arrival at the mansion. I'm told Lady Harting is quite overwhelmed and not yet in a state to be interviewed."

"Watson, your medical experiences and knowledge could be quite useful. My only involvement with carbon monoxide, if that is the cause of these deaths, was a mine accident several years ago. Several miners died, and a number were badly sickened."

"I'll be happy to come. I remember in the military having to treat a group of soldiers who foolishly lit a fire in their closed lean-to to keep warm overnight. They came very close to death. I think, however, we must hold off judgement until a more thorough examination can be held. Monoxide poisoning symptoms can be very elusive and are shared by other causes of death."

"Thank you. As you know, I am always reluctant to rush to conclusions until all the facts are assembled and checked. Shall we go?"

We told Mrs. Hudson we would return for a late dinner. She remonstrated with us about going out in the foul weather. I found myself agreeing with her.

Lestrade, Holmes, and I took our seats in the police carriage and we set off, slipping, skidding, and sliding in the noontime snowfall. I must confess that my nerves were in a sorry state by the time we arrived at the morgue. I was not looking forward to our subsequent trip to Park Lane and the Harting mansion.

At the best of times, the morgue is a forbidding place with dull grey walls, dim lights, antiseptic smells, and subdued sounds. There are no windows, but somehow that day the gruesome weather outside seemed to permeate the place. And of course, the atmosphere was topped off by the contents of the rows of drawers.

Three were open to reveal the bodies of a dark-haired man in his sixties with a full moustache and sideburns, a younger man bearing strong similarities to the older gentleman, and a woman, tall and full figured with a fall of jet-black hair, dominant mouth, and dark grey eyes. All three shared a ruddy complexion. They were clearly from the aristocratic class. Their hands showed no signs of ever engaging in labor, although the younger man's fingers were smudged with a dark substance.

The police surgeon and the morgue director were there to assist us. Holmes and I were familiar with both of them, having worked together in the past. The director, Doctor Redding, was a man of about fifty years, tall and gaunt, with a small hairbrush moustache and receding brown hair. He wore gold-rimmed spectacles, and seemed to have been perfectly designed for his role.

The police surgeon, on the other hand, might have been more at home in a music hall or a pub. Short and rotund with a shock of red hair, a booming voice, and twinkling eyes, he could have burst into a chorus of "*Daisy Bell*" at any moment. He stepped out in front of the retiring director and seized Holmes by the hand. "By George, it's good to see you again, Mister Holmes. I regret we keep meeting on such untoward occasions, but this one is a poser indeed. Hello Inspector! Hello again, Doctor Watson! How are you? Staying busy?"

"I'm doing rather well, Sidney, although the last few days have been taken up mostly with falls, sprains, and broken limbs. The wounds of winter are rather routine."

"Well, these three fatalities should satisfy your thirst for novelty. I must confess, and Doctor Redding agrees with me, they are most uncommon."

The director nodded his head and said, "I don't recall ever seeing the like."

Oddly, Holmes had remained silent during this repartee. That was about to come to an end. Looking sharply at the two, he asked, "What is it that you find so unusual?"

"Why, if it weren't for the blushes on their faces and bodies, I would have diagnosed natural causes, most probably heart attacks. There are no signs of violence. We haven't yet tested for the usual poisons. They succumbed together. A peculiar event in itself. I know the current wisdom suggests that they were victims of carbon monoxide poisoning from a fault in their automobile. However, I have reason to believe that they were dead before being placed in the car. *Rigor mortis* had begun to set in earlier than usual."

The detective smiled. "That may also explain why there was no driver when the constable found the car. He or she decided to abandon the automobile and its contents when it skidded off the street. I don't suppose there were tracks in the snow leading away from the scene."

Lestrade shook his head. "We looked for them, but the snow was falling so heavily that any footprints were filled in."

"Have you identified the woman?"

"No, and that's another peculiarity. While the two men were in evening clothes and capes, she was nude under some kind of heavy velvet cloak. She wore no jewelry, but she had a silver tiara dotted in blood red rubies. There was no purse, and the cloak had no pockets."

"Most compelling! I would like to examine their clothing and her head ornament. Did the men wear any jewelry?"

"They both wore signet rings." said the director. "Come, I'll show you their belongings."

We walked back to a room where the clothes and other effects of the morgue's occupants were kept. The men's outfits were classic evening wear. Each had a watch and fob engraved with an ornate letter "*H*" – no doubt Harting. Lestrade had already catalogued the sparse contents of their wallets. A few pound notes, several letters, and a fragment of paper containing an inscription in what looked like hieroglyphics. There were calling card cases identifying the Viscount and his son, Ewen. Two finger rings, plus the woman's silver-and-ruby studded tiara.

"I say, Holmes. Look at these rings. One is gold and the other is silver, but they are both representations of a coiled snake."

"Not a snake, Watson. A *dragon*. Ouroboros, the dragon that eats its own tail. It has been the symbol of alchemists, magicians, witches, warlocks, and shamans for centuries. Notice the symbol is on the woman's tiara as well, with the shape defined in the rubies. They were clearly interested in some form of arcane and deeply esoteric practices. I doubt very much, Lestrade, if we are dealing with a simple but fatal automobile accident. Please collect all these items and have them ready for my reevaluation. Meanwhile, I have intense research to embark upon. When do you plan to release the bodies?"

"The coroner needs to examine them, and we still must identify the woman. It will be at least another day or two. We have no clues yet as to who was driving the Mercedes. The Harting family driver is the obvious choice, but if so, his behavior is both peculiar and guilty."

The detective stared off into space. "I would not jump to conclusions, Inspector. There is the real possibility that an inexperienced driver, ill-equipped to drive in a snowstorm, may have been at the wheel and caused the accident. Still, we shall have to interview the Harting driver when we arrive at the mansion. Now, let us get on to Park Lane and console the bereaved widow and mother."

The snow had decreased, but travel was still a difficult task. Throughout our journey, Holmes was his calm and collected self, no doubt caught up musing over the problems presented by this strange set of events. Lestrade was an obvious nervous wreck. To compound the situation, he slipped getting out of the carriage and only missed falling thanks to Holmes's steadying hands.

"Come, Inspector! In spite of the ice, the game is afoot."

Chapter II

Harting Mansion occupies a relatively small but well-tended space off Park Lane. A four-storey affair built of stark red brick with white limestone trim, it cast a brooding image in the snow. Several of the ground-floor rooms were lit. Our driver had managed to reach a portico leading to the main entrance, and we only had to contend with slippery surfaces for a few feet. Lestrade took the lead and rang the ornate bell-pull.

A tall, grey-haired, formally-dressed butler opened the door as the wind blew snow into the elaborate foyer. "Good day, Inspector Lestrade. Well, it's hardly a good day, is it? Please come in, gentlemen, out of the elements!"

"Thank you, Hawkins. I'm back again as you can see. These two gentlemen are Mr. Sherlock Holmes and his associate, Doctor Watson."

At the mention of Holmes's name, the butler's brows rose. "I am familiar with your reputation, Mr. Holmes, thanks to your highly entertaining narratives, Doctor. Welcome."

"Is Lady Harting sufficiently recovered to meet with us?"

"I shall inquire, Inspector. At the moment she is with her personal physician, Doctor Millington, and her spiritual advisor, The Reverend Giles Abernathy. This has come as a great shock, as you can well imagine. If you will wait here in the Assembly Room, I will return shortly."

I looked at Lestrade. "To your knowledge, Inspector, are there any other Harting children besides the deceased Ewen?"

"There is a married daughter who lives on an estate in Hampstead. Her husband owns a very substantial metals manufactory. I doubt if she can get here due to the weather, but I'm sure she has been informed. Another son died in his teens in a train accident."

Holmes looked around the room and remarked, "I suppose you will be hearing shortly from the Viscount's solicitor."

"No doubt, Mr. Holmes, no doubt. I'm not sure who that is."

"Do you know this Doctor Millington, Watson?"

"We have met at several professional events. His practice caters to the wealthier members of London society."

The butler Hawkins returned and said, "Lady Harting will see you now. Please come with me. She is in her personal sitting room."

As we were about to enter the sitting room, Doctor Millington was saying his good-byes. "Good afternoon, Lady Harting. I shall be back to see you again tomorrow. In the meantime, get some rest and nourishment. Don't hesitate to use the sedative I have given you, but be careful to observe the dosage. Good day, Reverend Abernathy. Oh, hello, Inspector Lestrade. Is it still snowing out?"

"I'm afraid it is, Doctor, but not as heavily. May I introduce Doctor Watson and Mr. Sherlock Holmes?"

"A pleasure, gentlemen! Doctor Watson and I are acquainted, and I am familiar with you, Mr. Holmes, by reputation. Have there been any developments in this terrible tragedy?"

"None of consequence, Doctor. Our investigation has just begun."

"Well, if I can be of any assistance, do not hesitate to call on me. Hawkins, can you have my driver come to the door? This snow is treacherous."

Clearly the Reverend Abernathy displayed no intention of leaving with the doctor. He sat scowling in a chair next to Lady Harting. He did not acknowledge our entry.

The Viscountess reclined on a *chaise longue* with a cup of tea at her side. She was dressed entirely in black from neck to toe. A woman in her late forties or early fifties, she retained a clear and practically flawless complexion that offset her bright blue eyes, and her dark brown hair showed minor streaks of grey. She wore a necklace of black beads. I noticed that her hands did not display a wedding ring. In spite of the doctor's parting comments, she didn't seem unduly distressed.

"Come in, gentlemen." She addressed Lestrade. "I believe you are from Scotland Yard, are you not?"

"Yes, my Lady. Inspector Lestrade at your service. I was here earlier to bring the sad news to Hawkins. Our condolences. May I introduce Mr. Sherlock Holmes, a private detective who occasionally assists the Yard in its investigations. He is joined by his associate, Doctor John Watson."

In spite of his frequent dependence on Holmes, and in spite of Holmes giving the inspector credit for solving many cases, Lestrade gave little in return when describing or introducing the great detective. This rankled me, but Holmes seemed not to notice.

Lady Harting, on the other hand, was impressed. "Your fame precedes you, Mr. Holmes, and I am grateful for your interest in this situation. Doctor Watson, I have read several of your narratives and they are exceedingly well done. Let me introduce Reverend Abernathy. He has been a stalwart support for many years."

The clergyman condescended to nod in our direction.

"Now, what did you wish to tell me or ask me?"

Holmes took up the conversation. "Do you know where the Viscount and your son were last evening?"

She glanced over at the reverend and then back at us. "You should know that I have been estranged from my husband for quite some time. He keeps separate rooms here at the mansion, but spends most of his time at his establishment in Belsize Park. I own this mansion. My son shuttles back and forth between the two locations, but lately he has been spending a great deal of time with Godfrey – much to my chagrin. I have no idea where they were last night or any other night."

The clergyman was unable to contain himself. "Viscount Harting was a swine of the first order. His life was a continuous round of orgies, debauches, and carousing, and he had increasingly involved his son in his sinful ways. He has mocked me and my beliefs on a number of occasions. Whatever it was that brought about his demise, I am convinced it came from a vengeful God. His soul was captured by demons and is rotting in Hell at this very moment."

The lady sighed. "Giles, perhaps he and Ewen were forgiven in death."

201

"Nonsense! They are doomed forever. I have requested that the bishop forbid their burial in the consecrated ground of my church cemetery."

Holmes ignored the reverend's outburst. "But, Lady Harting, you have no idea where they were or what they were doing last night."

"Something clearly ungodly and sacrilegious!" shouted the clergyman.

"Giles, please! Ewen lived here, and we were still on speaking terms. Once, after he had too much to drink – and that was often – he confided in me that Godfrey was getting bored with revels and was exploring some arcane and occult activities. Ewen was fascinated by the idea."

Abernathy said, "Some pagan rituals, no doubt. Godfrey is doubly guilty for the loss of his own soul and that of his son."

"There was a third person found dead in the car. A woman."

Once again, the clergyman shouted, "One of his harlots – while his virtuous wife sits here deserted!"

"We do not have an identity for her."

"Godfrey and I have not had occasion to speak for quite some time, and Ewen has never mentioned any names. I cannot help you. I don't suppose this can be kept out of the press."

"I'm afraid not," said Holmes. "The minions of Fleet Street keep careful watch on the morgue, and it is the Director's obligation to reveal the identity, if known, of any bodies contained therein."

"Well, my reputation is already in tatters thanks to my errant husband. I don't suppose it could get much worse. My social life is at an ebb."

The inspector took up the questioning. "There is the matter of the car, which may have been the cause of the victims' deaths. A Mercedes. The registration papers gave this address as its location."

"That car was Godfrey's, Inspector. He housed it here whenever he was in central London. I have my own car and chauffeur."

"Did Lord Harting have a driver?"

"Not to my knowledge. He was an automobile enthusiast and wanted to drive himself. That Mercedes was his latest toy. Ewen drove it occasionally. In a way, I paid for that car, but I never entered it."

"Well," said Lestrade, "as soon as we clear the automobile from impoundment, it will be returned to you. It is up to your solicitor to ensure you retain ownership."

"I don't want the damned thing. The first thing I will do is sell it. If any of you want to bid on an almost new Mercedes, let me know. I suppose no one will want a death car."

Holmes replied, "If you don't mind, we would like to talk to your chauffeur, just to ensure he was not involved in transporting any of the victims last night. The weather may have made a professional driver a necessity."

"Please feel free. Ask Hawkins to summon him for you. Now, if we have nothing else to discuss, I would like to be alone to mourn my son. In spite of his faults, I still loved him. I can't say that about his father."

We repeated our condolences and said our farewells. The clergyman rose to leave with us. As we emerged into the hallway, he stood in front of us, clearly distraught.

Shaking with anger, he cried "You are on a fool's errand! Their deaths were not earthly in nature. God struck them down with avenging angels, and the gates of Hell have welcomed them. '*Abandon hope, all ye who enter here.*' He has punished them for their vile and illicit deeds. The children of Mammon shall perish, and the unjust man shall fall into perdition. The Viscount, his son, and their harlot have been cursed for all time."

As he turned and strode away, Holmes said, "Let us hope there is a more rational solution to this problem." I kept my peace, but wondered if Reverend Abernathy might not have some truth on his side. I shrugged as we went in search of Hawkins and the chauffeur.

That interview was brief and to the point. The driver said that he was at the mansion all night. He had dinner with the rest of the staff and could account for his time the rest of the evening. Ewen had taken the Mercedes earlier in the day before the snow storm had begun. The chauffeur suggested to him that with the oncoming snow, taking the car might be dangerous, but he was ignored. He didn't know where the auto was being taken. He assumed that it was to the Viscount's home, but he had no proof of that. He knew of no fault with the car's exhaust system or any other mechanism, but he seldom drove it. It was a remarkable piece of machinery, but he wasn't actually authorized to use or maintain it.

We thanked him and Hawkins and left. Lestrade's driver bravely took us back to Baker Street and the culinary wonders of Mrs. Hudson's kitchen. We bade the inspector a good evening and promised to meet again in the morning.

As we settled down to our remarkable meal, I queried Holmes on the Reverend Abernathy. "Is he simply an over-zealous cleric, or something more dangerous?"

He replied, "I can't be sure, but I believe our ecclesiastical friend may depend on Lady Harting's charity for a substantial part of his living. Nevertheless, his vengeful fanaticism and acute belief in the supernatural may overcome his good sense, if he has any. Do not be surprised if he is liberally quoted in tomorrow's tabloids. He has a keen hatred for Lord Harting, even in death."

"You don't suppose he could be responsible for what happened?"

"At this point, nothing is impossible, but I doubt it. I don't believe he has the technical knowledge to meddle with the automobile's exhaust, if that is what killed them. I'm not sure of that either. We will have to hear what the Mercedes technician has to say."

"The cleric could have had accomplices."

"He did. God's avenging angels."

While he seldom smiled or laughed, Holmes did have a keen sense of humour.

I rose and went to the window. The snow had stopped, and the skies were clearing. The moon was visible and what clouds remained were sparse and separated.

"At least the weather is improving. We'll have to contend with slush and ice, but we'll have visibility."

"That is what we need in this case. Some visibility!"

## Chapter III

The next morning dawned bright and clear. The sun reflected blindingly off the snow, which would shortly turn to dirt-encrusted slush. Holmes surprised me by eating yet another full breakfast, a thing that he seldom did. Mrs. Hudson was quite obviously pleased. "I'm glad you two gentlemen came back safely last night. I was concerned about you in that horrible storm." Then she said, "I almost forgot. The inspector sent a message saying he would call for you at ten."

Holmes looked up from his coffee. "That is just about now. No time for a pipe. Well, let's see what the automotive expert has to say."

The bell rang, and Mrs. Hudson went down to the door. In a moment we could hear the Scotland Yard Inspector say, "Good morning, Mrs. Hudson. This weather is a vast improvement although the streets are quite a mess. Are Mr. Holmes and the Doctor available?"

Before she could answer, Holmes shouted down the stairs, "We'll be with you momentarily, Lestrade!"

We took our coats, hats, and sticks and rushed down to join him. Once again, his trusty driver had the reins. Soon we arrived at our destination and Lestrade showed his police warranty card to get into the property, a converted dock where automobiles were stored. They were all covered in snow except for a large, silver limousine that had been brushed off and dug out. A young man in coveralls was under the car as a police constable looked on. He pushed himself out from under just as we were approaching.

"Mornin', gents. Name's Thompson. I suppose you are the detectives who want to know about this here beauty. Finest car in the hemisphere.

I've been servicing autos for years and I should know. I understand several swells were found dead in it. Well, the Merc here didn't do it. Aside from a crumpled wing and a cracked windscreen that was caused by an argument with a lamp post, this car's in perfect shape. The engine and the exhaust system, including the silencer, are all intact and working just the way they should. No one has tinkered with it that I can see. By the way, this closed body version has a venting device that keeps the inside air fresh, even when all the doors and windows are shut. Sorry, you'll have to look elsewhere for your killer. This car is innocent."

I asked, "Could anyone defeat the venting system?"

"Not without breaking it, and it's intact. Stuffing a rag or something else into the exhaust pipe would have damaged the silencer. It's working fine."

Holmes stared at the man. "Mr. Thompson, that's quite a strong statement. Would you be willing to make it in a court of law if it became necessary?"

"Absolutely, and I can bring along other experts to back me up. I'm as confident as can be."

Lestrade reached over and shook his hand, which was quite greasy. "Thank you, Mr. Thompson. Your agency may bill Scotland Yard for your time. Send it to Inspector Lestrade."

I looked at the two detectives and said, "I guess he's right. We have to look elsewhere."

Lestrade just shook his head.

We returned to the police carriage, where Holmes asked, "Can you please stop at the next newsagent. I'd like to pick up copies of today's newspapers."

We stopped, and Holmes bounded down. He was back in a few moments carrying a stack of papers. He frowned. "It's just as I suspected."

Chapter IV

"It seems the Reverend Abernathy summoned members of the press to his church this morning," Holmes explained, "and summarily damned Lord Harting, his son, and an unidentified 'harlot' as servants of Mammon who were condemned by God to everlasting torment in Hell. He further excoriated Scotland Yard and me for attempting to corrupt the workings of the Lord by suggesting their deaths were of natural origin. I am characterized as a heretic and an apostate, which is unusual, since I am a member of no organized religion. Fortunately, Watson, you are not mentioned. I suppose I could sue him for slander and defamation and the press for libel, but I will just charge it off to his fanatic insanity. I'm sure

205

Lady Harting is beside herself. I will leave this erratic cleric to her tender mercies."

"Holmes," I replied, "I ask again. How do you think they died?"

"Since I do not know the circumstances or even the nature of their deaths, I cannot venture an opinion without sufficient data. You know I refuse to theorize. Data, data! I am starved for it."

A little later in the day, some data did arrive. It seems the madam of a fashionable bordello had gone mysteriously missing. One of the fair maidens who plied her trade in her house of ill repute got up the courage to seek out the assistance of the police. They, in turn, took her to the morgue, where she acknowledged the female corpse was Mistress Fairburn, a popular hostess. The "harlot" had been identified.

Lestrade stopped by Baker Street and suggested a visit to the brothel. Holmes was willing to accompany him, and I reluctantly tagged along. When we arrived, the practitioners of the seductive arts were in a tizzy. Their leader was gone, and they were at the mercies of a bully named Jimmy Carson who owned and financed the enterprise and took most of its profits. Carson had made himself scarce when he heard about Letitia's (Mistress Fairburn) bizarre demise. We spoke with Kitty, the tart who had gone to the police.

"What can you tell us about Miss Fairburn's relationships with Viscount Harting and his son?"

"Coo, is that who he was? We always wondered about him. He was one of Letitia's few steady clients. She mentioned that her 'geezer' wanted her to participate in some sort of crazy ritual with him two nights ago. She didn't want to do it, but the pay was too much to pass up, and he swore she would be safe."

"Did she tell you about this 'crazy ritual'?"

"Somethin' about calling up the Devil, or some such swill. She was supposed to lie on an altar in a crypt and wait for Satan to arrive. She thought it was just for show. There was to be a hand-picked audience. The 'geezer' was playing at being a high priest, and the young man was his ackerlite."

Lestrade asked, "Now, come my girl. Where was this supposed to happen?"

"Letty didn't know. He was picking her up in his swell limousine. I saw it. It was a lovely car. I would have liked a ride in it."

"Given what has happened with that car," I thought to myself, "I doubt if you would, Kitty."

"Is that all you can tell us?"

"She never came back. Did he kill her?"

"We don't think so. He's also dead, as is his son."

"Oh God! Are we in danger, too? Is the Devil going to come and kill us? That swine Jimmy is only good for beating us and taking our fees. He couldn't protect a kitten."

Holmes replied, "I don't think you have anything to fear from the Devil. Inspector Lestrade, could you have a constable watching this premises for a few days?"

The policeman reluctantly agreed.

We left the sobbing girl, who promptly ran to tell the other wenches her tale of woe. I wondered what was going to happen to all of them.

Once we were back in the police carriage, Holmes frowned. "Well, now we have a better idea of what transpired. It seems the Reverend may not have been far wrong, but where is this crypt and how did it happen? Why are they dead? I refuse to believe this Devil-worship claptrap, although the Viscount may have. Kitty said there was supposed to be an audience. We need to find them. Whoever it was that killed them was probably in that group and drove the car trying to get rid of the bodies. He or she obviously couldn't handle a limousine in the snow. The more we find out, the less we know. Lestrade, have we heard anything further from the Police Surgeon?"

"He is still puzzled. He found no poisons in the bodies. But, now that we know there was some sort of ritual, it seems likely they had ingested something that did them in."

I spoke up. "He probably checked for only the most common forms of toxins. Holmes, in your previous cases, you have come up against some very rare and almost undetectable poisons. We should probably go over the conditions of the bodies again and search through your catalogue of venomous substances."

"You have anticipated me, Watson. We must return to Baker Street. I have some research to perform."

Chapter V

When we arrived, Mrs. Hudson greeted me with a message from Doctor George Fisher, Director of the Department of Infectious Diseases at Barts. It simply said, "*Please come by this afternoon. I have something interesting for you.*"

George and I had trained together at Barts and served as field doctors in Her Majesty's Army during the Afghan War. Since Holmes was about to throw himself into gathering data on toxic substances, I felt secure in leaving. The streets were a mass of slush and flowing water, and I took a cab to the imposing structures, saluting King Henry VIII's statue as I

207

entered the hospital's Main Hall. George's offices were somewhat isolated in one of the side annexes, as was the Infectious Disease Ward itself.

"Watson, old boy, come in, come in. Good to see you again. It's been too long. We must do dinner soon. How is that detective? Care for a brandy to ward off the cold?"

I nodded affirmatively. "Good to see you, too, George. Holmes is Holmes – intense and obsessive as ever. Now, tell me. What is this 'something interesting' in which you want to share?"

"Well, as you know, we are at the start of the influenza season, and such cases usually pack our halls, so I thought nothing very much when three aristocratic young men were admitted by their local physician last evening with some of the typical symptoms – headache, weakness, dizziness, nausea. congestion – you know the drill. It seems the men are related – two brothers and a cousin."

"That's hardly unusual with communicable disease."

"No, it's not. But according to their doctor, they are also related to that Viscount Harting and his son, whose deaths were in the tabloids. The police and your detective friend, Holmes, are investigating that, are they not? Their symptoms are flu-like, but there were additional symptoms that, at first, resembled something else."

"Such as?"

"Carbon monoxide poisoning."

"George, I need to send a couple of wires right away. Can your office help me?"

"Certainly, come with me. Do you want to see our three patients first? By the way, one of them has nasty bruise on his forehead and left arm."

"No, I want to send these wires to Holmes and Inspector Lestrade of Scotland Yard, summoning them here immediately. Then, I'd like to examine the three just as another physician you have called in – no mention of the Viscount."

After transmitting the urgent messages, I accompanied George to the Infectious Disease Ward. We donned sterile gowns and face masks and entered the disease-laden environment. To carry on the pretense of my being a consulting physician, I stopped at several beds and checked the patients there. The flu season was indeed upon us.

Finally, I reached the three young men that George had brought to my attention. Each was indeed ill, but they shared a flushed complexion that was not typical of the flu. They were, respectively, the brothers Edward and Gregory Hightower, and their cousin, the Honorable Eustace Portman. They seemed to be recovering rapidly from their symptoms and I would estimate that in twenty-four hours, they would be well on their way back to normal. I asked the Honorable Eustace how he came by his bruises and he said he had taken a fall, caused no doubt by his sickness.

In order to facilitate Holmes's inquiries, I suggested to George that we move the three to a smaller, isolated room. He concocted a story that the Ward had more incoming patients and the three were being moved to another location pending their next-day release. They seemed pleased by the prospect.

Holmes and Lestrade arrived within the hour. I introduced them to George. Both Lestrade and Holmes thanked the doctor profusely for his perspicacity. Lestrade had brought along a sergeant who was on hand to deal with any possible untoward activity on the part of our subjects.

The four of us entered the isolated room. George called a nurse to stand by and tend to any medical issues that might ensue. Holmes spoke first. "Gentlemen, my name is Sherlock Holmes, and this is my associate Doctor John Watson, with whom you have spoken a short while ago. You may have heard of me. I am a consulting detective working with Inspector Lestrade of Scotland Yard on the deaths of your relatives, Viscount Harting and his son, your cousin, Ewen, as well as the death of a woman, Letitia Fairburn."

The shocked expressions on the three faces spoke volumes. Eustace tried to project total ignorance of what Holmes was saying, but the brothers seemed to be on the verge of total breakdown.

"Come, gentlemen," said Lestrade, "let's not pretend you don't know what we're talking about. We have reason to believe that you three are suffering from the ill effects of carbon monoxide poisoning, not influenza, and were with the victims when they succumbed to a more intense dosage of the colorless, odorless, tasteless gas. We originally thought their deaths were the result of the exhaust fumes from the running engine of a limousine involved in an accident, but that is not the case. I suspect, Eustace, that you got your bruise from that accident. It will go much better for you if you share what really happened."

Edward Hightower broke first. "All right! We are not perpetrators. We are also victims."

His brother and the Honorable Eustace tried to silence him, but he continued, "Our uncle, the Viscount, and our cousin Ewen had been arranging a wild series of parties and revelries for quite some time. We participated in some of them – first for a lark, but then it became more addictive. Parties became debauches, and then the Viscount turned to a darker side. He started taking up Devil worship. We debated whether or not to join in, but Ewen threatened us. He would reveal our activities to our parents and friends unless we played along."

Suddenly Eustace broke in, "It's as Edward says. We had lost control. The Viscount told us we were to be present at a summoning of Beelzebub that he had planned. It was to take place in a crypt within a mausoleum on church property. Ewen said the delicious irony was the mausoleum was in the church cemetery of Reverend Giles Abernathy, a religious fanatic who was the spiritual advisor of his mother, the Viscount's wife. The Viscount and the churchman shared a mutual hatred, and this was his revenge."

Not to be left out, Gregory picked up the story. "The mausoleum was at the edge of the cemetery, away from the church and the minister's manse. It had started to snow. The Viscount, Ewen, and a prostitute they had engaged for the night arrived in the Viscount's Mercedes before we did in our own car. We're not sure how he broke in, but when we got there, the door was open and the three of them had descended down into a crypt below the floor. Ewen was tending a coal fire and the prostitute had stretched herself out on a small altar. "

"The Viscount had put on a cloak and was helping Ewen raise the fire. When we arrived, he looked up from the crypt and told us to watch from above. Beelzebub would soon arrive. He began a series of incantations that lasted at least half-an-hour. Nothing happened until suddenly the door to the mausoleum was slammed shut from the outside. We turned and started pounding on the locked door. The air was getting close and we struggled to open it. Finally after we pushed and pounded, we managed to break through. It was then we found the three of them lying in the crypt unconscious. I guess the monoxide was more intense down there."

Eustace said, "We went down in the crypt and dragged them up to the top. Our only thought was to escape. We put their unconscious bodies in the Mercedes and I drove it out, hoping to reach a hospital. Edgar and Gregory followed in their car. On the way, I skidded in the raging snow and the Mercedes hit a lamppost. It was then I realized that my three passengers weren't unconscious. They were dead. I panicked and ran from the Mercedes to the car with Edgar and Gregory. I shouted, 'They're dead! Let's go!' We drove off, but we were still sick as well. We're not proud of ourselves, but we didn't kill them."

The room was silent. Lestrade was in something of a quandary as to what charges to bring, but he told George that the police would take custody of the three and guard the room until they could be safely moved.

Holmes looked at me and we shared a question. Who had locked the door to the mausoleum? We had a suspicion.

The next morning, Holmes, Lestrade, and I went to The Reverend Abernathy's residence. He was his same confrontational self.

"So, have you come to apologize to me? Did I not tell you that God would destroy those offenders who dared to summon Satan? The Viscount, his son, and their harlot have all suffered the divine vengeance. Their souls are burning in Hell."

Holmes asked, "How do you know that? What did you do to hasten their destruction?"

"I locked them in, so that they could not escape their punishment. The avenging angels struck them down. They had the hubris to use the Lord's cemetery to practice their filth. They shall not be buried there. I have seen to that. Divine justice has been served."

Lestrade looked at him. "You have committed murder and attempted murder. That is the justice that must be served. Sergeant, please take Abernathy into custody."

The minister screamed, "You will be destroyed! I shall call down God's retribution on you all!"

As he was taken off by the police, a deadly silence fell upon us. Shaking his head, Holmes looked at me and asked, "Are you interested in buying a Mercedes?"

"I think not. Thank you all the same."

# The Solitary Violinist
## by Thomas A. Turley

In May of 1911, I received an unexpected visit from Mr. Sherlock Holmes. My readers will recall that by that date, my friend had long since retired to the South Downs, and I was happily ensconced in Queen Anne Street with a wife and stepchildren. As it happened, on the night of Holmes's arrival my family was away: Peter still at Eton, Priscilla and little Emily on a seaside holiday in Brighton. I remained at home nursing an attack of gout – a disquieting reminder of advancing years.

I was pleased to see that the great detective seemed much the same as ever. He was, indeed, a little greyer, but far less gaunt than he had been in London. Tranquil days of regular sustenance, walks along the chalk cliffs near his home, and the relaxing pastime of beekeeping – substituted for the stress and dangers of detective work – had wrought a considerable improvement in Holmes's health. However, on that evening the old obsessive gleam was in his eye, as he imparted his brother Mycroft's plan for a perilous but vital mission that would bring his partial retirement to a temporary end. Although neither of us knew it then, this mission would only be concluded on a night in August three years hence, when came the final reckoning with Germany that my friend had long foreseen. [1]

His news delivered, we sat a while in silence, sipping the whisky I had injudiciously decanted. I, for one, was pondering the long interruption in our friendship that was likely to ensue when Holmes – soon to be disguised as "Altamont" – left for Chicago. For men of our age, it seemed a far more ominous hiatus than my two-year sojourn in America nearly thirty years before. [2]

At last the detective remarked quietly, "I suppose you saw in *The Times* that Gustav Mahler died this week?"

"Yes," I said promptly, happy for a change of subject. "I've been following the case for several months. It was bacterial endocarditis, brought on by repeated streptococcal infections and a defective heart valve. The poor man had no chance of surviving, Holmes. It's a pity, for I remember how much you admired his conducting."

"Indeed, Doctor. I was privileged to hear him several times upon the Continent. A brilliantly innovative interpreter of the German masters. Moreover, the greatness of the vast symphonic landscapes he composed will one day be acknowledged."

"Certainly, it was *not* acknowledged at the concert you and I attended. The reviews, as I recall, were scathing. That was the only occasion on which I ever heard his music."

"Well, the *Fourth* can sound a bit naïve upon first hearing, and young Beecham was not up to it. [3] The result was very different when Mahler conducted his own work. I was fortunate to be in Munich last September when the *Eighth* premièred. 'The Symphony of a Thousand', it was called, and rightly so. I have never experienced a more remarkable performance in the concert hall. They cheered him to the rafters."

"I believe you mentioned once that you'd met Mahler. Was it at this concert?"

"Hardly, Watson. I could never have made my way through the throng surrounding him. No, it was now nine years ago – before, in fact, I'd ever heard his music."

My friend paused, regarding me with the puckish look I recognised (though I'd not seen it often in three decades past) as an invitation to pursue the topic.

"Go on, then," I said crossly, for I was in no mood to play his games that night. "I suppose you met him on one of your visits to Vienna. He the great conductor, and you what our American cousins call a 'fan'. [4] It hardly seems a role that suits you, Holmes."

"On the contrary. Our interaction was not primarily musical in nature. It was rather of the sort to which I have been long accustomed."

Thunderstruck, I sat up abruptly, wincing at the protest from my toe. "You mean to tell me that Gustav Mahler was your *client*?"

"He was, although the solution I provided failed to satisfy him. In my defence, it would have been impossible to solve the case as it was first presented to me. You see, Watson, the renowned conductor of the Vienna Opera and Philharmonic – a man of brilliant intellect and undoubted, if controversial, musical gifts – was convinced that he was being haunted by a ghost."

"And you *accepted* such a case?"

"I did."

"You astound me, Holmes! To hear you – of all men – tolerating even the mention of the supernatural is earth-shaking. Have you not always said of our investigations that 'No ghosts need apply'? What made this case so different?"

"I had my reasons, Doctor, and they did not include believing in the ghost myself. Would you like to hear the story?"

"Of course I would!" I made a move towards rising to retrieve my notebook, but my gout and my visitor united in restraining me.

"It is not for publication," he warned with a raised finger, "for it would add no luster to poor Mahler's fame. There was no heinous crime involved, nor even any prosecutable offense. It was merely a curious and rather shabby history, which in the end reflected credit neither on the man who prompted the investigation nor the one who undertook it."

"If you're trying to discourage me, Holmes, you're not succeeding." I settled back in my armchair and took another sip of whisky. "Now get on with it!"

My friend gave me a sardonic grin and took out his ancient briar. "Very well, friend Boswell," he began . . .

*Hereafter, dear Readers, I shall withdraw my presence from the printed page, for my questions and interjections would add little to the tale. Instead, I shall allow Sherlock Holmes to tell the story here as he told it to me then, on the last night I saw my friend before he departed for Chicago.*

. . . As you possibly do not recall, in the last week of February, 1902, I made a brief visit to Vienna. I had been summoned to present my conclusions on the dual tragedies that befell the House of Habsburg near the end of the last century. [5] Because the South African War had not yet ended, your military duties kept you occupied at Barts, as did a certain former client [Here Holmes smiled.] who would soon become your wife. [6] I therefore made the trip alone. After spending a long morning at the Foreign Ministry, and the afternoon in an audience with the Emperor Franz Josef, I was left with a free evening and three clear days in hand before my planned return to London.

Fortuitously, the Hofoper was premièring a new work that very night, and I was provided with a ticket. The opera, alas, was disappointing – a medieval farce, unsuitably paired with modern music sung by an overwrought soprano – but Mahler's staging and handling of the orchestra were both first-rate. He was an arresting figure on the podium: Small and wraithlike under a shock of coal-black hair. His contortions looked almost demonic as he spurred his minions towards a climax at the end of the last act. I took the liberty after the performance of sending him my card. To my surprise, it was returned with a note asking me to call at his home for luncheon the next day.

I arrived, as instructed, at precisely one o'clock. Herr Mahler resided in a handsome block of flats just off the Rennweg, a walk of ten minutes from the Opera House. After climbing a spiral staircase to the topmost floor, I entered a tiled hallway faced by a pair of oaken doors. Just as I knocked, the bell pealed loudly from the street below, and I heard someone bounding up the stairs at a far more rapid pace than I had done. The door was opened by a dark-haired young woman who gestured frantically for me to step inside. Rather breathlessly, she introduced herself in German as Herr Mahler's sister. I gathered that she also kept his house. Before I could enter, the Hopofer's director surmounted the last stair and joined us at the entrance to his flat.

"*Was ist los, meine liebe Justi?* [7] Must you keep our guest standing in the hallway? Come in, come in, Herr Holmes!" As Justi meekly followed, Mahler placed a hand upon my back and propelled me through the door into the dining room, where we found the soup course quickly being served. Seating me upon his right, my host attacked his bowl with an unseemly haste. I concluded – in part from Justi's nervousness – that he kept a strict, exacting schedule, to which everyone around him must comply.

I won't bore you, Watson, with a detailed exposition of our luncheon. Mahler began by enquiring as to my opinion of the opera. He was not offended when I answered that while I had enjoyed the performance, the work itself left much to be desired.

"Quite right! *Der dot Mon* is the merest rubbish. It will soon sink into deserved oblivion. You should have been here a fortnight ago for Strauss's *Feuersnot*. It, at least, is a little more substantial. [8] I am delighted to find, Herr Holmes, that you are a man of discernment where music is concerned."

After this transparent flattery, our conversation went rapidly downhill. Obviously, the *Herr Direktor* was accustomed to dominating the discussion at his meals. His sister spoke only to the servants, and I was required to say very little. Instead, I observed my host as he kept up a curiously insipid monologue: Hardly lighting on one subject before switching to another, posing questions only to answer them himself, and blinking at me through his spectacles as though surprised I was still there. I could not imagine a man of Mahler's intellect habitually babbling such drivel, so it dawned upon me that he must be extremely nervous. Certainly, he was the most relieved of all of us when the luncheon finally ended, although it was a near-run thing.

Afterwards, Justi was summarily dismissed, and the *Direktor* invited me into his study "to smoke a fine cigar". I accepted one and settled into an armchair while Mahler strode restlessly about the room. Normally, he remarked in passing, it was his custom to nap for an hour after luncheon before walking in the park.

"Pray do not allow me to keep you from your nap, Herr Mahler," I said blandly. It *was* a fine cigar, Watson, and I was curious to see what he would do.

*"Nein, nein,"* said Mahler hastily, "my abject apologies." With an awkward laugh, he pulled out the swivel chair behind his desk and perched on it across from me. "I am, you see, a very schedule-driven fellow. It is the only way in which a man of my responsibilities can function. Your honoured visit – while very welcome, I assure you – is quite outside my usual routine."

I sat and smoked, waiting for him to continue.

"May I enquire, Herr Holmes," my reluctant host eventually managed, "how much longer you intend to remain in Vienna?" He rose and retreated to the window while awaiting my reply.

"My train leaves on Tuesday at midday, *Herr Direktor*." To help him on his way a bit, I added, "Until then, I have nothing in hand and would be at your service."

"Excellent, excellent!" cried Mahler. He scrambled back into his chair and turned it to peer earnestly into my face. "You understand, I have a small commission for you – an *investigation*, if you would be so kind. When I received your card last night at the Hopofer, it was as though God Himself had sent the very man whom I required."

At last, my fish had struck the lure! Settling myself comfortably, I closed my eyes. As you know, Watson, I dislike any sort of visual distraction as I absorb the details of a case. To my irritation, however, Herr Mahler could not steel himself to take the plunge.

"Naturally, I would readily pay whatever fee is usual."

"My professional charges. . . ." I began. (You know the rest, Watson, so I need not repeat it.) When that aria was sung, I reminded the *Direktor* that I had at best three days in hand. "Now, if you would kindly state the nature of the problem?"

Unfortunately, this demand caused my would-be client to retreat to his window. I watched him for almost a minute as he gazed silently upon the street below. "It is an odd story, Herr Holmes," he muttered finally. "No doubt you'll think me mad."

I waited.

"For the past few weeks," Mahler haltingly began, "a month or more, six weeks . . . I have been haunted by the playing of a distant violin."

As you might imagine, I was disturbed by the word "haunted", but decided to assume that the *Direktor* had employed it as a figure of speech. I did not reply and waited for him to continue.

"It is always late at night . . . when I walk back from the Hopofer . . . or sometimes when I am here at home, sitting at my desk alone and working late upon a score. I often leave the window open slightly for a bit of night air."

"Describe the music."

"It is always the same. A single violin, quite faint at first. A low, ghostly, rhythmic scraping, exactly like the opening 'Adagio' of Mozart's *Dissonance Quartet*. You know this work?"

I nodded.

"But the music takes a direction the divine Mozart would never have conceived. Its dissonance becomes ever weirder – unearthly, almost atonal – *terrifying* as it erupts into a sudden frenzy . . . then trails away to nothingness, and all is quiet again."

I opened my eyes, Watson, looking carefully at the *Direktor* to be certain he was serious. "Always the same, you say?"

"Always."

"And you hear it only once on each occasion?"

"*Ja.*"

I gave an exasperated snort. "Then I can only conclude, Herr Mahler, that you are being 'haunted' by a street musician playing pranks! There must be dozens of them in Vienna, and what better target for a joke than the director of the Opera?"

To my surprise, my host suffered this outburst with equanimity. "I have thought of that, Herr Holmes," he answered calmly. "I know every street musician in the neighbourhood. I have questioned them, and they deny involvement.

"What of a disgruntled member of your orchestra? It is well known, *Herr Direktor*, that you are a most *demanding* taskmaster."

Mahler's face hardened, and he snarled, "They would not *dare!*" His ire diminished as another thought occurred to him. "No, that cannot be. The music I have heard would be unknown to them. Indeed, it is known to very few besides myself."

My host had already mentioned another, more unwelcome explanation of the matter. "The composer Robert Schumann," I reminded him, "is said to have heard the note of '*A*' resounding in his head for months before he went insane. Do you likewise fear madness, Herr Mahler?"

The *Direktor* answered with a bitter laugh. "God knows I have enough frustration in my life to drive me mad! I doubt you can appreciate the discomfort of an assimilated Jew who holds a Court position in Vienna. If I lose the support of Prince Montenuovo, I am out the door tomorrow! Half my musicians yearn to sleep through their performances as they did for Jahn or Richter [9] My critics – those infallible gentlemen of the press! – cannot understand that Beethoven's orchestra could not have played the *Ninth Symphony* the way *he* heard it in his deafness – certain augmentations are required. As if all *this* were not enough, '*the* Herr Direktor *Mahler will soon marry* [as our newspapers report it] *a beautiful*

217

*and accomplished woman half his age!' Also,* there have been times of late, Herr Holmes, when madness has not seemed unimaginable. It might even be the simplest solution to my woes. "

Wearied by this long tirade, I told him, "Then I should inform you, sir, that I am a detective, not a doctor, and therefore unqualified to minister to a mind diseased."

The *Direktor*, who had earlier resumed his seat for our discussion, sidled once more to the window. "There is, perhaps, one other possibility," he muttered.

"And that is?"

"This uncanny violin-playing – it is music that I seem to recognise. It reminds me irresistibly of a piano improvisation I heard once before." Mahler, who had turned to face me, dropped his eyes. "The man who played it is long dead," he whispered.

I rose to take my leave. "Am I to understand, *Herr Direktor*, that you believe you are being serenaded by a ghost? If so, I must add to my previous disclaimers that I am neither medium nor exorcist. I thank you inviting me to luncheon, but continuing this conversation can serve no useful purpose. I wish you a good afternoon."

Mahler intercepted me before I reached the door, placing his hand upon my sleeve. "*Please*, Herr Holmes," he insisted. "I know very well the idea is absurd, but to my shame I cannot rid my mind of it. Won't you hear me out?"

If nothing else, I could not doubt the man's sincerity. Something about this ghostly violin music was troubling him deeply. His ascetic, chiseled face was ashen, and behind their spectacles his eyes were rimmed with tears. No doubt it was the product of my admiration for his genius, but I felt a twinge of pity for the great conductor.

"Very well," I sighed, and took my seat. "You may have five minutes. Tell me, if you can, the identity of this persistent specter."

The *Direktor* hung his head. "I believe," he answered softly, "it is Rott."

No doubt it was highly unprofessional of me, Watson, but I threw back my head and roared with laughter. "Oh, I quite agree, Herr Mahler. It is assuredly rot! I am relieved to hear you say so."

My host smiled grimly. "I am aware of your English idiom, sir, but I do not employ it. I was referring to a lost friend of my youth, Hans Rott. We were students together at the Conservatory, now many years ago. Rott and I, Herr Holmes, were pursued by the same demons. He succumbed to them. I, at least so far, have not."

I stared at him in consternation, because he had suddenly cast an entirely different light upon the matter. You see, Doctor, I *knew* the name "Hans Rott."

During my first year at Cambridge, I became acquainted with an Austrian student of philology who was spending a term there in order to perfect his English. Our relationship was both brief and symbiotic – I utilised it to perfect my German – but Seemüller [10] was a decent chap, and we corresponded occasionally after his return to Vienna. Early in the year 1881, I received a letter from him asking for my help.

While at college, Seemüller had witnessed my developing powers of observation and deduction, and I wrote to apprise him when I first began to put those powers to good use. Now he offered me what would have been my first international case as a detective. However, the so-called case was utterly ridiculous! A friend of his – a budding composer named Hans Rott – wished to hire my services, but Seemüller proposed that I meet with my new client in Vienna's lunatic asylum! Rott had been institutionalised several months before, taken off a train to Mühlhausen after pulling a revolver on a cigar-smoking fellow passenger and shouting that Johannes Brahms had filled the train with dynamite. As Rott saw it, Brahms had in some way thwarted his musical ambitions, and the young man was also suffering – like many others of his ilk – from the effects of poverty and an unhappy love affair. Although in December he had attempted suicide, there was still some hope of his recovery. Seemüller wrote that it might be beneficial for me to investigate the "plot" against his friend, even though that plot existed only in Rott's mind. He offered to pay my fee and expenses if I would travel to Vienna, spend a few days conducting a specious investigation, and assure the poor young madman that the myriad dangers he saw lurking had been successfully resolved.

Well, Watson, I expect you will know how I replied. At the time, you and I had barely settled into our new digs, and several cases I had brought from Montague Street could hardly be abandoned. Moreover, in those days I was not inclined to foreign travel. Quite aside from all of that, I took Seemüller's absurd proposal as an insult to my new vocation. It would have done his friend no good whatever and made a fraud of me. I fear I answered his letter with more asperity than it deserved, and I heard nothing further from him, then or afterwards. Nor did I ever hear the name "Hans Rott" again until twenty-one years later – when Gustav Mahler informed me that the ghost of this young, unknown, and mad composer had begun to haunt him with a violin!

In a way, it seemed that Rott was haunting me as well. Having unexpectedly re-crossed this "path not taken", I could now atone for any lack of compassion I had shown the young man whilst he lived. Having nothing else to do in Vienna for the next three days, I was presented with an opportunity to tie up a loose end. I therefore agreed to hear out Mahler as he told me what he knew of his friend's story.

"Hans Rott and I, Herr Holmes," sighed the *Direktor*, "felt ourselves to be fruit of the same tree, brought forth by the same soil, nourished by the same air. We could have done great things together in the new musical epoch that was then dawning. *Alack!* Rott died – in want and unrecognised – on the threshold of a great career. What music has lost in him cannot be estimated."

"More data and less poetry," I murmured, "would be useful to the case at hand. Presumably, your relationship with Rott was not purely horticultural! What sort of young man was he? Was he your fellow student, your friend, or your rival? What in your past leads you to believe he may be haunting you, assuming – as I do *not* assume – that such a thing is possible?"

Mahler gave me a look of wry amusement. "It is true," he acknowledged, "that Rott and I could have been considered rivals. All Conservatory students, you may be sure, were to some extent in competition. We vied to impress the same professors, competed for the same prizes every year. It was much the same as in a school of law or medicine.

"But there was something wondrous about Rott. He had been born illegitimate – the son of an actor who married Hans's mother after his wife's death. The old man's fortune was exhausted by the time he died. Afterwards (as Hans would joke), rainwater had free discharge from his shoes! His dear mother – who had also borne an archduke's bastard – was dead by then as well. [11] Even so, Hans carried himself like a young prince! When this youth walked down the street, you forgot his old cap and shabby overcoat, his red-and-white striped butcher's trousers. You noticed only his gigantic stature, his lion's mane of tawny hair, his grey eyes alight with merriment. [12] Sneer if you wish, Herr Holmes, but I assure you that Hans Rott was quite a fellow!"

"And yet this paragon went mad. Tell me, if you know, what led to that event."

My client shifted with discomfort. "I know less than I should, I will admit. By then, we were no longer on close terms, but Rott's trouble had been coming for some years. It was not simply poverty, for the Conservatory had exempted him from fees after his father's death. Old Bruckner, who had taught Hans the organ and admired the boy, found a post for him as organist in the Piaristen monastery. *Natürlich*, it paid but a pittance, and the monks despised him. Still, between this work and his piano students, Rott could just get by with help from his wealthier acquaintances. His room in the monastery soon became a meeting-place for all of us: Wolf, the Krzyzanowski brothers, Löhr, Seemüller, and myself. [13] One came to it down a long and gloomy corridor, but Rott's window overlooked a spacious courtyard, shaded by big trees. Many were the nights we gathered there, talking, singing, and arguing as young men will.

"In those days, Herr Holmes, most of us were fervently Wagnerian. We made sport of our stodgy old professors: The tyrant Hellmesberger – who would throw my student compositions on the floor! – and even the great Brahms. Bruckner – his bitter enemy and Wagner's chief disciple – we idolised, eccentric fellow though he was. As it seemed to us, the struggle between them was for the very soul of music, determining its destiny for the new century as well as our own fates. But here, too, Rott was different. He refused to choose one path to the exclusion of the other. 'How many musicians are there,' Hans would say, 'and how few artists!' He studied and admired the music of both Wagnerians *and* Classicists, and elements from both were reflected in his symphony."

By this time, Watson, I was all but nodding in my chair. "Rott wrote a symphony?" I roused myself sufficiently to ask. "An unusual achievement for a student, surely?"

"Not at all," laughed Mahler, "for I wrote one myself. But *this* symphony was no mere student composition. Long before Hans completed it, it was revered among us as '*The Symphony*'. With this single work, Herr Holmes, Hans Rott became the founder of the new symphony as I understand it."

"And yet," I reminded him, "you left the orbit of music's bright new star. What was the cause of your estrangement?"

The *Direktor* gave me a sad smile. "It was a silly schoolboys' quarrel. At the time, Rott lived mainly on cheap sausages, called 'Extrawurst'. He used to hang them from the rafters of his room. I jested that any composer worth his salt should be able to subsist on quargel – a strong, and even cheaper, cheese. I derided Hans as 'a roast-beef composer'! He took offense, for even on my father's small allowance I was better off than he. After my stupidity, I was no longer welcome in his room. Then came the disaster at the student competition."

Mahler seemed reluctant to continue, but I encouraged him with an enquiring look.

"In his last year – the summer of 1878, it was – Rott entered the first movement of his symphony. It was the most Wagnerian portion of the work, ending with a great horn chorale like *Götterdämmerung*. Magnificent, even played on the piano! But at the end, only scornful

221

laughter was heard from the judges' table. Bruckner alone defended Hans, saying, 'Do not laugh, gentlemen – from this young man you will hear great things yet!' But he won *nothing*, while I took the prize with the scherzo of a quintet I never even finished! When I told my parents, my own mother shed tears of indignation. 'What injustice,' she cried, 'when Rott's composition was so much better than yours!'" [14]

My host chuckled rather bitterly. "From that point, matters went from bad to worse for Hans. He lost his job as organist with the Piaristens. The prior falsely accused him of stealing books from their library to sell, so he resigned in outrage. The lie was simply an excuse, for one can imagine the unsettling effect of a beautiful and pure young man in a cloister full of eunuchs! Afterwards, Rott had only his friends and his piano students to support him. Worse, he fell in love with one of them, but of course he lacked the income to support a wife. His health, I was told, began to fail as well. Yet, through it all, Hans kept on composing. He finished his wonderful symphony, as well as other works, and he hoped to redeem his fortunes by entering the symphony in the 1880 Beethoven Competition. Had he won, it might have been the saving of him. Instead, this plan led directly to his end."

"Another humiliation by the judges?" I surmised. Even I, Watson, had begun to feel a retrospective sympathy for the young man. But Mahler shook his head.

"Not precisely in the way you mean. Rott decided to make his case to each judge individually. Unhappily, he began with Brahms, who inherently disliked him – and the rest of us as well – because we were all friends of Bruckner, his great enemy. The master Hans admired was merciless, telling him his symphony was so full of trivialities and nonsense that its moments of great beauty could never be his own. Brahms became incensed because a theme in Rott's fourth movement resembled the one in his own *C Minor* symphony. It was intended as a tribute, but Brahms took it as a joke. He threw Hans out upon his ear, assuring him that he had no talent whatsoever!"

"Dear me! I shall not listen to *that* composer with quite as much enjoyment again! So this was the end of Rott's musical ambitions?"

"*Jawohl*, Herr Holmes, in essence. The faithful Bruckner urged Hans not to despair, so he tried again with Richter, pleading for him to place the symphony on a Philharmonic programme, which would have given Rott a bit of income. My future colleague was kinder, but he did not comply. *Also*, when a position as choirmaster in Mühlhausen – in far-away Alsace – arose unexpectedly, Hans was forced to accept it as a matter of survival. The last thing he desired, you see, was to leave Vienna. It seems little wonder to me that he at once went mad."

"Did you see Rott off before he left?" I wondered.

"*Nein*, Herr Holmes. To my shame, I did not join our comrades on the platform to wish my old friend well. Nor did I visit him in the asylum, for during the years of his internment, I was conducting in Laibach and Kassel and other dismal towns. The only occasion on which I saw Hans Rott again was at his funeral. Now, almost eighteen years later, it appears that he has come to visit me!"

I acknowledged this absurd speculation with a sigh. "Very well, *Herr Direktor*," I decided, rising to my feet, "I shall do whatever I am able to lay this ghost for you. Have you any suggestions as to how I should begin?"

In fact, my host had very few. He explained that visiting the Conservatory would be of little use, for Rott's professors, as well as Brahms and Bruckner, had all died years before. When I enquired about his old acquaintances, Mahler shook his head. Seemüller, he informed me, was now teaching in Innsbruck. One of the Krzyzanowski brothers was conducting opera in Weimar, the other writing novels in the Tyrol. Meister Hugo Wolf (whom I knew as the composer of many charming lieder) was confined in the same madhouse – the Provincial Lunatic Asylum of Lower Austria – where Hans Rott met his end. Although the asylum lay within the confines of Vienna, Mahler assured me that Wolf could be of no assistance. "He is dying of syphilis," the *Direktor* stated grimly, "and can no longer speak."

This left only Friedrich Löhr, an architect, who lived in Vienna and had been one of Mahler's closest friends. "We see less of each other nowadays," he admitted, "because my *Almschi* does not like him." From the fatuous smile that accompanied this verdict, I deduced that *Almschi* must be his fiancée. Nonetheless, he agreed to telephone Löhr on my behalf and request an appointment. "He and Seemüller did more than anyone for Hans in his last years, and Fritz still holds the poor boy's letters, journals, and surviving scores. I shall find out if he will see you in the morning."

"The afternoon might be more convenient for us both," I countered. "Tomorrow morning I intend to visit the asylum. Surely, someone on the staff remembers Rott, and there must be records from the time of his incarceration."

"*Sehr gut*, if you think it would be helpful," the *Direktor* agreed a little dubiously. "But how do you propose to examine such records? You possess no standing as a doctor and know no one there."

"You may rely on me to solve that problem," I assured him. "I have considerable expertise in gaining *entrée* into places where I am unknown – even lunatic asylums." Having delivered this airy rejoinder, I wished

223

Herr Mahler a pleasant afternoon, thanked Justi for her hospitality, and returned to my hotel. Once snugly installed in my own room, I telephoned our old acquaintance Sigmund Freud.

The next morning, I met Freud for breakfast at a café near the asylum. He walked from his apartment on the Berggasse – to which, in fact, he had invited me for an early *Frühstück*. I declined, feeling it inadvisable to disturb my equanimity during an investigation by returning to the scene of painful memories. [15] Freud seemed to understand my reservations. He asked about you, Doctor, and was pleased to hear of your impending marriage, which I had already deduced, although you had not yet announced it.

Our appointment at the asylum was at ten o'clock. While I had no idea what we might learn of the unfortunate Hans Rott, there was a more intriguing question on which I desired Dr. Freud's opinion. As we finished the last of our strudel and a third cup of excellent coffee, I asked him what might induce an otherwise sane man to posit that he was being haunted by a ghost.

The psychiatrist blinked at me, through his tobacco-smoke, with the same measured stare I well remembered. If stouter and greyer than when I saw him last, Freud appeared otherwise unchanged. As usual, he pondered a long moment before answering.

"Most often guilt, Herr Holmes, I do assure you. Whether or not you believe in the actual manifestation of a spirit, such men are truly haunted. A ghost, you see, is but a dream – either a benevolent or an avenging angel – but, most of all, a wish!"

"As I recently remarked to my client, a bit less poetry would be in order." I had not named Mahler to the analyst, telling him only that a client had directed me to research the asylum for any record of a long-lost friend.

*"Sehr gut!"* he laughed, "I shall be dull and clinical. Call it, then, the fear of death. We cannot cope with finding our loved ones in the worst condition in which we dread to find ourselves. Unable to accept their loss, we yearn to bring them back, even – if it must be – in a distorted, terrifying form. And always there is guilt – guilt over things unsaid, undone to reconcile ourselves with the departed."

"That sounds plausible," I mused, "especially in the present case. However, if the guilt's motivating offense happened many years ago, would a lingering sympathy for the wronged departed suffice in itself to evoke his specter?"

Again, Dr. Freud considered. *"Nein,"* he said at last, "it is unlikely. For so extreme a reaction, the motivating offense would need to be more recent. A ghost would require, I think, a fresher, urgent sense of guilt. I speak, you understand, in generalities, knowing nothing of the case you have in mind."

"Then matters are as I expected," I replied, for the vague suspicions that had lurked within my mind now coalesced. "I believe, *Herr Doktor*, that we should depart if we are not to be late for our appointment."

The Provincial Lunatic Asylum of Lower Austria was a massive edifice, composed of three full storeys and two wings. Although constructed in the 'Fifties, its interior had a modern aspect, with spacious rooms and long, well-lighted corridors. It being Sunday, the director was not on the premises. We were greeted by his chief clinician, Dr. Engel, a dapper, youngish fellow with an unwelcome air of condescension. Freud had already apprised him of the reason for our visit.

"*Es tut mir Leid*, Herr Holmes," said Engel, "but I fear I can provide you with little information on Hans Rott. His name appears in charts from our physicians' rounds in the early 'Eighties – a hopeless case of paranoia. We have many of them here. There are references to hallucinations, violent mood swings, forced feedings, and suicide attempts. He seems to have perished of tuberculosis in 1884. That was long before my arrival, nor would any of the other doctors now on staff have known him. As for Rott's case file, I regret that it was lost, with many others, when a broken sewer pipe flooded records in our basement storage room."

I snorted in disgust, for any useful knowledge of this young composer continued to elude me. Our host quickly reassured me that not all hope was lost.

"Do not despair, sir, for there is one person here who still remembers him. Our retired cook, *Frau* Hansum, says that she and her husband (an attendant in Rott's section) were good friends of this patient. Old Hansum died last year, but I have brought his wife, who still lives on the grounds, to speak with you. She is waiting in our conference room, if you would like to meet her." Obviously, Watson, I accepted with alacrity. Dr. Freud declined to join me, citing professional matters he wished to discuss with Dr. Engel.

*Frau* Hansum proved to be a stout, elderly woman with a kind, if wrinkled, face. It turned quite crimson when I entered, and she stood to bob a nervous curtsy. Happily, I possess (as you have noted, Doctor) a soothing manner with the fair sex when required. Once her shyness had been overcome, *Frau* Hansum talked volubly about Hans Rott, and it was clear that I had found a valuable informant.

"*Ach*, he was a sweet boy, *mein Herr*, that one," she sighed mournfully. "At first, it seemed he would recover. Hans wrote to a gentleman in Mühlhausen (wherever *that* may be!) of taking up his post

225

there soon. Many times, his friends would visit him. One day, they brought him a new hat, for Hans had thrown his own hat out the window! At other times, he would play the piano in our common room, working (as he told my husband) on new music of his own."

"So Rott continued to compose in the asylum?"

"*Ja!* Wonderful music it was, but very loud. The other patients would complain. Also, the attendants would have to make him stop. My good Otto let him play as long as possible when *he* was on the ward. *Der junge Mann* appreciated us, *mein Herr* – he said our kindness helped him to keep rosy expectations!"

"Sadly, I take it that these 'rosy expectations' did not last?"

"*Ach! Nein.* As months passed into years, poor Hans began to lose his hope. He would write out lists of debts and creditors and tear his hair, although (I heard it said) his friends were paying for his treatment here. Next, he began to rage against the doctors, shouting 'Herr Schlager's irony cannot deter me!' or 'Gauster's lies no longer have me in their thrall!' (I may safely speak these names, *mein Herr* – his doctors are all dead now.) [16] So they put Hans in the isolation ward, and would even turn a hose on him when he grew violent. My husband was in tears when he would tell me!"

*Frau* Hansum was likewise weeping. I decided to offer her my handkerchief and pat her hand, trusting that she would continue.

"Please forgive me," she murmured, dabbing at her eyes. "Since my Otto died, I cry so easily! When *junge* Hans came back to us, he was much crazier. At some times, he would rave for hours. At others, he sat indifferent and alone, speaking to no one, not even to my Otto. No longer did Hans play the piano, but still he would madly scribble out his compositions. Often, he saved them, but on bad days he would rip them into shreds, later using the expensive paper for, if you will excuse me (Here she blushed and whispered, Watson.), *quite another purpose!* At such times, the boy would laugh hysterically and tell my husband, '*That* is all the works of man are worth!'" [17]

"Did Rott's friends still visit him?" I wondered.

"*Ja, ja,* though not so much, for on most days he would refuse to meet them. There was only one person whom he wished to meet – but *she* never came, only her brother. It would not have been safe for her by then, for Hans was very sick. *Tuberkulose!*"

*Frau* Hansum hung her head, evidently weary, but I had one question left to ask.

"Did Rott ever speak of a friend – once a fellow student – by the name of Mahler?"

*"Mahler,"* the old woman pondered. "That is the name of the director of our Opera, *nicht wahr? . . .* Seemüller, and . . . Löhr, those names I remember. There *was* someone, a former friend, whom Hans – in the last days of his delirium – would rail against. This man, he said, was soon to steal his symphony, the one great work he had completed."

The hairs on my neck prickled, Watson, for I recalled a passage in that unheeded letter Seemüller had written to me long ago – a jealous rival whom Rott feared would one day steal his symphony. The man he dreaded – although the name meant nothing to me at the time – was *Gustav Mahler!*

While I sought to remain impassive in the face of this remembrance, *Frau* Hansum was removing a yellowed sheet of paper from her bag. "I have two things to show you, *mein Herr,* if you wish to see them. This letter, which my husband wrote, records Hans Rott's dying words. *Der junge Mann* came to himself briefly before he passed into a coma. Otto wanted to preserve his words, because he directed them to us."

"Please read me only the relevant portion."

"'*Herr Hansum,*'" she recited, in a voice that began to quaver halfway through. "'*. . . I wish to thank you and your wife from my innermost heart for your conscientious efforts and nutritious food. I dreamt once of a bright future. My works had been recognised by the great masters. I thought I could count upon a modest income, in order to sustain myself. But now I see that it has all been a delusion, and that I must die in the asylum.*'"

"And this," went on *Frau* Hansum, as she wiped her eyes, "is Hans's picture. It was taken in the year before he died. We asked *Herr Direktor Doktor* Maynert for a copy from the patient file, and he was kind." With a trembling hand, she laid a photograph between us on the table.

It was difficult to reconcile Mahler's description of his friend with the young man I now saw before me. The "lion's mane of tawny hair" still grew in profusion, but any trace of combativeness or merriment had left the handsome face. With a look devoid of all emotion, Hans Rott stared into the distance as into his own grave.

At that moment, the door into the conference room burst open, and Dr. Engel cried out heartily, *"Was gibts, gnädige Frau Hansum?* Still at it? You must not bore our honoured guest with so many reminiscences!" He swept in ahead of the embarrassed Freud, plucking Rott's photograph from the table before I could retrieve it.

*"Also!* Is this the patient you were looking for, Herr Holmes? Rather a sad-looking specimen, would you not agree, Freud? Note the utter lack of affect. Obviously, the poor wretch well knew the gravity of his situation. I'll wager he was not long for the Earth when this was taken!"

In the midst of this crass speech, *Frau* Hansum gathered her belongings – save for the cherished keepsake – and quickly fled the room.

"You must excuse me," I snapped to the clinician, snatching Rott's photograph and overtaking the poor woman in the hallway. By the time I had apologised and thanked her, the two psychiatrists were waiting, their respective visages reflecting complacency and shame.

"*Herr Doktor* Freud," Engel announced suavely, "has asked to visit one of our more famous patients, the composer Hugo Wolf. There is no longer much to see of him, alas, for he is in the last stage of general paresis."

"You will forgive me, Holmes," Freud muttered as we fell in step behind his colleague. "One of my new patients is in the same stage of this disease, which I have not treated for some years. I must see what the poor fellow has awaiting him. It will take but a moment." Dr. Engel, meanwhile, rattled on obliviously as he led us towards the first-class ward.

"Meister Wolf," he declaimed, "has been with us since 1898. When he arrived here, he imagined that *he* – not the great Mahler – was director of the Hopofer! That botcher of Beethoven's symphonies, it seems, declined to perform Wolf's only opera, which he had promised his old friend to do. Whereupon our patient – in his own mind, at least – superseded Mahler! It is wonderful how these lunatics will find ways of resolving such internal conflicts. Wolf held yet another grudge against his rival, whom he accused of stealing his idea for a libretto in their student days. I would not put it past our Gustav – the dirty Jew! *Ach!* Your pardon, dear Freud," he called across his shoulder to my grim-faced companion. "*Natürlich*," I exempt *you* from the insult 'dirty Jew'!"

"*Natürlich*, my dear Engel," Freud replied serenely, "just as I exempt *you* from the insult 'vicious anti-Semite'!"

Thankfully, we had at last arrived at Herr Wolf's door. "I have been informed by my friend Dr. Watson," I remarked to the clinician, "that part of a physician's duty is to respect his patient's privacy. Apparently, that portion of the Hippocratic Oath does not apply here in Vienna."

"It is quite irrelevant to the present case, Herr Holmes," sighed Engel. "Poor Wolf, I assure you, can feel no humiliation. In this final stage of syphilis, he is scarcely aware of what goes on around him. Come, gentlemen, and I will show you."

He opened the door softly, and we stepped into the darkened room. Meister Hugo Wolf lay comatose within a strange, lattice-like structure built around his bed. Simply put, the eminent composer was encaged, as surely as his lupine namesake in the zoo. The smiling Engel shook his head, seeming both pleased and regretful at the sight before us.

"It is necessary, you know, for his own protection." He had, at least, the decency to whisper. "Three years ago, Herr Holmes, Wolf and I would play duets of Bruckner's works on that piano, even though he was already quite insane. Now, the great *Meister* knows not his own name – he can neither see, nor hear, nor speak. The paralysis makes it difficult for us to feed him. [18] And yet he lives! Is *this*, Freud, what you wished to see?"

As you know, Doctor, I am seldom at the mercy of my emotions. But as I gazed upon the wasted, waxen figure on that bed, my first impulse was to run screaming from the room. Freud seemed equally shaken, although he had of course seen many more of an asylum's denizens than I. We turned away and left Wolf to his living death. After curtly thanking Engel for making *Frau* Hansum available to me, I fled the Provincial Lunatic Asylum of Lower Austria as though all the hounds of Hell were at my heels.

My pipe, and the cab ride back to my hotel, somewhat restored me. I spent the next two hours assimilating the data I had gleaned. During my ruminations, running through my head was a verse by the German poet Rückert: "*Ich bin der Welt abhanden gekommen.*" It translates, Watson, as: "*I am lost to the world.*" Some time later, Mahler himself would set this poem to music, and I have heard that he applied its words to his own life. Yet, if the words "*I am lost to the world*" applied to Gustav Mahler, how much more tragically did they apply to Hans Rott and Hugo Wolf, two friends whom he abandoned and possibly betrayed?

*Herr Doktor* Friedrich Löhr, philologist and secretary to the Vienna Archeological Association, had scheduled our appointment for four o'clock that afternoon. Entering his study, I found him in conversation with a dark-haired girl in her early teens, no doubt his daughter. Greeting me with no very friendly look, Dr. Löhr told the child quietly, "Leave us, Maja [19]. This is the gentleman of whom I spoke to you."

"*Jawohl,*" cried Maja saucily, "the great detective who would not help Hans Rott!" She gave me a hostile glare before departing, emphasising that my cold reception was in her opinion well deserved.

The archeologist laughed grimly as he waved me to a chair. "I regret my daughter's impudence, Herr Holmes, but I acknowledge that I share her anger. Seemüller and I had hoped to meet you twenty years ago, when you might have done poor Hans some good. What can I do for you at this late date? Or, rather, for my old friend Mahler, as it is only at his urging that I agreed to speak with you."

"Herr Mahler has taken a belated interest in Rott's fate," I began, "although no more belated – as you rightly remind me – than my own. I have visited the asylum where your friend spent his last years, and I have learned enough of Hans Rott to rue my refusal to act on his behalf. If an apology would still signify, *Herr Doktor*, I shall gladly offer one."

Dr. Löhr smiled at me behind his bushy mustache. "Well said, Herr Holmes! Your contrition is sufficient in itself as an apology. Now, how may I assist you?"

"I have a question for you, and also a request. The first, I will admit, is for my own edification, rather than for Mahler's. I have learned from a source at the asylum – an old woman whose husband cared for Rott – that he hoped to receive visits from the sister of a friend who was supporting him. I presume this friend was either you or Seemüller. I also recall Seemüller's letter stating that Hans Rott had suffered an unhappy love affair. If it is not too indelicate, can you identify the young lady whom he loved?"

"Quite easily," my host rumbled. "It was my sister Louise. She and Hans met when he came to our parents' home to give piano lessons to the younger children. Louise was seventeen, and they developed a mutual affection. By the summer before he went to the asylum, Hans had convinced himself that they would marry. Alas, it was impossible."

"Was Rott so unsuitable?"

"Not through any fault of his. You must understand the *milieu* in which Louise and I were raised, Herr Holmes. Originally, our family name was *Löwri*. It would have been unthinkable in that culture for a girl to act against her parents' wishes. Louise understood this, though Hans did not. When he composed a 'song of courtship' for her – consisting of three-hundred verses! Louise was not allowed, although she loved him, to read it or even accept it from his hand. With nothing more to offer her than his own ardent heart, it was preposterous for Hans to think of marriage."

"From what I have heard of this young man, I should imagine that he might take desperate measures rather than abandoning his hopes."

"Then you do Hans an injustice. The boy was mortified by his parents' sinful lives, by having an archduke's bastard as his brother. For *their* faults, as Hans saw it, *he* must make amends through purity! *Nein*, Herr Holmes. The only 'desperate measures' my friend contemplated were winning the Beethoven Prize, having his symphony performed, and assuring himself an income. And in these hopes Louise encouraged him. She begged Hans not to leave Vienna. Yet, I have no doubt that being thwarted in his love, as in his professional ambitions, brought on the poor lad's madness. Months before he took the train to Mühlhausen, Hans wrote to me: "*I am not far from lunacy!*""

I sat back, Watson, with a sigh. If ever a composer had sufficient reason to go mad, that composer was Hans Rott. "Where is your sister now?" I ventured.

"She is happily married and has become an artist. Herr Holmes, I believe you also mentioned a request?"

"Indeed." I considered how best to frame the matter. Obviously, the less said about a ghost the better. I did not want Dr. Löhr concluding that insanity had afflicted another of his friends! "I have been told," I said at last, "that you have custody of Hans Rott's papers, including the surviving scores of his musical works?"

My host nodded, but his face assumed what I saw was a forbidding air.

"Are there among them," I carefully resumed, "any solo pieces for violin – or any composition that might be based on Mozart's *Dissonance Quartet*?"

"I presume that Mahler prompted this enquiry?"

"Indirectly, that is so."

With more violence than seemed necessary, Dr. Löhr slammed his palms upon the desk. "*Verdammt!* I thought as much." He rose with a low growl and strode to a safe in the corner of the room. Opening it, he retrieved a pile of manuscripts and tossed them on the desk. "Here are Rott's surviving scores. You may have one hour. Please understand, Herr Holmes, that I cast no aspersion on your honour by stating that there is an inventory to the contents of that safe." Without another word, Löhr left me to myself and shut the study door behind him.

I spent the next hour, Watson, fascinated by the young composer's legacy. In all, there appeared to be some eighty works, though many were unfinished and I had time to examine very few. Besides a plethora of lieder, I found a serenade for strings, a pastoral prelude, two operatic overtures, and an oratorio entitled – prophetically – *Der Tod*. [20] There were even sketches for a second symphony. Naturally, it was to Rott's first symphonic essay that I devoted most of my attention. Taking the score – an obvious copy, for it was written upon newer paper and in a different hand – I sat down at Löhr's small piano and played my way through parts of it (even though I am no pianist, Doctor, as you know).

The symphony was all that Mahler said of it. I could readily understand how it had achieved almost legendary status among Hans Rott's friends. The first movement was, perhaps, excessively Wagnerian – building ever more dramatically upon the simple motif of its opening to end in a majestic brass chorale that indeed recalled *Götterdämmerung*. The slow movement, with its dignified sonority, paid Rott's debt to Bruckner for teaching him the organ, while the scherzo was a frenetically gay and swooping ländler. Interjected into the fourth movement was the noble string melody that had so infuriated Brahms. Soon it had transformed itself into a mighty march, joining the symphony's *idée fixe* to soar triumphantly before reaching a serene conclusion, which (like Hans Rott himself) tried to reconcile Wagnerians and Classicists before it quietly died away.

231

Although the symphony was oddly developed and marked by the naïvety of youth, I quickly saw – as Gustav Mahler would assuredly have seen – that this was music well worth stealing.

So entranced was I that an hour nearly passed before I remembered my real purpose: To find the ghostly violin music that appeared to haunt my client. Quickly, I searched again through the sheets of chamber works. There were none for solo violin, and all the trios, quartets, and quintets seemed to be unfinished. Then I found it, Watson: A complete *String Quartet in C minor*, which began exactly as had Mozart's in the major key. Mere moments after making this discovery, I heard Dr. Löhr's approaching footsteps, and the door into his study opened.

"Well, Herr Holmes, have you found the music you were looking for?"

"In fact, I believe I have. May I take this score to show to Mahler?"

Dr. Löhr considered for a moment. "When do you return to London?"

"My train departs at noon on Tuesday."

"Then you may borrow the score on one condition: That you *personally* place it in my hands before you leave Vienna."

"You have my word." Daring greatly, I turned to the copy of Rott's symphonic score. "This symphony, *Herr Doktor*, is a marvellous creation. I would be very grateful for an opportunity to study it at greater length."

"I am sorry, but I cannot allow that score to leave my possession. It is the only copy of Rott's symphony, and the original is in other hands. *Whose*," he added gruffly, "I am not at liberty to say."

For a long moment, we simply stared at one another. Then Dr. Löhr offered me a quizzical look, which I returned enquiringly. He dropped his eyes and turned aside, and I knew I had my answer.

When I telephoned Herr Mahler the next morning, Justi told me that he had already departed for the Hopofer. It was nearly midday before I heard from him – a note delivered to my room informed me that the *Direktor* would be occupied throughout the afternoon in a rehearsal. I was to come to his office at half-past seven in the evening, so that we might converse until Mahler's fiancée, *Fraulein* Schindler, arrived at eight to accompany him to the Café Imperial for dinner. There was, of course, no invitation for me to join them.

Although puzzled by my client's apparent lack of interest in his case, I passed the sunny afternoon by strolling in the Prater, then ate an early dinner in a coffee-house. It was precisely half-past-seven when I knocked upon Herr Mahler's door.

"Ah, Herr Holmes!" he greeted me. "Good of you to come so late. How goes your quest for Hans Rott's ghost?" Was it merely my imagination, Doctor, or did amusement lie behind the irony in the *Direktor's* smile?

"I fear," I sighed, "that I have been but partially successful. Your young friend's ghost, Herr Mahler, continues to elude me. However, I have at least been able to identify the violin music you have heard."

"*Have* you?" cried Mahler eagerly, moving towards me with his hand outstretched. "Then let me see what you have there!"

"I regret," I continued, keeping the portfolio that contained the string quartet tightly underneath my arm, "that I could not also bring you the score of Hans Rott's symphony. Unfortunately, Dr. Löhr was unwilling to release the only copy – the original being, as he said, 'in other hands'."

My client stopped short and scowled at me. "Did Fritz tell you that I have it?"

"He did not. Please remember, *Herr Direktor*, that I am a detective. My knowledge of the science of deduction includes the ability to add two plus two."

After we had glowered at each other for a moment, Mahler sighed deeply, walked to a cabinet behind his desk, and pulled out a thick roll of yellowed sheet music.

"How long have you possessed this astounding work?"

"Since the summer of 1900." [21]

"Nearly *two full years?* Why in God's name have you not performed it?"

"I feel that a performance," the *Direktor* answered, "would do little to enhance poor Rott's reputation. His talent was still raw and undeveloped." Herr Mahler began to stalk about the room in agitation. "It was as though a young athlete swings back to take the longest throw he can, and – still clumsy – does not quite hit the goal. Oh, I know well what Rott was aiming at, but what he wanted was not what he achieved!"

When I made no reply, my client turned away. "*Natürlich*, parts of the symphony are wonderful," he assured the passers-by beneath his window, "but many other parts are ludicrous! Did you know that Rott has a *triangle* clang incessantly throughout the whole fourth movement? *Nein, nein*, Herr Holmes. This work – magnificent and promising though it may be – is not performable."

Abruptly, Mahler's objections fell under their own weight, for he noticed the disdain with which I was regarding him. "Well, well," he finished lamely, collapsing into the chair behind his desk, "let us speak no more of this unhappy symphony! You say that you have found the ghostly violin music?"

"I have," I acknowledged, handing the *Direktor* the portfolio. Spreading the score beneath his desk lamp, he grew almost frantic with joy as he examined it.

"A *string quartet,* how charming! *Ja,* the cello – scrape, scrape, scrape – Ha! Just like Mozart! Now the violin – its high, atonal keening. *Ja! Ja!* This is indeed the music I have heard. It is the improvisation Hans played on his piano! Herr Holmes, you are a genius!" Mahler beamed on me beatifically but briefly, my anger routing his delight.

"But tell me," he said apprehensively, "why am I being haunted by Rott's ghost?"

"Ah, yes . . . the ghost." I waved my client back into his chair. "I have given the matter much thought, *Herr Direktor*, and I have even consulted experts on your problem. As I see it, there are two possible explanations for the ghost. The first – to revert to my original hypothesis – is that this eerie music *did* come from some street musician. Upon hearing it, the guilt you have long suppressed over your treatment of Hans Rott emerged and triggered a subconscious memory of similar music you once heard him play, leading you to believe – fallaciously, of course – that you were being haunted by Rott's ghost."

The *Direktor* did not seem altogether happy with this explanation. "Ah, I see you have been speaking with our Viennese psychiatrists," he grumbled. "I am not sure that I believe their mumbo-jumbo, but we shall let that pass. What is the alternate theory that you have considered?"

"Why, simply that there never *was* a ghost – except, perhaps, as a stalking-horse that you employed to acquire this piece of music."

"*Was!*" cried Mahler angrily, "You say that you do not believe me?"

"I am undecided as to whether I believe *you, Herr Direktor*, but I am certain that I do *not* believe in ghosts! Consider the facts. You borrowed Hans Rott's symphony and have held it for two years. Now, for whatever reason, you are anxious to acquire another piece by Rott. You are aware that a direct approach to Dr. Löhr may not succeed, unless you are willing to return the symphony. Therefore, you enlist Sherlock Holmes to be your advocate, under the cover of this ridiculous fable of a ghost. If *that* was your plan, Herr Mahler, I must offer my congratulations, for it succeeded brilliantly! You have the symphony, and now you have the string quartet. Best of all – if I may carry my idea to its logical conclusion – you are in a position to allow your friendship with Dr. Löhr to lapse (as I believe you have done with other friends before), pleasing your 'Almschi' and retaining Rott's compositions for as long as you desire – unless your hoodwinked friend should resort to legal action to recover them."

By this stage in my analysis, the director of the Opera was livid. "*Gott im Himmel*, Herr Holmes! You consider me not only a liar but a scoundrel!"

I must admit, Watson, that Mahler's outrage did seem genuine. I was closer to believing him at that moment than at any time before. Marching quickly to his desk, my client took out his cheque-book. "Name your fee, Herr Sherlock Holmes, so that I may pay it and we may be done with one another. Then you can get out!"

"I do not want your money, *Herr Direktor*," I said quietly. "All I wish to take from you is this." I picked up the score of Hans Rott's symphony.

"The symphony? But why?"

"So that I may return it to its rightful keeper, along with – as I promised him – this string quartet. In that way, *you* may retain the friendship of *Herr Doktor* Löhr and perhaps end these alleged nocturnal serenades." Not waiting for him to respond, I retrieved the string quartet.

Much to his credit, Gustav Mahler looked shamefaced. He even offered me a smile of resignation. "*Sehr gut*, Herr Holmes. I believe, after all, that you are right." He took a ragged breath and then said cheerfully, "Please return these scores to my dear Fritz. Give him my thanks and my apologies, along with my best wishes."

"I shall, indeed, *Herr Direktor*. Might I make one more suggestion?"

"*Ja?*" he responded warily.

"I have a friend named Sigmund Freud, an analyst who is quite knowledgeable on the subject of how guilt influences the mind's internal workings. Freud was extremely helpful to me on an occasion in the past. If ever you have need of him, I feel sure that he would do as much for you." [22]

The *Direktor* seemed put out by this proposal. "Should the need arise," he replied stiffly, "I shall consider it. *Danke*, Herr Holmes. *Guten Abend!*"

In the corridor, I was greeted with a radiant smile by Mahler's fiancée, who had obviously been listening outside the door. She was indeed lovely, Watson – albeit in the ponderous, Valkyrian fashion common to Teutonic beauties – much as our old friend the Duchess of Devonshire must have looked in the bygone days of her youth.

"*Guten Abend*, Herr Holmes. I am Alma Schindler, soon to be known as Alma Schindler Mahler. It is a great pleasure to make your acquaintance."

"Good evening, *Fraulein* Schindler. I had not expected to be recognised."

"*Ach, jawhol, mein Freund!* It is my destiny in life to be a muse to genius, and you have a *prominent* place upon my list of geniuses. Just now,

I found listening to the quarrel of *two* geniuses extremely stimulating! Do not forget me, *Meister* Sherlock Holmes. One day in the future, you and I shall meet again." She held out her hand to me, and I dutifully raised it to my lips.

"*Danke, gnädige Fraulein,* but I must take the liberty of doubting it. Until that day arrives, permit me to wish you and Herr Mahler *every* happiness on your forthcoming marriage." I bowed to the young lady, Watson, and departed the Hopofer with perhaps unseemly haste.

Sherlock Holmes laughed softly, lifting a hand to refuse my nod at the decanter. Instead, he settled back into his armchair to re-light his old briar.

"Quite a saga, Holmes!" I marvelled. "And I take it that you never saw either of the Mahlers afterwards?"

"We never met again. Several times in future years, I did see Mahler on the podium. It was less than four months later that I attended the première of his Third Symphony in Krefeld, its first complete performance. In 1907, I was privileged to attend the *Direktor's* valedictory concert with the Vienna Philharmonic, at which his *Second* was performed. On both occasions – and when I heard the *Fifth* in Antwerp – it was immediately evident how much Mahler's association with Hans Rott had (shall we say) *influenced* his own compositions. The great brass chorales, the cheerful ländlers in his scherzos – both might easily have been taken from his dead precursor's symphony. There were moments when I thought I recognised actual quotations from Rott's work."

"What you're saying is that the blackguard stole from Rott!"

"No, I do not accuse the man of outright plagiarism. Perhaps he intended, in those borrowings, to pay a tribute to his friend. Perhaps the two of them *were* stylistically (as my client poetically expressed it) 'fruit from the same tree'. In any event, no one who heard the *Eighth Symphony* in Munich – as I did – could doubt that Mahler's genius far transcended any debt he owed to Rott. Nevertheless, it was a debt the great composer never publicly acknowledged, and to my mind his legacy is the poorer for it. Had Rott retained his sanity, who knows what heights he might one day have reached? While I am convinced that Gustav Mahler's music is destined eventually to triumph, it saddens me to think that Hans Rott's music may forever be unknown." [23]

It was late, and I was rather weary. Not without discomfort, I hauled my aging body upright and pointed in the direction of my bed.

"I'll say goodnight, Holmes. Are you coming? Priscilla has prepared your room."

"No, old friend, I shall sit and smoke a while. A few matters still require consideration before my departure for America."

By now too accustomed to his ways to comment, I only grunted and limped towards the door. Before I reached it, the sound of my friend's voice halted me.

"There is one thing, Watson, that I have not told you."

"Yes?" I sighed reluctantly, propping on the sideboard as I turned to face him.

"On my last night in Vienna, I was standing at the open window of my hotel room, taking in a breath of air. It was long after midnight. Suddenly, I, too, Doctor, heard the sound of violin music coming from the street below."

Holmes seemed to expect a more theatrical reaction than I offered him. "No doubt some street musician," I said brusquely, "as you told Herr Mahler."

He shook his head. "I did not think so at the time, for I saw no one there. Though this was not the discordant, agitated music Mahler had described, it did sound hauntingly familiar. A theme of melancholy consolation, seeming even to contain a note of gratitude. Reflecting back upon my reading of the score, it came to me that I was hearing the *second* movement of Hans Rott's string quartet. But the music faded into silence before I could be sure."

"Pure twaddle, Holmes!" I snorted. "What is the maxim you have always followed? '*No ghosts need apply.*'"

"Quite so, Watson," my friend chuckled, saluting his maxim with his pipe. "Even I, it would appear, may occasionally be subject to the power of suggestion!"

## NOTES

1 –  A reference, of course, to "His Last Bow". For the initiation of Holmes and Watson's campaign against the German Empire in 1888, see "Sherlock Holmes and the Case of the Dying Emperor", Part 1 of my forthcoming collection *Sherlock Holmes and the Crowned Heads of Europe*, and currently available from MX Publishing as an e-book: *https://www.amazon.com/Sherlock-Holmes-Emperor-Crowned-Europe-ebook/dp/B07LCMVKDD*.

2 –  Watson told of his time in America during 1884-1886, and of his tragic first marriage, in "A Ghost from Christmas Past". The story was published in *The MX Book of New Sherlock Holmes Stories – Part VII: Eliminate the Impossible*, edited by David Marcum (London: MX Publishing, 2017), pp. 130-152. It later appeared, paired with an interpretive painting by artist Nune Asatryan, in *The Art of Sherlock Holmes: West Palm Beach Edition*, curated by Phil Growick (London: MX Publishing, 2019), pp. 196-211.

3 –  Thomas Beecham (1879-1961), who was later knighted, conducted this concert on December 3, 1907. It was the second performance in Britain of the Mahler *Fourth*, but the first (1905, under Henry Wood) had been no more successful. See *Henry-Louis de La Grange, Gustav Mahler, Volume 3, Vienna: Triumph and Disillusion (1904-1907)*, (Oxford: Oxford University Press, 1999), pp. 783-785. This monumental, four-volume biography is the definitive source on Gustav Mahler's life, although the author's revision of its 1973 first volume remains unpublished at this writing.

4 –  *Dictionary.com* dates this American slang abbreviation of "fanatic" as originating ca. 1885-1890.

5 –  Specifically, the apparent suicide of Crown Prince Rudolf in 1889, and the assassination of the Empress Elisabeth nine years later. Holmes's investigations of these events were chronicled in Watson's second Crowned Heads story, "The Adventure of the Inconvenient Heir-Apparent."

6 –  Not Mary Morstan, of course, in 1902. Watson's meeting with his third wife, Priscilla Prescott, was later recorded in "The Adventure of the Disgraced Captain".

7 –  This question might be colloquially translated as, *"What's up, my dear Justi?"*

8 –  Richard, not Johann, Strauss. Mahler had conducted his opera *Feuersnot* successfully on February 15th. For more on it and Josef Forster's ill-fated *Der dot Mon*, see *La Grange's Gustav Mahler: Volume 2, Vienna: The Years*

*of Challenge* (1897-1904), (Oxford: Oxford University Press, 1995), pp. 484-487.

9 – Wilhelm Jahn (1835-1900) was Mahler's predecessor as director of the Vienna Opera (1880-1897). Hans Richter (1843-1916) conducted the Vienna Philharmonic from 1875 to 1882, and again from 1883 to 1898, when Mahler succeeded him. Richter will be mentioned again later in this story.

10 – Presumably, Holmes (who entered Cambridge in the fall of 1874) is referring to Joseph Seemüller (1855-1920), who received his doctorate in 1877 from the University of Vienna. (His single term at Cambridge was not recorded in the sources I consulted.) In 1890, Seemüller became Professor of Old German Studies at the University of Innsbruck, and in 1905 he succeeded his dissertation supervisor as Professor of German Languages and Literature at Vienna:
*https://de.wikipedia.org/wiki/Joseph_Seem%C3%BCller*

Seemüller was also a close friend and supporter of Hans Rott. The two had spent a quiet vacation in the country shortly before Rott's breakdown in October 1880. Seemüller continued to visit his friend in the asylum, and to pay part of his expenses there, until Rott's death in 1884.

11 – On August 1, 1858, Hans Rott was born to an eighteen-year-old actress, Maria Rosalia Lutz. His father (aged fifty-one and married) was Carl Mathias Roth (Rott), then a famous comedy actor at the Theater an der Wien. Following his second wife's death, Roth married Rosalia in 1862. Meanwhile, she had given birth to Karl, the son of Archduke Wilhelm Franz. Roth legitimized both boys after the marriage, but their mother died at the early age of thirty-three. In 1874, Roth was forced to retire after a stage accident. His death two years later left eighteen-year-old Hans, by then at the Vienna Conservatory, orphaned and impoverished.

12 – Mahler's description of the young Hans Rott is quite similar to one recorded by Dr. Eva Gesine Baur in her article listed in the bibliography.

13 – Hugo Wolf (1860-1903), most famous as a composer of lieder, will figure in this story. While at the Conservatory, he shared a room with Mahler and Rudolf Krzyzanowski (1859-1911) until the three of them were thrown out for singing Wagner arias. Rudolf later conducted in Hamburg (where he assisted Mahler) and in Weimar. His brother Heinrich (1855-1933), a writer, claimed in his memoirs that "*there was no real friendship between Rott and Mahler*". Friedrich Löhr (1859-1924) also appears later in the story.

14 – There are several versions of this incident. From Rott's perspective, see Hawk and Leibnitz as cited in the bibliography. Both La Grange (*Mahler,*

Volume 1, Garden City, NY: Doubleday & Company, Inc., 1973, p. 49) and Alma Mahler (*Gustav Mahler: Memories and Letters*, New York: Viking Press, 1946, p. 107) record Mahler's mother's sympathy for her son's defeated rival.

15 – Holmes and Watson's initial meeting with Dr. Sigmund Freud is, of course, the subject of Nicholas Meyer's novel-length pastiche *The Seven-Per-Cent Solution* (1974). While other Sherlockian scholars dispute the authenticity of parts of this account (specifically, its depiction of Professor Moriarty as young Holmes's benign tutor, later unjustly vilified by the cocaine-deranged detective), we may at least accept that the novel established that Sherlock Holmes knew the renowned psychiatrist, who may have weaned him from the drug to which Freud himself had been addicted. Indeed, Freud's appearance in the present case offers additional verification of those facts.

16 – Hans Rott's relationship with these and other doctors is described by Hans-Roland Stegemeyer in his article cited in the bibliography below.

17 – Alma Mahler tells this tale (*Gustav Mahler*, pp. 8-9), but it is corroborated by other sources.

18 – Holmes's account of Hugo Wolf's last days accords with the one in the biography *Hugo Wolf*, by Ernest Newman (London: Methuen & Co., 1907), pp. 147-149. I found this source, through the courtesy of the Internet Archive, at:
*https://archive.org/details/hugowolf00newmuoft/*.

La Grange (Mahler, I, pp. 72-73) tells the story of Wolf and Mahler's student quarrel over which of them would write a libretto to the old German story Rübezahl. Ironically, although the feud damaged their friendship, neither produced a libretto. In September 1897, another quarrel between them caused Mahler to abandon his plan to produce Wolf's opera *Der Corregidor*. Wolf, already in the tertiary stage of syphilis, slipped over the edge into insanity. See La Grange, Mahler, I, 457-458; and II, 48-49 and 69-72.

19 – Fortunately, Dr. Maja Löhr (1888-1964) did far more than Sherlock Holmes to help Hans Rott. After her father's death in 1924, she began compiling Rott's surviving notes, letters, and scores, along with letters from his correspondents. In 1949, she completed the first biography of the composer. Although never published, it was included in Dr. Uwe Harten's more extensive biography published (in German) in 2000:
*https://verlag.oeaw.ac.at/mcgi/shop/produkt2.cgi?page=product&info=19 37*

In 1950, Maja Löhr gave most of Rott's papers to the Music Collection of the Austrian National Library. Its director, Leopold Nowak, created a catalog of Rott's surviving works.

20 – *Tod* is the German word for "death".

21 – See La Grange, II, p. 271. It quotes Mahler's letter to his friend Natalie Bauer-Lechner, which expresses most of his opinions about Rott referenced in Holmes's account. In 1900, Mahler took the score of Rott's symphony with him to his summer home in Maiernigg, where he did most of his composing.

22 – In 1910, after learning of his wife's affair with the architect Walter Gropius, Mahler did consult Dr. Freud and was briefly psychoanalyzed. See La Grange's fourth volume, *Gustav Mahler: A New Life Cut Short (1907-1911)*, (Oxford: Oxford University Press, 2008), pp. 884-899, 911-924.

23 – Hans Rott's *Symphony in E major*, in an edition prepared by Paul Banks, was finally performed by the Cincinnati Philharmonia (a student orchestra led by Gerhard Samuel) in 1989. That performance was recorded on the Hyperion label (CDA66366), and there have other good recordings since. Happily, Rott's symphony created a long-delayed sensation. His *String Quartet in C minor* was stirringly performed in 2008 by the Israel String Quartet. The CD was produced by Quintone Records (Q10002).

## A Bibliographical Addendum

By far the best source of information on Hans Rott's life and music is the website maintained by the Inter-national Hans Rott Society (IHRG) at:
*http://www.hans-rott.org/*.

Along with biographical material, the site provides a catalog of Rott's compositions and recordings of them. I am grateful to Dr. Uwe Harten and Martin Brilla, respectively president and secretary of the society, for sending me an article from their journal *Die Quarte* (cited below) on Hans Rott's last years in the asylum. Other articles from the IHRG and other online sources I consulted are:

> Dr. Eva Gesine Baur. "A Strange Man Worthy of Note: Hans Rott (1858-1884)"
> *http://hansjoerg-albrecht.com/entdeckung-hans-rott/?lang=en*

> Gustav-Mahler.eu.
> *https://gustav-mahler.eu/index.php?id=658:rott-hans-1858-1884*

241

Harten, Uwe. Hans Rott (1858-1884). *Biographie, Briefe, Aufzeichnungen und Dokumente aus dem Nachlaß von Maja Loehr (1888-1964). Wein: Verlag der Österreichischen Akademie der Wissenschaften*, 2000. [Sadly, I lacked the proficiency in German to make full use of this resource.]

Steven Eric Hawk. "Hans Rott's *Symphony No. 1 in E Major*: A Comparative Study and Conductor's Preparation Guide." Ph.D. Dissertation, University of Georgia, 2015 *https://getd.libs.uga.edu/pdfs/hawk_steven_e_201512_dma.pdf*

Tess James. "Hans Rott (1858-1884) – The Missing Link Between Bruckner and Mahler." *MTO: The Journal of the Society for Music Theory*. Vol. 5, No. 1 (January, 1999) *http://www.mtosmt.org/issues/mto.99.5.1/mto.99.5.1.james.pdf*

Jens F. Laurson. "Madness, Thievery, and a Train Full of Dynamite: The Story of Hans Rott, the Greatest Symphonist Who Never Was." *Listen Music and Culture*, 2019. *http://www.listenmusicculture.com/mastery/madness-thievery*

Dr. Thomas Leibnitz, librarian at the Music Collections of the Austrian National Library, Vienna. "Do not laugh, gentleman. . . . On the first performance of the *'Pastoral Prelude for Orchestra'* by Hans Rott" (2000) *http://www.hans-rott.de/leibnite.htm*

Hans-Roland Stegemeyer. "Hans Rott as a Patient of 19th Century Psychiatric Care in Vienna." *Die Quarte*, Vol. I+II. Vienna: International Hans Rott Society, 2008.

Walter Weidringer. ". . . An Intensive Talent. . . ." *Klangfocus*. Translation of article published in *Klang:punkte (Zeitschrift des Musikverlags Doblinger)*, No. 16, Spring 2003, pp. 3-5. *http://www.hans-rott.de/talente.pdf*

# The Cunning Man
## by Kelvin I. Jones

As Sherlock Holmes dipped his cut-throat razor into the water and lathered his cheeks, a feeling of immense weariness began to overwhelm him. And then he thought of Charles Whitaker.

It had come as something of a relief when the invitation had arrived from his old friend to stay with him for a short while. It would be a respite, a chance to recharge his batteries.

Later that morning, Mrs. Hudson entered, carrying a small breakfast tray, bedecked with silver dishes. A rich aroma of fried bacon tantalised his nostrils. She smiled warmly at him. "Sleep well?"

"Most comfortably, thank you, Mrs. Hudson," he replied. She had aged considerably over the years, but was still as sprightly as ever.

"I hope bacon and eggs are to your liking."

Not wishing to break with tradition, he smiled back at her.

"I'm sure they will do very well."

He had recognised the expensive cream envelope that she had brought him on a silver dish at once, for it bore the familiar ornate watermark of his old friend Charles Whitaker. He opened it.

*Dear Holmes,* (it ran)

> *I heard of Watson's marriage. Bill Hunter tells me you are still in the smoke. Why do you not quit the city for heaven's sake? For my sins, alas, I am still here in Cambridge, earning my usual pittance as a lowly professor of medieval studies – though nowadays, in a strictly part-time capacity. However, to come to the point: Now I'm in recess, and I thought you might care to take the great trek east to see me at my temporary Norfolk residence. That is, if you have no real objection to my tiresome company.*
>
> *Are you aware of the importance of the Thorsford Hill Figure, by any chance? It is one of those curious enigmas which I rather fancy turning my hand to solving. You are probably aware of its reputed links with Boudicca and the Iceni. Perhaps you will let me know and wire me if you could bear the company of an old curmudgeon.*

*Yours ever,*

*Whitaker*

Holmes finished his breakfast, refolded the letter, then smiled. Charles Whitaker: Old undergraduate ally, antiquarian, Cambridge don, clergyman, and author of *British Hill Figures*. He hadn't seen Whitaker for a year – a little matter that had occurred at Cambridge. His great domed head and piercing blue eyes often distinguished him from his contemporaries, as did the striking originality of his work. A pioneer in Anglo-Saxon and early medieval studies, his efforts included such titles as *The Maes Howe Inscriptions*, *Early Christian Crosses*, and *The Mythological Origins of the Weland Legend*. However, his most important work of recent years, *British Hill Figures*, was now regarded as the standard reference work.

Holmes pushed aside his plate and reached for his old pipe. Plugging the bowl with a fresh, aromatic supply of shag, he passed a lighted match across the rim and sat back, clouds of dense tobacco smoke spiralling above his head. The Thorsford Hill figure. Where had he heard mention of that before? A feeling of annoyance welled up in him as he tried to recall. And as for the Iceni . . . The Boudiccan revolt was a centrepiece of every child's history lessons, yet so far Boudicca had not been satisfactorily linked with any site in Norfolk. There was the Iron Age fort at Warham, near Wells, of course, and the post-Boudiccan town at Caistor built by the Romans to dominate the former Iceni tribal territory. Yet to his knowledge, Norfolk boasted not a single Iron Age hill figure. He would send a wire to Whitaker and accept his invitation. His ebullient and dynamic personality would assist him in pulling himself out of the slough of despond which had enveloped his spirit.

He strode downstairs, leaving behind him a trail of tobacco smoke.

"Mrs. Hudson, I shall be going away for a few days. Have you seen my *Bradshaw*?"

Heaving his large, battered suitcase into an empty compartment, Holmes collapsed onto the faded velour seat and consoled himself by mopping his brow with a huge, spotted blue-and-red handkerchief. The train lurched him forwards, his knee banging against the seat opposite, his suitcase sliding to the floor. Through the open window, the stale, soot-smelling effluence of the locomotive wafted in, making him cough. He stood up and shut the window, then spread-eagled himself on the seat. Reaching for his old clay pipe, he primed it with a plug of dark tobacco and within a minute had filled the small compartment with the equivalent of a London fog.

Occasionally in the newspapers, he would hear of Whitaker's exploits. There had been the case of the fraudulent medium, Madame Sophia, who had grown wealthy at the expense of numerous *nouveaux riche* families in Norwich; the episode of the Dunwich poltergeist, which was only resolved by the interment of certain bones which had fallen from the cliff; and, not least the terrifying case of the Cromer Black Shuck which had dominated the headlines in *The Anglian Post* for a week in the long, hot summer of 1902. Of course, Whitaker's expertise was not limited to the realm of the invisible. Although few of the lay public knew it, he was an expert in the realm of osteo-archaeology, and had contributed widely to the literature of the subject in various academic journals. He had also been consulted by Scotland Yard in at least three cases involving the exhumation of corpses from London cemeteries, and on one occasion was called upon to give evidence in court regarding the demise of Lady Eveline Gambon. In those days, of course, he had been unknown to the general public, and this facet of the case had passed unnoticed. However, it had been Holmes who had recommended him to the police.

Suddenly the compartment door was rolled open to reveal a tall, elegant woman wearing a broad-brimmed, purple hat. For a moment, she put down her case. Then, overcome by the acrid smell of the pungent tobacco smoke, decided to cut her losses and retreat, coughing and pulling the door shut, her face crumpled in disdain.

Holmes breathed a sigh of relief and peered out of the soot-lined window. Already the dingy grey suburbs had begun to bleed away. A diluted sun hung overhead, dappling the brown fields and scattered woodlands. At the far edge of the horizon, a flock of birds wheeled and turned in a frenzy of movement. He lay back against the compartment seat, again allowing himself to slip into a smoke induced reverie. The sunlight played on his face. An image of a beak-headed horse floated before his eyes, a face which seemed both animate and ancient. A shrill whistle pierced the rattling rhythm of the swaying locomotive as the train plunged into a tunnel and he was marooned in sudden darkness.

Later, Holmes stirred, only to find that he had slept on his arm, inducing a severe jabbing pain in his left elbow. He sat up, emitting a cry. The train had stopped. He pulled back the compartment door and stared out. Norwich Station. Half-a-carriage down, he caught a glimpse of a solitary news vendor, standing on the platform. He pulled down the window and summoned him. It was *The Norwich Post*, bearing the bold headline: *Sensational Murder of Norfolk Wizard*. He returned to his compartment and settled down in the middle seat, his pipe alight, scouring the lead story.

> *The funeral of a well-known Norfolk cunning man, who was discovered dead in strange circumstances last Tuesday, took place today at Thorsford. William MacBride, a former groom at Munnington Hall, and erstwhile labourer, was found dead in his cottage four days ago, but as yet, no clue has been offered as to the cause of his death. The ancient thatched cottage which lies on the outskirts of Thorsford village had been the home of the deceased for over twenty years.*
>
> *MacBride was well known in North Norfolk for his powers as a wart charmer and wizard, and was frequently visited by folk from Norwich for the purpose of having their charms renewed. He had also gained an impressive reputation for the procuring of stolen goods and was thought to have made considerable sums of money from his dubious craft.*
>
> *MacBride earned some notoriety a year ago when he was indicted under the Vagrancy Act for fortune telling and was sentenced to a month's imprisonment in Norwich. As we reported in yesterday's edition of* The Post, *according to the police, MacBride had been battered to death, his skull having been shattered by some blunt object. However, no murder weapon has been discovered. Almost every piece of furniture and the personal effects in the downstairs room had been smashed, and one of the downstairs windows had also been broken.*
>
> *The most singular fact was that before him on the table, completely untouched and unbroken, were four items: A bottle of whisky, a loaf of bread, a jar of berries, and a copy of the Holy Book. Nothing appeared to have been stolen from the deceased's collection of belongings, and his book of spells and conjurations had survived intact. Chief Inspector Alan Gould of the Norwich Police has stated that he is no nearer a solution as to the cause of MacBride's death, but that his investigation will continue undaunted.*
>
> *The Reverend Lewis Trenchard led today's funeral service, which was attended by about fifteen people, in itself a testimony to the popularity of this eccentric Norfolk wizard. An inquest will be held in Norwich on Saturday.*

Holmes folded the newspaper and stared out of the carriage window, reflecting on what he had just read. Was it not preposterous that in the age of reason, common folk still had recourse to the services of a self-proclaimed "wizard"? But perhaps he was not entirely right. He recalled Whitaker's own investigation into fraudulent mediums and the elaborate hoaxes of the spiritualist movement. One medium in particular, a large, coarse Glaswegian woman by the name of Helen Fitzsimmons, had produced ectoplasm by the yard and even fooled a professor of linguistics in her lodgings in Cannon Street. It had taken the forensic skills of Whitaker and Holmes to expose her machinations, which included the ingestion of yards of muslin through her mouth. The Fitzsimmons affair had been widely reported and earned the medium fourteen days in jail. Such cases were not unusual, so he should not really be surprised to read of the existence of a so called "cunning man" in a rural backwater like Thorsford.

The train slowed, entered a deep cutting, and then gradually climbed onto a broad plateau, rimmed by tall poplars on one side and on the other the cliffs of the Norfolk coast. To his left the sun was already low on the horizon, casting deep shadows across the adjoining woodland. Ancient oaks and birch trees loomed here, as if gathered in mute conspiracy. Holmes had forgotten the primeval power of this landscape. As a child, his parents had taken him on holiday to Cromer, that jewel of seaside towns, and his father, a keen amateur paleontologist, had roamed the scarred cliffs between Sheringham and Cley, dragging his infant son behind him like some diminutive mascot. But in young Holmes's mind, the immensity of sea and sky had carved out a place in his imagination to which he often returned in adult years. Here in the east, the primal power of nature with its severe, snow-bound winters and icy winds, suggested a haunted landscape.

It wasn't just the history of the place which interested him. Down the centuries, Dark Age queens jostled with Viking invaders, but there was more to it than that. The sheer immensity of the sky and the land pinned one down, and cut one down to size, so that one paled to insignificance. Once, during a summer holiday in their undergraduate days, he had found himself with Whitaker, digging in a trench near Hunstanton at the site of an Anglo-Saxon burial. It had been near sunset and he was bent low, peering at the outlines of a skull, half-buried in the sand. Without warning, the great orb of the sun had dipped westwards beneath the horizon. A darkness had slipped into the trench, so sudden and profound that he had scrambled for his paraffin lamp, filled with an irrational but compelling unease. Although he had seen nothing, the moment had haunted him down

247

the years. What was there to explain? Nothing in particular. Merely the power and eeriness of the landscape itself.

The train shunted to a stop. He picked up his suitcase, adjusted his fore-and-aft cap in the carriage mirror, and then made his way out into the gangway. Through the darkness he could see the glowing gas lamps of the station platform. A figure waved to him. He smiled and waved back.

It was his old friend, Whitaker.

A few days prior to Holmes's arrival, Whitaker had just finished his morning shave and was about to visit the post office when Mrs. Annis, his housekeeper, popped her head around the living room door, only to announce that there was a visitor anxious to see him.

"Can't it wait?" he had replied rather testily.

"He seems to be in a distressed state, sir," Mrs. Annis had replied assertively, fixing him with an unblinking stare.

"Very well, then Mrs. Annis. Who is it, for heaven's sake?"

"George Robinson, the blacksmith."

"Show him in then. Oh, by the bye, would you pop down to the post office and get me a copy of *The Times*?"

"I'll have to see," came the non-committal reply. "Maybe later when I've finished baking."

George Robinson was a short, squat individual of middle years with straight, jet-black hair, and pugnacious features. He was dressed in a shabby corduroy jacket, a pair of stained brown trousers and, somewhat incongruously, a battered brown hat.

"You'll 'ave to forgive me, sir," he began, "visiting you at this short notice, but to be frank, sir, we're at the end of our tether." His thoughts spewing out in an avalanche of words, his sonorous Norfolk accent booming in the oak-lined room.

"Let's cut to the chase, Mr. Robinson. And there's really no need to shout. What exactly has happened?"

The blacksmith sat down in a straight back chair opposite Whitaker, his ungainly form hanging uncomfortably over the edge of the seat. Whitaker noted that he was perspiring profusely, a broad band of sweat darkening his shirt front.

"It's my wife, you see. She has this condition – a bone ache in her arms and legs. She's had it for years, but recently it's got much worse."

"Go on."

"Well, about six months ago a friend of hers suggested she visit the wizard."

"The what – ?"

"The cunning man. William MacBride."

"And what sort of man is he?" Whitaker asked, a smile hovering about his lips. He had heard of cunning folk before. In his opinion, most of them were frauds.

"There's a lot of people hereabouts who rely on him for their charms. Farmers say he can cure beasts of disease."

"And your wife visited MacBride?"

Robinson produced a large red handkerchief, wiped his glistening forehead, and then blew his nose on it.

"At first he told her it would be easy to cure her of the condition. He used to give her a little packet of white powder which she had to throw into the fire and say a few words he'd written down for her."

"And she got better?"

"At first – yes, she improved a good deal. He charged her two shillings a month. But then she got worse."

"So what happened? You went back to complain?"

"I told him it wasn't working and she should have her money back. But he told me not to interfere. He said she must finish the course or he could not vouch for the consequences of her actions."

"So she continued?"

He nodded.

"She started to visit him more often. Recently it's increased to once a week. As a result, we've run so short of money, I've had to take on extra work to pay his bills."

There was a silence. Whitaker played with his watch fob as the big man opposite him shifted uneasily from side to side.

"So what do you intend to do about this affair?" he asked.

"I was rather hoping that, as a man of the cloth, you might speak to him – put him right, in a manner of speaking."

"You believe, then, that your wife is under some sort of spell?"

"She thinks that if she doesn't finish the course of treatment, some terrible calamity will befall her."

"And do you also believe that?"

"I don't know what to believe. I'm that worried about her."

Whitaker stood up. "I can't promise you anything, Mr. Robinson, but I'm willing to speak to this MacBride. We'll see what he has to say about the matter. Does your wife know you've come to see me?"

Robinson shook his head. "I wouldn't want her to know."

"Then for now we shall keep this between ourselves."

The small thatched cottage where MacBride lived lay on the eastern edge of the village. Robinson led the way past a battered wicket gate into a small unkempt garden bordered by large laurel bushes. Over the diminutive doorway hung a rusting horseshoe. The front door, which was open, led them into a dark, musty hallway.

"Mr. MacBride?" Robinson called, but there was no answer. Whitaker stepped forward in front of Robinson, putting his finger to his lips, then opened the door to the dingy living room. A smoking peat fire burned fitfully in the grate, but this was one of the few signs of domestic normality in an otherwise chaotic interior. Whitaker made his way round the room. For many years he had utilised his friend Holmes's methods. Observation, analysis, and logical deduction were not simply words. They were all-important strategies.

Books and papers lay strewn across the floor. A tall pine dresser was covered with broken china, and a number of jars had spilled their contents on its shelves. Windows had been broken. In the centre of the room, spread-eagled on a chair, sat William MacBride, his dark eyes staring, his face pale and bloodless, his mouth open in the rictus of death. There was a terrible wound upon his temple.

"Quickly," Whitaker instructed the blacksmith. "Go down to the post office and ask them to telephone for the police," When Robinson had left, Whitaker looked about the room, making a mental note of its condition. There was a small safe on the wall above the fireplace which remained unopened. A cash box lay on the table, but this also appeared to be intact. There was also a half-consumed bottle of whisky, along with a loaf of bread, a jar of berries, and a tattered copy of The Bible, opened at *The Book of Revelations*. The latter's placing struck him as somewhat odd until he recalled that cunning men would often use the Holy Writ as a tool in their divinations.

He peered at MacBride's still corpse. There was a small metal box beneath his hand. He opened the lid and found inside an *Ephemerides*, two books on the science of the stars, and three plates of brass which, when combined, formed an orrery. Engraved on their surface were tables and diagrams of the planetary motions. In addition, there were several small cloth bags which, on further examination, were found to contain herbs and powders.

Whitaker closed the box and replaced it on the table. Then he made his way across the wrecked room into the hallway and out into the daylight. Bordering the cottage was a wide flowerbed, and he noticed that one of the adjacent downstairs windows was broken. He peered down at the muddy earth but could see no evidence of footprints. Neither was the front door forced. The circumstances puzzled him. It occurred to him that Robinson himself might not be altogether above suspicion. Whoever had dealt the blow on MacBride's forehead must have possessed a great deal of strength. Moreover, he had opportunity as well as motive.

250

A sudden sound came from the heart of the laurel bushes. He turned and glimpsed the outline of a magpie, intent on some terrible act of predation. Whitaker made his way down towards the wicket gate and waited for the arrival of the police. He felt easier here, away from the oppressive gloom of the cottage with its staring, white-faced corpse, and the black-and-white, winged omen of bad luck. He shivered.

Far above him, on Thorsford Hill, the sun slipped from behind a bank of dense cloud and illumined the dark outline of the ancient hill figure. For a fleeting moment, he imagined he could see it in its entirety: A rearing, dragon-like creature, its elongated head turned towards him, the eye fixed and unwavering. He felt a sudden chill and drew his greatcoat about him.

Sherlock Holmes stepped forward into the glare of the station gaslamp and extended a broad hand to greet his old colleague. Whitaker smiled and shook the offered hand vigorously. He thought that Holmes had aged since last he saw him. There were deep crows' feet around the piercing grey eyes.

"Good to see you again. It's been too long."

"Caius College at High Table, as I recall," Holmes boomed back above the noise of the departing locomotive. Momentarily they were engulfed in a cloud of acrid smoke.

They walked side by side towards the station yard, Whitaker casting sidelong glances in Holmes's direction. His old colleague looked thinner.

"I have a fly waiting. It's not far. Good journey?"

Holmes nodded. Whitaker heaved the suitcase into the back of the vehicle, Mrs. Annis' strong arms guiding it to its destination.

"Holmes, this is my housekeeper, Sophia Annis. She shall be driving us. She has a way with horses."

"Pleased to meet you, sir. It'll not take long, sir. There's a cold supper waiting at the rectory."

As the fly rattled along the unmade road, Whitaker pulled the tartan rug across their legs and offered his friend a tot of brandy from his hip flask.

"That is most welcome," said Holmes. "Have you have read this edition of *The Norwich Evening Post*?"

"I haven't set eyes on it yet – just today's *Times*. I imagine you're referring to William MacBride's funeral?"

"I confess that I knew nothing of it before today."

Whitaker took the hip flask and replaced it in his great-coat pocket. "It was a most bizarre affair. I had the misfortune to discover the body."

"Really. And what did you glean from the scene of crime?"

"Very little, I'm afraid. There was no murder weapon."

Whitaker described the circumstances of his visit to MacBride's cottage as the fly rattled between two lines of giant poplars, the freshly risen moon casting shadows on the glistening road. At last the street lamps of Thorsford village came into view and they turned up a narrow lane, past the church, heading in the direction of the rectory gates, where Whitaker had taken temporary lodgings.

"What about motive?" Holmes enquired. "From what you've told me, he was well known in the area."

"Even in Norwich. Yes, his notoriety was widespread."

"Enemies?"

"I have no doubt of that. I can't imagine that George Robinson was the only malcontent."

"You've spoken to the police?"

"I made a statement, of course. Not that it was of much use to them. Chief Inspector Gould of the Norwich Police is heading the investigation."

"Any leads?"

"None so far. There's a coroner's court on Tuesday. I've been asked to attend. To be honest, I'd not expected to be plunged into a maelstrom of murder and mayhem while visiting down here."

"Hard lines. I shall do my best to assist you then. My, this is rather grand, isn't it?"

The fly trundled to a stop and they climbed out, Holmes staring with astonishment at the imposing frontage of the rectory entrance.

Later, after brandy and cigars, the two men retired to the comfort of the study. Whitaker lounged before a blazing fire as Holmes, pipe alight, peered at the collection of ecclesiastical volumes on the dusty shelves.

"They belonged to the former tenant, the late Ebenezer Oakenfull," explained Whitaker. "I obtained permission to stay for a while, as it was untenanted after his death. His reading was somewhat eclectic. Some of these titles suggest – "

" – That he was more preoccupied with folklore and superstition than theology or his ecclesiastical duties?" asked Holmes.

"Yes, I would agree wholeheartedly. There are several boxes of correspondence which I intend to go through when I get time to do it. He appears to have been conducting extensive research into the pagan history of the region. I suspect that he had intended to write a book on the subject."

Whitaker puffed at his cigar.

"Is there much to know about the subject then?" Holmes asked.

"I gather so. It seems there is some kind of continuity from Dark Age practices through to the witchcraft scares of the seventeenth century – "

"Ah, yes. The imposter, Matthew Hopkins."

"Yes indeed, our old friend the 'Witchfinder General' once made an appearance in these parts. A woman was burned at King's Lynn for causing her husband's death. An uncommon occurrence in those days, hanging being the preferred method of execution."

"And is there a link with the present? Have such practices survived the age of reason?"

Whitaker laughed and replenished their glasses.

By the following Monday, it had rained heavily, and the snows began to clear, rivers of slush pouring down the riverbank and spilling over into the eastern section of the churchyard. That afternoon the telephone rang and Chief Inspector Gould reminded Whitaker that he was required to give evidence at the coroner's court in Norwich. He explained that the main coach road was open and asked if he would be requiring transport. Whitaker politely declined, declaring that he had his own transport and would arrive in good time before the commencement of the proceedings.

After what seemed an interminable journey by fly through slush-bound roads, Holmes and Whitaker eventually arrived at their destination in Norwich, the old knap-flinted Guildhall in the centre of the city. They entered through the southwest doorway with its ornate jambs and foliaged spandrels to find themselves standing in a large room with fine stained glass windows and linenfold panelling and seats sporting curious beasts and grotesques.

The court was packed with an assortment of agricultural labouring men, tradesmen, and a scattering of professional types in dark suits and heavy ulsters. First in the stand was Chief Inspector Gould. A short, stocky man with a florid face and mutton-chop whiskers, he peered at his notebook through a pair of narrow-rimmed spectacles, coughed nervously, and then uttered his findings in a low, booming voice. Not much more could be deduced from his account, apart from the details which had already appeared in *The Norwich Evening Post*.

Next to the stand was the police surgeon, a tall, athletic young man with dark hair whose evidence was rendered somewhat comic by virtue of a slight lisp. However, his testimony was not without interest. The contents of the deceased's stomach revealed that immediately prior to his death, he had consumed a large meal and copious amounts of alcohol. The wound to his temple had caused an epidural bleed and subsequent brain damage. The fracture itself was semi-circular in shape and may have resulted from a blow from a piece of pipe, a wooden stake, or similar object. There was also a small subdural bleed at the back of the skull where the deceased had recoiled against the back of his chair, indicating that a person of considerable strength had administered the fatal blow. There was little trace evidence of any significance at the scene of the crime, save for a considerable number of long hairs which had attached themselves to the victim's jacket. However, these appeared to be of an animal, and not human origin.

Next it was the turn of Ronald Perceval Bloxham, the squire of Munnington Hall. A thin, ascetic-looking individual dressed in immaculate frock coat and scarlet waistcoat, he spoke in a low, scarcely audible voice, his phrases clipped and expressionless. It transpired that MacBride had worked for Bloxham on a part-time basis as a groom and handyman. On the day before his death was discovered, he had spent the afternoon trimming hedges on the borders of the estate. He had been dismissed at five p.m. by the head gardener for being drunk at work, but was seen by Bloxham at 5:30 p.m. heading down a narrow footpath in the direction of The Green Man Public House.

Next to give evidence was Henry Stanmore, landlord of The Green Man. He told the court that MacBride had sat sullenly at the bar from about six p.m. until closing time. He seemed unwilling to leave the premises and was much preoccupied, spending much of the evening making notes in a small, spiral-bound notebook.

Whitaker gave his evidence. He was questioned closely about the condition of the cottage and its contents which he observed on his arrival at the scene of the crime. He explained the reason for his visit to MacBride, whom he described as a man of "dubious reputation", and gave the coroner background information regarding the nature of Mr. Robinson's dilemma. The coroner questioned him closely at this point and Whitaker was able to reveal MacBride's function as a local cunning man. He commented on the large variety of abstruse astrological volumes in the deceased's collection, indicating that although MacBride was a common labourer, he appeared to be highly literate, and was evidently self-taught. He also revealed that he'd had an opportunity to glance at some of MacBride's correspondence, which demonstrated the breadth and social variety of his clientele. Indeed, he had been surprised at some of the names in MacBride's notebooks, indicating that some clients were members of the affluent classes.

At this point in the proceedings, the coroner raised his eyebrows, then coughed, but made no comment. Next to give evidence was Mrs. Ada Robinson. A thin, pale-faced woman with a hooked nose and lined features, she clung to the stand, her arthritic hands the colour of ivory. In a faltering, wheezy voice, she reluctantly gave her testimony.

"You are Ada Robinson, the wife of George Robinson?"

"I am."

"And what was your relationship with the deceased?"

"I asked him for help. I had been suffering a great deal of pain."

"So you went to MacBride for help?"

"That's correct."

"And how exactly did he help you, Mrs. Robinson?"

There was a pause as she gazed helplessly round the courtroom. The coroner repeated his question to her.

"He gave me some bags of salts which I was told to hang round my neck."

"And you were required to do this for how long?"

"For about four months, I should say."

"And I understand that your husband, Mr. George Robinson, was not entirely happy with this?"

"It was costing us a lot of money. No, he wasn't happy."

"And I understand that your husband consulted Mr. Whitaker in the hope that he might intervene?"

"George said MacBride ought to give us the money back because my condition wasn't improving."

"And how did he feel about Mr. MacBride? Was he angry about this?"

"Not angry, no. Just concerned about me."

"I see. Thank you, Mrs. Robinson. You may stand down."

The last to give evidence was George Robinson. Dressed in a baggy corduroy suit and looking distinctly apprehensive, Robinson gave his evidence in a faltering Norfolk drawl. He denied harbouring any feelings of animosity towards the deceased. Yes, he regarded MacBride as a cheat and an imposter, but he wished him no harm. At this point, Robinson began to flush and shift nervously from foot to foot. The coroner thanked him for his contribution and asked him to stand down.

In summing up the evidence, the coroner opined that William MacBride had been unlawfully killed by a person or persons unknown. In conclusion, he thanked the police surgeon, Whitaker, and Chief Inspector Gould for their detailed observations. The session having concluded, Holmes and Whitaker emerged into the cold air of a bright October morning and made their way back to Thorsford through slush-lined roads.

Holmes had never seen Munnington Hall before. He had read of its splendours, of course, but seeing it for the first time on a cold, cloudless October day, the soft autumn sun burnishing its limestone and brick facade, was an altogether surprising experience.

The hall lay at the end of a long, beech-lined driveway about a quarter-mile in length. On either side of the drive, sheep and cattle grazed on lush grass, and there was an air of undisturbed tranquility about the estate. Eventually the fly drew level with the main house, an impressive mansion built in the Dutch seventeenth-century style, two-and-a-half stories high with mullioned gables and elaborate pediments. Whitaker bade Mrs. Annis farewell and they were left alone, staring up at the great doorway with its detached, unfluted columns and heraldry.

Holmes pulled the bell pull and within a few minutes the door swung open. Facing them was a tall, aged butler dressed in an immaculate frock coat. Sallow skinned and entirely bald, he looked at them closely, hovering in the doorway like some ancient bird of prey.

"Whom may I say is calling?"

"Mr. Charles Whitaker and Mr. Sherlock Holmes."

He bowed slightly, then turned, muttering, "This way please."

He led the way down a dark corridor, lined with eighteenth-century paintings whose subjects, almost without exception, showed a series of studies of racehorses. They passed through a door on the left and entered a magnificent drawing room, fitted with Jacobean oak panels and a grand plaster ceiling. At the far end, dressed in a sober grey morning suit, stood Ronald Bloxham. At his side, clad in a long, diaphanous floral gauze dress, was a tall woman with long, lustrous blond hair. Her face was striking and reminded Holmes of Rossetti's painting of his wife. The eyes were large and dark, the nose Roman in shape, and the lips wide and sensuous. Deep lines were etched about the eyes and mouth, suggesting some prolonged period of worry or unhappiness. Bloxham stepped forward, greeting them in a voice which was faint and sepulchral.

"Gentlemen, we are so glad you could come. This is my wife, Augusta."

Mrs. Bloxham extended a thin hand.

"I am very pleased to meet you at last. Ronald tells me you are interested in our hill figure, Mr. Whitaker."

"Yes. I have invited Mr. Holmes, an old friend of mine from our university days to examine it."

The meal was as sumptuous as the surroundings. Afterwards, over brandy, the four of them sat in the drawing room before a blazing fire as Bloxham informed his guests about his passion for equestrian pursuits.

"I have always had a love for that noble beast," he explained, mellow with food and drink. "Horses are sacred animals. The ancients knew it. Yet in our own age we have treated them as no better than mere machines or beasts of burden. Call me extreme if you will, but I believe that the bond between man and horse is a purer and more noble thing than that between man and woman."

Holmes looked across at Augusta Bloxham. She looked slightly ill at ease.

"Did you know, Mr. Holmes, that the Celts who buried their warriors alongside these noble beasts believed that they would enter paradise together?"

"I have read of such burials."

"They understood more than we do."

"This man MacBride – I understand he acted as a groom for you?"

"In a part-time capacity, yes. MacBride may have been something of a rake, but he had a remarkable affinity with horses. He was a horse whisperer, you know. He had that ability to read their thoughts. It was a rare talent."

"To say nothing of his psychic abilities," interposed Mrs. Bloxham.

"Yes," agreed Bloxham. "He was also a talented medium,"

"I wasn't aware of it."

"Oh yes, he was of great assistance to us, especially after Leonard, our eldest, died in the war."

"I'm sorry to hear of your loss," Holmes observed. "You have my sympathy."

"Yes, MacBride was able to get through to the other side on a number of occasions. We were much comforted by that. MacBride had a strong spiritual presence. The fact that he often abused his powers is only regrettable. Now that he has passed on, we still maintain our séance circle, but it is not quite the same."

"You have a circle here in Thorsford?"

"At our neighbour's place – Eveline Da Costa's. We meet each Sunday evening at Glamis House. You would be most welcome to join us."

But Holmes politely declined the offer. They left Munnington Hall shortly after eleven o'clock, glad of the waiting fly and Mrs. Annis' presence. They drove back down the long driveway, the sky above them illuminated only by a weak, fogged moon. Mrs. Annis chatted amiably as, far off towards the east, low rumbles of approaching thunder began to break the silence of the still, cold night.

In Norwich the next morning, Holmes adjusted his scarf and made his way through the ticket barrier, past busy city commuters and out into the sunshine on Riverside Road. Here and there in the cobbled streets tradesmen and bowler-hatted clerks jostled for space en route to the courts, then passed him, their faces set and earnest, intent on the day ahead. As he turned into Tombland and passed the four-gabled house with its strange figures of Samson and Hercules, a pale-faced vagrant lurched towards him demanding money, but he fended him off with an outstretched hand and the thin, haggard figure melted into the shadow of an adjacent alley way.

The city had a gritty, murky feel to it. Grimed by coal smoke, and hazy with remnants of the early morning mist, the streets were lined with horse manure, decaying leaves, and litter. In the midst of this murk, the Erpingham Gate loomed above him, flanked by polygonal buttresses, decorated with heraldry and standing figures under leaf canopies. The easterly wind which had dogged him all the way from the railway station and along Friths Lane was absent here, blocked by the long gothic cloisters where he now strolled, his solitary footfalls sounding like pistol shots in the cold, crisp air. Past the rounded Romanesque east end of the cathedral, he took a short cut over the turf, making his way via a short path to the Bishop's Palace. Here he paused and reached for the brass bell pull, conscious of the stillness of the hour and the timelessness of the ancient building. Within, footsteps sounded on an uncarpeted staircase. The door opened, revealing a tall, bespectacled young curate with a hooked nose who stared at him inquisitively.

"Mr. Sherlock Holmes, to see the Bishop," he informed the owl-faced sentinel.

The young door attendant smiled weakly.

"I am expected," Holmes added impatiently.

"If you would like to sit in the anteroom, I shall inform the Bishop of your arrival."

Holmes waited in the oak-panelled room, eyeing the marble bust of Bishop Reynold as his feet began to thaw. There was a minute's delay, and then a door opened on the floor above and he heard heavy footfalls on the bare oak treads.

Bishop Bill Hunter strode towards Holmes, his corpulent torso tight beneath his purple surplice, his broad ruddy face as boyish as ever.

"Mr. Holmes!" he exclaimed. "Good to see you. I got your wire. Come up to my rooms and we'll talk."

Holmes followed Bishop Hunter's ample form up the wide oak staircase. He hadn't changed much since their last encounter a year back in the case of Jeakes' Summoning. A few more grey hairs, perhaps, a few additional pounds added to his already spreading figure, but the ebullient, generous personality remained unaltered. If ever a man beamed beneficence, it was Bishop Hunter. They stepped into a dark, oak-panelled study, lined with leather bound tomes ranging from ecclesiastical history to Gibbons' *Decline and Fall of The Roman Empire*.

Then Bishop Hunter opened a desk drawer and, placing a tin of tobacco ceremoniously on the table in front of his visitor, proclaimed,

258

"Feel free, Mr. Holmes. This is a very good quality shag. Now, what is all this about Ebenezer Oakenfull?"

Holmes filled his old, oily briar and soon the study was wreathed in a fog of blue tobacco smoke.

"The letter I referred to in my wire – "

"Ah, yes."

"I have it here. I think you should read it. I found this among Oakenfull's correspondence files. I'm a guest at his former home, and I've been going through some of his collections of books and pamphlets, left at the rectory after his death. I found it tucked in the flyleaf of a copy of Caesar's *Gallic Wars*."

He placed the letter in Hunter's chubby hand and he scanned its contents. The untidy scrawl and long spiky loops of the *G*'s and *Y*'s suggested to him that the author of the letter was a person of considerable strength and conviction.

> *This is the last warning I shall give you. I have repeatedly told you to stop interfering in my affairs, but you have consistently ignored my previous advice. As a consequence, I have lost a great number of clients. I tell you that if you do not desist, I shall have no option but to put a stop to your machinations. I do not stand in awe of your Christian God, nor do I bow to your false theology. Take heed. I am on to you –*
>
> *WM*

The Bishop passed the letter back to Holmes.

"Strong stuff," he commented. "And you believe the author was – ?"

"William MacBride."

Bishop Hunter leaned back in his chair and placed his fingers in a steepled position as if he were about to utter a prayer.

"To be frank, it does not come as much of a surprise to me."

"You knew of the enmity between them?"

"I was aware of it, though I believe that it was not public knowledge. Ebenezer had discussed the matter a few weeks before his demise. This man MacBride was a social pest."

"So I gather."

"He also had considerable influence in the district."

"I was aware of it."

"I am not sure you know the half of it, Mr. Holmes. Not only did he operate as a so called 'wizard', or cunning man. He had also started up a spiritualist group. His meetings drew followers from as far away as Kings

Lynn and here in Norwich. Ebenezer had become concerned about his sphere of influence. Then, of course, there was his reputation as a womaniser."

"I wasn't aware of that."

"Oh yes, he had a particular penchant for young women. His little peccadilloes caused quite a stir in the community, I can tell you. It was even rumoured that he had affairs with some of his more exalted female clients."

"Really?"

"Yes, but we shall not name names. Better not – especially as some of the ladies concerned are members of our congregation here at the cathedral."

There was a silence. Unabashed by the bishop's disclosures, Holmes sucked on his pipe. "You mentioned a spiritualist group?" he enquired.

"So I did. Apparently, MacBride had some reputation as a medium. He would advertise in the local newspaper. It was something that Ebenezer took great exception to. In fact, he went so far as to report MacBride to the local constabulary. As a result, MacBride was prosecuted under the Vagrancy Act. That was the start of the trouble. He never forgave him for it."

Holmes nodded. "Go on."

"Well, it developed into a feud. There was no other word for it. They exchanged letters in the local press. But that wasn't the half of it. Ebenezer even threatened to read out the names of the parishioners who patronised MacBride's sessions. In return, MacBride broke into the church and defaced the reredos. Of course, nothing could be proved. This battle went on for about a year as I recall. Then of course Ebenezer fell ill and died."

"But how exactly did he die?"

Bishop Hunter leaned forward on the table and adjusted his gold-rimmed glasses on the bridge of his thin nose. "It was terribly dramatic. He was at Sunday communion. It was coming up to Easter. Anyway, he was delivering a sermon based on the sinfulness of Sodom and Gomorrah when he was gripped by a series of violent convulsions. They took him back to the vicarage, but within a few hours he was dead."

"Heart failure?"

"No, it was some type of food poisoning. It was a terrible end, poor fellow."

Holmes removed the pipe from his lips, then relit the mixture, acrid fumes filling the study.

"It was said MacBride had a considerable number of enemies in the parish. Is that right?"

"Oh, I don't doubt it. He'd even cuckolded a number of husbands in Thorsford. But on the other hand, he had his allies. Squire Bloxham for one."

"I believe he worked for the squire as a groom?"

"That's right. He had an affinity with horses. Some even said he was something of a horse whisperer. Ebenezer always imagined there was some deeper bond between them, though he couldn't fathom precisely what it was. He was quite frequently seen at Munnington Hall. Yes, there's no doubt about it. MacBride had charisma. That was part of his appeal to the gentler sex, you see. What is it?"

He broke off abruptly, staring across at Holmes who appeared to be lost in thought. There was a long pause before he answered.

"I have a suspicion – a hunch, call it what you will – that Ebenezer Oakenfull was also murdered," he said at last. He was standing now, staring out of the window, watching the autumn leaves swirling about the quadrangle. The sky was dark and heavy with rain clouds and the air seemed ominously still as if it presaged a storm.

"How?"

"Poison. I may never be able to prove it, but I think it is a distinct possibility."

Bishop Hunter, who had now joined him at the window, placed a reassuring hand on Holmes's shoulder.

"You may be right, Mr. Holmes," he remarked. "But the question is, who then killed MacBride?"

When Holmes arrived back at the rectory, he found Whitaker and Chief Inspector Gould waiting for him. "I'm sorry to inform you, Mr. Holmes, that Ronald Bloxham is dead."

Holmes took out his old briar and began to fill it.

"You don't seem surprised, sir."

"I am not."

"The maid found him early this morning. She called the family doctor. It's thought that he died of food poisoning."

Later that day, after returning to the rectory, Whitaker mentioned that they had received an invitation to dinner that evening from Henry Stapeley, the noted art dealer. Holmes assented, and some hours later the two men set off to one of the large houses on the edge of the village. They arrived just as it was getting dark and walked down the narrow, tree-shrouded driveway.

Dressed in a dark green smoking jacket and voluminous Arabic-style pantaloons, Stapeley answered the door.

261

"So good that you could both make it. Do come in, gentlemen."

Stapeley led the way down a narrow hallway lined with books, and they entered a low-beamed living room, lit by candles and a roaring log fire. Stapeley bade them sit and took their coats into the hallway, his tall, thin form bending to avoid contact with the beams. Holmes inspected the room. A dark, eighteenth-century mahogany sideboard accommodated a variety of silver ornaments, a stuffed cat, and a Dutch tobacco jar. To his left, the silk-papered wall was lined with oil landscapes by members of the Norwich School.

"Admiring my Cotman, I see?" remarked Stapeley, who had entered bearing a drinks tray.

"It's a fine piece."

"I have three others by him upstairs."

"You're a collector, then?"

"Of paintings and antiques, yes. It has been my passion for over a decade, Mr. Holmes. It is also my living, of course. I understand that you are interested in prehistory, like myself?"

"I have read a bit about it, but it is Whitaker who has a deeper knowledge of the subject."

"Of course," replied Stapeley, exhibiting a toothy smile. "Charles here has told me much about his excavations and his theories about Boudicca. It's an exciting thought, isn't it?"

"But merely a speculation, I'm sorry to say," replied Whitaker. "It seems unlikely that Thorsford Hill has any connection to the grave of the warrior queen."

"Nevertheless, the whole area seems soaked in finds from the Iceni. I have one or two pieces upstairs which form the core of my collection, including a gold torc."

Whitaker raised his eyebrows.

"Oh yes, I'd be happy to show you my collection after dinner. Anyway, let us charge our glasses, gentlemen. A toast to the treasures of the past!"

Whitaker was quiet over dinner, a sumptuous affair consisting of roast duck, roast potatoes, and fresh vegetables, followed by a lemon pie. His silence was noted by Stapeley ,who spent much of the meal chatting to Holmes about the collections in the Ashmolean Museum. After the port had been consumed and the cigars lit, he turned to Whitaker.

"You seem rather troubled, Charles."

He briefly explained the circumstances relating to the discovery of Ronald Bloxham's body. Stapeley leaned back in his chair, his face serious.

"The whole thing's appalling – grotesque," he said, pulling at his goatee beard agitatedly. "We had our disagreements of course, but I would never have wished that fate upon him."

"Disagreements?"

"Oh yes, they were many. Mostly involving land disputes. When I purchased this cottage several years ago, I was told I had rights over several fields and their adjoining rights of way. They abutted the perimeter of the grounds of Munnington Hall. I made it my business to exercise my rights, you see. It didn't go down too well with Ronald. In fact, he became rather litigious over the matter. Cost me a deal of money, I can tell you. He even threatened to shoot me on one occasion. He was, in many respects, a dislikeable individual. But I wouldn't have wished that on him. Not at all. How is his wife taking it?"

"Not very well, I hear," said Whitaker.

"I feel for her. I do. She was never very happy in the relationship, you know. Hardly surprising really, considering her husband's complete obsession with equestrian matters."

"Really?"

"Oh yes. It was like a religion to him. Something he shared with that strange character MacBride. They were both members of a sort of secret society, you know. It was common knowledge around here – especially after MacBride made it public – more by chance than intention of course."

"Secret society?" asked Holmes. "What do you mean, precisely?" He leaned forward on the table, his eyes glinting in the firelight.

"Have you ever heard of something called 'The Horseman's Word'?" Stapeley asked.

"I confess I have not."

"Nor had I," Stapeley added. "I discovered it purely by chance through a friend of mine at Edinburgh University," he explained. "It was originally called 'The Society of The Horseman's Word'. Its origins are somewhat obscure. It seems to have been connected with Freemasonry and some of the medieval guilds. But unlike Freemasonry, it does not share that society's belief in the Christian creator. On the contrary, it believes in the power of Satan."

"And what has this to do with Squire Bloxham or William MacBride?" asked Holmes.

"MacBride was certainly a member, and I have every reason to believe that the squire was. They use a talisman, you see. I spotted it both at MacBride's cottage and at Munnington Hall. Look, I once made a drawing of it."

He stood up and, hunting until he plucked a scroll of paper from the bookcase. Then he unrolled it on the dining table.

"Here it is – a sort of cross made of riding crops, bisected with four horseshoes."

"Most curious," Whitaker said.

"I discovered from my Edinburgh colleague that members of this esoteric society all supposedly possess a great power over the horse. In short, they are horse whisperers. They have the power to stop a horse in its tracks or command it to do almost anything they wish. I have seen this in action with both men. MacBride, who was Squire Bloxham's groom, had the ability to work a horse into a frenzy when he so desired. Bloxham relied on him to calm his stallion prior to important race meetings. I have seen much the same thing with the Squire."

"This society," enquired Holmes. "Does it have any other distinguishing marks – a creed or ideology, for example?"

Stapeley pulled a small silver cigarette case from the pocket of his smoking jacket and offered the two men one of his Turkish cigarettes.

"It has its own initiation rite, according to McEwen – he's my Scottish contact incidentally. The order is hierarchical and is divided into six grades. Each represents what they term 'The Miracle of The Bread'. The grades are termed The Plough, The Seed, The Green Corn, The Yellow Corn, The Stones, and finally The Resurrection, the latter being the highest. Membership is available to men aged between sixteen and fifty. Each recruit is compelled to take what is termed 'The Horseman's Oath'. In it, the initiate swears that he will conceal and never reveal any part of his horsemanship, nor speak or write down the secret word of the brotherhood."

Holmes pondered for a moment. Then he said, "Doesn't it strike you as odd that both men were part of this society, and that both have met untimely ends? I'm intrigued by what you've told me about 'The Horseman's Word'. I should like to look further into the matter."

"I can help you there. I have some working notes on the society. I'll lend you them if you like."

When Holmes and Whitaker emerged later that evening, they discovered that a sharp frost had descended, riming the fields and trees. They made their way down the footpath that led back to the rectory, each in silent thought. When they reached the gate that marked the crossroads, Holmes glanced up towards Thorsford Hill. The sky was flooded with moonlight, which cast a silver sheen on the frozen landscape. From here, he could see the great hill with its humped summit and the dark trees beyond. Below, etched in white, lay the lines of the mysterious hill figure. He thought of the events at Munnington Hall. Some dark force was present here, the dark powers which had lain here for centuries beneath the earth.

They turned and walked down the yew alley. He had heard Whitaker say something about his plans for the following day and the completion of his scouring, but Holmes hadn't really been listening. He was thinking of The Horseman's Word, his hand gripping the packet of papers that Stapeley had lent him. As he glanced back along the alleyway, he thought for a brief moment he heard the whinnying of a horse, but realised it was only the sound of the wind in the branches.

The following day dawned fair and bright, despite a keen easterly wind which perpetuated the ground frost. Whitaker was up early and by eight o'clock had already completed his breakfast. Downstairs in the study, he met Holmes. The latter had already broached his after-breakfast pipe and was wreathed in pungent tobacco smoke.

"Up already?" Holmes enquired, glancing toward him from the study table.

"I want to make an early start. I have a feeling in my bones that today will be a remarkable one. What are you doing?"

"Following a hunch."

"The Horseman's Word?"

"Right."

"You really do think it had something to do with the deaths, then?"

"It's a hunch. Nothing more. But then, in my line of business, I have often come to rely on the irrational as a source of inspiration."

"Well, good luck then. I am armed with one of Mrs. Annis's sandwich boxes and a hip flask containing some excellent malt whisky."

"Perhaps I shall join you after lunch, time permitting."

The hard frost of the previous night hadn't made Whitaker's job easy. Using a Cornish shovel, his sticks, and a plumb line, he toiled away, breaking the iced sod, then clearing shovelfuls of earth from the limestone rock beneath. With the sun's heat on his back, he soon began to sweat and had to remove his thick sheepskin jacket in order to continue.

Holmes returned to the study and opened the packet of papers Stapeley had lent him the previous evening. For some while he poured over its contents, a collection of hand-written foolscap sheets entitled: "*The Horseman's Word: Some Observations, by Henry Stapeley, Esquire*".

> *A secret society with distinct pagan overtones* (he read), *The Horseman's Word, or The Society of the Horseman's Word, has existed for many centuries in both East Anglia and the far*

265

*north-eastern portion of Scotland. The cult originated in the town of Huntly in Aberdeenshire, and reached its peak in Scotland in the late 1870's.*

He skipped a page and his attention was caught by the following entry:

*The initiation ceremony of The Horseman's Word usually took place on Martinmas, otherwise November the First, and was held in an isolated barn. The number of people present at a ceremony had to comprise an odd, not even, number. When a sufficient number had been assembled, the word was passed round for members to attend. This was often done by passing a single horsehair in an envelope to each member. Each horseman was expected to bring to the ceremony a bottle of whisky, a loaf of bread, and a jar of jam or berries. This form of ceremony was also practised in certain areas of North Norfolk, although by the late 1860's this was no longer the case in Suffolk.*

*On the night in question, the novices were each taken blindfolded into a barn. When they reached the door, the horseman brother leading them gave what was termed "The Horseman's Knock" – three taps – and with this the leader would whinny like a horse. Each novice was then questioned and had to identify himself to the "minister" inside. The novice was required to say that he had been told by the Devil to attend "by the hooks and crooks of the road." He was then asked "What is the tender of the oath?" to which he replied, "Heal, conceal, never reveal – neither write, nor dite, nor recite, nor cut, nor carve, nor write in sand." In other words, no member of the group would ever impart the "Secret Word" to anyone who was not a member of the cult.*

*The initiation would then commence with novices, still blindfold, seated round the minister with the left foot bare and left hand raised in obedience. The minister then explained to the novices that Cain had been the very first horseman and that the Devil would be invoked by reading from the Bible backwards. Then he gave each "The Word" which, when whispered to a horse, would allow the horseman to control each horse who came within his sphere of influence.*

*The proceedings were ended by the minister cracking a whip across the knuckles of each initiate. As dawn*

266

*approached, and before the horsemen would return to their houses, they would sing the ceremonial toast:*

> *Here's to the horse with the four white feet,*
> *The chestnut tail and the mane –*
> *A star on his face and a spot on his breast,*
> *And his master's name was Cain.*

To this account Stapeley had added a note in green ink:

*Suspect Bloxham and MacBride are both members of this cult. Passed the barn Tuesday last at around ten o'clock and heard voices inside. Bloxham's stallion was leashed to a rail outside. I heard several men chanting inside something very similar to the words mentioned above. This appears to be some bizarre variation on Freemasonry. MacBride, I believe, is a man of power, as a man called Robinson may also be, the latter being a blacksmith, an occupation much revered from ancient times. I have it on good authority from Jennings that the Squire holds regular meetings at this venue. I have also witnessed MacBride's power over horses. He exhibits much the same influence over women – so I am told by Jennings.*

Holmes paused. A sudden noise had distracted him. He looked towards the study window and there, sprinting down the path between the tall beech trees, was the wild, dishevelled figure of Whitaker. He was gesticulating and appeared to be shouting excitedly, his hand clutching a cloth bag. Then he disappeared from view and Holmes heard the door to the rectory open and a cry of surprise from Mrs. Annis as the door to the study was flung open.

"It's gold!" Whitaker bellowed, his face suffused with joy. "I've found Boudicca's gold!"

Whitaker finished laying out the gold pieces on the white cloth and stood back to admire his bounty. On the other side of the table, Holmes picked up his magnifying glass and began to scrutinise the collection.

"The torc is really magnificent," he commented, "and, judging by the detail here and the weight of the thing, would have been made for a person of wealth and status. What a pity it's been damaged."

"This clean break would indicate to me that this has been done deliberately," Whitaker replied.

"But why would that be? For what purpose?"

"As part of a ritual – an offering to the gods. You remember how in Tacitus's account, Boudicca calls upon the goddess of war, Andraste, to lend her aid in the Iceni's uprising? The tribes would have provided a sacrifice of worth. What better than a piece like this? Just look at it. It's astounding."

"The enamelled brooch. That's been fractured too."

"Yes, and also this necklace. Judging by the type of work here, I would have no hesitation in placing them at just the right period to coincide with the Celtic uprising."

Their conversation was curtailed by Mrs. Annis, who announced that Inspector Gould had been spotted making his way up the driveway towards the rectory. Whitaker hurriedly collected up the pieces of treasure and beat a quick retreat to the living room in order to photograph the treasure.

When he entered the study, the inspector seemed haggard and disconsolate. Holmes offered him a whisky and the two men sat either side of the fireplace, cradling their glasses.

"Inspector, I thought you might like to know I have acquired some information about Ronald Bloxham which may be useful to you in your investigation."

"Really?"

Holmes leaned forward and gave him the papers he had perused that morning. "This was given me yesterday evening by Henry Stapeley, the retired schoolmaster. He believes that both William MacBride and the Squire were members of an occult society called The Horseman's Word."

"And what exactly is that?"

"It's rather similar to Freemasonry, but has pagan or occult leanings. As you are no doubt aware, the Freemasons are a Christian-oriented group, but The Horseman's Word pays lip service to the Devil. For that reason, I am dubious about their aims."

Gould perused the papers he had been given. "It seems an odd business, if you ask me."

"It appears to be a horse cult, and there are distinct degrees or grades of office. I would imagine that the Squire would have attained the highest of the ranks ,and from what I have learned about MacBride, I guess he was equal in status. Who the other members are, I have really no idea, save for Robinson, the blacksmith – that is, according to Stapeley."

"You are suggesting that this information may have a bearing on Bloxham's's death then?" Gould asked.

"I can't be certain. As you may recall, the two men were fairly close, and it strikes me as more than coincidental that both have met untimely ends. It's possible that one of the group may have had a motive for killing both of them. There is another factor to consider. Oakenfull, the former resident of the rectory, had made an enemy of MacBride by his constant attempts to humiliate him. Bishop Hunter has given me a deal of evidence about the background to their rivalry. By the way, are you aware that Oakenfull died of food poisoning, like the Squire?"

"I was aware that he'd died suddenly," said Gould, "but I recall there was nothing particularly suspicious about his death."

"I'm not so sure. What if they were both poisoned? Yesterday I spoke to Mrs. Annis about this business. She told me something very interesting. Apparently, the day before Oakenfull's death, some wild mushrooms were left on the doorstep of the rectory with a brief note."

"Was the note signed?"

"It was not."

"Did Mrs. Annis keep the note?"

"No, she didn't. She didn't read it, and no one knows what it said."

"Did she eat the mushrooms herself?"

"Mrs. Annis doesn't care for them, but wild mushrooms were a special delicacy of Oakenfull's. He ate them on a regular basis. It was several hours after the meal that evening that he began to develop acute abdominal pains from which he never recovered."

"So what are you suggesting?"

"That Oakenfull was murdered, of course."

"As you say, Mr. Holmes, these are interesting and plausible theories, but at present they are entirely unproveable."

Holmes stood up. "What worries me, Inspector, is the thought that somewhere in this community we may have a murderer who has struck not once, not twice, but three times. And as things presently stand, neither of us has any proof as to who that person might be."

"Very well, then, I admit it. I am a member of The Horseman's Word."

George Robinson had flung down the scissors he had been sharpening and wiped his hands on his apron. His face, which was bathed in perspiration. was twisted into a frown.

"I'm not here to judge you, Mr. Robinson," said Holmes. "It is of no consequence to me whether or not you are a member of a secret society. I am simply seeking information about two of that society's members, both of whom were known to you. Now, can we just sit down sensibly together and talk about this?"

Robinson passed a hand through his shock of wiry grey hair and subsided into a chair. He stared uneasily at Holmes.

"What do you want me to tell you?"

"How many members are there in your group?"

"Thirteen, prior to the deaths of MacBride and Squire Bloxham."

"Was there any enmity between the members of the group?"

"Not that I know of."

"And what grade did Squire Bloxham occupy in the society?"

"He was the master of our lodge. It was he who held the ceremonies of initiation."

"And how long had MacBride been a member?"

"I understood he'd been a member before he moved here from Cornwall, nigh on thirty years ago. He were the true master of the horse. Bloxham thought he knew a lot, but it were all book learning with him. MacBride was the master of the equestrian arts."

"Can you think why anyone should wish to kill the Squire?"

Robinson shook his head. "The members of our order had the utmost respect for him. Treated us fair, he did. With MacBride it was altogether different. He were unreliable. When the drink took him, he let things slip. That's why he came to a bad end, in my opinion."

"What do you mean?"

"He was seen twice summoning his horse in the market place. He used the secret word. The Squire heard him do it. He were warned about it, but he took no notice."

"You're suggesting that he may have resented MacBride for that reason?"

"I'm not saying that. I'm just saying MacBride was a liability. He didn't know how to control himself. If you ask my opinion, Mr. Holmes, I believe that no human being killed MacBride. It was the Devil's own work."

"Explain."

"Whatever killed MacBride was not of this world. Who in their right mind would have caused that amount of damage to his room? Why, even the window was smashed. Why should anyone bother doing that? All those things broken, yet the table in front of him was untouched. It makes no sense."

"What are you saying, man? That the Devil himself killed MacBride?"

"I don't know what to believe. All I know is that some force entered that room and gave a great blow to his head. I am sure that no human hand could have done that. That's all I'm saying. MacBride supped with the Devil, and maybe he came for him in the end."

The following morning, Mrs. Annis laid the breakfast table and soon entered, carrying a large bowl of porridge. Within a few minutes Whitaker also came in, dressed in plus-fours, hiking boots, a suede waistcoat, red shirt, and cravat. Mrs. Annis placed a silver platter in the middle of the table containing the morning post and a telegram. Then she retreated as Holmes entered. Whitaker greeted his old colleague. Then, opening the wire, Whitaker announced, "Ah, this may interest you, Holmes. The description that I sent to the British Museum of the torc and the other items."

"Oh yes?"

"They have been dated at around A.D. 60."

"Which means . . . ?"

"That we have a date contemporary with the Iceni's revolt against the Romans. The treasure was probably buried on Thorsford Hill as a sacrifice to the gods. I'm more certain than ever that this was a ritual burial."

"So does that mark the end of your quest?"

"Yes, I believe it does."

After Holmes had left the breakfast room, Whitaker scanned his post. Two bills, an enquiry about parish registers, and a long cream envelope embossed with the initials "R. H." Whitaker, who recognised the monogram instantly, opened the envelope to reveal two sheets of cream foolscap writing paper, written in an untidy hand. It was from his old friend, Robert Houghton of Morwenstow.

> *Dear Charles,* (the letter ran)
>
> *I was most pleased to hear from you again. I had imagined you were enjoying something akin to full retirement, but from what you have told me, you have chosen to surround yourself with murder and mayhem. How ignobly sensational of you! Life here in Morwenstow is, at present, unutterably dull, and I have nothing murderous to report – apart, of course, from my pursuit of the fox. Quite frankly, I miss the intrigues and skullduggery of Welcombe. Life in Morwenstow is, by comparison, a catalogue of monotony. I do very little these days, apart from sitting on the parish council, working on my histories of the Cornish saints, and acting as secretary for The Bristol Missionary Society. But to come to the point:*
>
> *You asked me about this fellow MacBride. He was indeed personally known to me during my time as Vicar of Welcombe. He was Romany by birth. In fact, his father was an immigrant who came to Cornwall by way of Ireland. During his time with us, he made a reputation for himself as a self-styled "wizard", or cunning man. People came from far and wide for their charms to be renewed. This would happen once a year,*

*usually in the spring. He was, however, a notorious swindler and confidence trickster, and gambled away much of his ill-gotten gains on horse-racing. You mention something called "The Horseman's Word". I fear I have no knowledge of this organisation, but I do know he had considerable influence over horses. I have personally witnessed his ability to stop a horse in its tracks by speaking to it in a certain way.*

*He had a book of astrological calculations and spells which he kept locked in a trunk in his cottage. It was an impressive looking volume, but I cannot vouchsafe as to its contents. He was, at one stage, a rival of mine, often conducting so-called "hand fasting" ceremonies. I complained to him, of course, but he simply took no notice. I suspect that quite a few of his female clients fell for his charm. Among them he numbered at least two women of wealth and position. There was something very dashing and Byronic about him which women found irresistible.*

*At one stage he had an accomplice – a young woman also of Romany extraction who came to the village with her parents for the annual horse trading. She soon set up shop with him and was equally proficient at the business of dispensing spells and charms, especially to young women. At one stage she acted as a midwife in the village and was reckoned to have remarkable healing powers. Eventually, however, they fell out and she moved elsewhere. She gave birth to a child, which was MacBride's, and I do not know exactly what became of her. Maybe she rejoined her parents. I don't really know. She called herself Tamson Bright, but I know that was not her real name. She was a striking woman, large-framed, with dark eyes and soft olive skin. There was something of the Spaniard about her.*

Holmes returned, and Whitaker greeted him, passing him the letter as they made their way into the study, where a large fire was blazing cheerfully. They had settled down in the leather armchairs by the fireside when the door opened to reveal Augusta Bloxham, shown in by the housekeeper. She was dressed in a long, black boucle dress, tapered at the waist, knee-high boots, and a short, green padded jacket. Her face seemed sad and wistful, and she seemed hesitant.

"Thank you, Mrs. Annis."

272

Holmes put down the half-read letter while Whitaker and ushered the tall, elegant, gaunt-faced visitor to a chair, where she sat, straight-backed, her hands folded in her lap.

"I felt I must see you both as a matter of urgency," she began. "There is something that you should know. I have kept it to myself for so long now and frankly, I cannot bear it anymore."

Whitaker smiled reassuringly and extended his hand in support.

"Go on," he said.

"I thought I should tell you both the truth about my husband and William MacBride, but you must understand that what I have to say now is strictly confidential. It may be that the police will have to be involved in this matter at some stage, but I do not wish it to become common knowledge in the village."

"We quite understand, Mrs. Bloxham. I can assure you your wishes will be respected," said Holmes, lighting his briar.

She released her hands and relaxed a little.

"May I offer you some tea?" asked Whitaker.

"No, thank you."

"Then please continue."

"You must understand gentlemen, that William MacBride was a truly remarkable man. Our association with him began when he was employed as a part-time groom for my husband. William was quite unlike other men. He was gifted."

"So we have heard," said Holmes.

"I know that he had something of a reputation for dishonesty, but he was a psychic of great power. My husband and I are – were, as you know – both spiritualists. When our son died, he offered to help us contact him beyond the veil. We said we would pay him for his services, but he refused. He had great success, and we were much comforted by the help he provided."

"MacBride and your husband were both members of a society known as The Horseman's Word?" asked Holmes.

She seemed surprised that he knew of it. "My husband had a great love of horses. He was initiated into the order many years ago when he was a member of the Norwich Freemasons. When he came to Thorsford, he was eager to establish a local chapter. He believed that MacBride was an invaluable member because of his psychic powers."

"And was he?"

She nodded.

"He had the ability alright. He would talk to the horses in such a manner that Ronald would rely on him before a race to ginger the animal up. It worked every time – every time he was sober, that is."

"He had a problem with drink?"

"He was very unreliable, especially when he'd been at the drink. In the end he crossed the line. Ronald could not forgive him for what he did."

"And what exactly did he do?"

"He spoke The Horseman's Word within the earshot of others – the secret word that no one must reveal outside the chapter. And this happened more than once."

"And what did your husband do about it?"

"He asked him to leave the order, but William refused. But there was something else."

She bent her head, revealing her long, slender neck. There was a silence. Then she spoke again, very softly, her head lowered.

"William and I – we were lovers."

"I see," said Holmes. "Did your husband know of this?"

"Not at first. I began to visit William's cottage in secret in relation to the séances. I needed his support, but I knew that Ronald would never forgive me. It was an innocent liaison at first. I would take him things that belonged to our precious boy – his hairbrush, one of his cufflinks, an old diary he had kept before he had enlisted. He would practise psychometry with them. He even spoke with his voice. I found it deeply moving. I was certain it was him, speaking to me from the Summerlands. I felt a great sense of reassurance, you see, in his presence. I know it may seem odd saying this to you now, but it was true. William possessed great spiritual strength, and I found that very comforting."

"And so you grew to love him?" She nodded.

"It was not a physical relationship – well, not at first. We would sit in that cottage and talk about all sorts of things. I learned about the beliefs of the Roma people, their customs and way of life. William was a mine of information. He had had no formal education, yet he was wise in the ways of the world. And he had lived a full life. He had loved women with all of his soul. I had never known a man with such a great and compassionate heart. It was on one of these visits that I told him that I loved him. I don't know what I expected. Maybe I thought he would reject me. But he didn't. He spoke to me in a way that Ronald never could – from his heart."

"And after that?"

"After that we kept meeting at the cottage. I suppose I thought that it would never end. That was folly, of course. I was deluding myself. One afternoon, Ronald must have been riding in the area. He saw me leaving. After I had gone, he called on William and interrogated him. He admitted everything and they had words. When Ronald got home that afternoon, he accused me of terrible things: Of being a whore and an adulteress, of bringing his reputation into disrepute. I told him I would leave

Munnington Hall the following day, but he said he would not allow it. That it would sully his reputation. So, in the end I stayed."

"And did your husband find it in his heart to forgive you?"

She shook her head. "From that moment onward, he turned his heart against me and I knew that he was intent on revenge."

"Revenge – against whom? You or William MacBride?"

"William. The night that William was murdered – I must tell you about that. William had been drinking again. He had been at The Green Man all afternoon. Ronald had left the Hall in the afternoon and I didn't see him again until late in the evening. When he did return, I noticed his clothes were dusty and he looked strange – preoccupied. I asked him where he had been, but he refused to answer. The following day, I heard that William had been bludgeoned to death. It is my certain belief that my husband killed him."

"But how can you be so certain?" asked Holmes.

"By his demeanour. A woman's instincts are rarely wrong."

"Then I will take your word for it, Mrs. Bloxham."

"I also found this among his belongings. It has bloodstains on it."

Reaching into her bag, she drew out a battered horseshoe and laid it on the study table.

Holmes peered at the item, turning it this way and that. Then he said at last, "And did you not think of speaking to Inspector Gould about your suspicions?"

"I did not."

"Even though you knew your husband may have committed murder?"

"My husband may have ceased to love me, Mr. Holmes but I consider the loyalty that exists between husband and wife to be a quality worth preserving."

Holmes gazed at her intently. Her own sense of loyalty had not been quite so robust when she had embarked upon her affair.

"Noble sentiments indeed, Mrs. Bloxham. However, I must tell you that we cannot just conceal this evidence from the police."

She bowed her head. "I understand." She rose to leave.

"Mrs. Annis will see you out," said Whitaker. "You may be required to give a statement to Inspector Gould, although I doubt you will have to appear in court."

"I shall do what is necessary, of course. Thank you for your time."

Holmes stood at the study window, watching her carriage leave. Flurries of snow were starting to fall, whitening the drive and the bare branches of the trees. He thought about the evidence that she had provided. If Bloxham had truly murdered MacBride in a fit of jealousy, then it was

275

also likely that it was he who had wrecked the inside of the cottage and smashed the windows, while leaving the various items on the table to suggest that MacBride had been the victim of some sort of ritual murder. But if so, who had murdered Ronald Bloxham – if he had in truth been murdered? Could that person have been Mrs. Bloxham herself? And did she have an accomplice? And how to explain the similarity between Bloxham's death and that of Oakenfull.

When Mrs. Bloxham had gone, Holmes picked up the telephone.

"I'd like to speak to Inspector Gould. Oh, I see. When will he be back then? This is Sherlock Holmes. Could you ask him to stop by the rectory when he has a chance? Thank you. The number is *Thorsford 375*." Then, leaving Whitaker to his own thoughts, he went out into the quite hallway and pulled the door shut, making his way through the quiet house to the room where Ebenezer Oakenfull's papers were stored. He had searched there the other day, when he found MacBride's letter, which he had later showed to Bishop Hunter. He had the nagging feeling that he hadn't searched carefully enough.

Inside the small room, there was a smell of age. On one side, a series of dilapidated bookcases were stuffed to the brim with old papers, box files, and cardboard boxes, marked in copperplate handwriting – certainly Oakenfull's by the look of it. On the other side lay a jumble of dusty furniture, old moth-eaten vestments, a broken rocking-horse, three oak chairs with holed seats, and a faded chintz sofa, spewing forth its horse hair. Holmes went to the window where he found a collection of small black candle holders and cleared them to one side to gain access to the window frame. He tried to open it, but found that it was stuck fast, having been painted in on the outside.

He began to rummage through the stacks of cardboard boxes, only partially searched the other day. A collection of damaged *Common Prayer* books, a large family Bible with a brass chain attached, and a set of English hymnals with faded gilt lettering were first. These he quickly discarded and began to rummage through the contents of another random box. An obsolete funeral service pamphlet, a guide for missionaries, and an All Saints' Day Order of Service. The next box was the same, and then another. He glanced through several letters from the Bishop – and what was this? A sealed foolscap envelope marked with the name *Sophia*. He hesitated for a moment, and then ripped it open. Out fluttered a collection of grainy black-and-white photographs and a small paper bag. He opened the latter and found inside a long lock of dark hair, tied by a pink ribbon. He picked it up and placed it under his nose. A rich, heady perfume, sweet and rose-drenched, drifted up to meet him.

He picked up one of the photographs. A woman, clearly Whitaker's housekeeper, though several years younger than the present Mrs. Annis, lay on a chaise longue, her head thrown back. She was smiling, her eyes half-closed as if she were half asleep. Her right hand dangled to the floor and her left clutched a glass. It was as if he were looking at an Old Master, for the porcelain flesh was etched against the darkness of the room. Above her, bending over, stood a tall man with greying hair, apparently Oakenfull. He was dressed in a long dressing gown which fell open, revealing his bare chest. He was smiling, as if he and the woman were sharing some joke. The depth of the photograph suggested it had been a slow exposure, for there was a slight blurring to the girl's hand where she had shifted slightly. There was something decadent about the picture, as if the participants had thought up the notion of the photograph in some drunken reverie. Across the bottom of the photograph, Oakenfull had scrawled the words: "*Sophia and me, Rectory, Summer, 1899.*"

Holmes lay the photo aside and leafed through the others. There was a photo showing the woman dressed as some sort of fairy. She wore wings and was dressed in a long, semi-transparent cloak. She was leaning against a tree, laughing. The photo appeared to have been taken in a wooded area. There were other pictures, much more explicit. These he didn't dwell upon, but returned them to the packet.

There was something strangely innocent yet obsessive about the images. He was about to thrust them into his jacket pocket when a piece of foolscap paper fluttered from the envelope and onto the floor. He picked it up and examined it. Written in Oakenfull's hand, it consisted of two paragraphs and was entitled "*The Goddess Andraste*":

*Who is this Great Goddess?* (Oakenfull had written) *Boudicca, Queen of the Iceni, invoked her prior to her great battle, supplicating her and praying for victory, yet she is mentioned but the once. Is this, in fact, the goddess called Andasta, worshipped by the fierce Vocontii of Gaul, a variant of Anu? Is she part of that great panoply of goddesses worshipped by the Celts, among them Dana, the Mother Goddess of the Tuatha de Danaan, associated with the hills of Kerry in Ireland, or in Scottish folklore the hideous hag Black Anu? Is this the same as the fearsome Morrigan, the death goddess, who wheeled as a raven over the bodies of slain warriors?*

*She is also Medb, the warrior queen of Connaught, of whom it was said that no king could rule unless married to her. Her armies invaded Ulster and killed its hero,*

*Cuchulainn, and she was possessed of voracious appetites. In my own way, have I not succumbed to her power in insatiable desire for this young woman? She inspires my every waking moment and I live only for the feel of her warm flesh and the consummation of my desire for her. I am nothing without the power that emanates from her body. I worship the temple. What am I saying? Sometimes I think I have gone down into the dark and will never return to the light of the Lord Jesus. Heaven help me, surely I am lost.*

Holmes looked up, observing that a spider was making its way slowly along a thin thread towards the dusty window, where its cocooned prey which lay at the centre of a web. He watched in fascination as the creature squatted over its helpless victim and began to suck from its inert body. A terrible feeling of suffocation began to overcome him. At that moment, he suddenly heard a sound – a cry? – from elsewhere in the depths of the house. He rapidly left the room.

When Holmes had departed, Whitaker had been lost in thought. Mrs. Annis had come in to see if he needed anything. He told her that he was fine. She then asked if Mr. Holmes was still about, and he realized that he didn't know. "I believe that he has stepped out," Whitaker replied, without really being certain. She nodded and pulled the door shut behind her.

A few minutes later, the telephone rang. After a few minutes, when it hadn't been answered, he walked to the door and pulled it open, peering into the hall. The ringing had stopped by then. He wandered through several nearby rooms without finding anyone. He returned to the study and peered through the window. The path outside was deserted, and slowly covering with snow. Where was Holmes? He scanned the hill, but could see no sign of his friend. He was apparently alone in the house.

He decided that he would to the village and see if Gould had any further news. He returned to the hall and was about to search for his boots when a door opened immediately behind him. Before he could turn, there was a sharp blow to the back of his head and he fell to his knees, his sight fading to blackness.

The voices came and went, faint echoes as if heard in a dream. Whitaker was fading, slipping back into sleep. He was cold, cold as ice. Cold as Death itself.

There was a voice now, somewhere just beyond his consciousness, a voice that was familiar to him. He wanted to turn around, but he didn't have the strength. Then, hovering in front of him, as if in a dream, he saw the face of Mrs. Annis.

Whitaker stirred in the chair. His head ached and his vision was blurred. He tried to move his hands but found that they had been tied to the arms with thick rope. Then he understood that his mouth was covered by a cloth, bound around his head. He made a noise, but it was nothing more than a muffled grunt trapped in his throat. He looked around, realizing now that he was in the abandoned east wing, a part of the vast rectory that he hadn't seen since first moving there. There had been no need to revisit it after his initial explorations, for it had been closed off for year. And now he was here, and he was beginning to understand why. Five women stood before him, all wearing flowing robes, facing away from him, their eyes fixed on a structure on the far side of the room. It appeared to be an altar.

Around the room were several figurines, ancient representations of the Great Goddess whom Hebrews and Christians had abjured for so many centuries. And at the centre of these statues stood the figure of an ancient white horse. Here in this room, these. . . *acolytes* had gathered to enact some arcane and ancient ritual. He could see clearly now as his housekeeper, Sophia Annis – dressed not in her normal clothing, but also draped in robes – stepped forward and lit two beeswax candles upon the altar. Then, she and the five women held hands and began to chant:

> *Mighty Horse Goddess, Andraste.*
> *She who is three parts in one,*
> *She who is the three phases of the Moon,*
> *She who waxes and wanes,*
> *She of the Three Mothers,*
> *She who is the Holy Trinity,*
> *Mother and Grandmother,*
> *Creator of all living things,*
> *She whose bright cloth is embroidered with threads of gold,*
> *We praise you.*
> *Loud is your war cry, sharp are your spears and arrows,*
> *You who flew across the battlefields, black as the blackest*
> *   raven*
> *Your bird cry filling the hearts of the living with dread,*
> *We celebrate your power.*

When they finished, their attention shifted from the altar to the bound man. He tried to scream then, but the gag was too effective. Mrs. Annis stepped in front of him. She had a cup in her hands. One of the other

women – she looked familiar, and he was sure that he had seen her in the village – moved forward and slipped the gag from his mouth. He was able to cry out, but it was quickly stopped when Mrs. Annis grabbed him by the hair and placed the cup to his mouth, tipping it up and pouring the bitter contents in. He tried to spit them out, but the other woman immediately put her hand over his mouth while pinching his nostrils shut. He had no choice but to swallow. Almost immediately, the face of Mrs. Annis, formerly so pleasant but now curiously filled with contempt, began to blur
. . . .

Whitaker shifted uneasily in the bed, then slowly opened his eyes. He tried to sit up but found that weakness prevented him. From the side of the bed, Holmes smiled.

"Feeling a little better?"

"Where am I?"

"At home. At the rectory. It's all right. Everything's under control. You have a visitor – Inspector Gould. Do you feel up to it?"

Whitaker nodded. Holmes helped his friend sit up in the bed and adjusted his pillows.

"What happened exactly?"

On the other side of the bed, the comfortable, stocky form of Inspector Gould looked at the bedraggled, pale-faced clergyman.

"You had a narrow escape, sir. A very close shave it was. Had it not been for this gentleman rescuing you when he did, we might have lost you altogether."

The memory of the abandoned room and the altar and the women flashed through his mind. He reached for a glass of water on the bedside table and took a sip to assuage his thirst.

"I was examining Oakenfull's papers when I thought that I heard a cry," said Holmes. "I returned to the main part of the house, only to find it abandoned. However, the door to the closed part of the rectory was standing open – which hadn't been the case ever since I've arrived. I saw footprints along the dusty floor – the housekeeper's, as well as those of another woman, and something being dragged – and followed them into the east wing.

"As I got closer, I could hear their chanting, and I approached cautiously. Looking carefully into the room where they had set up their altar, I saw you there, tied to the chair, I realised that something was horribly wrong. You were still semi-conscious, but doubled up with stomach cramps. I could see that you must have been given something poisonous as part of their ritual. It turns out to have been a deadly mushroom, *Amanida phalloides* – death cap. It took me a while to get you

280

out of there. It turns out that your housekeeper is a strong woman, by the way. She put up quite a fight. The others didn't seem to have much of an appetite for it and fled.

"Yes," said Whitaker. "Mrs. Annis. I was walking through the hall when someone hit me on the head. I woke up tied to the chair, with her and the others conducting some sort of pagan rite. Then, they forced me to drink a bitter liquid."

"Sophia Annis was the moving force behind it all," explained Holmes. "It seems that she established some sort of goddess-worshipping group of the sort that regards men as inferior. It was almost as if the women that she selected had no self-will left – as if they were mesmerized. Sophia was totally in control.

"After she had been subdued, I realised then that I had to do something about your condition pretty quickly, so I forced you to throw up. Drastic treatment, I'm afraid, but it had to be done. Once you'd vomited up the ghastly stuff, I knew you had a fighting chance of survival. They'd also given you a sleeping draught – a mixture of valerian and vervain, as she subsequently admitted – a knockout drink. That explains why you were so nearly comatose when I found you."

"Plus the bang on the head," intervened Gould.

Whitaker looked apprehensively about the room.

"Don't concern yourself," said Gould. "The women are all now in custody."

"The inspector arrived soon after," said Holmes, "having received my earlier telephone message. We've since interviewed Sophia Annis, and she has made a full confession – rather proudly – regarding the murders of Ebenezer Oakenfull and Ronald Bloxham. After some persuasion, I might add!"

"But what on earth was her motive?" asked Whitaker.

"Revenge, in a word – at least for Bloxham's murder. She killed him because he killed MacBride – who was her father."

Before Whitaker could consider the implications of that statement, Holmes continued. "Sophia Annis was the illegitimate daughter of William MacBride. This was the daughter referred to in the letter you received from your friend, Houghton. It appears that Sophia Annis was brought here when she was a young girl by her mother, who had followed MacBride from Cornwall, where both had set up practice as cunning folk. When the mother died, the familial connection to MacBride wasn't acknowledged, and Sophia was fostered by an elderly couple in the village. Then, when she was fourteen, she was put into service."

"And she remained friendly with her father?" asked Whitaker.

"She adored him, apparently. She became very concerned about his drinking bouts, and often got him out of scrapes. But they kept their relationship a secret all those years."

Whitaker coughed suddenly, his throat aching. When he had regained his composure, Holmes continued.

"As Mrs. Annis explained to us, she had an affair with Oakenfull. I had seen proof of it in Oakenfull's papers, so I knew to ask her about it. However, when he began to disparage her father, and then had him prosecuted for vagrancy, she decided that he must be sacrificed. She was in the habit of collecting wild mushrooms for Oakenfull. They were a delicacy of his. It was easy enough to slip him a portion of death cap – and he became her first sacrifice. It was the same treatment that she meted out to you, Whitaker."

"Only you were luckier," said Gould.

"I owe you a great debt, gentlemen," said Whitaker. "It seems you arrived in the nick of time."

"It appears that the day MacBride was murdered," continued Holmes, "Mrs. Annis had gone over to his cottage by way of the woods for a visit. She'd heard that he'd been sacked from his job with Bloxham. When she was halfway down the hill, she saw Bloxham and MacBride going into the cottage. It was obvious to her that MacBride was the worse for drink. She thought that she would wait until he'd got rid of his visitor, but when Bloxham left, she entered and found him in the same condition which you later discovered. It was obvious to her that there had been a violent struggle, and who had killed her father. Before he left, Bloxham had apparently added a few touches of his own – the Bible, the whisky, and the loaf of bread and so on – to confuse the issue.

"Knowing that Bloxham had killed her father, she arranged for him to be murdered. One of the serving girls in the house is a member of her little congregation. It was easy to add some of the deadly mushrooms to his food."

"But why kill me?" asked Whitaker. "I have only lived here for a few months, and certainly didn't have any involvement with the events related to her father's murder."

"No, but you did excavate the torc and the other items from the hillside. She saw it as a violation of her ancient religion. Remember, Whitaker, that Mrs. Annis had already sacrificially killed twice before, and both of the victims were men. The means of your intended death is horribly reminiscent of what the Celts once called 'The Triple Death' – a ritual sacrifice to the gods of the Celtic pantheon. You were to have filled the third spot. She believed that I was away from the house, and that it could be accomplished before I returned. When I arrived and intervened, Mrs.

Annis and her friends were chanting the name of the Morrigan – the warrior goddess of death and destruction.

"If I hadn't heard your cry," Holmes added, "and investigated, by now you would be on the other side of Hades, or whatever version of the underworld these ladies had prepared for you." He frowned. "I have been remarkably slow in this matter."

Inspector Gould shook his head in disbelief. "I can hardly believe that in the twentieth century we should even consider such events to be possible."

"Well, believe it or not, we have to accept it as fact," Holmes replied. "There is nothing more dangerous than religious zealotry. Wouldn't you agree, Whitaker?"

But Charles Whitaker was staring out of the window at the hills beyond. The outline of the old figure was stark and clear, its chalk contours picked out by the cold autumn sun. On one side stood the dark margin of the woods, on the other the hill swept down to a broad, open swathe of flat fields. Here, centuries before, the tribe of the Iceni had cultivated the land, grazed their animals, and performed their sacrifices to ancient gods. In the time that had passed since then, had humanity really changed or progressed? He didn't think so. He thought of the mass slaughter of the Boer War, and it struck him that in many ways men of his own age were more barbarous than any who had gone before. For a few moments his eyes filled with tears and he was lost in reverie.

# The Adventure of Khamaat's Curse
## by Tracy J. Revels

I called upon my friend Mr. Sherlock Holmes on a blustery December afternoon in 1902, only to find the Baker Street sofa occupied by a striking young woman. In her lovely features the English and the Middle Eastern were mixed to perfection, with flashing black eyes, a determined jut of the chin, and a wonderful wreath of ebony hair. She was dressed in a somewhat outdated fashion, however, with a hat that had been popular before our good Queen died. Everything about her attire suggested a genteel impoverishment, for I noted that even her shoes were worn and patched and seemed inadequate for our bone-chilling weather. Despite her battered bag and threadbare gloves, she radiated poise and dignity. I would have guessed her to be in her late twenties, and though her words were spoken in polished English, I caught just a hint of a foreign accent.

"Doctor Watson reveals in his tales that your clients call you a wizard," she said to Holmes, after introductions were made. Miss Salma Foster, of Luxor House, had greeted me warmly, assuring me that she was a great admirer of my stories. As always, hearing appreciation for my literary efforts – something I rarely received from Holmes – raised my spirits, so that I was especially intrigued by her prelude to her case. "If so," she continued to my friend, "can you lift curses?"

"That is a novel request, but perhaps not entirely beyond my repertoire," Holmes said with a low chuckle. "Who has cursed you?"

"My brother would have you believe that an ancient priestess has – the very woman whose mortal remains lie wrapped in bandages in our attic. But I get ahead of myself. I should give you some context for the problem in which my sister and I find ourselves ensnared."

"Please do," Holmes said.

"The basic facts are these: Our father was Roger Foster, the noted archeologist and adventurer, author of a half-dozen books on such things as Old Kingdom pyramids, the construction of Hittite chariots, and the strange cult of the crocodile god. He was offered prestigious chairs at several universities, both here and on the Continent, but turned them all down, for he was an unconventional man who preferred his freedom. He rendered great service to the Khedive of Egypt during the Urabi Revolt, and was rewarded with special permissions to dig in places where other explorers were forbidden. Once a year, he would forward his discoveries home to Luxor House for safekeeping, swearing that he would spend his retirement studying them.

"Our mother was named Choine, and she was an Egyptian woman who claimed the blood of the pharaohs. A gifted artist, she made sketches and copies of all the texts that Father found on the walls of tombs. My sister Rana is my elder by two years, and has just passed her thirtieth birthday. Until she was fifteen and I thirteen, we all lived as a happy family in a great house in Cairo, with a high wall and a lush garden and a date tree beside a little pool. When I close my eyes I can see our home, and often as I drift to sleep I think I can still hear, in the distance, the sound of the vendors in the marketplace or the imams calling the faithful to prayer. Rana and I were sheltered girls, our mother's pets, and she promised us that we would go to England someday and attend school and become fine ladies.

"Then disaster struck. An epidemic swept through the city, and my mother died after five days of burning with a fever. We had hardly passed this tragedy when a dirty, toothless native woman arrived at our gates, dragging a boy behind her. His name was Husani, the old woman said, and his mother had just died of the plague. Though we found her words difficult to comprehend as we eavesdropped from behind a curtain, we soon came to understand that she claimed the boy was our father's child, and that if he did not take him, the boy would be left to perish on the streets. Father was a kind-hearted man, and whether Husani was his blood or not, he took him in and told us that we were to call him brother. At first we were delighted to have a younger sibling, for he was only nine years old, but we soon decided that he was a pest, for he was also a bully and a cheat. Father told us to be kind, that the lad would learn better manners with time, but I confess that I was grateful when, toward the end of that year, rioters once again made trouble for the English and Father sent Rana and me to his family seat in England, entrusting us to the care of Mrs. Morton, his old nurse. Husani – whom father renamed Hugh – was packed off to a boarding school in Switzerland.

"For years we waited for Father's return. Rana and I hoped to go on to a lady's academy, or even a university, but Father's letters never contained instructions or enough money to make this possible. Hugh, however, was given an excellent education on the Continent and at Cambridge, and seemed destined to follow in Father's footsteps as an expert on antiquities. He was even allowed to go to Egypt on digs, while we were ordered to stay home. We found our lives lonely and purposeless, for Mrs. Morton was a strict chaperone and our neighbors were none too friendly because of our mixed race – and Father, despite all his promises, never came home. He died in 1901, on the same day as the Queen, murdered by a pack of grave robbers whom he was attempting to chase away from his dig site.

"I will not bore you with the details of our lives since Father's passing. Suffice it to say that Father's investments have been just enough to meet our most basic needs and to keep us in some manner of dignified spinsterhood. I have borne it better than Rana, however. After father's death, she became mentally unhinged. Her madness has taken a strange form: She dresses as an ancient Egyptian, worships their deities, and claims to commune with the spirit of Khamaat, a long dead priestess of Bastet, the cat goddess. Khamaat resides with us – or, rather, her mummy does, resting in a painted wood sarcophagus on an altar in our attic. Rana has turned this room into a shrine, complete with oil lamps, marble statues of Bastet, and a dozen devotees in the form of inky black cats, all of which have Egyptian names. Her paganism has made us pariahs, and it was only with great difficulty that I was able to employ servants, especially after the time Rana went around the village collecting stray cats, wearing nothing more than her linen nightdress. Father left the house and the collection of antiquities to my sister and me, but there is little in our home that is of true value, and I fear that in another year we will be forced to sell the property and make our own way in this cruel world."

"What of your brother?" Holmes asked.

"Hugh's education was his legacy from Father. Our brother has come for visits at Luxor House a few times since we left Cairo. Forgive me if I seem cold in my expression, but there has never been any real feeling between the three of us – he is a virtual stranger and we see very little of Father in him. He finds Rana's devotion to Bastet ridiculous, and in his last previous visit he spent most of his time mocking her and making me miserable, before he finally departed for America, to study under Professor Alexander Shaw of Harvard. As far as Rana and I knew, he was working on his doctorate degree, with plans to become a professor. It made me grateful to have an ocean between us. Then, exactly a month ago, he showed up unannounced on our doorstep, with a young woman in tow, prattling on about a curse.

"Hugh told us that in his research with Professor Shaw he had discovered the text of a scroll, copied by our mother, that had somehow been lost or stolen from Father's files in Egypt. It warned that a terrible curse would fall upon whichever blasphemer removed the Priestess Khamaat from her repose inside The Temple of Bastet, and that the curse would not be lifted until her sacred remains were restored to Bastet's sanctuary.

"'Don't you see?' he demanded, when we stared at him with stony faces. 'The curse is what killed your mother, my mother, and our father as well. We have been its victims all these years. Look at you both, pathetic spinsters, living on the knife's edge of poverty! Isn't this proof that Khamaat should be returned to her resting place?'

"'But how has the curse affected you?' I asked, for it was clear that no vindictive goddess had raised a finger to him – indeed, the death of his mother was exactly the thing that had elevated him in the world. He is handsome and healthy, he sports fine clothes, and wears a heavy golden ring on his finger. Furthermore, Hugh was given every opportunity to develop his mind, opportunities that were denied to Rana and me because of our sex, so I would hardly consider him cursed to any degree. Much to my annoyance, Hugh's companion, Miss Anna Wilkes, a buxom, blonde-haired girl who was presented to us as Hugh's 'research assistant', giggled at my question. She is a brainless thing. She is also as greedy as a child, demanding to know how much every curiosity in the house would bring on the auction block and staring at my sister's lapis lazuli necklace as if she wished to pull it apart and eat the stones.

"'The curse has harmed me in ways you could never understand!' Hugh snapped. 'Sisters, please – I can pay you five-hundred American dollars for that mound of rotten flesh and stinking bandages. What do you say?'

"This, naturally, was most offensive to Rana. She wanted to throw Hugh out, but I begged her, for Father's memory, not to quarrel with him. After a day of sullen silence, Hugh apologized and asked our permission to stay for a time and study some of the artifacts from Father's collections.

"It was two days later that the misfortunes began. Hugh must have gone into the village and talked of the curse, for our handful of servants suddenly became nervous and started jumping at shadows. The man who did all our outside chores fell ill with a strange fever and left our service. A day later our cook was sick. By the weekend she was also gone from our employ. Then, much to our dismay, old Mrs. Morton was found expired in her bed. She was very elderly, so her death was not completely unexpected, but Hugh and Miss Wilkes kept murmuring about the curse, and Hugh especially seemed unsettled by Mrs. Morton's passing. When our maid of all work began to shake and vomit the next day, she gave us notice, and so we were deprived of all our servants."

"Have you or your sister suffered from any illnesses?" Holmes asked.

"Rana seems immune to everything. She claims that it is Bastet who protects her. She spends all day attending to her prayers and devotions in the attic, and sleeps there as well, seldom letting her dear Khamaat out of her sight. I, meanwhile, have been plagued by constant headaches and nausea. Miss Wilkes also claims to be frequently indisposed, though she giggles merrily enough when left alone in a room with my brother. More

287

than once I have caught them in inexcusable familiarity. Mr. Holmes, I confess I am a bit prudish and my sister's queer ways have made me ever more concerned for the family's honor. Because of this, two days ago, I asked the village vicar to tea, hoping that his presence might shame Hugh and Miss Wilkes into more respectable behavior. He was perhaps too gentle a man to upbraid them – he never even fussed at Osiris when the cat knocked over his cup and scratched his ankles. Later that evening, we received a visit from the vicar's wife, who was out searching for him, as he had failed to come home. It was not until the next afternoon that his body was found, collapsed in some bushes. It seems he had been ill, stepped away from the thoroughfare, and perished there, but from what cause we do not know. Upon learning that sweet man had died, perhaps because of . . . *No!*" the lady said, with a violent, angry shake of her head, "I cannot – I *will not* – believe in curses from antiquity! Yet I cannot deny that some evil has come among us."

Holmes was sitting with his fingers pressed together. "Miss Foster," he said, "I want you to think very carefully – who do you suspect of causing the sicknesses and deaths?"

"My brother, of course, but I do not know how. I feared, at first, that he might be poisoning us, so I have taken charge of all the food preparation. Nothing noxious has passed through our lips. We have gas in the house, and two weeks ago I had a man out to inspect it, to assure me that nothing could be administered to us that way. If Hugh is causing our pains, I do not know how he is accomplishing it."

"What about his paramour?"

"She is far too stupid, I think. She talks of nothing except the jewels that Hugh will buy for her when he becomes a famous professor. Does that not tell you something of the limitations of her intelligence, that she thinks a professor will be a wealthy man? Besides – she does not have the heart to hurt anything. You should have seen how upset she was about the dead cats."

Holmes sat straighter in his chair. "How many cats have died? And when?"

The young woman shrugged her shoulders. "It is difficult to say, since Rana has collected every unclaimed feline in the neighborhood, along with her prize clutch of pure black 'sacred' specimens. Let me think . . . . There was a pair of gingers that we found in the barn, and the big gray tom that stayed in the kitchen with our cook. The blind one – what a mean, devilish thing she was – I believe Rana found her dead two weeks ago. Old Osiris perished this morning. Miss Wilkes was still mourning for him as I was departing for the station." The clock on the wall chimed and Miss Foster gave a start. "I must hurry, or I will miss my train. Can you help me, Mr. Holmes?"

"I believe that I can," my friend said. "I will be at Luxor House by mid-morning tomorrow. When you return home, it would be best if you removed yourself and your sister to a friend's house for the evening."

The young woman raised her chin defiantly. "We have no friends we could impose upon, and Rana would never agree to leave Khamaat in the house alone with Hugh. Are you implying there is danger to us?"

"I fear that there may be."

Much to my astonishment, a little golden hilted dagger suddenly appeared in the lady's hand, flicked masterfully from within somewhere within her sleeve.

"Then I am ready for it."

The next morning, when I met Holmes at the railway station, he was not alone. He introduced me to a trim, freckle-faced young woman with chestnut hair cut in a mannish bob and golden spectacles perched on the end of her nose.

"Watson, a consulting detective knows when he must consult. This is Miss Hypatia Brown, an expert in hieroglyphics and ancient languages."

Holmes rattled off a further string of intellectual honors. The lady turned a pleasant shade a pink at his praise. I wondered how anyone so young could have achieved so many academic credentials, but did not ask where Holmes had found her. His network of associates was vast, and while most were people of the criminal class and lower orders, a few were simply unusual individuals of high specialized skills.

"Do you believe in curses?" I asked Miss Brown, as we settled into our compartment. The lady answered in a soft voice.

"What I believe is unimportant, but what the intended victim believes matters greatly. For example, there are a number of verified cases in America, from before their Civil War, where a slave who was informed of being 'hexed' by a conjurer rapidly sickened and died in just the manner that the spell prescribed."

"Superstition," I tutted.

"Or the power of suggestion," Holmes corrected. "The human mind is a wonderous thing. And, my dear Watson, before you allow yourself to indulge in prejudice against all things not English, recall that even Shakespeare placed a dire warning on his tombstone:

*"Good friend for Jesus sake forbeare*
*To dig the dust enclosed here*
*Blessed be the man that spares these stones*

289

We arrived at Luxor House at ten o'clock sharp as the village bells rang in the distance. The house showed many signs of neglect, yet there was something strangely picturesque about it in the bleakness of the winter landscape. My eyes were drawn to the quaint, unexpected details that marked it as the former home of an Oriental adventurer. Stone sphinxes, rather than lions, guarded the iron gates, and instead of a Grecian or Gothic folly, a tumbledown replica of the great temple of Rameses rose above the brambles in the frozen remnants of a garden. The house was fronted by white columns fluted in the Egyptian style, while the massive door bore the carved likenesses of Thoth and Horus. Miss Foster opened the door at our first knock, and immediately we knew that she was nearly undone by anxiety. The face that had been so composed the day before was now flushed with emotion and stained with tears. Her lips were bitten raw. Before any words could be spoken, she seized Holmes's hands and tugged him forward.

"Oh thank God that you have come! It is too dreadful, the argument they have had! Please, Mr. Holmes, if you have any paternal feelings, you must intervene. You must help me put it all to rights!"

"My dear lady," Holmes said, as I closed the door behind us, "do try and calm yourself. What has happened?"

"This morning, when Rana awoke to perform her devotions, she found another of her cats dead. She stormed down to shriek at Hugh and his lady, accusing them of slaying her precious creatures. Hugh laughed and told her that Khamaat was displeased, and that the animal's death was what she deserved for refusing to surrender the mummy to him. They both began to scream horrible oaths at each other, and suddenly the dishes were flying, leaving Miss Wilkes cut on the face and bleeding. Rana ordered them to leave, and Hugh said they would gladly depart on the evening train. He and Miss Wilkes have gone upstairs to pack, while Rana has gone to bury her pet. Oh, Mr. Holmes, maybe there is such a thing as a curse, to have set us against each other and – "

Her words were broken by a hideous wail, a banshee cry that seemed to roll and echo and swell to fill the entire house. For an instant all we four could do was stare stupidly at each other, and then Holmes was racing for the staircase, charging upward in the direction of the sound. As I galloped behind him, I had the fleeting impression of an elegant home that had been transformed into something no longer quaint or curious, but dark and sinister. Walls were painted to resemble the inside of a tomb, with scenes of jackals devouring the hearts of evildoers. Statues with strange heads and contorted bodies lured in dark alcoves. The cloying aroma of incense blended with the unpleasant smell of cats. A dozen or more felines darted into corners or beneath chairs, hissing and spitting at us as we ran toward the attic.

Holmes pushed the hatch door open and I came up the narrow steps after him. I will never forget the horror that lay within that large but low room, which was lit only by the glow of a few oil lamps which dangled from the ceiling. Two bodies rested on the floor just a few feet apart, both of them drenched in gore. Hugh Foster was a robust, darkly handsome man, but now he laid on his side with his knees curled and his open eyes staring sightlessly at the ceiling, his throat viciously slashed. It had been done just moments before, and his warm blood had pooled around him. His sister was crumpled to one side, a jewel-encrusted knife still clutched in her hand. I knelt to see if there was any aid I could offer her. Hugh Foster was beyond succor, and to my dismay I found that Rana Foster was also deceased, the back of her skull smashed in. The murder weapon was a black marble statue of a Bastet, about the size of a dumbbell, which had been discarded beside the body. Just inches from the two victims was a strange altar, with the wooden sarcophagus propped against it. The mummy of Khamaat had been removed from its casket, and bits of it were scattered about the altar, as if someone had been breaking it apart, limb by limb.

In the far corner of the room, Miss Anna Wilkes crouched like a frightened child, her hands pressed to her mouth. As the ladies entered the attic behind us, she began to wail.

"I'm sorry, I'm sorry, I didn't mean to do it! She killed Hugh – she had a knife, she tried to cut me too. She was she was going to kill me! I didn't mean to hit her so hard!"

Miss Foster ran forward, screaming at the sight of her sister's body. She lunged toward Miss Wilkes, her own golden blade suddenly in her hand, but Holmes seized her before she could strike. Miss Brown – by some feminine magic that neither of us could comprehend or hope to replicate – got her arms around the furious woman, whispered words in her ear that quickly calmed her, then escorted her from the room. Holmes stood still, his eyes roaming over the grim tableau. In the corner, Miss Wilkes continued to weep.

"Someone must go for the authorities," I said.

"Yes – please do so, Watson."

I could tell from his dark expression that this sad event would weigh heavily upon my friend's conscience. I took it upon myself to bundle up Miss Wilkes and lead her down to a bedroom on the second floor, where I administered a strong sedative. I then hurried downstairs and found that one of the Fosters' employees had returned and was standing at the door, hat in hand, curious as to why his knocks had received no answer. I gave the man the briefest of sketches, bidding him to go and summon the police. Pale-faced and trembling, he rushed off, and I returned upstairs.

"Careful, Watson," Holmes said as I once again stepped within the strange sanctuary to Bastet. "Do not let the cat out."

I looked down and saw a large black cat giving me an evil stare. He was wearing a leather collar with his name engraved on a brass bar. I consulted it from a safe distance.

"Do you plan to question Mr. Ra as a witness?"

"He has his role to play," Holmes answered. "In the meantime, let us see if we can accurately reconstruct what occurred. I have no doubt that Miss Foster assaulted her brother, infuriated by having found him at his work."

"His work?"

Holmes pointed to the casket and the broken pieces of the mummy. "Hugh Foster had been seeking his chance for days, but Miss Rana Foster's devotion to her idol thwarted his attempts. She also would not fall victim to the sickness he created with his 'curse'. It must have been infuriating to him." Holmes gestured to the jagged wrapping that were half-torn from a leathery arm. "He had no time to spare on the niceties of unwrapping. Clearly, Miss Rana surprised him in the act, and her passion to guard her relic was unquenchable. Like her sister, she went about armed and did not hesitate to use her blade."

I looked down at the tiny woman on the floor. She was a pitiful creature, hardly larger than a girl, dressed only in a thin linen gown, barefoot, her exposed arms covered in gaudy bangles and bracelets. Her thick hair hung almost to her waist, but was heavily shot through with gray. I shook myself, recalling that she was only thirty years of age.

"How did such a small woman manage such a brutal act?"

Holmes considered the position of the man's body. "I believe he was on his knees when she struck. Perhaps he was picking up a piece of the mummy or seeking something he had dropped. She rushed up in a fury at his desecration – maybe he even laughed at her. If so, that was his fatal mistake. A man should never underestimate a woman, especially when a woman is defending what she loves, be it a child or a cat or a dead body."

"And Miss Wilkes?"

Holmes backed away and pointed to the nearest wall, which was almost lost in the gloom of the attic shrine. A host of statues rested on shelves, but one was niche was empty.

"She stood there. She had no interest in Hugh's grisly work, so she amused herself by toying with the décor. It is darker at the wall, these oil lamps do not illuminate the room adequately, and Miss Foster was focused intently on the vengeful task at hand. The placement of the wound makes it clear that Miss Wilkes struck Rana Foster from behind. Our American lady may have been in fear for her life after witnessing her lover's demise, but she was not being chased or assaulted by Miss Foster when she struck the blow. We must leave it to the authorities to decide her level of culpability in this crime."

His reasoning seemed impeccable, but questions still formed in my mind. "What did you mean about Hugh creating a sickness?"

Holmes crouched down beside the man's body. With twitching fingers, he began to examine the contents of the dead man's pockets. At first there was little of interest: A gold watch, a railway ticket, a handkerchief, a piece of hard candy. Then Holmes uttered a cry of satisfaction and held up a small blue bottle. Holmes pulled out the stopper and gave a short, cautious sniff. He frowned as he shook the bottle.

"I should have expected it to be empty."

"But . . . how did you know you would find a bottle? And what was in it?"

"A simple thread of reasoning told me that there must be a container for the 'curse'," Holmes said. "I knew I would find some type of toxin which brought illness and, perhaps unintentionally, death." Before I could speak, Holmes shed his travelling cloak and began stalking the big black cat. "Come here, Puss. We mean you no harm. Watson, hold these."

He tossed me an item from his pocket. It was a large pair of nail clippers.

"Ah – *Gotcha!*" Holmes enveloped the squirming feline in his cloak. At just that moment, Miss Brown returned to the attic and, intuiting the problem, hurried to assist my friend. They wrapped the angry, squalling feline until he was a helpless, bound bundle of fur and fabric with just the tips of his paws exposed. I moved closer, still wary, as the cat continued to emit low, spectral-sounding moans. "Take the clippers, Watson, and trim off his claws," Holmes instructed, much to my displeasure. "Put your gloves on first – I wouldn't want you infected. Be sure to gather up the nails in a handkerchief. They will put my skills at chemical analysis to the test."

I suddenly understood what he had only hinted at. "Hugh Foster coated the cat's claws in poison!"

"Yes, and it is a cunning preparation. His goal was to bring fear and terror to the house, to make his victims feel they were being sickened by a supernatural entity. He knew that in a house swarming with cats, scratches were inevitable – no doubt the servants hardly noticed the occasional wound. But the merest scrape from a cat's tainted claws could bring fever and nausea. Poor Mrs. Morton and the vicar were already in delicate health, and what made for a few uncomfortable hours for younger people ushered them into the afterlife. I doubt that was Hugh Foster's intent, but he was a murderer just the same."

"And the cats, when they licked their paws, were poisoned as well."

"I suspect the cats were like their human counterparts – the heartier ones crept away to be ill in a corner, while the older ones, including ancient Osiris, were killed by the toxin. Not a single cat that Hugh could catch would have been spared the treatment. Miss Rana escaped the plague because she doted on the cats and they returned the favor. Unlike the others in the household, she was never scratched." I finished the last paw, and Holmes released the ungrateful animal on the floor. "We should attend to all the cats we can find. The more samples I have, the easier my work will be."

I folded the handkerchief into a little packet. "But why was Hugh willing to kill to acquire this particular mummy?"

Holmes turned to his expert, who was now standing over the sarcophagus. The appalling scene on the floor did not seem to affect her, and she worked with quiet, quick motions, picking up pieces of the damaged mummy's body and reassembling them in proper order.

"The answer is elementary," Holmes said. "The body in the coffin is not that of Khamaat, a priestess of Bastet."

"Why would you think it is an imposter?"

Holmes smiled as he watched the young woman pull out a magnifying glass to study an inscription on the linen wrappings.

"Another simple chain of reasoning, Watson. Hugh Foster was a trained archeologist and familiar with his father's collection. He knew of his sister's obsession with this mummy. But suddenly he returned from his studies in America with a startling new revelation. We may brush aside the concern over a curse. As a man of science, Hugh had no such fears. He was desperate to get his hands on his sister's favorite relic, and he thought that by mimicking the results of a curse, he could obtain the mummy, due to her superstitious nature. There can be only one conclusion that explains his actions: The mummy had not changed, but his *knowledge* about the mummy had changed. He had learned that the mummy was not the body of a priestess, but the corpse of someone more famous and, therefore, more valuable."

"Yet he was breaking it apart," I argued, sensing a flaw in Holmes's argument. "That would make it worth less to a collector or museum."

"You are both right," Miss Brown said. "Hugh Foster discovered the mummy had been misidentified by his father. I have deciphered the cartouche on the wrappings. This is not the priestess Khamaat, but rather the Pharaoh Kumet, a king who ruled for less than a year in the fifteenth dynasty. Hundreds of years ago, someone charged with protecting the dead pharaoh placed his mummy in Khamaat's sarcophagus. It was not such an uncommon practice, as grave robbers were active and in search of royal loot. The unknown guardian must have reasoned that no thief would bother to disturb a mere priestess, for her mummy would have little to offer."

"You said we were each correct. So there is something *inside* the mummy?" I asked.

"Yes – see here." The lady handed us a small golden talisman, an image of a hawk with an emerald for an eye. "These are called funerary amulets, and are placed throughout the wrappings and against the body. They were said to provide protection during the soul's journey to the afterlife. For a pharaoh, they would be made of the finest gold and gems. They could be worth a fortune."

Holmes sighed as he looked down at the bodies of the archeologist and his deluded sister. "Are those ancient trinkets worth the lives of four humans and a yet unknown number of cats? If there was not a curse on this house before, most assuredly there is now."

My readers will be curious to know what became of the case of the Fosters of Luxor House. Holmes collected the claws of all the whiskered residents of the manor, but his chemical experiments were inconclusive. Whatever poison the treacherous Hugh Foster had placed on the cats' nails could not be positively identified, though Holmes believed it was derived from a certain noxious plant common in the rocky soil of New England and used by native shamans as a purgative. Miss Wilkes was briefly held for the murder of Rana Foster, but was able to convince the police that she knew nothing of her lover's plot and had struck the insane sister in self-defense. Holmes provided the local authorities with his thoughts on what had occurred, but I believe that a certain prejudice against "amateurs" – even one as famous and respected as my friend – combined with the accused lady's great beauty, timid demeanor, and doe-like helplessness, persuaded the authorities not to take a stern attitude with her. I also suspect that the Christian community's disapproval of Miss Rana Foster's avowed paganism may have contributed to the release of her killer.

Miss Selma Foster, now not only orphaned but deprived of all her kin, took some time to recover from the tragedy. A month or so later we received word that she had invited a young archeologist, Professor Edward Peterson – a man with a distant kinship to another famed investigator of antiquities, Mr. Howard Carter – to make an assessment of the damaged mummy of Khamaat/Kumet. Peterson arrived at Luxor House and documented the find, eventually unwrapping the mummy completely and confirming that it was, indeed, the corpse of a pharaoh lost to time.

However, the funerary amulets and other goods dug from the wrappings were not as valuable as the greedy Hugh had anticipated, and did not restore the previous wealth of the Fosters. Yet for all these misfortunes, the story had a remarkably happy ending.

A basket arrived at Baker Street on a spring morning, just as I was paying Holmes a call. It was a strange wicker concoction, much like one designed to transport a fisherman's catch. Holmes glanced at the note attached, then thrust it at me with a request that I read it aloud. I cleared my throat.

> *My Dear Mr. Holmes,* (I read)
>
> *By the time you receive this, you will have learned that Professor Edward Peterson, recently appointed to a chair in the study of ancient cultures at Camford University, has done me the honor of asking for my hand in marriage. We have been thrown together a good deal as he studied the mortal remains of Kumet, and in him I have found my heart's companion. Luxor House is to be sold, and I pray that all my bad memories of my wicked half-brother will go with it.*
>
> *You were too kind to refuse any reward for solving the mystery of Khamaat's curse. Please, do not continue to blame yourself for my sister's demise. I believe Rana happier now, her soul residing in some heavenly place where she may bask in Bastet's splendor. I beg you to allow me to bestow on you this memento of our strange family and one of your more peculiar cases.*
>
> *Sincerely,*
>
> *Selma Foster*

"Watson, the basket is moving."

Cautiously, I lifted the lid of the container. What I glimpsed within caused me to laugh heartily, especially when I turned and saw the alarm on Holmes's face. I reached inside and drew out a little black kitten, no doubt the offspring of one of the felines that Holmes's claw-trimming had spared from an untimely demise, perhaps even the son or grandson of the mighty Ra. The little fellow had a ribbon tied around his neck, and he purred with delight when I gave him a fond scratch under his chin. Holmes sighed.

296

"I have had unusual compensations before, but this is truly one for the annuals." Holmes took the kitten, studying its bright green eyes. "However delightful a companion you might make, little gent, my rooms are hardly a safe place for a cat, with all the poisons lying about – not to mention the dangerous characters who pass through these doors at all hours. I think I can find a much more suitable home for you. Mrs. Hudson!" he shouted, "I have a surprise!"

# The Adventure of the
# Weeping Mary
## by Matthew White

"It really is no good, Watson," said Sherlock Holmes as I stepped into our old sitting room at 221b Baker Street. It was a chilly February morning, and I had decided to abandon my practice for the day and pay a visit to my friend. I found him slouching in his chair by the fire in his old mouse-coloured dressing gown, one arm draped over the armrest, a letter held loosely between his long fingers. The remains of his breakfast were still on the table, and the room was in its customary state of orderly disorder, with stacks of papers and books covering the table, chairs, and nearly every other flat surface. Holmes would never suffer the landlady, Mrs. Hudson, to tidy the room, on the objection that every item in every pile was placed for maximum convenience, and the slightest disruption would ruin his entire scheme of organization.

"What is it, Holmes?" I asked. Rising from his chair, he moved a stack of books off my old familiar chair by the fire and poured a generous measure of brandy into two glasses, one of which he offered to me and I gladly accepted.

"Bah!" he ejaculated in annoyance as he resumed his seat, curling his legs under him and wrapping himself tightly. "I had hoped that the morning post would bring something of interest. I have been so wretchedly bored since I concluded the affair of the fraudulent Shakespeare folio."

"I wish I could have accompanied you for that," said I. My friend waved his hand dismissively.

"It was quite trivial in the end. Nothing, I dare say, that would have been especially exciting to your loyal readers."

"Even so," I said, "I'm always pleased to follow you on your cases for my own personal satisfaction, and for another chance to study your remarkable methods."

"You are very kind," said Holmes, obviously pleased by the compliment. "But I fear you will be disappointed today."

Holmes languidly extended his arm and offering the letter for my inspection. I took it and read:

*Dear Mr. Sherlock Holmes,*

*I am writing to you in hopes of obtaining your help with a matter which is weighing on my conscience. It is possible you have heard certain sensational rumors regarding a statue of the Blessed Virgin in the Church of St. Anne, which is reputed to weep blood. There is such a statue, and I have seen the blood for myself. Despite the evidence of my eyes, I suspect all is not as it appears, and a great fraud is being perpetrated. If convenient, I will call upon you at ten o'clock and tell you more in person.*

*Yours faithfully,*

*Mrs. Mercy Driscoll*

"How extraordinary," said I after reading the letter. "You don't feel it warrants your attention?"

"It hardly takes an expert to point out that statues do not weep blood," said Holmes irritably, "or at any rate not for supernatural causes. It is, therefore, no great revelation that, in our correspondent's words, '*all is not as it appears.*' Why, I can describe three methods a clever man could use to produce the effect, and a further two so simple that no cleverness at all is required in their application."

My friend sighed.

"Ah, the Baskerville case – now that was clever! The priory devil – that was imaginative! Compared to that, weeping statues seem positively mundane!"

"Surely," I said, "it would not hurt to hear the details. It is nearly ten already."

"Yes, yes," Holmes said, waving his hand with a dismissive air. "It will, at the very least, provide a quarter-of-an-hour of relief from complete boredom. Ah, Mrs. Hudson, there you are! Do clear the table, won't you? The Good Doctor and I are expecting visitors."

"You wish me to stay, then?" I asked.

"Naturally, if it is not inconvenient."

"Never, my dear fellow," said I, gratified as always by the invitation.

The long-suffering landlady had just gone downstairs, and I was engaged in a vain effort to make the room presentable, when the bell rang. We heard light footfalls on the stair, and the page boy entered the room, followed by our guest. She was a tall woman, middle-aged but with an ageless elegance. Her features were soft, her hair dark, and despite the austerity of her dress and the pained expression on her face, she carried herself with as much poise and confidence as any noble lady I have ever seen.

"Mrs. Driscoll," said Holmes in soothing tones. "I am Sherlock Holmes, and this is my friend and colleague, Dr. Watson, who is sometimes kind enough to help me in my investigations. Please, do have a seat," he said, indicating the basket chair. "May I offer you some refreshment? Please, do sit down at once, for I perceive that your long walk has aggravated your right foot. I take it that you are not in the habit of riding an omnibus?"

"I won't deny it, Mr. Holmes," she said in a startled tone. I poured her a glass of brandy, which she gratefully accepted. "I have heard you have a talent for revealing a person's secrets within moments of meeting them. I suffer from a bunion on my right foot, as a matter of fact. I suppose that was plain enough to see, but I am curious how you knew I don't often ride omnibuses."

Holmes smiled. "The bunion was, indeed, plain enough. I could hear that it was difficult for you to climb the stairs – twice you stopped for a brief pause, and when you entered the room, I observed that you favour your left foot. The manner in which you twist your right ankle to minimize pressure against your great toe is quite characteristic of the affliction. As for the omnibus, that was a simple process of elimination. You are not dressed for long travel. Therefore you began your journey in London, but it is obvious by the fresh dirt on your boots and skirt that you did not take a cab. Neither could you be expected to walk the entire way, so, naturally, the omnibus is the obvious choice. That same accumulation of dirt, and your obvious signs of pain, indicate that you walked much farther than would be required if you had taken the most efficient omnibus route. It is reasonable to assume that you are not familiar with them."

"It does sound rather simple, when you put it like that," our visitor said, and I saw the briefest flicker of disappointment on Holmes's face before he resumed his calm, charming manner.

"Mrs. Driscoll, I have read your letter. Sadly, the lack of details prevents me from offering useful counsel to you in this matter, so I shall need you to supply more. I gather that you believe some fraud is being committed?"

"Yes, Mr. Holmes, it is exactly so."

"Pray, take your time, and when you feel ready, give me the details, as clearly and completely as you can."

My friend stretched his legs and leaned back into the chair, putting his hands together fingertip to fingertip. Our guest took a few moments to collect her thoughts and sip her brandy before she began her story.

"My late husband was a steamship captain, and earned us a good living. Sadly, his ship was lost at sea, and the past ten years have not been kind to my children and me. Our circumstances compelled us to take up residence, I am ashamed to admit, in a tenement house in Spitalfields, where we take such work as we can get. Being Catholic, I attend the Church of St. Anne there."

"St. Anne, St. Anne . . . Ah, yes, on Underwood Street."

"Yes, that's the one," Mrs. Driscoll nodded.

"It is rather new, is it not?"

"Yes it is, Mr. Holmes, only recently completed. Nonetheless, we serve many people in great need. I'm sure I do not need to tell you that the slums of Spitalfields are havens of criminality and filled with unfortunate souls who drown, year by year, in poverty the likes of which many of their neighbors in the city can scarcely imagine. It is a place without hope, Mr. Holmes – without light. I am ashamed to admit that living in such a place has, on occasion, caused me to doubt the goodness of Our Lord. With some of the other lay women, I take part in some small charitable endeavors for the less fortunate – providing food and clothing, or helping them find productive work. It is my own small way of bringing some light to that awful place."

"That's very commendable of you," said I. "If only there were more women like you in the world."

"Thank you, Doctor Watson, but I do not do it for praise. In any case, I was very close for a number of years with the parish priest, Father Murray, an elderly gentleman and the kindest, most godly human being I have ever met. Six months ago, a new priest, Father Lester, arrived at the parish. Almost immediately, Father Murray's whole attitude changed. He became irritable, sullen, and sad. He and Father Lester didn't get along. Why, one evening I was walking past the priory when I heard the two of them having a terrible row. I couldn't hear everything they said, but it sounded like it was about money. The next day, Father Murray resigned and Father Lester became our new priest. His resignation was so sudden that I did not have the chance to see him again."

"Did Father Murray give any reason for his abrupt resignation?" I asked. Mrs. Driscoll shook her head.

"Not that I know of, Doctor Watson, but I am certain Father Lester was the cause. I gathered that he was stricken by some sudden illness, and had a mind to send him a letter, but when I inquired after an address, I was told that it would be quite impossible."

Holmes frowned. "Pray continue, Mrs. Driscoll."

"I was disappointed to learn that Father Lester is rather less interested in charity than Father Murray was. The two men may look very much alike, but they could not be more different. He doesn't seem to have much regard for the needs of his parish, or for the charity Our Lord expects of us. Indeed, he rarely speaks to anyone, and spends most of his time in the priory. It was shortly after his arrival that . . . ."

Our guest looked uncomfortable. Holmes leaned toward her and spoke in a soothing voice.

"Say whatever is on your mind, Mrs. Driscoll. You may trust us."

His reassuring manner seemed to put her at ease, for she smiled at him, sat up straight, and continued her narrative.

"It was shortly after his arrival that a statue of the Blessed Virgin in the church began to weep tears of blood. I've seen it myself. The blood wells up in the corner of the eyes and trickles down the statue's face. Oh, you must think me mad."

"Quite the contrary," he assured her. "I believe completely that you saw what you say you saw."

"I am relieved to hear it. Many people believe it's a miracle. They come to see it every day, morning and evening, and bring offerings – sometimes all the money they managed to make the day before, hoping that the Virgin will bless them with health, or money, or whatever their heart desires."

"Father Lester encourages these offerings?"

"Oh yes," Mrs. Driscoll answered. "Often, those without offerings are denied admission to see the statue. He lectures them on the story of the widow's mite."

"I know the passage," Holmes said. "What do you think of the statue, Mrs. Driscoll?"

"I do not consider myself an overly superstitious woman, but what else could it be but a miracle?"

"And yet, from the contents of your letter I glean that you have doubts?"

Mrs. Driscoll frowned and looked at her hands as if searching for words.

"I cannot tell you why, Mr. Holmes. As I said, I do not see how the weeping statue could be anything less than a genuine miracle. Nor do I have proof that Father Lester is doing anything dishonest. I only know that something feels wrong. I feel it in my bones."

"The circumstances you describe also strike me as suspicious," Holmes said. "The only detail you have omitted, so far as I can tell, is how exactly you would like me to help you."

"Put simply, Mr. Holmes, I want you to investigate St. Anne's and discover if I am right. If all is as it should be, well and good. But I fear I

302

shall not rest until I can put my suspicions to rest. I have little money, but I am prepared to pay what I can."

Holmes closed his eyes and sat in silence for a number of minutes. Mrs. Driscoll looked at me in evident confusion, and I gave her what I hoped to be a reassuring smile. Even I, however, had begun to fear my friend had fallen asleep when his eyes snapped open again.

"I fear, Mrs. Driscoll, that your intuitions are correct. There is certainly fraud being committed at St. Anne's."

"Oh?"

"Before you arrived, I remarked to Doctor Watson how easy it is to make a statue weep. It seems to me clear that this Father Lester has produced a counterfeit miracle in the hope of profiting from the desperate men who offer their money and goods in exchange for divine favour."

"But why in Spitalfields, Holmes?" I asked. "Surely his gains would be greater in a more prosperous neighborhood?"

Holmes shrugged. "Perhaps Father Lester believes that desperate men are easier to fool. I have certainly found that to be true in my own experience. In any case, Mrs. Driscoll, if you wish to pursue the matter, I think you would do well to appeal to the Archbishop of Westminster."

"But I have done, Mr. Holmes, and he has promised an investigation, but no investigation seems to be taking place. And in the meanwhile, these poor people continue to get poorer and poorer."

"You might try the police," I suggested. Mrs. Driscoll's features curdled into a look of disgust.

"They don't seem to care what happens in Spitalfields, Doctor," she said. "Is there nothing else you can do to help, Mr. Holmes?"

"The matter seems to be a perfectly simple one, Mrs. Driscoll. I have given you my professional opinion, and I have no doubt that it can be cleared up without any further intervention on my part. As for my fee, you needn't trouble yourself. Good day."

With that, he pulled some tobacco from the Persian slipper by the fire and concentrated on filling his pipe, apparently disinclined to take any further notice of our visitor. I took it upon myself to escort Mrs. Driscoll to the door, and gave her an amount which I hoped would be adequate for cab fare.

"I think," said I when we were alone, "that that was rather insensitive of you. Surely there is more you could do to set that poor woman's mind at ease?"

"As I said, it is a perfectly simple case, and not one which requires action from me. It is within the power of the police to investigate further, if they see a need. I fancy even Athelney Jones, for all his faults, would not be fooled by anything quite so obvious."

"But she has said the police refuse to help!"

"And I am not under any obligation to supply their deficiencies, as I've said before."

"And the priest?" I asked.

"He is obviously party to the trick, and probably the main perpetrator."

"Holmes," said I, "for all your experience of the minds of criminals, I think I may boast a superior experience of the minds of women. I am not speaking of Father Lester, but Father Murray. The lady was plainly worried for her friend. Indeed, I believe she my think something has happened to him. Do the circumstances of his departure not strike you as suspicious, as well?"

His only reply was a monosyllabic grunt. He tucked his knees under his chin and assumed a look of intense concentration. Being familiar with Holmes's habits, I recognized that he had no further need of company, being occupied now with a mental problem to unravel. I left him there with a cloud of tobacco smoke growing about his head, like a great storm cloud gathering above a mountain peak.

Though I went to sleep with the puzzle still on my mind, the toil of the next day swiftly pushed it from my memory. I had quite nearly forgotten it entirely when, the next afternoon, a commissionaire arrived at my practice with a telegram addressed to me. The message was characteristically brief:

*Come to Baker Street tonight at five. – H*

Accordingly, at the appointed hour my hansom pulled up at the door of 221b and I alighted, bundled up to ward off the chill. Mrs. Hudson took my coat, hat, and stick, and I ascended the stairs. Before I could knock on the sitting room door, Holmes flung it open, clutching a letter in his hand.

"Watson, do come in."

"Has something happened? A new investigation, perhaps?" I inquired, pointing toward the letter.

His manner was spry and energetic.

"Not quite, Watson, not quite. As a matter of fact, I must confess that I erred by dismissing Mrs. Driscoll's case so soon."

"Oh? What changed your mind?"

"Have a seat, dear fellow," said he, indicating my customary chair by the fire and flopping down on his own.

"I have been very busy today, but I mustn't get ahead of myself. The fact is, although I was satisfied with my explanation for the situation described by Mrs. Driscoll, something still puzzled me. I determined that

I would be remiss if I did not, at the very least, see things for myself. This morning, therefore, I was at St. Anne's."

"You?" I gasped in astonishment, for I had never known my friend to have any affinity for the Roman Catholic Church.

"In disguise, of course. I admit, it was rather different from what I expected."

"The church?"

"The statue, Watson."

"You saw the weeping Mary?" I asked with an eyebrow raised.

"If it is counterfeit, it is more cunningly done than any I have heard of before."

"You say 'if' it is? Then you think it may be genuine?"

"One must be open to all possibilities in order to provide against them," said Holmes sagely, like a tutor lecturing his pupil. "How many times have I told you that once you have ruled out the impossible, whatever remains, however preposterous it may seem, must necessarily be the truth? But once again, I am getting ahead of myself."

"Tell me everything!" said I.

"My disguise was very well done, if I may say so myself. I dressed myself in rags, and gave myself an unkempt white beard and the rosy complexion which always marks the man who has lost himself to drink. I joined a motley pack of unfortunates who filed into the church once the mass proper was concluded and the respectable worshipers had dispersed. The spectacle which followed was, based on my own admittedly limited knowledge of Roman Catholic liturgy, quite unusual.

"The statue is situated in an unassuming little shrine in the north aisle, near the west end of the church. Father Lester held out a gold plate on which we newcomers deposited coins and notes. Twice, the Father turned away supplicants whose offerings were inadequate. Afterwards, we assembled in the aisle before the shrine of Saint Mary, and the Father got on his knees before the statue, and the rest of us did likewise. He began to recite that old familiar prayer: *Ave María, gratia plena*, and so on. I had positioned myself so that I had a view of the statue behind him. It was most remarkable, Watson – as he prayed, the statue began to weep, exactly as Mrs. Driscoll described! I admit, it took me by surprise."

"How so?"

"Because it did not behave like a forgery at all. A common method of producing a weeping statue, if one does not simply apply the liquid to the surface directly, is to fill a hidden reservoir with some fluid, which will slowly seep through a porous material behind the eyes and appear on the outer surface. But the weeping, or so we may call it, occurred much too quickly for that. And the timing – you might say it was *immaculate*."

Holmes grinned wryly. "It was exactly as you would expect from a miracle."

"And you know of no method of trickery which could account for it?" I asked. Holmes looked thoughtful.

"One or two possibilities occur to me, but I shall need to examine the statue more closely before coming to any conclusions. The statue is not the only interesting puzzle in this case, however."

"What else?"

"The question of why Father Murray is hiding in the parsonage."

"What?" I gasped. "How can you be sure?"

"Because I have seen him."

Holmes looked at me in amusement, clearly pleased by the dramatic effect of this revelation.

"After leaving the church, I took some time to observe the parsonage, which a rather stately building directly beside the church. I was peering over the garden wall when I noticed some movement in an upper window. The windows beside it were fully shuttered, but this particular window was only partly done, so that it was just possible to see a face looking out. For a brief moment, I thought it was Father Lester, but this face was much older, careworn, and pale. He wore an expression of despair such as I have seldom seen on a man's face."

"How very strange," I remarked. "What do you suppose it means?"

"I have my suspicions. It certainly elevates this case above the commonplace, and into the realm of the sinister. But it is a mistake to theorize in the absence of data, and data is what I need."

Holmes reached for his tobacco and began to fill his pipe. I could see from his expression that he was deep in thought, and so I kept quiet, not wanting to disturb him. After some time, he arose and paced to-and-fro, before turning on his heel to face me.

"Perhaps you would like to accompany me on an errand, Watson?"

"Certainly," I said.

"There's a good fellow."

A few minutes later, we descended the stairs, Holmes taking them two at a time, and went outside into the chilly winter air. Holmes appeared to be in a good mood, and spent the walk to the post office speaking excitedly about a number of topics, including an article he had read about a breakthrough in the study of chemistry which particularly excited him, and news of sensational crimes on the Continent which had recently come to his attention. He must have found his current endeavor quite stimulating, for I have seldom seen him behave so energetically for any other reason. At the post office he collected a telegram, which he studied for a moment before pocketing it and going back outside to hail a passing cab. He instructed the driver to take us to St. Anne.

"You're going back?" I asked.

"*We* are going back," he corrected me. "I have a few questions about Father Lester, and I intend to get my answers directly from the source."

"I see. But surely my presence is hardly necessary?"

"My dear Watson, you are invaluable to me! Four hands are better than two."

As we neared our destination, the nauseating reek of nearby Spitalfields filled my nostrils.

"It is a striking contrast, is it not, Watson?" said Holmes, evidently noticing my discomfort. "How many citizens of our blessed metropolis, the capitol of the world, the beating heart of the Empire, go about their daily lives heedless that they have only to cross a street or two and see men no different from themselves reduced to living little better than beasts? All the modern wonders which the mind of man can invent, side by side with the worst squalor the mind of man can imagine."

"'*Ye have the poor with you always* . . . .'" I quoted.

"Quite so," said Holmes with a sardonic smile. "Pithy, Watson. I confess that you sometimes take even me by surprise."

After a time the hansom pulled up at St. Anne's and we climbed out onto the pavement. Holmes caught my attention with a look and nodded across the street. A ruddy-faced fellow with a strong jaw and pronounced chin was crossing in our direction, clad in clerical garb with a pair of gold-rimmed spectacles perched on his nose. With the graceful swiftness of a feline predator, Holmes moved to intercept the priest, who had not seemed to take any notice of us.

"Father Lester, I presume?" said Holmes as he stepped in front of the man. The gentleman, who had the look of a man in his early fifties, seemed surprised and annoyed at my friend's approach, and the forced smile he assumed did nothing to dispel the impression.

"Forgive my intrusion into your busy day," Holmes went on, "but I have heard so much about you from my friends in the parish, and when I noticed you crossing the street I simply couldn't resist introducing myself."

"No trouble at all," said Father Lester, unconvincingly. "Mr. – ?"

"Scott," replied Holmes at once, tactfully removing the glove from his right hand. "William Scott. It is an honor, sir."

Holmes extended his hand, which the priest perfunctorily grasped. I glanced around and noticed that we were observed – a short, rather petite woman was standing under the shadow of the church, watching the conversation between Holmes and Father Lester. There was something in her face which I found familiar, but before I could study her further, she disappeared behind the church building.

I looked back toward Holmes in time to see him part ways with Father Lester, who was walking to the parsonage with more haste than before, no doubt to escape any more unexpected conversations. Holmes approached me with a smile on his face.

"Holmes," I said, "there was a woman watching you."

"Yes, I noticed her the moment we disembarked from our cab. Did you get a clear view of her face?"

"Well, yes. She looked ordinary enough. But what was the meaning of that brief exchange just now?"

"Simply that I wished to know more about Father Lester," Holmes replied.

"And you learned it by shaking his hand?"

"I'll explain in good time, Watson. For now, let us see if we cannot get a closer look at Father Lester's putative miracle."

Together we entered St. Anne. It was not large, as churches go, but every bit as majestic on the inside as the oldest and grandest English cathedrals. The steeply pitched, vaulted ceiling and grand arches between the cluster pillars made the space seem far greater than the drab exterior would cause one to suspect. In the aisle to our left, close to the door which connected the church to the parsonage, was the weeping Mary herself. After assuring myself that we were alone, I followed Holmes as he went to inspect the statue, and I looked over it carefully in order to satisfy my own curiosity as Holmes's keen eyes swept the rather ordinary-looking likeness of the Virgin Mary ensconced in a finely-wrought shrine.

"Would you be kind enough to sit just there, Watson, in that pew, and ensure that we suffer no unexpected interruption?"

I did as he asked, keeping a watchful eye on the doors while following Holmes's movements. He felt the statue's head, as though probing for some abnormality. Shaking his head in disappointment, he drew his lens out of his pocket and commenced a methodical inspection of the statue and its base, looking for all the world like a bloodhound fixated on some interesting scent. He did not speak during this process, aside from the occasional "Oh!" and "A-ha!" which he quietly breathed when he saw something of interest. I confess that I had seen nothing out of the ordinary, but my friend's superior powers of observation doubtless permitted him to observe things that I could not. After a minute or two of examining the statue, he turned his attention elsewhere, lightly tapping the adjacent wall with his finger and crawling on his hands and knees to examine the floor directly in front of the shrine.

"Remarkable," he murmured. "I've never seen anything like it."

I heard footsteps and voices coming from behind the nearby door. Someone was crossing from the parsonage to the church. Holmes heard it as well, for he stood up at once and motioned to toward me, pointing at the door and then tapping his ear. I nodded to indicate I understood, and Holmes beat a hasty but silent retreat to the church door while I bowed my head and clasped my hands, assuming an attitude of a prayer. I heard the parsonage door open, and heard two sets of footsteps – one heavy, the other light and rapid, like the hurried walk of a person trying to keep up with a longer-legged companion.

". . . it'll be too hot for us soon. Perhaps we made a mistake," whispered a woman's voice.

"No one knows he's here." This was clearly the voice of Father Lester. "Once we're ready, we'll do him in and leave him in the street in some beggar's rags – that will throw the police off the scent. By the time they find out who he is, if they ever do, we'll be long gone."

I heard a sharp hush and the footsteps stopped. Taking that to mean I had been seen, I kept my eyes closed and moved my lips to imitate a man deeply engaged in prayer. Despite my facade of tranquility, I was shocked and distressed. My time in the army had acquainted me with mankind's propensity for cruelty, and my experiences with Holmes on his cases had, to a considerable degree, hardened me to the depravity of criminals. Nonetheless, the nonchalance with which those two had discussed the murder of another human being appalled and disturbed me. Happily, my ruse seemed to work, for the footsteps receded. When I judged it safe, I rose to slip out of the church and rejoin Holmes, whom I found waiting for me a little down the street.

"I suspected as much," said Holmes after I had told him what I had overheard. "We shall have to move quickly. I think I shall have to pay another visit to the post office."

"Holmes," I said as we walked, "you never did tell me what you learned about Father Lester by shaking his hand."

"You know my methods, Watson. The eye may be the window of the soul, but the book of a man's whole life is written on his hands, and Father Lester is no exception."

"And?" I asked, becoming exasperated by my friend's reticence.

"I perceived from the thickness of his skin that he has done much manual labour, but several pronounced scars, grooves, and nicks told me that in more recent years he has taken up some more complex trade, one requiring skill and specialized tools. He also has a tattoo on his wrist, just barely covered by his cuff. It is crudely done with poor ink – the kind of work which might adorn the wrists of dock workers or common toughs. By the look of it, I should say it is no more than six or seven years old."

"Wait a moment, Holmes," I said, "do you mean that Father Lester is not really a priest at all?"

"I am entirely convinced that he is not."

"The scoundrel!" I said. Holmes held up a hand.

"That is not all we can deduce, Watson. He is no ordinary member of the working class. He is well-spoken, with no hint of lower-class vernacular in his speech. He is clever, and educated enough to pass as a priest. His teeth, as far as I can tell, are only now beginning to degrade in condition. Inference: He lived his early life at a higher station than he now occupies."

"Remarkable," I said.

"Furthermore, it is quite plain that he is naturally intelligent. It is difficult to advance from manual labor to skilled work at his age, suggesting that he taught himself. Combined with the obvious fact that he has made several very delicate repairs to his own spectacles, this suggests a clever mind and an aptitude for tinkering."

"Why, that is just the kind of person who might be able to fake a weeping statue!" I said, excited by this revelation.

"A penetrating insight, Watson," said Holmes dryly. "But it also raises a difficult question: Why choose to commit fraud in such an *outrè* manner? There are countless other ways for a clever man to make money dishonestly, most of which would be simpler and attract far less curiosity."

"Yes, and what of Father Murray?" I asked. "Keeping such a well-respected member of the community prisoner in his own home, not to mention murdering him, must surely entail great risk to his plans."

"Indeed," said Holmes. "Our picture is yet incomplete. Despite his meticulousness, Lester – as we may call him, for he is no Father – has some personal motive beyond mere financial gain." He rubbed his hands together, but from cold or satisfaction I couldn't say. As we entered the post office, he had the look of a hunter preparing an ambush for his quarry. "This case goes much deeper than mere fraud. Mark my words, Watson, Father Murray is the key to this case, and the case is nearly complete."

Holmes filled out a telegram and sent it off before we marched once again out into the chilly evening. By now the sun was setting, and the sky was painted orange and red with its fire. I shivered, and my leg ached where the Jezail bullet had wounded me long ago, so that I was obliged to return to St. Anne at a slower pace than before. Holmes, to his credit, seemed not to mind, and talked as we went.

"Mrs. Driscoll is rather more observant than she realizes," said he, "but she failed to realize the true import of what she observed. Recall, for example, when she told us that Father Murray and Father Lester – that is, simply Lester, for he is no priest – had a vicious row over money. An unusual thing for priests to argue about, would you agree? But still, not so suspicious on its own. In light of other circumstances, however, it becomes very suspicious indeed. The suddenness of Father Murray's resignation and removal to somewhere beyond the reach of the postal service, for example. And this," he said, withdrawing a letter from his pocket.

"It is the letter I received this morning from the office of the Archbishop of Westminster, in response to my query about the goings on at St. Anne. In it, the Archbishop, or his secretary, informs me that he has been assured by Father Murray that nothing untoward is taking place. Father Murray, *not* Father Lester. The implication is clear: Father Murray, or an impostor, is complicit in the fraud. Since we know Father Murray is in the parsonage, and does not wish to be seen, I think it likely that he himself wrote to the Archbishop to cover up Lester's misdeeds."

"But why on Earth would he do such a thing?" I asked.

"Lester clearly has the means to blackmail Father Murray, for blackmail is the most likely explanation for the priest's cooperation."

By the time we arrived back at St. Anne, I was nearly limping from the pain in my leg. Holmes noticed, for he implored me to wait in the church.

"Wait?" said I. "Wait for what?"

"For the moment of revelation, Watson. I assure you, I can manage quite well on my own, and I don't wish your leg to cause you any more pain than necessary."

After some persuasion on his part, I at last agreed to sit in the church. I entered and resumed my seat on a pew near to the north aisle, where the shrine was. I must have fallen asleep very quickly but slept very lightly, for I remember some things in a haze: Movement, the darkening of the windows, Father Lester and the short woman arriving from the parsonage. I heard a door close and a loud click, which woke me fully from my slumber. I rose to go find Holmes only to discover that I had been joined by a company of people walking into the church and congregating in the aisle by the shrine, where Father Lester was standing. The short woman, however, had disappeared, no doubt having left by the parsonage door. I rose and joined them out of curiosity. One by one, they handed some money over to Father Lester, who stood with a gold plate held out, waiting to accept the gifts. Realizing what was about to happen, I hastily dug some coins from my pocket and dropped them in. When the collection was finished, Father Lester indicated that we should kneel before doing so himself and beginning a prayer.

I have never been an especially religious man, being content to keep my devotion to the Almighty a private affair. Although I have seen many strange and unlikely things, I certainly never anticipated to witness anything that could be called a miracle. Though I knew what to expect, it was still quite a shock to see the blood pool in the corners of the eyes at the very moment the priest began his prayer. I looked closely for any sign of a mechanism to account for it, but could see nothing. In spite of myself, I began to wonder if it could be real.

"Was it worth the price of admission, Watson?" asked Holmes from over my shoulder. I nearly jumped with fright, but he put a hand on my shoulder to steady me. Behind him, I saw Inspector Tobias Gregson of Scotland Yard and an old man leaning against a nearby pillar.

"Perhaps you would be kind enough to tend to Father Murray, Watson." Holmes said.

"Of course," I answered, still somewhat dazed by this sudden turn of events. I helped Father Murray sit down and offered him some brandy from my flask.

"What can I do for you, gentlemen?" Father Lester asked nervously. "We are at prayer, if you would care to join us."

"I think it would be better," said Gregson, "if you would join us at the station, Mr. Lester, and answer some questions."

"That's Father Lester," the false priest replied with an air of wounded dignity.

"I think not," said Holmes with a look of triumph on his face. He suddenly strode past the startled priest, withdrawing a putty knife from his pocket and jamming it into the shrine.

"What on earth do you think you're doing?" cried Father Lester, but Holmes payed no attention. He rushed at Holmes, but I, with a burst of energy like that of the young rugby forward I once was, leaped across the space and caught him around the shoulders. Several of Lester's audience members fled the scene as I helped Gregson apply a pair of handcuffs to my captive's wrists as he wriggled and thrashed in a vain attempt to throw us off.

Holmes continued to probe the shrine with the putty knife. A sharp click was heard, and at that sound Father Lester stopped struggling and merely hung his head. I released my grip, and he collapsed on the floor. Holmes swung the front of the shrine outward like a cabinet door to reveal a truly remarkable sight. The short woman I had seen before was sitting inside the shrine, which was only just big enough to accommodate her. Rubber tubing connected a pail of red fluid to a little pump she held in her hand, and another tube went upwards into the statue itself.

"Miss Lester," said Holmes, "kindly step out."

The embarrassed woman awkwardly extricated herself from the contraption and stood up straight, looking each of us in turn. She was red-haired and rather pretty, with a fiery, defiant gleam in her eye.

312

"Miss Lester?" I asked, thoroughly confused.

"The false priest's sister," Holmes explained, "and Father Murray's daughter."

I turned in shock to look at the elderly priest behind me.

"Is this true?"

"Aye, it's true," Father Murray answered.

"Perhaps we ought to get more comfortable before we start asking questions," Holmes suggested. "The parsonage should suffice. Here, Gregson, allow me to lead Mr. Lester while you restrain his charming accomplice."

We settled into a little sitting room. The handcuffed Lesters were made to sit in chairs while Father Murray was stretched out on a sofa. From the look of him, I determined he had been deprived of adequate food and drink for some time, and his body was bruised over from what appeared to be numerous violent blows.

It was Mr. Lester who spoke first.

"Looks like you figured us out, Mr. Scott. If your real name's not Holmes, I'm an old woman."

"That is, indeed, my real name. But we are both guilty of using an alias. Am I correct in thinking I stand in the presence of Donald and Molly Neeson, the tricksters and con artists of Dublin?"

The woman hissed, but the man only glowered.

"It looks like you are just as good as they say, Mr. Holmes. Why, I never suspected it was you until it was too late."

Gregson interrupted. "The law compels me to tell you both that anything you say may be used against you in court."

"It's not our first time," Molly Neeson said.

"We always seem to get clear in the end," added Donald.

"Not this time, I'd wager," said Holmes. "You have gone rather out of your depth. Defrauding hundreds of people. Kidnapping, assault, and nearly murder. These are very serious crimes indeed."

"I suppose you know everything about the matter?" said Mr. Neeson.

"I know much," Holmes replied. "I know you blackmailed Father Murray into allowing you to use the statue to persuade desperate people to part with their already meager wealth. I know you kept him hidden, a prisoner in his own home, where you beat him, starved him, and forced him to help cover your tracks. I know you planned to murder him. I know you built that statue yourself – a cunning piece of work, I grant you, but I was able to discover its secrets all the same. You see, it is really no use to attempt to deceive me. I dare say your scheming days are at an end."

Donald Neeson looked more and more defeated as Holmes went on.

"To do all this to your own father . . . ." I said indignantly.

313

"He was never any father to us," Molly Neeson growled. "We were only children when he up and left, but we saw how it broke poor mama's heart. He left her an unmarried mother, without honor or reputation or a friend in the world. Thought you could get away with it, old man? Thought we'd die in the Hunger, and no one'd be the wiser? Oh, but we found you in the end!"

Father Murray sat up and hung his head, a pained expression on his face.

"What became of your mother?" asked Holmes.

"She died of pneumonia, working her fingers to the bone in a Magdalene laundry," answered Donald. "My sister and I were lucky enough to be raised by a great-uncle, who could afford to give us some education. He died fifteen years ago, and we were left penniless, for his entire estate was claimed by creditors."

"We're the only family either of us has, now," said Molly.

"So you wanted to punish and humiliate your father as revenge for your abandonment," I said. "That's why you used the church."

"No one robs people better than the church," Donald Neeson said. "What's the harm in getting a share for ourselves? It's the least we're owed, after what the pious Reverend Father over there did to us. He left his children behind to starve while he became a priest and got fat off the church."

"You must have known your ruse couldn't last forever."

"We didn't need it to. We had a bit saved up, once we had a bit more we were going to leave the country for foreign parts, have a decent life for the first time."

"And your father?" Holmes asked quietly.

"At first we only thought to let him take the blame once we'd left and the trick was discovered," Donald Neeson said. "But a little revenge only leaves you wanting more. In the end we planned . . . well, it seems you know the answer to that too."

"It'd be no more than he deserves," said Molly Neeson defiantly.

"It's true," spoke Father Murray for the first time. "It is what I deserve."

All eyes were now on the priest.

"How many times I have cursed myself over the years! I should have done the right thing and married your mother. Instead, I left her forever dishonored and left my own children behind!"

Father Murray put his head in his hands. "Later, when I repented my actions and wanted to find you, it was impossible. All your mother's family died in the famine, and I came to believe you had died too. I thought there was nothing to do but move on and try to forget, and for a while I did. But my sins found me out at last. God forgive me."

"God?" roared Donald. In his face I saw the hatred of decades expressed all at once, a terrible mask of pure malice and spite. "God forgive? What has *God* got to do with it? It's *us* you sinned against, not *God*! It's us you should be groveling to."

"It's easier to ask forgiveness from God, isn't it?" said Molly, her voice dripping with contempt. "You don't have to look into his eyes. You're a coward, and always have been."

The old man began to weep bitterly.

"I know there are no amends I can make. It is far too late for that. I cannot expect you to forgive me. I cannot even forgive myself. If God can forgive me, it will be far more than I could ever ask or deserve."

His children, unmoved by his words, stared at him with cold hatred. At length, Holmes stirred.

"Well, Inspector, my part in this drama is done. It's all in your hands now."

"Much obliged to you, Mr. Holmes," Gregson replied.

Without another word or glance and the three seated figures, Holmes left the room, and I followed him out into the crisp night air, where after some waiting we found a cab and commenced the ride back to Baker Street.

"I suppose, Watson," said Holmes, "that you there are points which seem unclear to you?"

"You have kept me somewhat in the dark," I answered. Although I was thoroughly used to my friend's penchant for the dramatic, his habit of withholding his plans in order to achieve the desired effect remained a source of annoyance throughout our partnership.

"You must forgive me my little conceits," he said in an apologetic tone. "I will be very happy to answer any questions you may have."

"That's very generous of you," I answered, allowing a hint of sarcasm to colour my tone. "Firstly, how did Inspector Gregson come to be at St. Anne?"

"I invited him. I suspected from the first that 'Father Lester' was no true priest. That was one reason I visited the church this morning – to see him for myself and provide a description to Gregson, who can be quite discrete when the situation calls for it. His reply, which I collected on our way here, was to inform me that the description was a possible match to Donald Neeson, and gave me two clues to look for – namely, the tattoo on his wrist and the presence of a female accomplice. The telegram I sent later was simply a confirmation of the man's identity and an urgent request for Gregson to arrive at once with a warrant in order to recover Father Murray from his captivity. This he did within the hour, a testament to the man's tenacity."

"Very well," said I, "and how did you know that Father Murray and the Neesons were related?"

"Why, the family resemblance between the three was as plain as day! Even Mrs. Driscoll saw it, not realizing what it meant."

"And the statue?"

Holmes smiled. "I admit, the statue was a difficult puzzle, but an inspection of the shrine and the floor told me what I needed to know. The first clue was a brown stain on the floor which our tricksters had failed to entirely scrub away. The position of the stain was such that it revealed a cunningly concealed gap, which I was able to trace. It was clear that the front of the shrine was a door, so well made that it was hardly visible and so perfectly fitted that it did not move or shift when touched. It was clearly designed to open widely enough to accommodate a person the size of Miss Neeson. It was not difficult, then, to suppose that the bafflingly perfect timing of the weeping was due to her directly controlling the flow of fluid, most likely with the sort of pump we saw. This was the hypothesis which I put to the test with the putty knife, hoping I could force the door to unlock itself, as indeed it did. I have never heard of this method ever being used before to create a weeping statue. Those two may well be pioneers in that particular field."

"Splendidly done, Holmes!" I exclaimed. "But wait a moment. You said that something about Mrs. Driscoll's account still puzzled you after you dismissed her. What did she say that caused you to reconsider?"

"My dear fellow, it was something that you said."

"Me?"

"I've said before that you have a remarkable gift for stimulating genius in others. It was you who pointed out that Mrs. Driscoll was more worried about Father Murray than about the statue, though she herself may not have realized it. Still, feminine intuition is a powerful thing, and not to be lightly disregarded. You were quite right to argue with me before. If I am annoyed by the obstinacy of the official police, it is because I must work tirelessly to check the same tendency in myself. Alas, despite the exaggerated accounts of my abilities which you present to the public, I am bound to fail at times. So be a good fellow, and if ever you feel I am being too obstinate, simply remind me of the weeping Mary."

Very little about the affair of the weeping Mary of St. Anne appeared in the papers. The Diocese of Westminster, keen to avoid scandal, removed the statue and assigned a new priest to the parish within a week, refusing to make any comment on the matter. The Neeson siblings were found guilty on several charges: Donald served a sentence in Newgate gaol

316

and was eventually freed on parole, while Molly was sent to a hospital run by the church in the hopes that she might be reformed. As far as I am aware, she remains there to this day. Little was ever heard of Father Murray again, but I understand that he retired to life in a cloister, and spends his days in prayer and contemplation.

# The Unnerved Estate Agent
## by David Marcum

F rom where he stood by the hives, my friend Sherlock Holmes couldn't see the young man approaching us. However, when I pointed out the fact that a visitor had arrived, he turned and frowned.

It was late in the afternoon, and the sun, low in the in the sky, was quickly vanishing behind a bank of clouds building to the south. Already there was a chill in the air as the threat of an autumn rain pushed a cold breeze around us. Darkness was falling suddenly, so that the features of the fellow walking our way were indistinguishable. I could see that he wore a dark suit, which would likely have been hot earlier in the day, but now his choice of clothing was quite appropriate.

I knew that even Holmes was unlikely to be able to see more of the man than I could at this distance, but I asked anyway, "Do you recognize him?"

"No," was his reply. "But he is striding with purpose, and no attempt to hide himself – unlike Fryston last month.

I knew to what he referred, even though I hadn't been present. Fryston, a convict, had escaped with the sole purpose of revenging himself upon Holmes, the man who had originally discovered his schemes. In first revealing the miscreant's imposture of a railway clerk, additional facts had been exposed. While the police would have been happy to simply prevent the theft that was planned for a special train to Norfolk, Holmes had seen something that didn't ring true about the fellow's uniform, alerting him to persist and dig a bit further.

After his arrest, Fryston had been quite cheerful in his capture, agreeing that it had been a fair catch. Like many criminals, though, he talked too much, and his casual mention of growing up near Corby, along with the unusual *J*-hooked scar that crossed the back of his left hand, had sent Holmes rooting through his scrapbooks, brought down with him from London when he retired, and still updated when he had the chance. An old news article about the senseless murder of an entire family ten years earlier for the theft of a small cache of old Roman coins discovered on their property had allowed Holmes to determine that the accused killer, never identified and still uncaught to the present, had carried the same scar.

It didn't take long to determine that Fryston and the murderer were the same man. Following the accusation, the cheerful demeanor sloughed off as fast as if he'd shed a cloak to reveal a raging madman. His sanity

318

now in question, he was eventually delivered to Broadmoor instead of standing trial for the failed train robbery. Once ensconced there, he had subsided again into bland anonymity until, seeing his chance, he escaped, killing a guard in the process. There was no indication as to which way he'd gone until he appeared at Holmes's farm one September morning, just a few weeks earlier, hiding in the gardens planted for the bees. Holmes, who happened to be in residence at the time, had perceived the insects' agitation and had gone to investigate. At Holmes's approach, Fryston leapt forward, a large knife raised. But his motion had disturbed the bees, several of whom attacked him. As he swatted at them, more and more bedeviled him, giving their lives and allowing Holmes to gain the advantage as he waded in and disabled the man. Apparently seeing that the danger was past, the bees calmed and resumed their business, the threat to one of their own now removed.

I had seen in the newspapers that Fryston was captured near Birling Gap, and had suspected the possibility of Holmes's involvement, but I had no idea of these dramatic events until they were relayed to me when I arrived for a visit on the previous night. Now, standing so near Holmes's hives, I couldn't help but hold myself still so that the occupants wouldn't take issue with me as well. Still, they had known me for quite a while by that point, and in any case, they were hurrying home ahead of the approaching weather with no thought to my presence.

Since his supposed retirement here to the Sussex Downs in late 1903, Holmes had walked a delicate balance. He'd left London while giving the very public impression that he was retiring. Thus, a certain amount of public attention had to be directed toward his new residency at what he called his "villa" near Birling Gap and his seeming new life as a reclusive apiarist. On the other hand, he was in actuality spending a great deal of his time working as an agent of the British Government, usually under the aegis and direction of his brother Mycroft, traveling here and there as needed to investigate incidents or facilitate matters that helped Britain prepare for the upcoming war with Germany, which was at that point recognized by many – including the Holmes Brothers and myself – as inevitable, and not *if* but *when*. As such an agent, he obviously didn't want visitors bringing him distracting cases when he might need to depart at a moment's notice, with the very real possibility of not returning for weeks at a time.

That early October day happened to be one of those periods when he was again in residence at his farm, a comfortable habitation consisting of several acres enclosed by a rock wall, just north of the tallest Beachy Head cliff. We had returned from a late afternoon walk to the top, looking down upon the lighthouse and noting the Coast Guard houses off to the west in

Birling Gap. Holmes had pointed out a long crack running in the cliff-top near us, parallel to the edge, and had talked while we ambled and occasionally stopped to catch our breaths about how that piece would eventually separate and collapse, as had so many others along there for eons. He pointed out the cliff faces at Birling Gap and mentioned how in the past the road there had sloped gently down to the beach, perhaps hundreds of yards further south in an area now reclaimed by the ocean. What had once been an easy sea access for smugglers was now gone. Eventually, long after we had vanished, Birling Gap, the lighthouse, Holmes's farm, and even East Dean, a mile inland, would be swallowed by the sea as well. He and I had discussed this before, and it seemed to be a thought that had crossed his mind several times.

We had walked down the sloping hill to his villa, crossing the road, entering through the gate, and angling away from the house in order to take a turn through the hives before a late tea. Over the years, I'd come to trust the bees as my understanding of them grew, but never to the point that Holmes did. He walked among them will complete assuredness, and they sensed it, and totally accepted him.

Now, a stranger approached us, and Holmes led me away from the hives to meet him halfway.

He was young, not much older than twenty. As he pulled a cloth from his pocket to wipe his face, I noted that he was tall and slim, nearly Holmes's height, with an angular skull and brown hair that likely wouldn't stay combed for very long. He had light blue eyes, perhaps the legacy of some long-ago Scandinavian invader to our shores, and a face that looked like it smiled more often than not. But on this day his eyes had dark circles under them, as if he had recently missed a great deal of sleep, and he seemed to shed tension that was almost visible.

"Mr. Holmes," he asked in a deep voice, looking directly at my friend. By that time, there was no question as to which of us was which – unlike the early days, when visitors to our Baker Street sitting room might occasionally direct an initial hesitant question my way before things were sorted.

"I'm sorry to disturb you," the young man continued. "I would have sent a wire first, but I was in Eastbourne on business and decided to visit on the spur of the moment, to ask your advice. If it's inconvenient, I shall depart immediately with my most sincere apologies."

I could tell that this approach had softened whatever comment that Holmes might have offered in regard to trespassers. He glanced at the rapidly darkening sky. "To turn you out would be unkind," he replied, "and I happen to have some time, Mr. – ?"

"Tenbury," was the reply. "Matthew Tenbury." He turned to me. "And you must be Dr. Watson." He stuck out a hand, which I shook, and then he offered it to Holmes, who shook it as well. Holmes indicated that we should step toward the house, where tea would be waiting.

It was, and after we had settled ourselves in the comfortable parlour, Holmes took a sip, set the cup on the octagonal table that he had brought with him from Baker Street, and leaned back. "Well, Mr. Tenbury, you have found me at home, and in for the evening, apparently. What would you like to tell us?"

Tenbury cupped his tea in both hands, as if seeking warmth, and then took a long sip and set it aside. Crossing his legs, he sat back, and then closed his eyes for a moment before opening them again to look from one to the other of us. "Now that I have my chance to tell my story," he said, "I feel rather foolish. But I know that something is going on, and before another day has passed I may be under arrest, and my chance to speak with you might be gone forever."

Holmes raised an eyebrow. "Indeed? And what charge might you face?"

"Murder."

The word, which had been said to us in one form or another on countless thousands of occasions, and in countless contexts, never failed to provide a small thrill of horror. A life lost, a murderer's soul damned, and disruptions and disasters of all degrees spread to those involved.

Holmes glanced up and to the left, thinking for just a moment before he found the fact which he sought. "The recent death of an old spinster named Lanham."

Tenbury seemed surprised. "That's it? But how did you know?"

Holmes shook his head, as if this were a waste of time. "Clearly you're employed locally – the signs on your clothing tell me that much, although you were raised in Essex. Your manner of speaking reveals that. Mostly likely near Chelmsford. The only recent murder that I can recall, still unsolved as of what was printed in this morning's newspaper, was of the Lanham woman, near Chailey."

"It's true. And I fear that I shall be charged with the crime, if you don't help me. But there's more than that – more that I cannot tell the police, for they will think that I'm simply trying to confuse the issue. Or that I'm mad."

"Pray continue," said Holmes, leaning back and closing his eyes.

Often at this point, clients would look to me in confusion, thinking that Holmes was no longer listening, or possibly that he had chosen to take a nap. However, Tenbury seemed to realize that Holmes was actually engaged more intently, and he began without hesitation to relate his tale.

"I work for a large estate agent in Brighton – Hoddard and Stanton. I've only held the position since the spring and, while I very much enjoy the work, I feel that I'm still proving myself. I also realize that I have a great deal to learn. There is a competitive rivalry amongst the agents, especially those like myself without much experience or seasoning, and with only so many permanent positions, we have to prove ourselves to advance.

"Two days ago, a routine letter came to the office from an old – " He stopped suddenly, and awkwardly, with an innocently horrified expression on his face as he realized that he was addressing two men in their mid-fifties – clearly ancient from his perspective. I glanced toward Holmes to see that one corner of his mouth had twitched in something like a smile. I turned back to Tenbury and nodded reassuringly for him to continue.

"The letter was from an . . . a woman – the same Miss Lanham who ended up murdered. She requested that someone from the agency visit to begin an evaluation of her property in order to determine its value, as well as that of its contents. She had lived there her whole life, inheriting it from her parents, and had decided to sell and move away to the seaside while she had good enough health to appreciate it.

"Mr. Stanton – he runs the agency, as Mr. Hoddard has been quite ill for a number of years – called me in and explained the situation, indicating that he would be away for several days, and that he wished me to carry out the investigation, stating that it would be a good experience. 'This won't be the final estimate by any means,' he said, 'but you've seen enough by now to get a sense of whether there is any value there, or if instead it's a hovel filled with a lifetime of collected sentimental trash that she's held onto because she believes that there is one single person somewhere out there in the world who will pay her a fortune for a certain broken chair or water-damaged magazine.'

"He's become rather cynical, has Mr. Stanton, but I knew what he meant. I've already seen enough of the houses of the type that he'd described to know that there are more of those than not. With a nod, I gathered what I would need to make an assessment and headed that way.

"It was late afternoon when I arrived, about the same time as now, but the clouds that day gave the sun a brassy look, and there were long shadows already falling as I found the house. It was in a lonely spot, five or more miles from the station, and while I'd had enough money on me to pay for a man to take me out there, I knew that I'd have to walk back. Along the way, I'd tried to get something out of the driver about Miss Lanham, or about the house, but he wasn't in the mood for talk – although he apparently had enough talk in him to tell the police about me after she was found murdered!"

Holmes cracked his eyes. "Relate it in order, Mr. Tenbury. You were taken to the house."

The young man swallowed. Outside, the wind had continued to rise, and the limbs in the trees over Holmes's cottage could be heard sighing as the remaining autumn leaves gave up the struggle and turned loose, to be carried who knew where, before settling and returning to the earth from whence they had come.

"I watched the wagon go back in the direction of Chailey. Then, deciding that I should get on with my business, I looked at this house that I was supposed to adjudicate. It's a wooden structure, three stories and an attic, and it looks taller than it really is due to the narrow width of the place. It has a wide covered porch spread across the whole front. As I approached, I was struck by its loneliness, and how, except for an area immediately surrounding the house, the grounds around it have been left wild, likely for decades. There appear to be no close neighbors in any direction.

"I stepped up and knocked. After a moment with no response, I tried again, and this time I sensed rather than heard that someone was approaching the door. Perhaps it was the vibration of the joists being felt outside where I stood, for when Miss Lanham opened the door, I realized that she was a surprisingly . . . substantial woman.

"She stood peering at me, wheezing a bit. There was an unpleasant warm smell that flowed past her from inside the darkened building, something that suggested an animal. Or animals. Unexpectedly my eyes watered a bit, and then I understood when a cat, and then another and another, appeared on the floor beside her, twining in and about where her skirt dragged the floor. One hissed at me

"'Yes?' she asked in a whispery kind of voice. I swallowed and introduced myself, explaining that I was from Hoddard and Stanton, and that I'd come about her letter.

"I expected a bit more enthusiasm than I received. Her mouth tightened, and I feared that I had made an amateur mistake by coming there directly rather than writing first for an appointment. However, she seemed to decide to make the best of it and stepped aside to allow me in.

"As she shut the door, I saw at least two more cats silhouetted before me in the darkness, one on the back of a sofa with the window behind it, and another passing into another room toward the rear of the house. It was the movement of the second that startled me a bit, for it seemed rather more rat-like in its motion – although I doubt that any rat, let alone anything smaller, could survive long in that feline sanctuary. Later that evening I was able to ask her about the cats, and she told me that the one I'd seen was lame in its hind legs. She also explained that she had eleven of them – or so she believed, as the number might change at any given moment, depending on how many wandered off and how many more arrived. She believed that they somehow spread the word amongst themselves that they were welcome there, and had a cozy billet if they wanted it. But I'm getting ahead of myself." He picked up his tea-cup and took a sip.

"We seated ourselves in the darkened parlour, she on the very weary-looking sofa, while I was on a tall narrow chair placed at right angles to where she rested. I began to ask questions as I'd been taught, and learned that she'd inherited the house as a young woman in her twenties – over forty years ago. She'd never married, and had lived there, for the most part in solitude, except for occasional visits from tradesmen making regular deliveries. Her late father had established a number of investments that, while never making her rich, had provided a steady income throughout her life.

"I couldn't imagine such an existence as she described, or that she could have stood it for so long. I asked why she wished to leave now, for I perceived that she'd been satisfied with the arrangement for quite a while.

"She couldn't provide an adequate answer. 'I don't know, really,' she said in that raspy way she had of talking. 'I receive a number of periodicals along with my groceries, and somehow the stories of other parts of England have taken root in my head after all this time. I realized that I'm sixty-eight years old and that I've never been more than ten miles from where I sit right now.'

"'But,' I said, 'you could take short journeys here and there. Are you ready to make such an abrupt change? What if you don't like some other place, but only discover it after you've made it permanent?' Even as I asked, I feared that I might be talking her out of selling the place and the contents, and I'd have to explain to Mr. Stanton how I'd lost a contract. I clapped my mouth shut.

"In any case, she seemed to have no answer, and after a silent moment or two, she heaved herself up and, picking up the lamp, began to show me the house, starting with the ground floor.

"It was growing much darker, and like now, the wind was starting to rise. If you recall the weather night before last, one of the equinoctial gales was just beginning, and I very much feared that I faced a terrible trek back to town when our inspection of the property was complete. Miss Lanham appeared indifferent to the worsening weather, walking from room to room, carrying the lamp and leading me around, first through the ground floor, and then upward to the first.

"So far I felt that I could make a good report to Mr. Stanton. The house was mostly empty, and seemed to be well built. It was beyond my experience whether the overpowering smell of the cats could be removed, however, and I would have to defer to his opinion on that matter. We had reached the second floor and had looked through several more empty rooms there when she reached a door at the end of the landing, explaining and apologizing that this was her lumber room, and was therefore much more cluttered. I didn't feel that one roomful of materials would be much of a problem.

"She handed me the key, as if my unlocking the room meant that I was somehow taking responsibility. When the door swung back, I could see that, unlike the other rooms, this one was filled with boxes from near the door all the way to each wall. There was a small open space near the door for it to swing clear, but otherwise there was a vast amount of accumulated material. Apparently, this is where Miss Lanham, and her ancestors before her, had chosen to store their family treasures – and other trash that they couldn't quite set free as well – cramming it all here while keeping the rest of the house clear.

"Immediately to the left of the door as one entered the room was a staircase, leading up into the ceiling, three or four feet wide. On the right side, each of the steps was piled with boxes at every level, leaving only a space of two feet or so on the left to pass up or down. 'That goes to the attic,' she gasped, for she was still out of breath from climbing to this level.

"I had barely heard her, however, for my heart was suddenly pounding in my ears. I knew that it went to the attic, although from that floor it was no great deduction. Still, I was already certain of it because I realized that I had been there before!"

He stopped then, his silence only serving to emphasize the increasing winds outside. Elsewhere in the house, I could hear the bustle of the evening meal being prepared, and I smelled the slowly drifting aroma of a savory stew. It would be a perfect night for it.

Holmes had opened his eyes when his visitor fell silent, and he used the opportunity to rise and pour brandy for the three of us, apparently feeling that by this point in the story, something stronger than tea was required. Tenbury took a sip and held it in his mouth for a few seconds before swallowing, making the face of someone who didn't initially realize its excellent quality. Then he resumed, but on a surprising tack.

"You need to know something of my past," he explained, his voice much quieter now. "To understand why I was so shocked." He took another sip, as if deciding how to explain. "I'm an orphan, you see. I was raised by a kindly vicar and his wife, living on the Sandford Road near the barracks – in Chelmsford, as you realized. I was taken in by them when I was three years old, after I was found abandoned.

"I don't have many memories of my life before then. I know that I had a father, a tall gaunt man who always left me feeling terrified. In the few memories I have of him, he was always either looking down at me with disappointment, or possibly even anger, or he was close before me, repeating my name over and over, as if it were a lesson that I couldn't not master. 'Matthew Tenbury!' he would bark into my face, insisting that I repeat it as best I could. 'Matthew Tenbury!'

"As I said, I have very few memories of those days, but besides my father, I have one other strong recollection, and that was the house in which we lived. I remember that there was a woman there, although I seemed to know somewhat that she was not my mother. She was quiet, and no more than a shadow at the edge of my perception, moving dreamlike along the edges of what I recall. I have the sense of a few rooms, but no details remain – that is, except for one. And it was that room that Miss Lanham led me into, so crowded with boxes, and with steps leading up to the attic above.

"I cannot tell you both how often that room has haunted my dreams in the years since. As I grew, over and over again, I would wake from nightmares where I was back in that room once again. It seems to me that I must have slept in the attic, and that I had to walk into that crowded room and then up those same steps every night to reach my little bed, tucked into the eaves amongst a great deal more collected trash, such as what was in the room below. I have memories of sounds around me as I cowered under my sheets – mice probably, but to my young ears, they were the rustlings of monsters, creeping closer every night. Worse, I can still hear whispers from the room below after I would be in bed, my father and the woman, talking low at the foot of the steps before carrying the light away and leaving me in darkness.

"Through the years, the dreams would vary, but they would always repeat themselves, ending at the foot of the stairs leading to that dark attic. In all the dreams I would find myself wandering through a house, but its shape and mood would vary with every occurrence. It might be a large hall, or a cottage, or somewhere almost institutional, like at a university. Always deserted, and always very dark, as if the sun has already gone down. In every case, I move from room to room, looking here and there, but for nothing in particular. Eventually, regardless of the initial setting, I find myself at the foot of the stairs – those same stairs in Miss Lanham's house – looking up in the blackness above me, and hearing rustles and whispers just out of earshot – sometimes beside me, behind or under the boxes and abandoned parcels in the room at the bottom of the stairs, or worse, coming from the darkness above me, where I know that I have to go. And in each case, in spite of my terror, I begin to climb the stairs, no

326

matter how much I want to avoid it. I feel cold all over, and there is something preventing me, as if my limbs are paralyzed, or like the sensation when trying to walk in the sea through deep water. And yet, I rise toward the darkness, inevitably, step by step by step – and then I awaken, shaking . . . and sometimes, weeping." He lowered his head in shame, and his voice became even quieter. "It was that way when I first had the dream, when I was very small, and it was the same when I had the dream again last night. Except now I know that I've been dreaming of that same room at the top of Miss Lanham's old house!"

The first of the rain arrived then, suddenly hitting the parlour windows like shot. I was glad that I didn't jump. Holmes, of course, paid it no attention. "You were abandoned?" he said. "What were the circumstances?"

"From what I was told years later, I was found wandering the streets of Chelmsford, a lost three-year old boy who knew his name and nothing else. I couldn't tell where I was from, or give anything but the vaguest description of my father. All that I knew was my name. A wide search was carried out, but no reports were found of anyone named Tenbury, at least with a missing child, and it was assumed that my father was perhaps from one of the colonies, or even America, though I had a British accent. I've always believed in my heart that he is dead – else he would have found me. When nothing could be discovered as to my antecedents, the vicar and his wife took me in. They kept in touch with the authorities over the years, in case anything about my father ever turned up, but it never did."

"And in what year did this occur?"

"Why, twenty-one years ago. In the fall of 1888."

Holmes rose then and abruptly walked out of the room without comment, leaving Tenbury looking rather puzzled. I was long used to Holmes's sudden impulses, but it would have been too amazing even for him to walk deeper into his house and return a moment later with an entry from his scrapbooks providing the young man's identity. And in fact, that wasn't the reason that Tenbury was here. He'd yet to reach the part of his narrative about Miss Lanham's murder, and how he might be charged with it at any moment.

Holmes was back almost before I could truly consider why he'd left. "We're having stew for our little supper, and bread from the local baker," he explained. "It isn't quite ready yet. Of course you'll stay, Mr. Tenbury."

The young man looked surprised, but nodded and offered thanks. Holmes's invitation wasn't unexpected. He was a fine host when he tried, and the rising weather meant that Tenbury would have had a miserable walk back to Eastbourne – or more likely I'd have been drafted to drive him there in my little but rugged automobile, a trip that I wouldn't enjoy.

We certainly hadn't learned the entire story yet, and it was entirely possible that Holmes had observed something that made him want to observe more. The fact that a man or woman was a murderer – and there was nothing yet to exonerate this particular young man – had never stopped Holmes from spending time with them in the past if there was something to be learned.

"Pray continue," said my friend to Tenbury. "You recognized the room. What happened then?"

Tenbury looked rather sheepish. "I faltered a bit just then, losing track of what Miss Lanham was saying, apologizing for all the 'clutter' in that one room, but she didn't seem to notice. She asked if I wanted to see the attic as well, and of course I did. She excused herself, saying that she was too weary to climb the stairs. So, taking the lamp, I did so without her, leaving her leaning against the newel post.

"I must confess that the first few steps were quite difficult. Two decades of the dream in all its forms weighed on me, and I expected at any second to hear the low whispers begin above me. And yet, I looked at the prosaic staircase in front of me, littered with dust and boxes and piles of paper and realized that, unlike my fearful dream world, this was real, and it was rather shabby."

"You mentioned the dust," said Holmes. "Do you happen to recall if anyone had recently been on the steps before you, possibly leaving footprints?"

Tenbury frowned. "I . . . I don't believe so, Mr. Holmes, but I cannot say for sure. I was staring intently at each step as I ascended, but at the same time my thoughts were quite distracted. I believe that I would have noticed footprints, but I'm not certain. I'm sorry."

"No matter. Please continue."

"I reached the top and saw that the attic stretched across a good portion of the house. Like the room below, it was quite cluttered with boxes, trunks, and the like. I had to wonder why these things had been carried up to such an inaccessible point at such likely great effort, instead of keeping them in one of the empty lower rooms, or simply removing from the house to be burned, or hauled away, or given to charity. There was nothing that seemed to be worth keeping – but I've already learned how people will hold on to the most unlikely items."

At this point, I had to smile to myself, recalling Holmes's constant accumulation of objects – souvenirs of past cases, relics of famed criminals, and ever increasing stacks of documents that constantly threatened to tumble to the floor, and yet could not be tossed, for he had a horror of destroying them. I found it ironic that, while Mrs. Hudson was his landlady in Baker Street, and was then unable to exert any influence on him toward reducing his collection of detritus, she had put her foot down since coming down to Sussex as his housekeeper after his supposed retirement, forcing him to maintain the cottage in a much more presentable fashion indeed.

"I looked around," continued Tenbury. "All of it was vaguely familiar. And then, right where I knew it would be, surrounded by what was so typical throughout the attic, was a little bed – *my* little bed, from when I was three years old, left there in terrible fear night after night by my father. The blankets were still turned back as if I had just awakened."

He faded into silence, and then Holmes prompted him, asking, "What happened next?"

"Hmm? Well, after a moment, Miss Lanham called up to ask after me, saying that she wanted to get back downstairs. With a last look around, I went down and joined her. When she heard me coming, she stepped into the hallway and I shut and locked the door. I turned to hand her the key, but she was already walking away, so I slipped it into my pocket. We proceeded to the ground floor. During all that time, however, the weather had closed in upon us, the same as it has done here this afternoon. When Miss Lanham finally noticed, at the end of our tour, she seemed to be paralyzed as to what to do. When I half-heartedly said that I'd best get on my way, and wondered if I might borrow an umbrella – as if such a thing would be any protection at all on a five-mile night-time walk in a hurricane! – she reluctantly offered to let me stay the night, obviously hoping that I'd refuse. However, as there was no way that I could travel back to town, in spite of how much I wished to avoid staying there – because of the cats and the smells and most of all my feelings about the attic – I knew that I'd be a fool not to accept. And truth be told, I was curious about my memories of the place, as poor as they were, and wanted to see if I could learn more from her about what they meant.

"I had no success, however. She had no servants, so she warmed up some left-over soup and we each had a bowl at her kitchen table. There was very little of it, and it was thin and tasteless. With no bread or anything else to join it, we were soon finished, and there had been practically no conversation while I ate. Seeing how uncomfortable we both were, I said that if she could show me where I'd be sleeping, I'd turn in for the night. She lit a second lamp, handed it to me, and then led me along a hallway to one of the empty ground-floor bedrooms that looked out upon the wide porch. Wishing me well, she turned away.

"I had every intention of trying to sleep. I pulled back the dusty blankets, sending myself into a coughing frenzy. The sheets didn't look any too clean, but at least the door to the room seemed to have been shut, for there were no signs that the cats had been allowed in there.

"I found that I seemed to fear falling asleep, as if being this close to the attic and the stairs would somehow intensify the dream. I would nearly drop off, and then a thought of it would set my heart to pounding once again. Finally, a thought took hold and I knew that I wouldn't rest until I'd once again looked on the little bed several floors above me, trying to understand how I could have ever been in this house.

"I redressed, wondering so many things. Had Miss Lanham been the woman who was at the edge of my memories, in the background during those few interactions that I could recall with my father? She would have been in her late forties then, so it wasn't impossible. But who was my father, and why would we have been here, at this place? I regretted over and over not simply asking her, yet I somehow sensed that if I had, I'd not only receive a denial, but somehow put her on her guard as well.

"I knew that her room was on the other side of the house, and with the storm raging outside, there was no way that she would know that I was up and about. And yet, I stepped into the hall with the lamp unlit, my eyes having adjusted enough to the dark that I could move with some confidence toward the stairway. I went up to the next floor, and then the next – they were just steps, but it seemed as if my dream was coming true. I was moving through a dark and nearly empty house, gradually approaching those terrifying stairs to the attic. Before I knew it, I was at the door to the cluttered room. I could just make out the knob in the darkness, and I decided that I would leave my lamp unlit – at least until I was in the attic. That is, if I could force myself to make the last ascent to get there.

"I silently unlocked and opened the door – there was no squeak to announce what I was doing, and besides, the storm seemed to be even worse. With a deep breath full of resolve, I stepped over the threshold and turned immediately to my left, resolutely intending to put my foot on the bottom step to the attic. I believe that I did so, but I cannot be sure, because what I saw then pinned me to the ground in terror.

"For above me, at the top of the stairs, was a dim glow, seeming to highlight the shoulders and face of a man. He was at the top of the steps, seemingly looking my way, but his eyes – or where they should have been – were black pools, empty sockets, giving the skull-like appearance of Death himself. But if he was Death, he wore a face that I knew, one that I have envisioned for most of my life. It was the visage of my own father, whom I hadn't seen for over twenty years!

"I gasped – I couldn't help it – and his head turned my way, just a small movement, but enough to show me that there were eyes in those sockets after all, as the light that seemed to glow around him gave a small flash from them as he focused in my direction.

330

"My nerve broke then, and all the years of anxiousness seemed to drown me. I couldn't breathe, and before I even know what I was doing, I had turned and fled back into the hallway. I don't recall setting down the unlit lamp – or perhaps I dropped it in my haste. I ran downstairs without it and into the sitting room, my chest heaving and heart pounding,

"While I stood and attempted to catch my breath, I realized that I was being foolish. I am a grown man, and shouldn't be afraid – even of what I had seen – to obtain the answers to a lifetime of questions – something that was now within my grasp.

"Yet suddenly I was overwhelmed by the smell of the cats and the closeness of the room. I craved fresh air. I opened the front door and stepped outside. The storm was furious, and I could see the violent lashing of the trees in the occasional lightning flashes. I was standing in a protected area, where the wind had yet to direct any of the drenching deluge. I fumbled in my pocket and found my cigarettes, jumping every time there was a crack of thunder. I lit one, walking back and forth across the porch as I tried to calm my nerves.

"I had circled once or twice and found myself outside the room where I was supposed to sleep for the night. I was idly staring at the window, not really seeing it as one does when deep in thought, when suddenly, with a loud ringing noise, I saw a hand, palm and fingers open, lying flat against the glass where it had just been slapped. It was white, and the very lines were seemingly etched across the flesh on the palm where they were pressed tightly against the glass pane, which itself was still rattling and vibrating within the frame. And even as I watched, the hand yanked itself away and vanished!

"Without pausing to consider, I threw aside my cigarette and dashed back into the house, charging down the hallway, intending to confront whomever was doing this, certain then that I would find my father, and the answers that I had sought my whole life. But I discovered that the room was empty! It had only been a few seconds, and yet whomever – or *whatever* – had slapped the glass had thoroughly vanished.

"I was becoming angry then, although the hair on my neck was standing up and I felt all the terror of my recurring dreams returning and slowly overtaking me. Resolved to find answers, stepped into the hall, only to stop short with a gasp – for a pair of eyes seemed to hover before me, glowing terribly. Then I realized that it was one of the cats, nearly invisible as it sat upon a table across from my bedroom, only its reflective eyes visible in the dim light. My anger returned, and I crossed the house to Miss Lanham's room, knocking over and over upon the door to awaken her, but getting no answer. Finally, I opened it, but I couldn't see a thing. Striking a match, I found that the room was empty. The match went out, burning my fingers. With a curse, I lit another, walking across to light the lamp on her dressing table. Her bed hadn't been slept in at all. Taking up the lamp, I proceeded to search the entire ground floor, without discovering her – or anyone else – whatsoever.

"I went upstairs and repeated my search on the first floor, and then the second as well. And then, I once more found myself outside that crowded box-room. Through the doorway, I could see the foot of the attic steps. There was nowhere else in the house to look. I had looked in every other room. There were none that had connecting doors, so Miss Lanham couldn't have stayed ahead of me as I searched, and anyway I would have heard her. She had been quite clear during our tour that there was no cellar. My breath was coming in gasps as I tried to force myself forward, to the foot of the steps. Then, with a dreaded resolve, I took one step, and then another, finally placing my foot on the bottom step. But just then, a terrible shriek came from the black void above me, rising and rising as if a soul was being ripped asunder. I couldn't tell if it were man or woman – or something worse. I lost my nerve and ran. In seconds I was at the front door, throwing it open and rushing headlong into the storm.

"The wind whipped around me, and I was immediately drenched to the bone. At least it seemed to be a warm rain, pushed here from the south I suppose, or else I might have ended up in hospital the next day. As it was, I was quite miserable. I didn't look back, but instead ran toward the road, barely able to see my way from the water running into my eyes. I found that I still carried the lamp, clenched in my numb fingers, but the rain had almost immediately extinguished it. I stopped and tried to relight it, but my shaking fingers couldn't ignite the wet matches, and then, with my fingers cold and wet and shaking, I dropped it, whereupon it shattered on the ground.

"I pressed onward into the darkness, and my night vision was constantly ruined by lightning flashes. I must have gone a mile before I saw a small building built near the road, really nothing more than a shed with three walls and a roof. I cast myself inside, trying to catch my breath and walking back and forth across the small space, trying to warm myself while hoping that I might dry, just a little bit.

"Eventually I calmed down a little and huddled up against one of the walls to sleep. I didn't dare explore further past the shed to see if there was a nearby house that might take me in – I certainly wouldn't have welcomed anyone like me if I'd shown up at that time of night in my condition. And so the night passed, somehow, and if I slept it was only some sort of continuation of the questions about what I had seen.

"I was back on the road before dawn, the storm having finally blown itself out. Thankfully my return ticket, though soaked, was still legible enough to obtain my passage on the train, and I was back home an hour later. With my clothes changed and my perspective quite a bit more positive than it had been just hours before, it all began to seem like something that had happened in a feverish dream. With that sensation foremost in my mind, I went to the office, thankful that Mr. Stanton was still away for several days and that I had time to plan my report to him regarding my initial assessment of Miss Lanham's house.

"However, I never got the chance. Not long after lunch, I looked up to see two men in the lobby, being directed my way by one of the other agents. My coworkers all had dark looks as they tried to surreptitiously watch what was happening, while the man who had pointed me out was moving from one small group to another, whispering. I understood why when the two men introduced themselves as Inspector Heaton and a sergeant, stating that they wished to ask me a few questions. We adjourned to one of the small conference rooms, where the inspector and I sat down. The sergeant remained standing nearby. Without comment, the inspector then laid an object that he'd carried with him upon the table. I was surprised to see that it was my own binder, with all of the notes that I'd made while inspecting Miss Lanham's house.

"I only remembered it then, as it hadn't crossed my mind before that time. I'd taken it with me, and had used it during our inspection. It had several of my cards, which had given the police my name. They explained where it had been found in my bedroom, and asked me how it got there.

"I warily told how I'd been to visit Miss Lanham the following day, and asked if there was a problem. It was then that the Inspector informed me that Miss Lanham was dead, found strangled at her open front door that very morning by the lad who came to deliver her groceries.

"I was stunned, remembering how I'd just spent several hours with her less than a day before. I haltingly explained about the letter that she'd sent – they said they'd found it folded in my binder – and that I'd arrived in the afternoon. The inspector said they'd also confirmed the fact from the driver who took me out to the house.

"'What did you do after you arrived?' asked the inspector.

"I related that Miss Lanham and I had spent an hour or so looking over the house while I made the notes that they'd found.

"'And when did you leave?'

"'Last night,' I said vaguely, suddenly a bit wary. His question seemed just a little too loaded, and I realized that I was on dangerous ground, having likely been the last person at the house – and that my curious story would only add to the suspicions that he was already displaying.

"'Had you arranged to be driven back to the station?'

"'No,' I replied.

"'Did you leave before the storm?'

"'No.' My previously garrulous answers had suddenly altered to obvious reservation.

"'You left after the storm started?' he asked with over-exaggerated surprise, turning his head to look at the sergeant, standing beside him. His countenance offered no reaction. I realized that the idea of someone choosing to walk out at night into such a tempest, with a ten-mile journey ahead of him, truly sounded mad. And yet, I believed that I could not share the rest of the story – my memories of the place, and seeing what appeared to be the ghost of my own father on the very steps that I had feared for most of my life.

"It was then that inspector added his next comment. 'We found your binder in one of the bedrooms. It was the only one where the door was open to the hallway. The bedspread was turned down, and the sheets looked as if someone had slept there.'

"He left the statement hanging, as if I would confirm or deny it. Instead, I did nothing but shake my head, as if I were as puzzled as they were.

"Both men looked at me with seeming suspicion, but I held my tongue, and eventually they announced that they need not bother me any more today. However, they did suggest that they might have further questions for me as the investigation developed – and that I shouldn't travel.

"I explained that I had a certain amount of traveling to do as part of my job – today's visit to Eastbourne, for example. They nodded, thanked me, and departed.

"After they had gone, I settled back into my chair and considered my situation. Then, with nothing else that I could do, I set about my daily tasks, returning home last night. It was then that I noticed that I was being followed. I have no doubt that it was a policeman, as he made no real effort to conceal himself. I considered approaching him, to make assurances that I had no intention of fleeing, but I thought that would be suspicious in itself. Today I went to the office, and another man followed, the same as before. I stayed in until mid-day, then stepped out for lunch before taking the train to Eastbourne, where we are acquiring the effects of a bookstore owner who recently passed away. I was careful to do nothing that would excite suspicion, but I realized that this was intolerable – and yet, I felt that I couldn't tell my story, for fear that it would only seem more suspicious. I was walking down the street to the station, intending to catch the return train, when I recalled that you lived near here, Mr. Holmes. I found a cabbie who knew the way, and here I am."

Holmes nodded toward the front of the house. "And I expect that one of the policemen is parked somewhere out in the storm in a following cab, curious as to why you visited here."

Tenbury nodded. "I suppose so. At least I hope that he's in a cab, and not hiding across the road under a bush, as wet as I was two nights ago." He leaned forward. "Can you help me?"

Holmes nodded. "I expect so. But not tonight. The weather is expected to clear tomorrow, and then we can settle this affair. Of course you'll stay over."

It was a statement rather than a question, and Tenbury nodded, thanking him several times as we rose and reassembled at the dining table for our evening meal.

Mrs. Hudson had made a beef stew flavored with red wine, and she'd obtained a crusty loaf of bread earlier in the day during a visit to nearby Eastbourne. It was a perfect choice for the terrible night, and I asked if she'd planned it that way. She gave a knowing smile, neither confirming nor denying it.

Throughout the meal, Holmes made seemingly meaningless small talk, and yet he was able to pull additional details about Tenbury's background – his childhood and education in Chelmsford, attendance at university, and then his current job at Hoddard and Stanton. The young man's education had been extensive, and it explained his impressive manner of speech when telling his story. I found that the more he spoke, the more he seemed to ring true, and I didn't doubt that the story he'd related was true. And yet, I withheld complete trust, as my decades of experience with liars – courtesy of being friends with Sherlock Holmes for over two-and-a-half decades and meeting so many of the people encountered during his investigations – informed me that some people can lie as easily as taking a resting breath.

After our meal, it was clear that Tenbury was exhausted, and Holmes had Mrs. Hudson show him to one of the villa's guest rooms. Then, as the rain washed against the windows, we sat on either side of the fireplace in Holmes's study and discussed the matter.

Holmes agreed that the young man's education was obvious from the way he had related his story. "'Drenching deluge' indeed," he said. "This fellow has a literary bend. Perhaps you can give him some advice about writing."

I waved a hand toward the nearby shelves. "When you left the room, did you go to check on Mrs. Hudson's progress with dinner, or instead to consult your scrapbooks?"

Holmes smiled. "The latter. Something about his story rang a small bell."

"1888?"

"You have become rather adept at this over the years, Watson. Yes, there is something significant about that period of time, when our three-year-old client was discovered abandoned."

"And you would prefer to reveal it all tomorrow?"

"Well, nothing is certain yet. I need to send a few wires in the morning for verification. But I believe that I have a dim understanding of some of what has gone on – although the murder itself is just an untidy appendix to the affair."

He rose then and wished me good night. I nodded, finished my brandy, and stood as well. I could have gone to my own room then, but I stepped to one side, pulling out his commonplace book for 1888.

It was a massive thing, and really needed to be split into multiple volumes. And yet, I knew that it only represented the merest fraction of what we had truly done in that terrible year.

I flipped through it, uncertain as to what I should see. I saw references to cases early in the year, after my sorrowful return to Baker Street – the Birlstone murder, and the terrible affair of The Eye of Heka soon after, where the world might have been plunged into war if Holmes hadn't decided one morning to visit the British Museum. I saw with a smile Holmes's own notes on the trip to Norbury later that spring, and then the documents that he had saved related to the Sholto murder, and soon after the events in Dartmoor. But nowhere did I find anything about the Whitechapel Murders. All of those – along with my own extensive notes – had long since been delivered to Holmes's brother, Mycroft.

I almost missed it, having realized that I'd become distracted when reading of long-ago adventures. It was a small news clipping, from October 1888. While it in no way explained the matter of Miss Lanham's murder, I felt that I dimly understood what had occurred to Holmes, and that I would be better caught-up when morning came. Putting the clipping into my coat pocket, I replaced the volume upon the shelf and I went up to bed.

The day dawned bright and clear, the storm of the previous night having left behind amazingly blue skies. I was speaking to Mrs. Hudson while she finished cooking breakfast when Tenbury stepped in from the back of the house, even as Holmes appeared, having clearly been outside. I asked if he'd been checking the hives after the storm, and he acknowledged it, while also announcing that he'd also been to Eastbourne to send a few telegrams. Mrs. Hudson clicked her tongue, and Holmes explained.

"I was up rather early, as is my custom. After seeing to the bees, I walked the five miles into town – quite refreshing I assure you – and sent a few inquiries. I expect the answers to arrive shortly. Then I had Etchison drive me back – and just in time, I see."

Mrs. Hudson moved past him, an amused look on her face, as she placed our eggs and bacon upon the table. Tenbury assured us that he has slept well, although his haggard expression belied his polite reply. Clearly he wanted to ask Holmes what he thought or planned, but he wisely held his tongue. Holmes was feeling rather loquacious, describing some of the new plants that he was setting out throughout his little farm, experimenting with attempts to flavor the honey. "American clover provides a particularly pleasant-flavored honey, as I found when passing through there in '93. It was while stopping at that curiously British settlement of Rugby, in Tennessee, that I was able to – "

He was interrupted by the sound of a knock on the front door. He stood, his breakfast only partially consumed but now forgotten, and left the room. Tenbury looked curious, but refrained from asking aloud the obvious questions. In a moment, Holmes returned, smiling.

"That was fortuitous," he said. "I received answer to both of my inquiries. We should depart soon to meet Inspector Heaton at the Lanham house near Chailey. Watson, do you mind conveying us in your automobile?"

I did not, and soon we were on our way. The trip took a bit longer than I'd estimated, as there was a bit of storm damage along some of the smaller roads. We skirted Llewes and then turned north. From Chailey, we were given useful directions from Tenbury, and by mid-morning we'd arrived at the Lanham house.

It stood alone, with no other buildings anywhere close. It was at the end of a long drive that wound about so that soon all view of the road was lost upon reaching the building. It was as Tenbury described – three stories, with the ground floor sporting a wide and covered porch across the whole front of the building, looking like some veranda that one might find on an American home. It was rather worn and neglected-looking, with the vegetation overgrown and encroaching upon the building. At the top of the structure were a few dormer windows – the terrifying attic which had so haunted Matthew Tenbury's dreams for much of his life.

I glanced at him, and saw that he was looking at those windows as well. I wondered just how often that he'd had the nightmares he described.

Waiting on the porch were a several policemen. One was Inspector Heaton of our acquaintance, and another fellow who was introduced to us as Sergeant Pembroke. He nodded, and seemed to give Holmes special attention, seemingly deciding whether this fellow truly lived up to his reputation.

After introductions had been made, Holmes thanked Heaton for bringing the requested officers, and asked that they be spread around the house. This was done.

We hadn't seen the inspector since the little surprise of the salacious investor, a couple of years before. None of us had been either surprised or saddened when that man had been found hanged in his cell.

Heaton gave a knowing look at Tenbury, which was not missed by Holmes. "Your report, of course, will show that Mr. Tenbury visited my home last night to retain my assistance."

Heaton nodded. "That's what I thought when I heard that he'd gone there." He looked then at Tenbury. "That's either very wise, Mr. Tenbury, or foolish, depending. The prisons – either the cells or their graveyards – are full of guilty men that tried to trick Mr. Holmes into helping them."

Tenbury started to speak, but Holmes beat him to it. "I think that I can cut through some of this when I tell you that Miss Lanham was Jack Lanham's sister."

The inspector's eyes widened. He glanced at Pembroke, and then at Tenbury. I could almost see his suspicion of the young man bleed away – not entirely, of course, as his policeman's instincts would certainly inform him that there are many parts of a story, but something about hearing Jack Lanham's name seemed to shift the ground entirely.

I, of course, knew nothing, and cleared my throat. Holmes smiled. "Jack Lanham was a notorious thief – but perhaps I slander the man."

"No slander, Mr. Holmes," interrupted Heaton.

"Quite, then," continued Holmes. "Although he tried his hand at any number of illegal enterprises, he was mostly known throughout the south of England, if only by reputation, as the guiding mind of some notable robberies, usually at various upper-class country houses, but he was never caught – at least for that. He started on his own in the early 1880's, came under Moriarty's thumb, and then, during the trials of 1891 and 1892, he was sent to prison. However, this was for some of those alleged activities related to what he did for the Professor, as the case against his own activities was not proven. I had evidence against the man, but either Inspector Patterson did not choose to use it, or it was misplaced or swallowed up during the dozens of other prosecutions at that time.

"After serving his sentence, Lanham left prison. I kept an eye on him, following my return to England, and he never did anything that was overtly criminal, although there were several robberies that seemed to have his touch. Then, during one of them a few years ago, a footman was killed, and it became a murder job. At that, he tacitly seemed to confess his guilt by vanishing, not to be seen since."

"And you think that he's been hiding here, Mr. Holmes? So you said in your wire."

"A hunch, Inspector, based on the fact that robberies displaying his *modus operandi* have continued to the present throughout Sussex, and also because I've heard the rest of Mr. Tenbury's story." He then indicated that Tenbury should share with the inspector what else happened that night. The young estate agent did so, and even though we were standing in the sunlit yard in front of the house, I still felt the same chills run across me when the terror of the attic was once again described.

Heaton stood silently for several minutes, pondering what he'd heard. Then, looking at Tenbury, he stated, "I can see why you withheld that, although not answering a policeman's questions is always a terrible policy. Still, if you had told me that, I'd have locked you up on the spot, instead of letting you have a little rope to see if you'd hang yourself."

He then glanced back at Holmes. "You believe that this was his base of operations?"

"I do," replied my friend. "And that it still is. Then his sister – the only legitimate and public owner of the house – decided to sell out and relocate to the seaside. I suspect that a disagreement between them, after Mr. Tenbury fled two nights ago, resulted in her death."

"Then he's long gone," said Pembroke, speaking for the first time.

"Not necessarily," replied Holmes. "Mr. Tenbury, you inspected the house. Did you see anything that might make you believe that Jack Lanham's lair is located here?"

Tenbury, however, did not reply, for he was staring into the distance, a look of growing horror upon his face. Holmes, recognizing it for what it was, said, "Mr. Tenbury! I see that you fear that this man that we've discussed, Jack Lanham, is your father, making you the son of a thief and murderer, and the nephew of the murdered woman. I assure you that this is not the case. For now, can you answer the question?"

Tenbury swallowed and took hold of himself. "No. I didn't see anything like that."

"I believe that Miss Lanham told you that there is no cellar?"

"That's right."

"Then let's see if that's accurate." And then he walked off by himself, taking a turn once around the house before returning on the opposite side in just a moment. Then he led us to the front door.

I had thought that he might spend time looking around the entryway, where it was reported that Miss Lanham's body had been found. Apparently Heaton thought so too, for he mentioned that the area had been preserved to protect any clues, even as Holmes waved a hand as if brushing aside a pestering insect. Instead, he wandered off through the house, bent down and studying the floors.

When he finished with a room, he would let us know and we would follow along while he advanced further into the building. Soon he went upstairs, investigating the first floor, and then the second, the same way. He appeared to be paying particular attention to the baseboards in both the rooms and hallways. Finally, he stopped at the door to the room leading to the attic. The wood around the lock was splintered. Holmes looked at Heaton with raised eyebrows.

"It was the only room that was locked," was the reply. "We didn't know but what the killer was hiding in there."

Holmes looked at Tenbury. "According to your story, this room was unlocked when you departed."

"It was. I still have the key." He took it from his pocket and handed it to Holmes, who then leaned down, slipped it into the lock, and turned it back and forth, showing that it was indeed the correct key for that lock."

"Did you find another key for the door when you searched the house?" he asked the inspector.

"We did not."

"Then someone with another key relocked this door after the murder." He then stepped into the room, glanced at the mounds of boxes filling the space to eye level, and then went upstairs.

I mounted the steps curiously, seeing in daylight what had terrified Tenbury since his early childhood. I looked behind me to see how he was doing, but he only appeared curious, as if exploring the room in the bright daylight through the dormer windows, and in the company of skeptical policemen and Holmes and myself, was finally enough to exorcise the memories of this place.

Looking back, I could see that there was nothing frightening here. It was just a dusty attic, filled with more clutter similar to what was in the room below. I saw the little bed to our left, in a nook between mounds of boxes, and could only wonder why the boy hadn't also feared being crushed if some of that had collapsed and fallen on him.

Holmes had no interest in any of it. Instead, he was looking at a single line of footprints that led off past the bed, farther than any of the others. "Your footsteps stopped here, Mr. Tenbury," said Holmes softly, pointing just past the bed. "Those others belong to the policemen who searched up here – there's no mistaking that regulation print. But that one shabby set, continuing to the far wall – those are of greater interest."

"Do you think Jack Lanham is still up here then?" asked Heaton, his voice low.

"No, but I think that we can get to him from here." And he walked quietly to the far end of the attic. Surprisingly, there were no squeaks from the floorboards, and I recalled Tenbury indicating that he hadn't heard any either from the solidly built house.

By the time we joined Holmes, he was kneeling against the far wall, feeling along the baseboard. "On the two floors below us are empty bedrooms. I saw no sign of entrances there. But beneath that, on the ground floor in Miss Lanham's bedroom, I did see indications – "

Before he could finish, there was a soft snapping sound, and a panel in the wall swung open, exposing a narrow opening at the base. Holmes produced a small electric torch that he'd taken to carrying the last few years. Its beam revealed a narrow staircase, descending through the wall at the end of the house.

"There is an opening in Miss Lanham's bedroom," Holmes whispered. "I believe that after Mr. Tenbury went to bed the other night, she opened it and went into the unknown part of the house. That's why he didn't find her when he searched. Later, after he departed into the storm, after having been frightened away by Jack Lanham, the two of them argued, and the brother killed the sister. I suspect that he's still here – wherever this leads – and that we can catch him, or drive him outside into the hands of the constables. I'll go first."

And without waiting for further questions, or for Heaton to insist that it was his place to lead the party, Holmes dropped into the darkness.

I didn't wait for the policemen or Tenbury to follow next, instead stepping forward and then carefully placing my feet upon the narrow steps. There was a wooden handrail of sorts nailed to the side, and I gripped it thankfully. At the next level down, there was a turn onto another flight, and then again at on the first level. Below that, I could perceive light, and in a moment I saw where Holmes had thrown open the door to Miss Lanham's bedroom. But he wasn't there. Rather, he'd continued on down, into the cellar level that was not supposed to exist.

At the bottom, I found him, standing behind a partition rather than another door. He'd extinguished his torch, and had a small mirror in hand, holding it out past the edge of the partition to see into the chamber beyond. Even as he nodded, I heard a scuffing sound of someone's shoe upon the rough concrete floor.

When Heaton and the others had joined us, Holmes stepped out into the cellar, dimly lit by a lantern hanging from the ceiling.

I could see that the space stretched much farther than the footprint of the house above us. The crude ceiling was built of roughly-hewn beams, supported by similar wooden posts. However, the space around us was forgotten when one saw the mounds of various materials stacked here and

341

there, on both the concrete floor and upon heavy tables. Later inventory would discover a fortune in stolen loot, along with smuggled goods on an incredible scale. And standing in the middle of it all, having just become aware of us, was a haggard-looking man in his middle-sixties, tensed like an animal that is unexpectedly encountered in the wild. And just like one of these, he bolted.

He reached a wooden ladder that was standing in the middle of the space, leading to the wooden ceiling above. He was up in two leaps, pushing at something which gave way, flooding the room with sunlight. He had wiggled through before any of us besides Holmes even thought to move. It was no surprise to see that Holmes had made it through the same opening just seconds after Lanham.

I climbed much more slowly than the two of them, but still more quickly than normal. Crawling through the opening, I looked back to see that one side of the base of the house, disguised to look like part of the foundation, was actually a door of sorts. But that was of no interest compared with the struggle occurring several feet away, where two constables were holding a wildly frantic Jack Lanham. He only gave up when Holmes stepped in front of him, saying nothing, but allowing the man to recognize who had finally caught him.

Unlike many instances when a criminal breaks down and explains what he had done, or confirms Holmes's explanation, Lanham refused to speak whatsoever, even when Matthew Tenbury stood before him, staring into his eyes, as if willing that some sort of explanation regarding his mysterious past might be revealed. Heaton assured Lanham that, with his past record and what was found in the house, the man was certain to be convicted, and that was before the matter of his sister's murder was added to the charges.

Tenbury was full of questions as we drove back to Holmes's villa. In short, Holmes explained that he'd verified details of Lanham's past last night in his scrapbooks, after hearing the name and the location of the Lanham house in Tenbury's story. I recalled the news clipping from late 1888, still in my pocket, and wondered if I'd perhaps been on the wrong trail after all. But no, as we were soon to discover.

"When I heard of this lonely Lanham house," continued Holmes, "I conceived of six – possibly seven – explanations that would account for the circumstances as we had heard them. I believed that I now knew where Lanham had gone to ground after the footman's death several years ago. He had continued to lead the odd excursion into burglary, but clearly his business methods had developed more on the lines of fencing and smuggling. When we arrived at the house, I knew that I was right about that, as the road to this lonely house showed an excessive amount of wear for a place where only an old woman lived. When I saw the house, I understood the layout, and a look around outside showed where a door to the non-existent cellar might exist. Believing that he was still in the house, it seemed best to catch him there, or drive him in front of us.

"Although he may never confirm it, I believe that he and his sister disagreed about her wish to sell and move to the seaside – for that would mean abandoning his carefully constructed hidey-hole – and clearly it was well-devised, and was surely built when the house was constructed. Lanham was apparently only carrying on the family business started by his father decades ago.

"When you arrived without an appointment, Mr. Tenbury, Miss Lanham decided to go ahead and proceed, showing you around the house, while Jack Lanham hid and fumed. Then, worse, you were invited to stay overnight. And when you unexpectedly encountered him at the attic's entrance, highlighted as he was by a dark lantern, things began to spiral out of control. He saw that he'd scared you, and he followed you downstairs. Seeing that you were on the porch, he must have decided to add to your nervousness, slapping the window. Then he ran to Miss Lanham's room and urged her into the secret passage, so that you'd only find an empty house. His further scream from the attic sent you running into the night, but who knows what else he might have done to frighten you away.

"Might he have murdered me?" Tenbury wondered.

"I doubt it. In spite of his sister's strangulation, which was an act of spontaneous rage, likely when they argued following your departure, Jack Lanham has never been known for violence. Even the dead footman was not his doing, but rather carried out by an ill-chosen henchmen." Holmes smiled at me. "I wasn't unaware, Watson, that you seemed to question my allowing young Tenbury here to join us as we descended into Lanham's cellar. I was fairly certain that we would be safe, based on the man's past history."

I shook my head, disagreeing. At that point, Lanham was wanted for murder, and had very little to lose. He might very well have shot us on sight. But it was moot at that point, and by then we had arrived back at Holmes's farm. A very modern Rolls Royce was parked in the yard. As we walked by, the chauffer nodded at us. I wanted to stop and admire it, but I was also interested in seeing who was inside, as I was certain that it related to the 1888 newspaper clipping that I carried in my pocket.

Therefore, I wasn't surprised when we found Lewis Bernard, the chemical magnate, and the man mentioned in the article standing in the doorway, looking toward us anxiously. But beside me, young Matthew Tenbury, seeing the famous industrialist step forward into the mid-day light, was suddenly shocked. He stopped, and I feared that he might have sagged to the ground if I hadn't taken his arm.

I could understand his reaction. I would have felt the same way if I'd looked up and seen a mirror image of myself – tall and slim, with an angular skull and brown hair that was out of place, and eyes hinting at some Scandinavian ancestor. The only differences between them was that Lewis Bernard was more than two decades older than Matthew Tenbury, and his face was lined as if he'd faced a long grief that had worn him down. Now, however, those same lines had pulled back into a smile that rivaled the sunshine, and his face gleamed with uncontrolled tears as he managed to gasp, "My son!"

He was in front of Tenbury in an instant, and the two looked at one another, before the same smile crossed the young man's face as well, and they hugged one another desperately. I looked toward Holmes, already standing in his doorway and observing from the shadows. I couldn't see his reaction, as my own eyes were burning just then as well.

Later, we were seated inside as a beaming Mrs. Hudson served tea, and I pulled the article from my pocket, handing it to Holmes. He nodded, acknowledging my insight.

"When your son was kidnapped twenty-one years ago," Holmes said, "in October 1888, Watson and I were rather distracted by other matters, so I'm sorry to say that I wasn't able to offer any assistance. In truth, I only became aware of the matter a few months later, when I was asked to examine the affair by my brother, and by then the trail was cold." He leaned forward to hand the clipping to Matthew Tenbury. As the young man read it, Holmes continued. "Earlier this morning, we arrested a long-time criminal for murder – your son can tell you the details later. But when he came to me for help last night, and told me his story, he related some of his past – how he had been found as a three-year-old child in 1888, only knowing his name – Matthew Tenbury – and with the memories of a man whom he thought to be his father. This was the man, he explained, who went to great lengths to teach him that name, if nothing else.

"I checked my own records and confirmed that your own son had vanished at about the same time, causing me to communicate with you this morning that he might have been found. I recalled, from seeing your photograph in the newspapers, that the two of you bear marked resemblances to one another, so the connection was likely.

"Apparently Jack Lanham, the man who kidnapped your son, was willing to try some of everything, especially in those days, when he was an agent of Professor Moriarty. I believe that you were in the Sudan then, in the Army, much involved in the skirmishes that led up to the Battle of Suakin later that year."

Lewis Bernard nodded. "I was. I had no idea that little Michael – that's your name," he said to Matthew Tenbury – "was kidnapped. My wife didn't want me to be told, for she feared that it would upset me – make me careless, or get myself killed. She kept it out of the press and didn't immediately notify the police – instead paying one ransom after another. It was only after I returned home weeks later, after receiving letters from concerned friends who ignored her wishes and wrote to me, that I read her diaries, and saw how despondent she had become in those days before she . . . before she . . . ."

"She killed herself," I said quietly.

Bernard nodded. "By the time I made it back to England, she had died – she blamed herself, and feared to face me, believing that she had failed me – and the trail to find my son was cold." His voice drifted away.

"I am sorry that I wasn't more effective or successful at the time," said Holmes. "It has been my experience that the most successful murderer is able to go undetected when he commits a random crime – when he or she has no connection to the victim. The same is true for in the case of the kidnapper. Jack Lanham apparently targeted your family without any other reason than he noticed you first. He took your son, hid him at his sister's house in Chailey, and set about teaching him the false name 'Matthew Tenbury' so that, if questioned, the boy wouldn't say that he was Michael Bernard.

"After repeatedly obtaining additional ransom payments, he probably became fearful, or realized that he had bitten off more than he could chew. He took the boy to Chelmsford and abandoned him in the streets, where he was then taken in and raised by a kindly clergyman and his wife. No connection was made between you and your kidnapped son. The boy, however, continued to have nightmares for years afterwards about the house where he had been kept, and when he ended up at that same house a few days ago as a routine part of his professional duties, the memories came rushing back.

"Meanwhile, the kidnapper, Jack Lanham, had his own problems. He was being forced to abandon his long-developed headquarters by his sister's desire to live elsewhere. Their quarrel apparently led him murder her, setting in motion the events that resulted in his subsequent arrest a few hours ago. And here we are."

Within a few moments, the two men had left, talking excitedly. Lewis Bernard expressed an interest in meeting the couple in Chelmsford who had done such a fine job in raising his son. Holmes's house seemed strangely quiet when they were gone.

As Holmes lit his pipe, I said, "I suppose that there's no doubt that Tenbury is Bernard's missing son?"

He shook his head. "You saw them – the younger is the spitting image of the elder. The dates coincide as well. And possibly Lanham may be persuaded to verify a few details before he is hanged."

As will be remembered, he was willing when, in a strange twist, Lewis Bernard provided legal counsel for him in exchange for the information confirming how Matthew Tenbury – or Michael Bernard as I learned to think of him – had been kidnapped. It did no good, however, and the wily old criminal finally received his just punishment on a cold January morning the following year.

On that October day, however, I was still trying to fit it all together in my own mind. "It's an amazing coincidence – " I began, but Holmes cut me off.

"Nonsense. The world is full of curious plannings, cross-purposes, and wonderful chains of events, working through generations that lead to the most *outrè* results. If we could see it all from above – the connections, the near-misses, the causes-and-effects constantly set in motion, it would make all fiction seem most stale indeed. This was not just coincidence. And this reconnection of a son with his father is almost mundane compared with another in which I was peripherally involved, only a couple of months ago. Perhaps you'd like to hear about it – although I don't know the end of the story yet myself."

And he told me how, just the previous August, he'd been called to Paris to examine a set of fingermarks, discovered in the diary of a survivor of the ill-fated *Fuwalda*, lost off the coast of Africa in 1888 – "An interesting coincidence of years, wouldn't you say?" Holmes pointed out. The child of two of the only two survivors, a young married couple, had recently been found to be alive, having been raised to manhood under most curious circumstances on the West African coast, and the matter of his fingermarks, as compared to those that he had made in his father's journal when he was a baby, had decidedly confirmed that he was in truth the heir to a title and the vast estates associated with it.

"This young man's father, presumed lost on the *Fuwalda* with his young wife back in '88, was one of Mycroft's agents – I believe that you knew him years before in India." He repeated a name that I did recall. "The son's identity was conclusively verified by the fingermarks in the journal, and yet, word has reached me that he refuses to take possession of his inheritance. Now the reasons for that, to me at least, are worth pondering."

And he pulled at his pipe, his thoughts drifting toward that other matter, while I rose and relocated to the back of the house, where Mrs. Hudson was preparing lunch.

# Death in The House
# of the Black Madonna
## by Nick Cardillo

### Chapter I

"Ah, Sherlock. Dr. Watson," said Mycroft Holmes without rising from his overstuffed leather chair. "It does me good to see two such familiar faces after so long a time."

It had been several years – seemingly several lifetimes – since I had stood within the Stranger's Room, the only location in which speaking was permitted within the austerity of the Diogenes Club, and it felt nearly as long since I had clapped eyes upon my old friend, Mr. Sherlock Holmes. On that particular day in the early summer of 1919, I felt as if I were separated by oceans of time from the man I once was at Holmes's sid: Friend and colleague to the world's first unofficial consulting detective. At the dawn of the Great War, I had assisted Holmes in some official state business, but in the intervening years, we had drifted apart. I heard tell from Holmes's occasional correspondences that he had been employed once more by his brother and the British Secret Service to carry out matters of state, and I do confess that a part of me felt jealous that my friend was still continually challenging himself just as he was so many years earlier. For my part, I did all that I could to aide in the war effort and resumed my practice with a zealous attitude that was unrivaled since my earliest days as a practicing medico. It was stimulating work, but each time I received a letter from Holmes – the man positively detested the modern convenience of the telephone – I yearned to be at his side once again.

So, when I received an urgent telegram from him that morning informing me of his presence in London and requesting me to meet him at noon precisely in the Stranger's Room of the Diogenes Club, I couldn't have been more surprised or more thrilled.

As my eyes fell upon Sherlock Holmes once more, I was amazed to see that he had changed little since last we had met. He was just as tall and lean as ever, though age had begun to show upon his pointed, aquiline features, and his temples had gone the way of grey. He leaned upon a silver-handled walking stick, and even at a glance I could see that there was a stiffness to his legs which spoke of some recently sustained injury which, even for a man as healthy as Holmes, was not the kind of damage that could be easily sustained by a man firmly in his sixties. His grey eyes twinkled as I drew into the room, the door of which was promptly closed behind me by the porter who had shown me in, and I barely had a chance to greet him before Mycroft Holmes was addressing the both of us and waving us with his large hands into the two empty chairs that were facing him.

"I must admit, Sherlock," Mycroft was continuing, "that there was some reticence upon my part when you suggested to me this morning that you should like to involve Dr. Watson in this affair. However, seeing as the man does have a habit of bringing the best out of you, I acquiesced to your wishes."

I had never known Mycroft to speak so highly of me, and I blushed in spite of myself.

"You shall want your wits about you, brother mine," Mycroft continued, "as this case is a matter of international security."

"You have been characteristically taciturn about the details of this case, Mycroft," Holmes said, as he eased into his own chair and stiffly crossed one leg over the other. Then, settling back in his seat, he withdrew his silver cigarette case from the breast-pocket of his coat, coaxed a cylinder from amongst its brethren, and lighted it. "However, you promise much, and I expect much for having traveled so far from my bees at so volatile a time for the colony."

Mycroft scoffed. "You shall find this business more fruitful to your constitution, Sherlock, than your bees and your honey ever could be. I do know how you crave mental exercise."

Holmes blew a ring of smoke about his gaunt head. "Then, please," he said, "do not hesitate any longer in telling to us the details in full."

Mycroft shifted his girth in his chair. "It could hardly have escaped your attention, gentleman, that precisely one year ago, the kingdoms of Bohemia and Moravia united into one country, Czechoslovakia. This peaceful transition of power was admired the world over, particularly as it came so close on the heels of the Great War. When that conflict came to an end, and word began to spread through the seats of power in Europe that such a unification was imminent, His Majesty's Government sent an agent, a reliable man called Fitzroy, to be our own eyes and ears on the ground. He reported to Prague in April of last year and oversaw the official process from afar. We received bi-weekly reports from Fitzroy, oftentimes encoded should they be inadvertently intercepted in transmission from the Continent, and in each report he spoke of what progress was being made within the country.

"Six weeks ago, however, the nature of Fitzroy's reports began to change. He alluded to a scheme of some variety. However, details were

348

sparse and he dared not reveal too much, even in the form of a coded message, should it fall into the wrong hands. We received two messages of this nature from Fitzroy before all communication stopped. We haven't heard from him at all since his last communication, which confirmed that something was afoot in the city of Prague. We immediately dispatched another man to the Continent in search of Fitzroy, but his efforts yielded nothing. When he returned with only one piece of information, it was decided that we should bring in someone else to oversee the location of our man. I suggested you, Sherlock."

Mycroft Holmes sat back in his seat as Holmes smoked his cigarette in silence. I stared from one brother to the other, waiting for this informal standoff to end. It did when the younger Holmes said, "So you wish for us to go to Prague?"

"Yes. Your mission is to locate Fitzroy and – if possible – to elicit from him the details of this plot onto which he has stumbled."

Holmes crushed the cigarette into an ashtray and hoisted himself from his seat. "I daresay that you could have selected a better man for this job, Mycroft. This espionage work is hardly the business of an old man like me. And, you can hardly forget what happened in Constantinople." Holmes gestured with his cane at his leg. The injury was sustained during some mission, then.

"I can think of no better man than you, Sherlock." Mycroft then added as an afterthought, "And of course you too, Dr. Watson."

I bowed my head resolutely.

"This matter should hardly require of you the same physical prowess as the Turkish Job," Mycroft said, as he pulled himself out of his chair. "Fitzroy and our second man, Jones, are two of our best operatives and, combined, they do not have the cognitive abilities to adequately investigate this business. You, alone, Sherlock, can handle this matter."

I saw Holmes stare at a point in the floor and consider. This business was so far afield from the little matters which were presented to us in our Baker Street rooms years ago. This was a matter of international consequence, and despite Holmes's considerable efforts in the past, I could tell that he felt daunted by the task before him. Then, miraculously, the ghost of a smile crept across Holmes's thin lips and he turned his gaze to me.

"I shall be happy to 'handle' this investigation for you, Mycroft, provided Watson is keen to accompany me. Even after all these years, I should be lost without my Boswell."

I felt a sudden surge of joy rush through my breast and I all but jumped out of my chair. "I should like nothing more, Holmes!" I cried.

349

"Splendid," the detective replied. Then, rounding on his brother with newfound alertness and energy, he said, "I shall, of course, require a few hours preparation time before Watson and I make accommodations to catch the boat train. If my memory of the time tables is still exact then we should have no difficulty in catching the 3:06."

"That would be the 3:08," Mycroft countered with a wry grin.

"But of course," Holmes retorted, acquiescing to his intellectual superior. "I did myself the service of packing a few spare clothes before I departed Sussex, but I should expect that the Good Doctor will need an opportunity to obtain a spare shirt and pair of trousers for the Continent."

"I should welcome the opportunity," I replied.

"And do be a good fellow and slip your old service revolver between yours things," Holmes added. "That is, provided you still have the thing about."

I nodded in the affirmative.

"Excellent!" Holmes exclaimed. "I shall require one more crucial piece of information from you, Mycroft: You say that this second man, Jones, discovered something while he was in Prague searching for Fitzroy. What did this man discover?"

"An all-important but ultimately fruitless lead, I am afraid," Mycroft said. "According to Jones, Fitzroy is still alive. Jones' contacts in the city have heard word that he is in hiding. Fitzroy has done a good enough job that even Jones could not locate him."

"These contacts of Jones'," Holmes said. "Could you supply me with their names as well?"

"I shall examine his report and send you their names this afternoon."

"And a photograph of Fitzroy shall be of great assistance."

"Of course," Mycroft replied.

Holmes beamed. "Then I don't think we should waste another moment here," he declared. Turning to me, he said, "Come, Watson. Once more the game is afoot!"


Chapter II


We did part ways after we had left the Diogenes Club, rushing out into the teeming streets of St. James. I called out for a passing cab while I watched Holmes rush off down the street, already in the midst of setting some plan into action. I returned home and hurriedly packed a bag, making sure that I tucked my old revolver amongst my things as Holmes requested. I then traveled by automobile once more and arrived at Victoria Station just in time to meet Holmes for the 3:08 train to Dover.

Situated within a train carriage opposite from my friend melted away the years, and for a brief instant I felt as if we were back on opposite sides of the hearth in Baker Street. Holmes regaled me with tales of his recent exploits, though in his habitual tight-lipped fashion, he never indulged on the details and often left me yearning to know more. The fabled mission to Constantinople, for instance, he never once mentioned. He was also kind enough to press me for information of my life since last we had met and I was happy to share my successes as a practicing physician. A light came into Holmes's eyes as we sat in the undulating carriage and watched the countryside pass us by.

"It does me good to see you again, old man," he said.

"And it does me good to see you too, Holmes," I replied with a great grin. "This is just like old times."

"We may be older and greyer, but indeed, this is like old times," Holmes replied bemusedly.

"And if this is indeed like old times," I continued, "then I ought to know you well enough to know that you have already set into motion some scheme. I saw you hurry out of the Diogenes like a man possessed. What is to be our plan of action?"

Holmes smiled and leaned forward conspiratorially. "I should think it best, my dear fellow," he began, "that we should maintain a discreet profile once we have arrived in Prague. I fear that we tread in dark waters, and making our presence known would be a mistake of a cataclysmic kind."

I agreed with my friend, though his gloomy words unnerved me.

"In spite of this – or perhaps as a result of it – I have been forced to make contact with some of Prague's more shadowy operatives, a task I set into motion this afternoon. I secured the name of one of Jones' contacts in Prague, a man called Palan, who has agreed to meet us as soon as we arrive. It is through Palan that I hope that we shall find our way to Fitzroy."

"Was Mycroft able to supply you with a photograph of the man?"

Holmes nodded and withdrew a folded picture from his inner pocket – a portrait of a youngish, handsome man with dark hair and a prominent jaw. I studied his features for a moment – enough I felt confident that I could recognize the fellow on sight – and then returned it to Holmes.

"We have a long journey ahead of us, Watson," Holmes said as he leaned his head back against the plush seat. "I recommend getting some sleep now. I think that we shall need all of our wits about us very soon."

Yet it felt as if it took ages for us to eventually reach the city of Prague. Our connecting train in France crawled through Central Europe, climbing through mountains and forging through deep valleys, so that for many hours I felt as if I were in a state of total disorientation, unsure of what way was what. Holmes was silent for much of our journey, and I wondered if – as we wound our way through the land I should forever think of as Bohemia – he cast his mind back to the regal figure of that land who stood within our very Baker Street sitting room so many years ago and hired Holmes for a job – a job which would bring him into direct contact with *the* woman, Irene Adler. Of course, Holmes's face was a mask as he cast his eyes out of the train compartment window, and I knew full well that I would never know what he was thinking.

I heaved a great sigh of relief, then, when our train finally reached Prague. Night had fallen over the city and, after we collected our bags and found an automobile that was willing to convey us to our hotel, I was thoroughly exhausted. Once instituted within the confines of my room, I sat upon the edge of my bed and let out a deep sigh of total fatigue. Sherlock Holmes, however, was totally unmoved by the long journey and, as he stood in the doorway to my room, a look of impatience upon his face, I knew that I had to muster all of my energy to follow him once more. I slipped my revolver into my inner pocket and followed him out into the night.

Our small but comfortable lodgings were situated in Old Town Square, a remarkable open-air location that was surrounded on two sides by churches and on the other the Old Town Hall, a great stone edifice that had been standing for nearly six-hundred years. We set off that night, Holmes traversing a path through the square as though he knew the place like the back of his hand. The city was eerily quiet as we made our way through its narrow streets and across its ancient cobblestones. Somewhere in the distance, tolling the hour from one of the city's many church steeples, I heard bells signaling the passing of one o'clock in the morning. I felt drained of life as Holmes pulled me down another side street, and I very nearly let out a thankful breath when he whispered that our port of call was at the end of the street.

I saw it at once: A sign for a pub which hung beneath a single streetlamp affixed to the side of a stone building. The sign read something in Czech that I could not divine, but Holmes knew full well that this was the place we needed to be. Approaching the door to the establishment, I thought it very unlikely that anyone should answer Holmes's knock, but much to my surprise, the door swung open from within and we were confronted by a tall, skeletal-looking man with a countenance that spoke of many years' hard labor. Holmes addressed him briefly in Czech, to which he bowed his head and then gestured for us to draw in further. The door closed behind us and I found myself standing in a low, dingy room, illuminated only by a few guttering candle flames that stood upon table tops. The pub was empty save for a few disreputable-looking figures hunched in the shadows. There sat one man, however, at one of the tables, his face lit by the glow of the little candle flame, and it was to him that the stranger at the door gestured.

Holmes approached the man and I tentatively followed. As we drew nearer, I could make out the man's features. He stood, and I could see that he was tall and lean with an athletic build, and an ovular head which sat atop his strong neck and shoulders. He was almost completely bald, but his face was covered in prematurely-greying whiskers, and I could tell – even in the low light – that there was a twinkle in his humorless eyes.

"Mr. Lukáš Palan?" Holmes said inquiringly, yet I believe he already knew the answer.

The man nodded his head in the affirmative and wordlessly gestured for us to sit as he returned to his own chair. He then reached for the glass at his elbow and downed a swig of the heady brew within.

"You were most vague in your correspondence, Mr. Holmes," Palan said in his heavily-accented voice.

"I think the same could be said of you, Mr. Palan," Holmes retorted. "Yet I know that if there is anyone in this city who can help me locate our man, Fitzroy, it is you. You should be pleased to know that you name is not an unfamiliar one in London."

Palan arched an eyebrow. "That is most distressing, sir," he answered. "I have done my utmost to keep a low profile."

"The London criminal fraternity is like one great spider's web, interlaced with another," Holmes began, overlapping his long bony fingers as he spoke. "Word spreads from one thread of one web to a thread of another, and so on and so on. However, Mr. Palan, these words are spoken in voices no louder than whispers. Your work is still secret to most."

"Most men are not Sherlock Holmes," Palan retorted. "Yours is a name which we know all too well in this country."

"This is why I must insist upon your absolute discretion, Palan. It has become apparent that our man, Fitzroy, was onto something while here in Prague. Should it be a plot of some kind, we cannot allow its perpetrators to know that we are onto them at all."

Palan nodded understandingly and took any drink from his glass. "Well then," he said, "how can I be of assistance to you?"

"First of all," Holmes said, "tell us what you told our man, Jones. He was your contact. We learned from Jones that Fitzroy is still alive and in this city. How did he come across such information?"

Palan considered. "The criminal network of London may be like a great web, Mr. Holmes," he began, "but here in Prague, we are a tighter-knit community (for the lack of a better word). It is unlikely that if some crime is carried out that someone else would not have heard word of it being perpetrated. This includes, surprisingly enough, murder. It was therefore no mean feat to ascertain whether there had been word of any murders perpetrated recently and, if that was the case, who the dead man was. I learned quite easily for Mr. Jones that no dead man matching Mr. Fitzroy's description had turned up anywhere."

"But what if his appearance was altered to conceal his identity?" I asked.

"Such mysterious deaths of that kind had not been reported by anyone in the criminal classes," Palan answered.

"What is more, Watson," Holmes continued, "Fitzroy was traveling virtually incognito. He would have been a total stranger in this city. No one would have known him and to conceal the identity of a complete stranger does seem rather superfluous."

Holmes returned his attention to Palan. "If you are quite certain that Fitzroy is still alive, where would you suggest looking for him?"

"Prague is an ancient city, Mr. Holmes. There are plenty of places in it that one might disappear, should they wish."

Holmes considered. "How many men do you have? Can you scout the city for Fitzroy, provided I supply you with a description?"

"Our numbers aren't strong, Mr. Holmes, but they are not feeble. My eyes and ears on the streets can certainly make an effort at finding him."

Holmes smiled. Then, the ghost of a grin was gone from his face as he added, "Tell me, Mr. Palan, no matter how trivial it may seem: Has there been anything *unusual* going on in this city of late?"

"*Unusual?*" Palan said, sitting bolt-upright in his seat. "Whatever do you mean?"

"I mean precisely what I say," Holmes retorted coldly. "What has been occurring in this city that is beyond your explanation? I note your obvious concern now, but I perceived that something was amiss from the moment I entered this room. Your man at the door is clearly concealing a stiletto blade within his coat – the uncomfortable position of his arm directly above the handle is a dead giveaway – and I think such precautions are unneeded after one in the morning in this secluded pub . . . even for a man of such a dubious reputation as yourself."

Palan drew in a deep breath. He also chuckled as he spoke next: "Have you heard of the *Golem*, Mr. Holmes?"

In the darkness of that pub and at the sudden fear which clouded Lukáš Palan's eyes, I felt a chill pass up and down my spine.

"The legend is not unfamiliar to me," Holmes replied, "though I can hardly claim to have an exact knowledge of it."

"Shall I tell it to you, then?"

Holmes let out a sigh of contempt. Never one for stories, I knew full well that hearing the tale of the Golem would not benefit Holmes in any way. However, Palan added, "I can assure you, sir, that it is of vital importance to you to know it."

With a wave of his hand, Holmes sat back in his seat and Palan began again.

"There are hundreds of tales of the Golem throughout the world, Mr. Holmes," Palan said. "However, it is in Prague that perhaps the most famous tale is said to have taken place. the Golem has become a fixture of this ancient city's legacy. We all know the basics of the story. But what if it was not simply a story? To put it simply, Mr. Holmes, in the sixteenth-century Rabbi Loew is said to have created the Golem – a monolithic creature born from clay from the banks of the Vltava River – to protect the residents of the city's Jewish Quarter from pogroms. The creature was brought to life, but soon Loew lost control of his creation and it became more and more powerful. The thing escaped its confines and went on a rampage through the city. According to legend, Loew caught up to the Golem and stopped it. Some say that he pulled the *shem* from the Golem's mouth and incapacitated the creature, while others suggest that with his staff Rabbi Loew struck from the Golem's brow one of the carved Hebrew letters which had brought the thing to life and, in doing so, the Golem crumbled before his eyes. However, once it had been destroyed, the Golem (or what was left of it) was placed in an attic room of the Old New Synagogue, should its services ever be needed again.

"There are many in this city that believe that that day has come."

Holmes leaned forward in his chair. "I think you had better explain yourself, Palan."

"For some time now," Palan continued, "there are have been sightings of a creature that could only be the Golem. At first, these were reported only by children and not taken very seriously, but there have been more and more people who have said that they have seen something – a beast in the shape of a man, but larger than any mortal man could ever be. He keeps to the shadows and his features are caught only in fleeting glimpses, but that is enough to convince many in Prague that the Golem has returned. Whether he is a good omen to mark our independence or a harbinger of doom, we do not know."

Holmes considered for a moment. "None of your contacts have anything to say about this Golem?"

"Nothing at all," Palan answered. "I should have thought that I would know such a character, but his shadowy nature concerns me."

"You don't believe that this thing really is the Golem, do you?" I asked incredulously.

"I do not know, Dr. Watson," Lukáš Palan answered. "I wish that I could be more firm in my beliefs. But I simply cannot be sure."

We left Palan, I with trepidation and uneasiness coursing through my body as we traversed the empty streets of the city once more. My eyes were darting into every darkened doorway, down every alleyway looking for long, looming shadows. I could tell that Holmes was reserving his quiet judgment and at length I could only say to him, "Were you not at all intrigued by the tale that Palan had to tell?"

"It is an interesting bit of local trivia," Holmes rebuked, "though I doubt that it has much bearing on our present situation."

"But how can you explain it?" I asked.

Holmes shrugged his shoulders. "I shall not explain it away until I need to do so," he said. "At present, these sightings of the Golem have little to do with the disappearance of Fitzroy, and I fear that our visit did little to supply me with direction. We are no closer to finding him, I'm afraid."

We returned to our hotel in silence after that, and Holmes shut himself away in his room. I slept fitfully that night, tossing and turning on an uncomfortable bed, my dreams filled with visions of *things* beyond human comprehension. It wasn't long before I abandoned all hope of sleep and sat up waiting for the dawn.

I was taking breakfast in my room, wearily pouring a cup of coffee, when Holmes swept into the room. He took a seat and happily poured himself a cup.

"Your mood is definitely improved," I said as I applied some jam to a slice of bread.

"I underestimated Palan," Holmes replied. He produced a folded sheet of paper and tossed it across the table to me. I opened it and read the hastily-scrawled message thereon:

*We have located Fitzroy – L.P.*

"That correspondence was slipped under my door only a few hours after we returned," Holmes said. "Not only did I underestimate Palan and his men's ability to locate Fitzroy, but I underestimated his ability to find our own lodgings."

"Well, this is wonderful news," I said. "What do we do now?"

No sooner had I asked then there came a knock on the door. Holmes stood to answer it and we found an enthusiastic Lukáš Palan standing on the other side.

"We have no time to lose!" he cried. "One of my men is on his way to intercept Fitzroy now. When he found out that we had located him, he made immediate plans to flee Prague. If you do not want to lose him, we must act quickly."

Holmes eagerly grabbed for his hat and stick as I threw down my piece of bread and rushed after the two men.

"He was under our nose the entire time," Palan said as we walked side by side through Old Town Square once more. I was doing my utmost not to be distracted by the beautiful ancient architecture in the daytime, which in the early hours of the previous night had loomed ominously above us. Now, the city took on a much more beautiful aspect and I drank in the pastel-colored buildings and centuries-worth of architectural styles standing side-by-side. "We located him in a flat just off of Old Town Square, and he should be coming through here any moment."

No sooner had Palan spoken than I could sight of a familiar-looking man across the square. He was tall and dignified in appearance, his dark hair and prominent handsome jaw conjuring up images of the photograph Holmes had shown me on the train in my head. Even from a distance, he knew at once that we were looking directly at him and, locking eyes with our small party, I saw his eyes go wide with alarm and then, shockingly, he turned and bolted away from us.

"Quickly!" Holmes hissed. "We don't want to lose him!"

The detective broke away from our group, charging after Fitzroy across Old Town Square. One would never have suspected that Holmes was as old as he was or that he had sustained an injury of any kind, watching him run as he did. I had always reckoned Holmes a man fleet of foot, but I doubt if I had ever seen a man run faster than my friend did that day. So startled were both Palan and I at Holmes's sudden change that we were left momentarily stunned before movement took over our own legs and we ran after.

Fitzroy had the advantage of youth and he was quite a ways ahead of Holmes, but I still was able to see him through the small crowd of people who had gathered in the square that morning. Fitzroy ducked down a side street in an effort to evade Holmes, but the detective kept his eyes locked on our quarry. As I followed, I felt my legs begin to give way under me and my lungs burning, but I had to power on. If Holmes could keep up the chase, I told myself, then I certainly could do so too. Palan ran alongside of me, his face a quizzical mask. In the midst of our run he turned to me and cried out, "I haven't any idea where the man could be going!"

We kept running until we saw Holmes come to a stop ahead of us, bent over double catching his breath. We stopped and I did much the same, drawing deep gasps of air into my lungs that felt as if they were on fire.

"I'm afraid that I lost him," Holmes said through gritted teeth. He looked to Palan for his knowledge of the city.

Our informant's eyes full upon the building before which we stood. It was a three-story building that did not match our surroundings at all, a strange, Cubist monstrosity with great bay windows looking out over the cobblestone street. On the corner, where a stone edifice once stood, was the figure of a woman clinging to the wall.

"The House of the Black Madonna," Palan said. "This is the only place that Fitzroy could have sought refuge. It is a department store," Palan said, "but where better to hide than in plain sight?"

"Then we are doing ourselves a disservice by remaining out here," Holmes said, pushing past us and striding into the shop.

At first I believed the building to be empty, save for a shopkeeper who was milling around the showroom. He addressed us in Czech, but Holmes brushed the man off, his eyes darting around the premises. And then his gaze fell upon an open door leading further into the shop. Rushing forward, he disappeared into a separate room. I followed and stopped suddenly when I saw what lay within: Sprawled on the floor of the room near the opening to a passageway leading out into the street, in a horrible, twisted heap, was all that remained of our man Fitzroy.

## Chapter III

Of course the proper authorities were notified immediately, and we soon found ourselves in the curious position of having to communicate with the Czech police. Palan, our guide and translator, had disappeared upon discovery of the body for fear that his face, a familiar countenance to the police, might implicate him in this affair. Therefore, Holmes and I had a devil of time trying to explain ourselves without giving ourselves up entirely. Luckily, in time, a tall, stout official pushed his way through the assembled crowd of onlookers that had gathered outside The House of the Black Madonna. He was clothed in a tweed suit and homburg with wire-framed glasses on his round face, and jutting from the corner of his thin-lipped mouth was the stump of a pipe. I watched several of the officers with whom we had been attempting to converse address this man and then he turned his attention to us and addressed us in heavily-accented English:

"Mr. Sherlock Holmes!" he said to my friend. "Your name is a familiar one. And if you are Holmes," he stated, then turning to me, "then you must be Dr. Watson. It is an honor to have two such personages in my city. But how unfortunate that you should be present at the scene of a murder. That is your line of work, though, is it not, Mr. Holmes?"

"At one time," Holmes said airily. "I am now very much retired, and was simply here on holiday with Dr. Watson."

A grin crossed the man's face as though he did not believe us in the slightest. "I have forgotten to properly introduce myself," he said with a courtly bow, "I am Inspector Jan Horák of the Prague Police."

"It is a pleasure to meet you, Inspector," Holmes replied.

The mischievous grin did not leave the inspector's face. "You must forgive me, Mr. Holmes," he said. "It is certainly a once in a lifetime opportunity to work a case alongside a detective as esteemed as you. If you were investigating this matter – hypothetically, of course – what would your first thoughts be?"

Holmes considered, feigning ignorance. "I should make a thorough examination of the body," he said. "Luckily, it seems as though you and your men have left it *in situ*. I must congratulate you. Many moons ago, my friends at Scotland Yard were not so thorough."

"Would you be interested in making such an examination?" Inspector Horák said. He was tempting my friend as though he were the serpent in the Garden of Eden.

"I should leave such examinations to Dr. Watson," Holmes replied. The inspector leveled his gaze at me and arched an eyebrow.

"If I may be of any help," I said, "I should be happy to examine the body."

"Excellent," the inspector replied. He gestured for us to follow him back into the building.

Indeed, the police had taken the proper precautions of leaving everything intact and as we returned to the room in which Fitzroy had been murdered, I realized for the first time that this was the first opportunity I had had to truly oversee the body. I knelt down over the corpse and made a cursory investigation before I stood again.

"The poor fellow has taken a pretty bad beating," I said. "I shouldn't be surprised if nearly every bone in his body was broken, but it was his neck which did the poor man in."

"*Every bone broken?*" the inspector echoed.

"Yes," I replied. "It was quite a strong hand that did this nasty thing."

"An inhuman hand?" I heard Holmes mutter. Both the inspector and I turned surprised gazes towards him. "I have heard recently, Inspector, that there has been a spate of sightings of the mythical Golem in your city. I cannot but think that the two cases are related."

"You are not seriously suggesting that the Golem is responsible for this?" Horák said incredulously. "I believed you were a rational man!"

"It was a theory and little more," Holmes said with a dismissive wave of the hand. "My apologies that I could not be more helpful to you, Inspector. And I am afraid that Dr. Watson and I must keep an important appointment."

So saying, Holmes took a hold of my arm and whisked me out of the building.

"What is going on, Holmes?" I asked once we had walked far enough away from the crowd and the penetrating glares of the police officers.

"I fear that I spoke too hastily when I dismissed any connection between the Golem and the disappearance of Fitzroy. Now that the man has been murdered – no doubt to prevent him from telling to us the particulars of the plot he stumbled upon – I can see that the two incidents are not unrelated at all."

"Tell me: Why did Fitzroy run from us in the first place?"

"No doubt he thought we were part of the plot. Put yourself in his place: You are roused early this morning by Palan's men. You do not know them – it was Jones who made contact with them, after all – and fearing that your location has been compromised, you leave immediately. And then you see three strangers across the square that run after you. Surely in his last moments of life, Fitzroy was convinced that we were not there to lend him a hand, but to kill him. Unfortunately, someone else did just that.

"However, Fitzroy's last actions do tell us something important: If he was not even aware of all the players in this plot, then it is one of a large scope. That is suggestive in itself."

I saw the familiar contemplative look cross Holmes's face as his mind was transported elsewhere as we walked.

"What do you intend to do now?" I asked at length.

"Going through Fitzroy's things will be most instructive," Holmes said, "and we had best do that before the police find out just who he was. We need not run into the scrutinizing Inspector Horák again."

We returned to our hotel where Holmes spent some time getting in touch with Lukáš Palan. When we had finally discovered the location of Fitzroy's hideaway – only a short distance away from where we had been staying – we hurried off at once. Holmes gained ingress by convincing a man stepping out of the building that he was a relative of the newest tenant in the building and we were admitted without question. We stealthily ascended a cramped, narrow staircase to the first floor of the building, making sure that there were no police officials that had found their way there before we did. From his coat, Holmes produced his lock-picking kit and went to work on the door, which he opened in only a matter of minutes. Stepping inside, we were met with an overwhelming sight.

The cramped flat that Fitzroy had called home was overstuffed with papers – stacks of pages stood upon every flat surface, and other sheets lay scattered across the floor, the window seat, and on bookshelves which were overcrowded with aged tomes. Stacks of books challenged the papers for dominance of the space, and I suddenly felt lost amidst all of the paper that was found on the other side of that door. Holmes was undaunted as ever, and stepped further into the room, his head swiveling about like a great predatory bird's. He ducked into the adjoining room and I followed, happy to find that it was Fitzroy's bed chamber and in quite another state altogether. This room was tidy. The man's bed made and his clothes neatly stacked atop his traveling trunk. Holmes stood in the doorway of this room and tapped his lips in consideration.

"It strikes me as odd. Wouldn't you concur, my dear Watson?"

"What strikes you odd?" I asked.

"These rooms," Holmes said with a broad gesture. "The outer room is a disaster – over-brimming with books and papers, while Fitzroy's own room is perfectly-kept. It strikes me as incongruous and suggestive."

"Suggestive of what?"

"Deception," Holmes replied. "Think, Watson – Fitzroy knew full well that he had been found out. He was hiding for good reason, and knew that should his location be compromised, the perpetrators of this mysterious plot would go searching through his things. Would they not be discouraged by a room which looked as if it had already been ransacked? Would their search for answers not be greatly inhibited if they couldn't find a thing to begin with?"

"So Fitzroy kept the room purposefully cluttered?"

"Precisely," Holmes replied, "and I would wager anything that that means the answers we seek are to be found in that room."

Holmes paced back into the room, his eyes darting around him. He suddenly let out an exclamation. "Oh, what a clever, clever man he was, Watson! Mycroft told us that Fitzroy sent all of his communications back to London in code. The key to that code is somewhere in this room. The key must be a book, hidden amongst these other books."

"But which book?" I asked aridly. "There are quite a few here."

Holmes's eyes scanned the shelves. "Fitzroy would want to keep it in a place that shouldn't arouse suspicion. A book cast about on the floor would be the first to be searched. The bookshelf seems the most likely hiding spot then."

Holmes proceeded to pluck a few volumes from the shelf with his long, dexterous fingers. "It would a well-thumbed volume," he said more to himself than to me, "no doubt held open for long periods of time as he wrote his messages. A book with a creased spine and broken binding seems, then, most likely."

At length his fingers stopped over the spin of a hefty volume which he pulled down. Glancing at the cover, I knew Holmes to have found the right one: *The Legend of the Golem and Other Tales of Ancient Prague*.

"Well," I said, "we have the key but –"

Before I could finish, Holmes had opened the book and a few loose sheets fell from its pages. I stooped to pick them up and read the hastily-drafted message written thereon:

*Should this message be found, then I am surely dead. It is an eventuality that I foresaw. What I regrettably cannot foresee is who shall find this message. If you are one of the perpetrators of this plot, then everything I have to say shall be familiar to you. Should you be one of His Majesty's men enlisted to find me, then I can only hope that this shall prove helpful to you. I speak now not in riddles and in code for, beyond the grave, I am past being in danger.*

*Not everyone, I have discovered, has approved of the unification of the German kingdoms of Bohemia and Moravia. The formation of Czechoslovakia has incited dangerous nationalism in quarters of the country, and there are some who have gone so far as to plot separation. These groups have, since the unification, remained dormant, but I fear that one of them is plotting for something much grander. My gathered intelligence suggests that this group is plotting to bomb Wenceslas Square, the great boulevard of this city, and this action shall only be the first in a series of calamitous occurrences which are designed to weaken the city of Prague. From there, splinter groups throughout the county shall carry on this deadly plot, crippling Czechoslovakia in revenge for their unification.*

*I hope that I am still alive on 25 June when this deadly action shall commence, but I fear that my time is running short. Should you be one of my fellow King's men, I trust that you shall do with this information what you will. Report it to the proper authorities and prevent tragedy from befalling this beautiful new country. If you are my enemy, take solace in the knowledge that you have eliminated me. But know that your secrets have been exposed. I went to my grave knowing the full truth of your devilish plot, and I sincerely hope that others out there will take up my work and quash your plans.*

*God Save the King,*
*G. Fitzroy – 1919*

Holmes and I stood in silence reading and re-reading Fitzroy's last words. At length, he set the paper aside and drew in a deep breath.

"What do we do?" I asked.

"Though I am loath to do so," Holmes said after a moment of consideration, "I think it best that we do as Fitzroy says: '*Report it to the proper authorities*'. We have luckily made the acquaintance, and I daresay an impression upon, the good Inspector Horák. We had best come clean about our true involvement in this matter. He is made of more manpower than we, my dear fellow, and they can be put to good use – especially since Fitzroy claims this deadly action is only twenty-four hours from now."

Holmes stopped and considered for a moment more. "However," he added, "I should think that our part in this has not come to an end. There is still one principle player that we haven't yet encountered, and I should very much like to meet him."

"And who is that?" I said.

"Someone I rather think shall warrant the use of your service revolver," Holmes said grimly. "I speak, of course, of the Golem."

## Chapter IV

I consulted my watch and saw that it was gone nine o'clock of the following evening and, despite the fact that Holmes and I had been out-of-doors all day, I was beginning to feel pent-up. We had paced the length of Wenceslas Square more times than I could count throughout the day, both of us keeping our eyes open for any suspicious activity. I did my part not to make eye contact with Inspector Horák's plain-clothed men who had sat at café tables for much of the day, doing just as we had.

It had been a tumultuous day since we'd located Fitzroy's hiding place and discovered the nature of the plot he'd uncovered. We did as Holmes had suggested and delivered Fitzroy's letter into the hands of the inspector at his office. He gave us a knowing smile as we entered his rooms, plucking the pipe from his mouth, and standing to greet us. "When Mr. Sherlock Holmes is to be found in your city," he said, "one should know that he is there on official business."

We had given him Fitzroy's correspondence and the inspector immediately jumped into action, designating tasks to his officers and preparing for the day-long vigil that we now all undertook. For hours which masqueraded as a lifetime, we watched the comings-and-goings of the city, kept an eye out as people disembarked the electric tram cars that ran through the square, and acquainted ourselves with the countenances of those men and women who seemed to linger just a little too long in one spot. More than once, I pressed the cold steel of my revolver into my breast as my hand closed around it, but it was for naught.

And now, as the sun had disappeared beneath the city sky, I felt even more on edge. The crowds in the square had dwindled, but those who did pass through were luxuriously dressed, no doubt on their way to a night at the theatre or returning from a sumptuous dinner somewhere else in the city. I suddenly had the strangest feeling deep in my chest that something was amiss and if any attack were to take place, it would be now.

No sooner had this curious pang welled up inside of me, than Holmes suddenly reached out and grasped hold of my arm, subtlety pointing in the direction of a tall, lean man who was disembarking from a tramcar, dressed in a mackintosh with a dark trilby pulled low over his eyes. Tucked under his arm was a package wrapped in brown paper and tied with a length of twine. To the untrained eye, one wouldn't have suspected anything, but Holmes and I were certain that that was our man. I had the sudden urge to rush forward and subdue him at once, but Holmes held me back, no doubt reading the compulsion in my eyes.

"Steady yourself, man," he hissed. "Wait for it."

Our man approached a bench and took a seat, nervously crossing and uncrossing his ankles. He removed a watch from his pocket and checked the time before stowing it away again. Then, setting the package down gingerly upon the bench, he stood and hastily began to cross the square.

"Now, Watson!" cried Holmes, rushing forward. "Now!"

From his inner pocket, Holmes withdrew a police whistle and, touching it to his lips, he let out one long, shrill blast. The man cast an anxious look over his shoulder and then broke out into an all-out run. By this time, three officers had approached us. Holmes gestured towards the package left upon the bench and then, after cautioning the men to its deadly contents, grabbed me by the arm and pulled me away from the throng and after our man. For an instant I was conscious of a moment of extreme clarity in which I could not understand how I had done so much running in two days' time. Surely, I reasoned, this was the work of a much younger man, and not someone entering his dotage. If Sherlock Holmes felt any strain upon his constitution, however, he did not show it, for he was already ahead of me, closing the gap between us and our quarry.

We had gradually been running uphill and, coming to the top, we watched our man flee down a side street. No longer surrounded by the crowds in the square, I pulled my revolver from my pocket and prepared to aim and fire in an effort to wound him and quell his attempts at escape, but Holmes stopped me.

"Think what other tricks he may have up his sleeve," he said. "We cannot risk it."

Then he was off again, sprinting after the man, all the while clutching his silver-headed stick in hand. I rushed to follow, the now all-to-familiar burning sensation returning to plague my lungs. We had entered the mouth of the side street into which our man had flown, but he suddenly appeared to have vanished. Holmes and I stopped, looking about us for any sign of him, but our attention was arrested by the sound of a man's voice from very nearby.

"You may have foiled my plans," he said in a heavily German-accented voice, "and for that you shall not escape this street alive."

Then, out of a pool of shadows, he stepped and stopped before us, a malign smile upon his face. I leveled my revolver at him and pulled back the hammer, but I was suddenly stopped by a sight that I couldn't fathom.

Out of the same inky darkness stepped another figure that I took at first not to be human. Indeed, even as my eyes became accustomed to the mountain of a man before me, I couldn't believe my eyes. The thing that stood before us must have been at least seven feet in height and broad all over, his massive shoulders and arms easily the thickness of an uprooted tree. He was barefoot and dressed in little more than a simple white cloth, for I couldn't think how such a beast could find clothes that would fit its immense frame. But it was the beast's visage – somehow not entirely human – which chilled me even more to the core. I stood transfixed, my unbelieving eyes simply not comprehending the figure that stood before us, the thing that had lurched out of the night at us, and it was a feat in itself to pry my gaze from the beast – the Golem – and cast a glance at Holmes, who stood just as rooted to the spot as I.

I must have steeled up enough courage, however, to take aim at the beast before us and fire, but my hand was unsteady and my shot was wide, embedding itself in the stonework of the alleyway which closed in around us and trapped us with the thing that would surely mean our deaths in time. The shot must have angered the creature, for the Golem lumbered towards me even as I attempted to fire again. My sweaty fingers slipped over the trigger and suddenly the revolver had fallen from my grasp. I contemplated clambering for it on the ground, when I felt a great hand upon my neck and then the horrible feeling of air beneath my feet. The Golem had hoisted me up from the ground, and I felt its grip on the back of my throat begin to tighten. This was how it was to end, I contemplated, with my life squeezed out of me by a thing not truly human in this back alley. I tried to flail and kick my way out, but my body was failing me.

And then, from the corner of my eye I caught sight of Sherlock Holmes as he wildly swung his cane over his head. Its silver handle made contact with the Golem's ribs and I swore that I heard the beast let out a groan of pain. Its grip on my neck loosened ever so slightly, and I began to wriggle my way out of its harsh grasp. Holmes swung his cane again and I took this chance to muster up what little energy I had and deliver a powerful blow with the back of my heel to the creature's stomach. The Golem let out another cry and dropped me entirely. I made hard contact with the ground and, though winded, I had enough wherewithal to run my hands over the cobbles and land upon my revolver. Turning over onto my back, I saw Holmes with his stick raised over his head once more face-to-face with the Golem, holding the creature at bay as best he could. I pulled back the hammer of the revolver, listened to its satisfying click, and then squeezed off a shot.

The Golem clasped a massive hand to its own throat and then, like a felled tree, toppled to the ground dead.

Sherlock Holmes had little time to celebrate such a victory, however, for he was already looking for our other man, but it seemed as if he had used our struggle with the beast as an opportunity to take to his heels and flee. Dejection evident on his face, Holmes helped me to his feet.

"You needn't worry about it," I panted breathlessly. "You got a good enough look at him. And if you did not, then I certainly did. We can supply Horák with as much information as he needs."

"You are, of course, right, my dear fellow," Holmes said, clapping me upon the shoulder. "If there is one thing that we can take away from this little adventure of ours, it is that sometimes the combined forces of Sherlock Holmes and Dr. Watson are not enough. Occasionally we need the outside help of others."

I turned my attention to the behemoth that lay prostrate at our feet, my eyes traveling to the still-warm gun in my hands. For an instant, my mind clouded in confusion. Could the thing really have been the Golem – the creature born out of clay so many centuries earlier? Surely not – and yet, I was inclined to believe almost anything when I had felt its great grip on the back of my neck. Sherlock Holmes, seemingly always able to divine my thoughts, regarded me with a bemused grin.

"This is not the storied creature that we have heard so much about of late," he said. "Look upon his visage now, Watson, and you shall see what tricks the mind may play upon you."

I did as my friend said and saw that, although the dead man was hardly handsome, there wasn't anything particularly remarkable about his appearance at all. Indeed, it had been my mind playing tricks on me in the low light of that alleyway that had conjured up the demonic countenance that had so terrified me. I almost felt like laughing.

"It is a face I do believe I recognize," Holmes added. "I should have known earlier. Had I divined the link between the Golem and the radicals sooner than I did, all would have fallen into place. In my researches, I have more than once come across the name Klaus Schneider, commonly known in some circles as '*The Goliath*' or '*The Golem*'. If a foreign element was to be involved in this business, and there were reported sightings of a creature believed to be the legendary Golem, then Schneider's ought to have been a name on my mind from the start. Luckily, we have brought an end to the Golem's reign of terror once and for all."

Two days later we found ourselves once more in a train compartment trundling across the continent. We had spent the intervening time clearing up loose ends with Inspector Horák and, from our description of our man, it sounded as though finding him should hardly be a challenge. Indeed, as we packed our things for our return trip, we received word from Horák that he was in police custody.

Holmes was in a communicative mood as our train drew out of Czechoslovakia, and he was happily discussing the case:

"I really should have been more on the trail sooner, my dear fellow. Should you ever find reason to draw up this case for your records – a personal account, only, for Mycroft should never let such a tale reach the public – then you really must put it down as one of my failures. My suspicions ought to have been aroused as soon as Palan told us that he knew nothing of what happened to Fitzroy. If someone in the Czech underworld had been responsible then some whisper of the business would surely have made its way back to him. However, since it was a ring of German radicals responsible for this plot, then it stood to reason that Palan should have been totally unaware.

"I just thank god that we were not too late," I said. "When we discovered Fitzroy's letter, we had only twenty-four hours' time to foil the plot. Imagine if we had even been one day later."

"From time to time," Sherlock Holmes said, "I am inclined to believe in the hand of Fate. These past few days have been one of those times, and fortunately for us, Fate appears to have been on our side."

Holmes cast a glance out of the train window.

"It is a changing world, my dear Watson," he mused quietly, "and we have played our small part in facilitating that change. With luck that change is for the better. Only time shall tell, Watson. For us. For Czechoslovakia. For the world. Only time shall tell."

# The Case of the
# Ivy-Covered Tomb
## by S.F. Bennett

"But it's like I was saying to Mrs. Elkins, we've all got our problems, dear, but there's no use moaning about it, because in this day and age there's no one to listen, and the young – well, they've got their own lives to lead, what with all this gadding about and jazz and whatnot, and then there's them like my old man, Bill, who never listens to a word I say, so it's just you and me, Mrs. Elkins, trying to put the world to rights – well, that's what I always say anyhow, Mr. Holmes."

One of the perennial problems of living in the countryside is the difficulty in finding suitable staff. When the admirable Mrs. Hudson decided her retirement was long overdue, I was forced to consider the question of her replacement as housekeeper. The first candidate I interviewed had the dubious distinction of having never stayed in a post longer than six months. This was on account, so she said, of her previous eight employers having had the misfortune to pass away soon after she started working for them. After a few judicious enquiries, I was satisfied there had been no suspicious circumstances in any of the cases and I was about to tempt fate when another applicant came to my door. Mrs. Bracegirdle, from a neighbouring village, was affable, efficient, and came with excellent references.

Indeed, if Mrs. Bracegirdle has any fault at all, it is a tendency towards garrulousness. At first I attributed it to the solitary nature of her work and a felicitous arrangement of her husband's working hours, whereby the couple rarely shared the same roof for longer than was necessary. Whether by art or design, I cannot say, except that Mr. Bracegirdle, in his occupation as a railway guard, was always ready to take on those unsociable shifts so disparaged by his comrades.

It was for this reason, and my sanity, that I purchased a wireless and licence to keep Mrs. Bracegirdle company whilst at her work. When that failed, I took solace in my bees, the only thing guaranteed to keep the woman at bay. On this particular morning, however, in the late spring of 1925, when the lingering cold had brought on an attack of rheumatism, I was obliged to remain indoors and endure the full brunt of her one-sided conversation whilst trying to bring some semblance of order to my commonplace books.

"Because you never know, sir," she went on, "when you wake up in the morning, if it's going to be your last – well, I don't have to tell you, Mr. Holmes, what with you being nearer to the grave than the cradle – so what I say is, we might as well make the most of things."

I deplore this modern fashion for assuming everyone over a certain age is liable to pass away at a moment's notice. When one reaches maturity in years, it has been my observation that one of two approaches is taken. In the case of my brother, Mycroft, who slipped from middle age into later life without ever leaving the comfort of his armchair, he has embraced the notion of his inevitable demise with gusto – hence the missives I regularly receive bemoaning the paucity of my visits and reminding me that "you shall regret it when I'm gone". Since this has been the burden of his song for the last five decades, I dare say I have become inured to its effect.

Watson, I fear, has gone to the other extreme, and now attempts to make the most of all that this busy century has to offer. He has swapped the racecourse for the race *track* and, if one may judge from his letters, Brooklands has become a second home to him. He is as enthusiastic a supporter of mechanised horse-power as one may hope to find outside the pages of *The Journal of Modern Motoring*. There has been talk of late of his intention to purchase a motorcycle of the model favoured by Mr. T.E. Lawrence. When first I advised caution, I was informed that I was "hopelessly old-fashioned", which, considering Watson is two years older than I am, was something of a conceit on his part. I had hopes his dear wife would make him see sense – otherwise I predicted an unhappy ending for all concerned.

As for Mrs. Bracegirdle, since my many attempts to correct these views of hers have fallen on stony ground, I tend now to let her have her head on the matter. The alternative involves going through the rigmarole of finding another housekeeper, for which I have neither the time nor the patience.

"I mean to say," she continued, "it's like that new vicar over at Fishcombe Regis way. Oh, he came with all these newfangled ideas, and how does he end up? Dead one morning, with his head in old Mr. Fossgate's urn."

"Most unfortunate," I murmured.

"I'll say. The Fossgates paid a lot of money for that urn. I mean, you don't expect it, do you, to find the vicar face down in your dearly departed's ashes?"

"I meant, unfortunate for the vicar," I said.

"I dare say it was, but you know what these incomers are like, Mr. Holmes. Never listen to a word the locals have to say. Him being from

London, he had his own ideas of course – well, you know how it is with these London types, sir, they think they know everything."

"I came here from London," I reminded her.

She waved a dismissive hand. "But you've lived here years, sir. Why, you're practically a local."

Given that Mrs. Bracegirdle had been a resident in the area for some ten years herself, I wondered by what criteria she had formed such an opinion. Indeed, in some parts of the district, only those who can prove three generations of settlement can ever justifiably consider themselves locals.

"But as I was saying before you interrupted me, sir, that young vicar – well, the curse got him in the end. We all knew it would. He was warned – ”

"Curse, Mrs. Bracegirdle?" I interrupted her.

Those readers of Dr. Watson's accounts of my work will know the little store by which I set tales that attempt to render myth and superstition as the motive for crime. There are few things calculated to both pique my interest and raise my ire more keenly. I dare say had Mrs. Bracegirdle practised the economy of language which I often recommend, I might have missed this single stem of wheat amongst the chaff of her verbiage.

"You must have heard of the curse of Farmer Jack, sir," said she.

"I would not be asking if I had, Mrs. Bracegirdle."

I had no concern that she might take offence. Any invitation to share her knowledge was never refused.

"Well, Farmer Jack owned the manor over Kimblecombe way years ago," said she, warming to her subject. "A more black-hearted ruffian never drew breath. He used to terrorise the people hereabouts, riding through the village in the dead of night, raising hell and striking down those who tried to stop him. Word is he once tried to buy a champion bull from a neighbouring farm and, when his offer was refused, he cursed the animal and it died the very next day, it did." She pursed her lips in a gesture of disapproval. "A lawless fellow, by all accounts, and in league with the Devil too."

"They usually are, Mrs. Bracegirdle," I said, returning to my work. I had heard enough of these tales of lore and legend to know that supernatural forces were bound to make an appearance in the story somewhere.

"But when his time came, he tried to get out of his bargain with Old Nick," she continued, lowering her voice as if she feared the forces of Hades might hear her. "You see, the Devil said he would come to claim his soul at the age of threescore and ten and, Farmer Jack thinking he was clever, he agreed. Only he knew he would never be seventy because he

370

was born in a leap year and his birthday only came round every four years. So when the Devil came calling, 'Oh, no,' says Farmer Jack. 'You can't have me, I'm only . . .' well, however old he would have been."

"Seventeen and one half," I said.

"But the Devil he says: 'Seventy years is seventy years', and Farmer Jack fell down dead. And then the day after they buried him the churchyard at Fishcombe, the vicar came out to find the tomb was all overgrown with ivy and brambles, like the Devil had bound him to the earth to stop him escaping. The vicar told his sexton to cut the ivy away and, as the man made the first cut, he dropped down dead."

She nodded, as though this explanation should be enough to please anyone.

I looked up at her expectantly. Having got this far, I was mildly interested to see how a dead vicar related to an overgrown tomb.

"Well, it's like I said, Mr. Holmes. It's a curse. And a warning," she added hurriedly. "Not to cut the ivy away from the tomb of Farmer Jack, otherwise you'll die."

"I assume," I said, forsaking my work to sit back in my chair, "the new vicar wanted the tomb cleared."

"He said it was ugly and made the churchyard look untidy," said Mrs. Bracegirdle earnestly. "He was warned but he would have his way, sir, and he declared he would do it himself that very night. At dawn the next day, they found him, sir, dead with horrible staring eyes."

I could not deny that certain aspects of the business appealed to me. "I presume the police investigated?"

"Yes, sir. His doctor said he had a weak heart. Well, there were no marks of violence on the body, excepting where he hit his head on old Mr. Fossgate's urn when he keeled over, so the coroner said he must have died of fright."

"Did he not find it curious that the vicar had attempted to tackle the unsightly growth on this tomb in the middle of the night?"

Mrs. Bracegirdle frowned. "Why would he, Mr. Holmes? The vicar was a man given to sudden flights of fancy. When the mood took him, there's no saying what he might get up to."

I had heard enough, both in quantity and quality, to come to a decision. I threw aside the blanket I had placed over my knees and rose abruptly with a speed that took Mrs. Bracegirdle by surprise, if her bemused expression was anything by which to judge. "Fishcombe Regis," I said. "I might take a walk in that direction this morning."

"But it's seven miles or more, Mr. Holmes."

"Indeed. If I set out now, I should be there in time for lunch."

"But what about your rheumatism, sir?"

"A walk and fresh air will do me the world of good, Mrs. Bracegirdle. I heartily recommend it."

As it happened, there was something invigorating about being out of the house, with only the birds and the singing breeze for company. Nature is at its finest in the spring after the hardships of winter. The trees are newly-enrobed in green mantles and every meadow wears a painted face. Poppies dance beside the lane, vying for sunlight with ox-eye daisies, whilst purple orchids peep their shy heads from the grassy verge. And yet, in the midst of such abundance, death is always with us. Be it a lamb in a nearby field or a vicar in a neighbouring parish, it is the one constant that binds us all.

I had made good time and arrived at Fishcombe Regis before the few shops in the High Street closed their doors for lunch. It is a quaint village, girt by fields of wind-swept corn on one side and the sea on the other. The main road runs down to the harbour, where the fishermen sell their catch safe from the fury of the ocean. For myself, I selected a tea shop situated down a side road, a place frequented by locals away from the milling mass of wandering visitors who come to admire and pause a while before moving on.

As I was one of the few customers, the elderly lady who brought my tea was happy to pass the time of day.

"I am something of an enthusiast for local legends," I said, when our conversation had moved on from the lamentable state of the weather to the nature of my business in Fishcombe Regis. "A lady in the next village mentioned something about a fine tale you have of your own."

The proprietress folded her hands before her and shook her head. "It's no legend, sir," said she. "It's as real as you or me."

I smiled politely, as I was once again regaled with the tale of Farmer Jack, this time with embellishments of how he danced with the Devil on Fishcombe Harbour and regularly visited murder, violence, and rent rises on the locals.

"Now I'm no fanciful woman," said she. "But only two months back, the curse struck again. Our last vicar, Mr. Tipton, why he laughed in the face of the devil and said he would clear Farmer Jack's tomb even if it was the death of him. And the Devil, fearing Farmer Jack would escape his clutches, he killed Mr. Tipton, sir. Struck him down where he stood, he did."

That I had heard none of this before came as no surprise. The local newspaper covers an irregular area, which includes a town some twenty miles distant, but not a village within walking distance. If not for Mrs. Bracegirdle, I should know nothing of the affairs of my neighbours at all.

372

"Most distressing for you," I remarked. "But surely one such death might be something other than the curse?"

She looked affronted. "Who said it was the first? There's been more deaths and mishaps in that churchyard over the years since Farmer Jack was laid to rest than is decent. Last winter, old Mrs. Formby went to lay flowers on her husband's grave and tripped over one of Farmer Jack's brambles and did herself a mischief."

"Which is presumably why the vicar wanted them cleared," I suggested.

"Then there was that courting couple, who came from over Harfield way. Crept into the churchyard to see if they could call up the Devil. He starts pulling the ivy off the tomb and the Devil came after them both and stole their souls."

This sounded more promising. "When was this?" I asked, not wishing to appear overly interested.

She wrinkled her brow in an effort of remembrance. "Why, it must be two-hundred years back."

I was beginning to lose heart in what had seemed an intriguing line of enquiry.

"Then there was that fellow from London." She squeezed her eyes tightly shut and tapped her forehead. "Now what was his name? Ah, yes, now I remember. John Datchett. They said he was a criminal – come looking for Farmer Jack's pot of gold. They do say as how he was buried with it, you know."

Yet another variant on a well-worn tale, I gave it no more credence than legends of Devil-bound tombs. The name, however, was one with which I was familiar.

"But, for the life of me," she continued with a sigh, "I can't remember how long ago that was."

"Eight years," I said.

"Well, bless you, sir, now I come to think of it, yes, it *were* eight year ago. However did you know that?"

I told her it was nothing more than a lucky guess. What I did not mention was that I had a good memory of the case. Datchett, a member of the notorious Guildford Gang, had targeted small museums throughout the provinces with his fellow thieves to relieve them of ancient hordes of gold and jewels. Roman jewellery, Anglo-Saxon coins, Elizabethan silver – nothing was beyond their grasp, however small. Priceless treasures which had never been recovered had in all probability ended their days in the melting pot. When over-confidence finally brought about their downfall, four members of the gang were arrested.

It had been suggested at the time there were others, including a ringleader, who had evaded justice. If so, Datchett and his comrades never betrayed their fellows. Nor would they reveal the location of the stolen items. I had been in France during the height of the Great War when the press had made passing mention of how Datchett had been found dead in an East Sussex graveyard the day after his release from prison. Until now, I hadn't made the connection with Fishcombe Regis.

It seemed to me a visit to this ill-famed churchyard was in order. The Church of St. Giles sat on a slight incline above the town, reached by several flights of uneven steps. The graves were arranged in terraces on the slope, with the lower ones bearing obvious signs of subsidence so it appeared as though they were slowly slipping down to the sea. Where the ground levelled out, a hoary-headed gravedigger was at work, busily smoking a battered clay pipe as he leaned on his shovel while a younger man stood in the six-foot pit, pitching dirt onto an ever-growing pile at the graveside.

I hailed them. The elderly gentlemen looked up and acknowledged me with the merest bob of his head. The younger man spared me a glance before continuing with his work.

"A pleasant part of the world," I said.

"So they tell me," said the elderly man. "Leastways, I don't hear no complaints from this lot."

He gestured with his pipe to the graves around him. I gathered this was by way of his attempt at humour.

"Perhaps you could help me," I said in the manner of a visitor to the area. "I've heard there's an unusual tomb in the churchyard."

The man sucked thoughtfully on the end of his pipe. "An unusual tomb, you say. Well, can't say as I know which that might be."

At this, the other man stopped his digging, thrust his shovel into the soil, and looked across at me. Of about five-and-twenty years, he had the bronzed complexion of a man who spends his working life outdoors. Well-built, economical in his movements with his tools, and with a mottling of fresh cuts and old scars along his forearms, I gathered that this was not his regular employment.

"And what would you be wanting this 'unusual' tomb for?" asked he.

"Curiosity," I replied. "The lady in the tea shop was telling me the story of 'Farmer Jack'."

"That'd be Maud," muttered the elderly man. "Never could keep nothing to herself."

"It's over there," said the younger man grudgingly. "North side of the church. Can't miss it."

374

As he said, the tomb of Farmer Jack stood out from its fellows. Heavily clad in centuries-worth growth of old ivy, only the vaguest shape of what had once been a large chest tomb, standing over four feet tall and surrounded by rusting railings, could be discerned. What had been inscribed upon it had long since deteriorated. Whilst all around the grass was cut and the headstones weathered to an attractive mottled buff, the tomb of Farmer Jack alone was overgrown and neglected. It was a striking anomaly in an otherwise picture-perfect scene. Whatever the truth about the soul interred within, I could understand why legends had grown up around this decaying monument.

A few feet away, a broken urn indicated the place where the unfortunate vicar had met his end. Set in its own plot with a low raised curb enclosing a gravelled area, I almost tripped over it. In the dark of night with only a lantern for illumination, I could envisage that the vicar might have made a similar mistake – a more plausible theory certainly than those involving otherworldly beings.

Having gleaned what I could, I headed back to the gravediggers. "A curious thing, indeed," I remarked. "Tell me, why has it never been cleared?"

The younger man gave me an unfriendly stare. "You one of them reporters up from London?"

"No, upon my word," I said. "I am merely eager to learn of local customs."

The older gentleman chuckled. "Come here after dark and you'll see a few of them going on too, so the young folk tell me."

"That's enough," said his companion harshly before directing his attention back to me. "You'll have to excuse Malcolm, sir. We've had our fair share of trouble-makers up here since the last vicar died."

"So I heard. A tragedy."

"Not unexpected though. The man had a weak heart, so the coroner said. He would insist on trying to clear that tomb himself. A man like that had no business undertaking hard labour in his condition."

I nodded and leaned thoughtfully on my stick. "You place no store then by these tales of devilry?"

"I've been trimming the ivy on that grave for eight years and I've never seen anything, save the odd mouse and blackbird."

"But the placement, on the north side of the church? Does that not speak of local disapproval?"

"Look around you." He gestured to the crumbling terraces, where the gravestones were packed in as tightly as any London traffic. "We don't have the luxury of making distinctions here. You're lucky these days if you can get in the churchyard at all. I dare say they'll close it to new burials soon."

"I'll be out of a job when they do," said Malcolm.

"They'll still need a gardener," said his young companion consolingly.

"And what of you?" I asked him.

"I only come here to help Malcolm with the heavy work when he needs it. I have a trade."

"Thatching?"

The particular muscular development and the scratches left by cut stems upon his arms and neck spoke of someone accustomed to carrying sheaves of straw on his shoulder. A farmer would be too occupied with his own affairs to worry about the local churchyard, but an apprentice thatcher might have time when his work was done for the day.

He glanced up at me, his eyes sharp and shrewd. "That's right, sir. Now, either that's a lucky guess or you're that London detective what I've heard lives around these parts."

Since I had been discovered, there was no point in denying it. I introduced myself.

"Well, there's been no murder round here for you to solve, Mr. Holmes," said the young man dismissively. "No devils either."

"'Cepting that man what your father found years back, Hoggy," said Malcolm. "He were a wrong 'un by all accounts."

The look the younger man threw him made him retreat back into silence.

"That were a long time, Malcolm." Too late, he saw I had heard and an explanation was required. He sighed resignedly, as though it was a story he was tired of telling. "He's talking about that criminal from London what died here a while back. I expect you know all about that, Mr. Holmes."

"I had heard rumours," I replied. "It was your father who discovered the body?"

He nodded. "My father, Bert Hogarth, he used to dig the graves here. He found him here in the churchyard, impaled on the railings of Farmer Jack's tomb. They said he'd been trying to climb in when he slipped." He grunted. "Another one looking for devils."

"Turned Bert's mind, it did," added Malcolm. "Ain't ever been right since."

"The shock brought on a stroke," said the younger Hogarth. "My father has never recovered. This churchyard meant a lot to him, which is why I help out when I can. He can still see it – his house is over yonder." He indicated the windows of a cottage which could just be glimpsed through the trees. "Our family has been buried here for generations."

"Your own roots are somewhat north of here, I fancy," I said. His accent, though worn, still bore traces of a London heritage. "Barnet, perhaps?"

"That's right, Mr. Holmes. My father left Fishcombe when he was a young man with some notion of setting up his own book and printing shop at St. Paul's Churchyard. He moved us all back here when I was eleven. Said he'd had enough of London life and wanted to retire. Well, I'm sure you can understand that, sir."

"I do indeed." From Hogarth's demeanour, it was evident our conversation was at an end. "Well, good day, gentleman. This has been most interesting."

With the church bells ringing out the hour, there was time to use the public telephone box in the village square before I set off for home. I spent several hours sifting through a lifetime of newspaper cuttings before I eventually located the piece in question. According to an account of the trial of the Guildford Gang in 1911, Datchett had been given six years for his role as their sentinel, with the other three members receiving sentences of twelve to fifteen years hard labour, having been caught in possession of the stolen artefacts. Whilst Datchett had been released, the other three men had died in prison.

The afternoon was wearing into evening when I caught what sounded like the rumble of approaching thunder. Glancing out to see only a clear sky, a figure suddenly came into view. Half-obscured by the garden wall, he appeared to be wearing a tweed jacket coupled with a leather flying helmet and goggles. With Mrs. Bracegirdle thrown into a quiver about this vision, I went out to investigate, knowing full well who I was about to find.

"Good afternoon, Watson," I said. "I assume it is you, although it is hard to tell under that paraphernalia."

He was laughing as he pulled off the helmet and attempted to bring his ruffled hair into a state of respectability.

"Why, who else could it be?" said he, offering me a leather-gloved hand. "How are you, old fellow? You look well, in any case."

"Well enough. This contraption is yours, I presume."

He beamed with all the pride of a new father as he patted the polished petrol tank of the purring motorcycle. "A beauty, isn't she?" said he. "A Brough Superior SS100. Custom made, you know – even the handlebars."

As if to demonstrate, he swung his leg over the seat and tried to look as though he knew what he was doing as the machine swayed under his weight.

"Custom made, you say," I remarked. "But you do not mention for whom, Watson."

He chuckled. "For me, of course. You know I've been talking about getting one for ages. Well, here she is. What do you think, Holmes? Want to come for a spin?"

It was on the tip of my tongue to mention something about the proper conduct for gentlemen of our age when it occurred to me it was something Mrs. Bracegirdle might say. I trust I am not one of those fellows who denies the value of new technology, but I had hoped for so much more. When I had telephoned Watson earlier, I had been hoping he would come in his car. Instead, he had presented me with this gleaming metal monster. One could admire the artistry of engineering that allowed a man to travel at speed in the midst of traffic built for a more elegant era, but that it should have fallen into the hands of my old friend troubled me more than I cared to say.

"No, Watson, I do not wish to 'come for a spin', as you put it," I replied. "I would rather you came inside where I can enlighten you as to the case."

"Ah, yes," said he with enthusiasm. As low as it was, I noted he still managed to catch his foot as he got off the motorcycle. "In matter of fact, I was pleased to hear from you, Holmes. I wanted to give her a good run. I came as fast I could."

"I dare say. How fast is that?"

"Well, she has a top speed of one-hundred-miles-per-hour."

I gave him a disapproving stare.

"Not that I did that," said he quickly. "No faster than fifty for me. Well, it might have been sixty. I suppose. Seventy at the most."

"On your way to the cemetery, no doubt."

He shook his head. "Holmes, you really are—"

"'Hopelessly old-fashioned'," I finished for him. "If by that you mean I have an aversion to seeing an old friend risk life and limb in an effort to recapture his youth, then yes, that is exactly what I am."

Watson looked in turn both crestfallen and annoyed. "At least I haven't buried myself away in the countryside," he retorted. "I knew you would disapprove, as you always do."

"My dear fellow, you mistake concern for disapprobation. It is a very pretty thing, Watson, but I could wish for you a safer mode of transport, especially for tonight." I became aware that we were under scrutiny from Mrs. Bracegirdle, who was watching us from the kitchen window. "Come inside and let me tell you about the case."

Watson mellowed, as did I, after several cigars and a pot of Mrs. Bracegirdle's strongest tea. I ignored an oblique reference to something stronger. With little between himself and the road save good tweed and a leather helmet, he needed all his wits about him.

"So what did you have planned for tonight?" he asked, idly gesturing in my direction with the remains of a cream scone after I had outlined the particulars of the case.

"Grave-robbing." I saw his eyebrows rise. "The tomb of Farmer Jack to be precise. It occurs to me, Watson, that someone has gone to a great deal of trouble to keep people at bay from that particular tomb. I want to know what it contains, other than the bones of the departed."

"If you think that, Holmes, why don't you contact the local constabulary? I'm sure they would oblige, with the proper authority."

"That would take too long. Time is of the essence before our mark takes flight."

"Well, then I am your man," said he.

"Capital!" I declared. "I thought I knew my Watson. Dependable to the last."

"Should we be armed?"

I unlocked the drawer of my desk and removed my old revolver. "Several deaths have been attributed to this 'devil', Watson. I think certain precautions are necessary."

He considered for a moment, watching as I placed the weapon into my jacket pocket. "Tell me, Holmes, how will we get to this Fishcombe Regis?"

"We will walk, naturally."

"Walk, yes," he mused. "It is seven miles, Holmes. In the dark."

I noticed the gleam that had come to his eye. He clearly had something particular in mind. Which is how we came to arrive at Fishcombe under cover of darkness on Watson's Brough Superior. Seven miles never seemed quite so long. I had had my doubts about Watson's ability behind the wheel of his car. Sitting behind him on the motorcycle, I was certain my last days had come. We stopped on the outskirts of the village to avoid waking the residents and made the short trek down to the church. Save for the call of the nightjar, all was silent. I had brought along my dark lantern, and by its meagre light we threaded our way through the gravestones.

Then, to my ears came what sounded like a scuffle over by the open grave, followed by a short scream, easily mistaken at first for one of those unearthly calls made by foxes. We dropped down behind the nearest monument and waited. I thought I caught the drum of running feet and looked up just in time to see a figure heading at speed towards the lychgate.

"Watson!" I cried. "There he goes! After him!"

To our credit, we put up a fair chase. Watson fell behind before ever we had left the churchyard and, from his cry of consternation, I took it he had met with an accident. Our quarry was fleet of foot, however, and finally I was forced to watch as his dark shape advanced ever further away up the hill while I stood trying to catch my breath. A warning shot would be wasted, I decided, especially when I heard a familiar roar in the distance.

I returned to the elder graveyard to find Watson nursing his ankle beside the grave that had been dug earlier. I had worse news for him.

"He got away?" he asked.

"I'm afraid so. On your motorcycle."

His face fell. The pain of the loss was evidently more severe than any twisted ankle.

"Not my Brough, Holmes?"

"Courage, my dear fellow. He won't get far. A motorcycle like that will be sure to attract attention. He must be rid of it as soon as possible if he is to evade capture." I offered him my hand and hauled him to his feet. "Come, a visit to the local police station is in order."

I gave him the support of my arm and with slow, painful steps, we edged our way around the grave. When Watson suddenly caught his breath, I thought he had aggravated his injury, only to find him pointing down. The thin light caught a glint in the darkness as I lowered the lantern into the grave, and we found ourselves looking into the dead face of the gravedigger, Malcolm.

It was not the result for which I had been hoping when I had persuaded Watson to join me on the night's escapade. The local constable took a sanguine view of the matter and was more concerned with our reasons for wandering round a churchyard in the dead of night.

"Another death for Farmer Jack," he had said when the old man had been removed from the grave. "The Devil makes work for idle hands, and there was none idler than old Malcolm."

"On the contrary, Constable," I was obliged to inform him. "An earthly presence brought about this fellow's demise, although I do not entirely disallow that it was an accident."

The constable chuckled. "Now, now, Mr. Holmes, this isn't London, you know."

"City or countryside, discovery of the cause of death is of paramount importance – especially in this case, as it creates an element of doubt."

"Doubt, Mr. Holmes?" said the constable. "No doubt about it, if you ask me. His neck is broken, consistent with a fall from such a height. He was running from something and fell in. He was old. His bones snapped like a twig."

"Running backwards?" I said. "When we found him, he was face up."

The constable looked bemused. "Then what is your suggestion, sir?"

"That he was running from someone who caught up with him. With your permission, Constable." He nodded his assent and I demonstrated by gripping his lapels. "They struggled and old Malcolm fell backwards into the grave."

"Why would they be struggling?"

"Perhaps because of what Malcolm had stolen. You observed the dirt on the old man's coat."

The constable gave it due thought. "He was in the grave, sir."

"This dirt was on the front. Here," I said, holding my hands before my chest as if holding before me. "He was grasping something which was wrenched away from him. Something pulled from the dirt – from the very grave of Farmer Jack!"

"Now, Mr. Holmes," said the constable with exaggerated patience, "you don't want to go believing those tales about Farmer Jack's pot of gold."

"Rather a pot of gold belonging to another person entirely, I fancy."

"My, my, you do have a vivid imagination, sir. And who's responsible, would you say?"

"The miscreant who stole my friend's motorcycle in an effort to elude the police. The son of Bert Hogarth. Malcolm's assistant."

At that moment, the telephone rang and the constable stepped away to answer it. When he returned, he was ashen.

"Well, sir, we've had a surprising turn of events," said he. "The county police have arrested a man over at Finchingham. Seems he crashed a motorcycle into a lamp post. It's the young man you mentioned, sir. Jim Hogarth. They're bringing him back to Fishcombe now."

From behind me, Watson, with his foot up on a chair, let out a groan of the deepest misery.

"Did he have anything with him, Constable?"

"No, sir."

"Then it must be still in the graveyard. It is imperative we organise a search straight away."

We did not have far to look. The box had fallen in the struggle and had come to rest behind a decaying headstone, riven with holes. We bore it back to the police station, where another policeman was waiting with a subdued prisoner. When I placed the box on the table before him, he started up, only to be held back by the attendant officer.

"I hope it was worth it," said the constable severely. "Now, Jim, what's all this about?"

Hogarth glared up at me. "I knew you were going to be trouble, Mr. Holmes."

"On the contrary, I am about to spare your neck a stretching," said I. "The explanation, Constable, is simple. To coin a phrase, 'the sins of the father'. Am I right in saying your father, Mr. Hogarth, had what might be called a nefarious past?"

"He had his faults," Hogarth grunted. "No one's saying he was perfect."

"Far from it," I agreed. "He was a member of the Guildford Gang."

"Who?" asked the constable.

"Before your time, I dare say. They made a name for themselves stealing priceless artefacts from small museums. You may be familiar with another member of the gang – a certain John Datchett." The constable's mouth fell open. "Datchett and three other men were sent to prison for the crimes of the Guildford Gang. They kept silent about Hogarth – I imagine he was responsible for the storage and disposal of their ill-gotten gains. Another man was also involved, the ringleader of the gang."

I looked to Hogarth, who was keeping his lips firmly pressed together.

"Come now, what does it matter now when all is known?" I urged. "His name to save your life."

"William Leadbetter," came the grudging reply. "When the others were arrested, he gave my father the gang's box of stolen treasure. Told him he was to keep it safe. Only when all the others were released from prison would he come back and divide up the money between them. That's what my father was told and that's what he's been doing all these years. He had told Leadbetter and the others about Farmer Jack and how no one would ever think of looking in a tomb cursed by the Devil. That's where he stored the box, and he took care to keep that ivy growing so it covered it all over. Whenever he saw anyone lurking in the graveyard at night, he would dress up like a devil and go out and frighten them."

"It didn't work with John Datchett."

"No," said Hogarth solemnly. "He came wanting his money. Said he wasn't prepared to wait for the others. He tried to break into the tomb, Mr. Holmes. He and my father fought. He didn't mean to kill him." He bowed his head. "It broke him, it did."

"And you took over from your father, keeping watch over the tomb. What happened with the priest?"

"I only meant to scare him. But no sooner did he see me than he started gasping and clutching at his chest. I would have got help, but he was dead as soon as he hit the ground."

"And Malcolm?" I asked.

Hogarth shook his head. "He got suspicious, what with you asking all those questions. 'Why would the great Sherlock Holmes be interested in

382

our Farmer Jack?' he kept saying. Well, sir, I kept my eye on him after that, and sure enough he went poking about where he had no business to be. I saw him take that box out of the tomb. I caught up with him and tried to take it off him. Only he fell and ended up in the grave. That's when I saw you, Mr. Holmes. I didn't know what to do, so I made a run for it."

"On a stolen motorcycle. I do hope it was insured, Watson?"

Another pained groan informed me that was not the case.

"But why, Jim?" said the constable. "All these deaths for a few trinkets?"

"It's more than my father's life is worth to lose that box!" Hogarth yelled. "Before Leadbetter left, he said if anything happened to it, my father would be responsible. If Leadbetter doesn't find that box when he comes back, he'll kill him. I know he will."

"*If* he comes back. Constable?"

I stepped back as the policeman brought up a shovel and struck the clasp several times before the padlock came off. Throwing back the lid, he let out of a cry of surprise. The box was empty. Hogarth got to his feet before the other policeman could stop him and ran to it. Scrabbling at the splintered wooden base with his fingers, he tipped it from side to side before letting it fall in utter disbelief.

"I don't understand," he uttered. "Where did it go?"

"Leadbetter isn't coming back," I said. "Your father has been guarding an empty box all these years. I imagine Leadbetter's idea was that the others would think your father had stolen their money, when all along he had taken it."

"Then where is he?" asked Hogarth.

It was a good question. Further investigations confirmed that Leadbetter had left England in 1911, soon after the trial of his comrades began. By chance, he had booked passage to America on the ill-fated *S.S. Solara*, which sank off the coast of Ireland in a freak storm with the loss of all hands. Should the wreck ever be salvaged, I am confident a treasure trove is waiting to be found. On my testimony, Jim Hogarth was spared the gallows when the deaths were reduced to manslaughter.

Watson, I am pleased to report, lived to fight another day, but was persuaded to forgo the purchase of another motorcycle for the safety and the sanity of those around him. In any case, it seemed our escapade had caused him to lose interest in the venture. When last he wrote, he claimed to have found a new hobby in aviation.

Perhaps the leather flying helmet was not a wasted purchase after all.

# About the Contributors

The following contributors appear in this volume:
**The MX Book of New Sherlock Holmes Stories**
**Part XVIII – Whatever Remains . . .**
**Must Be the Truth (1899-1925)**

**Kareem Abdul-Jabbar** is a huge Holmesian, the National Basketball Association's all-time leading scorer, a Basketball Hall of Fame inductee, and a *New York Times* bestselling author. In 2016, he received the Presidential Medal of Freedom, the USA's highest civilian honor, from former President Barack Obama. Currently he is chairman of the Skyhook Foundation, which "gives kids a shot that can't be blocked", a columnist for *The Guardian* newspaper, and a cultural critic for *The Hollywood Reporter.* He has written a number of books, and is a two-time NAACP aware-winning writer and producer. With Anna Waterhouse, he is the author of *Mycroft Holmes* (2015), *Mycroft and Sherlock* (2018), and *Mycroft and Sherlock: The Empty Birdcage* (2019).

**Brian Belanger** is a publisher and editor, but is best known for his freelance illustration and cover design work. His distinctive style can be seen on several MX Publishing covers, including *Silent Meridian* by Elizabeth Crowen, *Sherlock Holmes and the Menacing Melbournian* by Allan Mitchell, *Sherlock Holmes and A Quantity of Debt* by David Marcum, *Welcome to Undershaw* by Luke Benjamen Kuhns, and many more. Brian is the co-founder of Belanger Books LLC, where he illustrates the popular *MacDougall Twins with Sherlock Holmes* young reader series (#1 bestsellers on Amazon.com UK). A prolific creator, he also designs t-shirts, mugs, stickers, and other merchandise on his personal art site: *www.redbubble.com/people/zhahadun.*

**S.F. Bennett** has, at various times, been an actor, a lecturer, a journalist, a historian, an author and a potter. Whilst some of those things still apply, she has always been an avid collector, concentrating mainly on ephemera and other related items concerning Sherlock Holmes and British science-fiction of the 1970's. To date, she has written articles on aspects of The Canon for *The Baker Street Journal, The Sherlock Holmes Journal,* and *The Torr,* the journal of *The Sherlock Holmes Society of the West Country.* When not collecting, she can be found writing science-fiction and mystery stories, and has contributed to several anthologies of new Sherlock Holmes pastiches. Her first novel was *The Secret Diary of Mycroft Holmes: The Thoughts and Reminiscences of Sherlock Holmes's Elder Brother, 1880-1888* (2017). She is also the author of *A Study In Postcards: Sherlock Holmes in the Golden Age of the Picture Postcard* (*Sherlock Holmes Society of London,* 2019).

**Thomas A. Burns, Jr.** is the author of the *Natalie McMasters Mysteries.* He was born and grew up in New Jersey, attended Xavier High School in Manhattan, earned B.S degrees in Zoology and Microbiology at Michigan State University, and a M.S. in Microbiology at North Carolina State University. He currently resides in Wendell, North Carolina. As a kid, Tom started reading mysteries with The Hardy Boys, Ken Holt and Rick Brant, and graduated to the classic stories by authors such as A. Conan Doyle, Dorothy Sayers, John Dickson Carr, Erle Stanley Gardner, and Rex Stout, to name a few. Tom has written fiction as a hobby all of his life, starting with The Man from U.N.C.L.E. stories in marble-backed copybooks in grade school. He built a career as technical, science, and medical writer and editor for nearly thirty years in industry and government. Now that he's truly on his own as a novelist, he's excited to publish his own mystery series, as well as to contribute stories about his second-most-favorite detective, Sherlock Holmes, to *The MX anthology of New Sherlock Holmes Stories.*

**Nick Cardillo** has loved Sherlock Holmes ever since he was first introduced to the detective in *The Great Illustrated Classics* edition of *The Adventures of Sherlock Holmes* at the age of six. His devotion to the Baker Street detective duo has only increased over the years, and Nick is thrilled to be taking these proper steps into the Sherlock Holmes Community. His first published story, "The Adventure of the Traveling Corpse", appeared in *The MX Book of New Sherlock Holmes Stories – Part VI: 2017 Annual*, and his "The Haunting of Hamilton Gardens" was published in *PART VIII – Eliminate the Impossible: 1892-1905*. A devout fan of The Golden Age of Detective Fiction, Hammer Horror, and *Doctor Who*, Nick co-writes the Sherlockian blog, *Back on Baker Street*, which analyses over seventy years of Sherlock Holmes film and culture. He is a student at Susquehanna University.

**Harry DeMaio** is a *nom de plume* of Harry B. DeMaio, successful author of several books on Information Security and Business Networks, as well as the ten-volume *Casebooks of Octavius Bear – Alternative Universe Mysteries for Adult Animal Lovers.* Octavius Bear is loosely based on Sherlock Holmes and Nero Wolfe in a world in which *homo sapiens* died out long ago in a global disaster, but most animals have advanced to a twenty-first century anthropomorphic state. "It's Time" is Harry's first offering treating Holmes and Watson in their original human condition. A retired business executive, consultant, information security specialist, former pilot, and graduate school adjunct professor, he whiles away his time traveling and writing preposterous articles and stories. He has appeared on many radio and TV shows and is an accomplished, frequent public speaker. Former New York City natives, he and his extremely patient and helpful wife, Virginia, and their Bichon Frisé, Woof, live in Cincinnati (and several other parallel universes.) They have two sons living in Scottsdale, Arizona and Cortlandt Manor, New York, both of whom are quite successful and quite normal – thus putting the lie to the theory that insanity is hereditary.

**Sir Arthur Conan Doyle** (1859-1930) *Holmes Chronicler Emeritus.* If not for him, this anthology would not exist. Author, physician, patriot, sportsman, spiritualist, husband and father, and advocate for the oppressed. He is remembered and honored for the purposes of this collection by being the man who introduced Sherlock Holmes to the world. Through fifty-six Holmes short stories, four novels, and additional Apocryphal entries, Doyle revolutionized mystery stories and also greatly influenced and improved police forensic methods and techniques for the betterment of all. *Steel True Blade Straight.*

**Matthew J. Elliott** is the author of *Big Trouble in Mother Russia* (2016), the official sequel to the cult movie *Big Trouble in Little China, Lost in Time and Space: An Unofficial Guide to the Uncharted Journeys of Doctor Who* (2014), *Sherlock Holmes on the Air* (2012), *Sherlock Holmes in Pursuit* (2013), *The Immortals: An Unauthorized Guide to* Sherlock *and* Elementary (2013), and *The Throne Eternal* (2014). His articles, fiction, and reviews have appeared in the magazines *Scarlet Street, Total DVD, SHERLOCK,* and *Sherlock Holmes Mystery Magazine,* and the collections *The Game's Afoot, Curious Incidents 2, Gaslight Grimoire, The Mammoth Book of Best British Crime 8,* and *The MX Book of New Sherlock Holmes Stories – Part III: 1896-1929.* He has scripted over 260 radio plays, including episodes of *Doctor Who, The Further Adventures of Sherlock Holmes, The Twilight Zone, The New Adventures of Mickey Spillane's Mike Hammer, Fangoria's Dreadtime Stories,* and award-winning adaptations of *The Hound of* *the Baskervilles* and *The War of the Worlds*. He is the only radio dramatist to adapt all sixty original stories from The Canon for the series *The Classic Adventures of Sherlock Holmes*. Matthew is a writer and performer on *RiffTrax.com*, the online comedy experience from the creators of cult sci-fi TV series *Mystery Science Theater 3000* (*MST3K* to the initiated). He's also written a few comic books.

**Steve Emecz**'s main field is technology, in which he has been working for more than twenty years. Following multiple senior roles at Xerox, where he grew their European eCommerce from $6m to $200m. Steve worked for eCommerce provider Venda, mobile commerce platform Powa, collectAI in Hamburg (Artificial Intelligence) and is now back in London with CloudTrade. Steve is a regular trade show speaker on the subject of eCommerce, and his tech career has taken him to more than fifty countries – so he's no stranger to planes and airports. He wrote two mystery novels (one a bestseller) in the 1990's, and a screenplay in 2001. Shortly after, he set up MX Publishing, specialising in NLP books. In 2008, MX published its first Sherlock Holmes book (Alistair Duncan's wonderful *Eliminate the Impossible*), and MX has gone on to become the largest specialist Holmes publisher in the world. MX is a social enterprise and supports two main causes. The first is Happy Life Children's Home, a baby rescue project in Nairobi, Kenya, where he and his wife, Sharon, spend every Christmas at the rescue centre in Kasarani. In 2014, they wrote a short book about the project, *The Happy Life Story*, with a second edition in 2017. The second is the Stepping Stones School, of which Steve is a patron. Stepping Stones is located at Undershaw, Sir Arthur Conan Doyle's former home.

**Mark A. Gagen** BSI is co-founder of Wessex Press, sponsor of the popular *From Gillette to Brett* conferences, and publisher of *The Sherlock Holmes Reference Library* and many other fine Sherlockian titles. A life-long Holmes enthusiast, he is a member of *The Baker Street Irregulars* and *The Illustrious Clients of Indianapolis*. A graphic artist by profession, his work is often seen on the covers of *The Baker Street Journal* and various BSI books.

**John Atkinson Grimshaw** (1836-1893) was born in Leeds, England. His amazing paintings, usually featuring twilight or night scenes illuminated by gas-lamps or moonlight, are easily recognizable, and are often used on the covers of books about The Great Detective to set the mood, as shadowy figures move in the distance through misty mysterious settings and over rain-slicked streets.

**Arthur Hall**, who also has stories in Parts XVI and XVII, was born in Aston, Birmingham, UK, in 1944. His interest in writing began during his schooldays and served as a growing ambition to become an author. Years later, his first novel *Sole Contact* was an espionage story about an ultra-secret government department known as "Sector Three" and has been followed, to date, by four sequels. The sixth in the series, *The Suicide Chase*, is currently in the course of preparation. Other works include five "rediscovered" cases from the files of Sherlock Holmes, two collections of bizarre short stories, and two novels about an adventurer called "Bernard Kramer", as well as several contributions to the ongoing anthology, *The MX Book of New Sherlock Holmes Stories*. His only ambition, apart from being published more widely, is to attend the premier of a film based on one of his novels, ideally at The Odeon, Leicester Square. He lives in the West Midlands, United Kingdom, where he often walks other people's dogs as he attempts to formulate new plots. His work can be seen at *arthurhallsbooksite.blogspot.com*, and the author can be contacted at *arthurhall7777@aol.co.uk*

**Paul Hiscock** is an author of crime, fantasy, and science fiction tales. His short stories have appeared in several anthologies and include a seventeenth century whodunnit, a science fiction western, and a steampunk Sherlock Holmes story. Paul lives with his family in Kent, England, and spends his days chasing a toddler with more energy than the Duracell Bunny. He mainly does his writing in coffee shops with members of the local NaNoWriMo group, or in the middle of the night when his family has gone to sleep. Consequently, his stories tend to be fuelled by large amounts of black coffee. You can find out more about his writing at *www.detectivesanddragons.uk.*

**Christopher James**, who also has a poem in Part XVI, was born in 1975 in Paisley, Scotland. Educated at Newcastle and UEA, he was a winner of the UK's National Poetry Competition in 2008. He has written two full length Sherlock Holmes novels, *The Adventure of the Ruby Elephant* and *The Jeweller of Florence*, both published by MX, and is working on a third.

In the year 1998 **Craig Janacek** took his degree of Doctor of Medicine at Vanderbilt University, and proceeded to Stanford to go through the training prescribed for pediatricians in practice. Having completed his studies there, he was duly attached to the University of California, San Francisco as Associate Professor. The author of over seventy medical monographs upon a variety of obscure lesions, his travel-worn and battered tin dispatch-box is crammed with papers, nearly all of which are records of his fictional works. To date, these have been published solely in electronic format, including two non-Holmes novels (*The Oxford Deception* and *The Anger of Achilles Peterson*), the trio of holiday adventures collected as *The Midwinter Mysteries of Sherlock Holmes*, the Holmes story collections *The First of* Criminals, *The Assassination of Sherlock Holmes*, *The Treasury of Sherlock Holmes*, and the Watsonian novels *The Isle of Devils* and *The Gate of Gold*. Craig Janacek is a *nom de plume*.

**Roger Johnson** BSI, ASH is a retired librarian, now working as a volunteer assistant at the Essex Police Museum. In his spare time, he is commissioning editor of *The Sherlock Holmes Journal*, an occasional lecturer, and a frequent contributor to The Writings About the Writings. His sole work of Holmesian pastiche was published in 1997 in Mike Ashley's anthology *The Mammoth Book of New Sherlock Holmes Adventures*, and he has the greatest respect for the many authors who have contributed new tales to the present mighty trilogy. Like his wife, Jean Upton, he is a member of both *The Baker Street Irregulars* and *The Adventuresses of Sherlock Holmes.*

**Kelvin I. Jones**, who also has a story in Part XVI, is the author of six books about Sherlock Holmes and the definitive biography of Conan Doyle as a spiritualist, *Conan Doyle and The Spirits*. A member of *The Sherlock Holmes Society of London*, he has published numerous short occult and ghost stories in British anthologies over the last thirty years. His work has appeared on BBC Radio, and in 1984 he won the Mason Hall Literary Award for his poem cycle about the survivors of Hiroshima and Nagasaki, recently reprinted as "Omega". (Oakmagic Publications) A one-time teacher of creative writing at the University of East Anglia, he is also the author of four crime novels featuring his ex-Met sleuth John Bottrell, who first appeared in *Stone Dead.* He has over fifty titles on Kindle, and is also the author of several novellas and short story collections featuring a Norwich-based detective, DCI Ketch, an intrepid sleuth who investigates East Anglian murder cases. He also published a series of short stories about an Edwardian psychic detective, Dr. John Carter (*Carter's Occult Casebook*). Ramsey Campbell, the British horror writer, and Francis King, the renowned novelist, have both compared his supernatural stories to those

of M. R. James. He has also published children's fiction, namely *Odin's Eye*, and, in collaboration with his wife Debbie, *The Dark Entry*. Since 1995, he has been the proprietor of Oakmagic Publications, publishers of British folklore and of his fiction titles. He lives in Norfolk.
(See *www.oakmagicpublications.co.uk*)

**David Marcum**, who also has stories in Parts XVII and XVIII, plays *The Game* with deadly seriousness. He first discovered Sherlock Holmes in 1975 at the age of ten, and since that time, he has collected, read, and chronologicized literally thousands of traditional Holmes pastiches in the form of novels, short stories, radio and television episodes, movies and scripts, comics, fan-fiction, and unpublished manuscripts. He is the author of over fifty Sherlockian pastiches, some published in anthologies and others collected in his own books, *The Papers of Sherlock Holmes*, *Sherlock Holmes and A Quantity of Debt*, and *Sherlock Holmes – Tangled Skeins*. He has edited nearly fifty books, including several dozen traditional Sherlockian anthologies, including the ongoing series *The MX Book of New Sherlock Holmes Stories*, which he created in 2015. This collection is now up to 18 volumes, with several more in preparation. He was responsible for bringing back August Derleth's Solar Pons for a new generation, first with his collection of authorized Pons stories, *The Papers of Solar Pons*, and then by editing the reissued authorized versions of the original Pons books. He is now doing the same for the adventures of Dr. Thorndyke. He has contributed numerous essays to various publications, and is a member of a number of Sherlockian groups and Scions. He is a licensed Civil Engineer, living in Tennessee with his wife and son. His irregular Sherlockian blog, *A Seventeen Step Program*, addresses various topics related to his favorite book friends (as his son used to call them when he was small), and can be found at *http://17stepprogram.blogspot.com/* Since the age of nineteen, he has worn a deerstalker as his regular-and-only hat from autumn to spring, and often summer as well. In 2013, he and his deerstalker were finally able make his first trip-of-a-lifetime Holmes Pilgrimage to England, with return Pilgrimages in 2015 and 2016, where you may have spotted him. If you ever run into him and his deerstalker out and about, feel free to say hello!

**Sidney Paget** (1860-1908), a few of whose illustrations are used within this anthology, was born in London, and like his two older brothers, became a famed illustrator and painter. He completed over three-hundred-and-fifty drawings for the Sherlock Holmes stories that were first published in *The Strand* magazine, defining Holmes's image forever after in the public mind.

**Tracy J. Revels**, who also has stories in Parts XVI and XVII, has been a Sherlockian from the age of eleven. She is a professor of history at Wofford College in Spartanburg, South Carolina. She is a member of *The Survivors of the Gloria Scott* and *The Studious Scarlets Society*, and is a past recipient of the Beacon Society Award. Almost every semester, she teaches a class that covers The Canon, either to college students or to senior citizens. She is also the author of three supernatural Sherlockian pastiches with MX (*Shadowfall*, *Shadowblood*, and *Shadowwraith*), and a regular contributor to her scion's newsletter. She also has some notoriety as an author of very silly skits: For proof, see "The Adventure of the Adversarial Adventuress" and "Occupy Baker Street" on YouTube. When not studying Sherlock, she can be found researching the history of her native state, and has written books on Florida in the Civil War and on the development of Florida's tourism industry.

**Roger Silverwood** was educated in Gloucestershire before National Service. He later worked in the toy trade and as a copywriter in an advertising agency. Roger went into business with his wife as an antiques dealer before retiring in 1997, and he now leads a fairly happy existence with his wife Mary in the town of Bromersley in South Yorkshire. The Yorkshire author excels in writing crime books and is known for his sensational series featuring the fictional Detective Michael Angel.

**Robert V. Stapleton** was born and brought up in Leeds, Yorkshire, England, and studied at Durham University. After working in various parts of the country as an Anglican parish priest, he is now retired and lives with his wife in North Yorkshire. As a member of his local writing group, he now has time to develop his other life as a writer of adventure stories. He has recently had a number of short stories published, and he is hoping to have a couple of completed novels published at some time in the future.

**Gareth Tilley** is a writer whose works include several scripts for Imagination Theatre's *The Further Adventures of Sherlock Holmes.* One of these was included in *Imagination Theatre's Sherlock Holmes*, where the contributor royalties benefit the Stepping Stones School at Undershaw, one of Sir Arthur Conan Doyle's former homes.

**Thomas A. (Tom) Turley** has been "hooked on Holmes" since finishing *The Hound of the Baskervilles* at about the age of twelve. However, his interest in Sherlockian pastiches didn't take off until he wrote one. *Sherlock Holmes and the Adventure of the Tainted Canister* (2014) is available as an e-book and an audiobook from MX Publishing. It will also soon appear in *The Art of Sherlock Holmes – USA Edition 1.* In 2017, two of Tom's stories, "A Scandal in Serbia" and "A Ghost from Christmas Past" were published in Parts VI and VII of this anthology. "Ghost" was also included in *The Art of Sherlock Holmes – West Palm Beach Edition.* Meanwhile, Tom is finishing a collection of historical pastiches entitled *Sherlock Holmes and the Crowned Heads of Europe.* The first story, "Sherlock Holmes and the Case of the Dying Emperor" (2018) is available from MX Publishing as a separate e-book. Set in the brief reign of Emperor Frederick III (1888), it inaugurates Sherlock Holmes's espionage campaign against the German Empire, which ended only in August 1914 with "His Last Bow". When completed, *Sherlock Holmes and the Crowned Heads of Europe* will also include "A Scandal in Serbia" and two additional historical tales. Although he has a Ph.D. in British history, Tom spent most of his professional career as an archivist with the State of Alabama. He and his wife Paula (an aspiring science fiction novelist) live in Montgomery, Alabama. Interested readers may contact Tom through MX Publishing or his Goodreads author's page.

**Matthew White** is an up-and-coming author from Richmond, Virginia in the USA. He has been a passionate devotee of Sherlock Holmes since childhood. He can be reached at *matthewwhite.writer@gmail.com.*

*The following contributors appear*
*in the companion volumes:*
## The MX Book of New Sherlock Holmes Stories
### Whatever Remains . . .
### Must Be the Truth
### Part XVI – (1881-1890)
*and*
### Part XVII – (1891-1898)

**Josh Anderson** is twenty-four and lives in Wales, UK. He enjoys running, tennis, video games, and reading, and is currently training to be an English teacher. His favourite Sherlock Holmes author is James Lovegrove. This is his first story.

**Derrick Belanger** is an educator and also the author of the #1 bestselling book in its category, *Sherlock Holmes: The Adventure of the Peculiar Provenance*, which was in the top 200 bestselling books on Amazon. He also is the author of *The MacDougall Twins with Sherlock Holmes* books, and he edited the Sir Arthur Conan Doyle horror anthology *A Study in Terror: Sir Arthur Conan Doyle's Revolutionary Stories of Fear and the Supernatural*. Mr. Belanger co-owns the publishing company Belanger Books, which released the Sherlock Holmes anthologies *Beyond Watson, Holmes Away From Home: Adventures from the Great Hiatus* Volumes 1 and 2, *Sherlock Holmes: Before Baker Street*, and *Sherlock Holmes: Adventures in the Realms of H.G. Wells* Volumes I and 2. Derrick resides in Colorado and continues compiling unpublished works by Dr. John H. Watson.

**Hugh Ashton** was born in the U.K., and moved to Japan in 1988, where he remained until 2016, living with his wife Yoshiko in the historic city of Kamakura, a little to the south of Yokohama. He and Yoshiko have now moved to Lichfield, a small cathedral city in the Midlands of the U.K., the birthplace of Samuel Johnson, and one-time home of Erasmus Darwin. In the past, he has worked in the technology and financial services industries, which have provided him with material for some of his books set in the 21$^{st}$ century. He currently works as a writer: Novelist, freelance editor, and copywriter, (his work for large Japanese corporations has appeared in international business journals), and journalist, as well as producing industry reports on various aspects of the financial services industry. Recently, however, his lifelong interest in Sherlock Holmes has developed into an acclaimed series of adventures featuring the world's most famous detective, written in the style of the originals, and published by Inknbeans Press. In addition to these, he has also published historical and alternate historical novels, short stories, and thrillers. Together with artist Andy Boerger, he has produced the *Sherlock Ferret* series of stories for children, featuring the world's cutest detective.

**Bob Bishop** is the author of over twenty stage plays, musicals, and pantomimes, several written in collaboration with Norfolk composer, Bob McNeil Watson. Many of these theatrical works were first performed by the fringe theatre company of which he was principal director, The Fossick Valley Fumblers, at the Edinburgh Festival Fringe between 1982 and 2000. Amongst these works were four Sherlock Holmes plays, inspired by the playwright's lifelong affection for the works of Sir Arthur Conan Doyle. Bob's other works include the comic novel, *A Tickle Amongst the Cornstalks*, an anthology of short stories, *Shadows on the Blind*, and a number of Sherlock Holmes pastiche novellas. He currently lives with his wife and three poodles in North Norfolk.

**Andrew Bryant** was born in Bridgend, Wales, and now lives in Burlington, Ontario, Canada. His previous publications include *Prism International*, *Existere*, *On Spec*, *The Dalhousie Review*, and second place in the 2015 *Toronto Star* short story contest. His first Holmes story, "The Shackled Man", was published in *The MX Book of New Sherlock Holmes Stories – Part XIII*. The story in this collection, "The Blue Lady of Dunraven", is situated at Dunraven Castle, a few miles from where he was born, and he remembers walking the house and grounds as a child. Tragically, the Castle was demolished in 1963, robbing the nation of a fascinating and mysterious historic landmark. Hopefully, The Blue Lady wanders the ruins still.

**Chris Chan** is a writer, educator, and historian. He works as a researcher and "International Goodwill Ambassador" for Agatha Christie Ltd. His true crime articles, reviews, and short fiction have appeared (or will soon appear) in *The Strand*, *The Wisconsin Magazine of History*, *Mystery Weekly*, *Gilbert!*, *Nerd HQ*, Akashic Books' *Mondays are Murder* web series, *The Baker Street Journal*, and *Sherlock Holmes Mystery Magazine*.

**Bert Coules** BSI wandered through a succession of jobs from fringe opera company manager to BBC radio drama producer-director before becoming a full-time writer at the beginning of 1989. Bert works in a wide range of genres, including science fiction, horror, comedy, romance and action-adventure but he is especially associated with crime and detective stories: he was the head writer on the BBC's unique project to dramatise the entire Sherlock Holmes canon, and went on to script four further series of original Holmes and Watson mysteries. As well as radio, he also writes for TV and the stage.

**Anna Elliott** is an author of historical fiction and fantasy. Her first series, the *Twilight of Avalon* trilogy, is a retelling of the Trystan & Isolde legend. She wrote her second series, *The Pride & Prejudice Chronicles*, chiefly to satisfy her own curiosity about what might have happened to Elizabeth Bennet, Mr. Darcy, and all the other wonderful cast of characters after the official end of Jane Austen's classic work. She enjoys stories about strong women and loves exploring the multitude of ways women can find their unique strengths. She was delighted to lend a hand with the Sherlock & Lucy series, and this story, firstly because she loves Sherlock Holmes as much as her father does, and second because it almost never happens that someone with a dilemma shouts, "Quick, we need an author of historical fiction!" Anna lives in Pennsylvania with her husband and their four children. Learn more about the Sherlock and Lucy series at *www.sherlockandlucy.com*

**David Friend** lives in Wales, Great Britain, where he divides his time between watching old detective films and thinking about old detective films. Now thirty, he's been scribbling out stories for twenty years and hopes, some day, to write something half-decent. Most of what he pens is set in an old-timey world of non-stop adventure with debonair sleuths, kick-ass damsels, criminal masterminds, and narrow escapes, and he wishes he could live there.

**Tim Gambrell** lives in Exeter, Devon, with his wife, two young sons, two cats, and seven chickens. He contributed "The Yellow Star of Cairo" to *Part XIII* of *The MX Book of New Sherlock Holmes Stories*, and has a story in the forthcoming collection *The Early Adventures of Sherlock Holmes* from Belanger Books. Outside of The World of Holmes, Tim has written extensively for Doctor Who spin-off ranges. He has recently had two linked novels published by Candy Jar Books: *Lethbridge-Stewart: The Laughing Gnome – Lucy Wilson & The Bledoe Cadets*, and *The Lucy Wilson Mysteries: The Brigadier and The Bledoe Cadets* (both Summer 2019). He also has a novella, *The Way of The Bry'hunee*, for the Erimem range from Thebes Publishing, which is due out in late 2019. Tim's short fiction includes stories *in Lethbridge-Stewart: The HAVOC Files* 3 (Candy Jar, 2017), *Bernice Summerfield: True Stories* (Big Finish, 2017), and *Relics . . . An Anthology* (Red Ted Books, 2018). Further short fiction will feature in the forthcoming collections *Lethbridge-Stewart: The HAVOC Files – The Laughing Gnome*, and *Lethbridge-Stewart: The HAVOC Files – Loose Ends* (both due later in 2019).

**Jayantika Ganguly** BSI is the General Secretary and Editor of the *Sherlock Holmes Society of India*, a member of the *Sherlock Holmes Society of London*, and the *Czech Sherlock Holmes Society*. She is the author of *The Holmes Sutra* (MX 2014). She is a corporate lawyer working with one of the Big Six law firms.

**Paul D. Gilbert** was born in 1954 and has lived in and around London all of his life. He has been married to Jackie for thirty-nine years, and she is a Holmes expert who keeps him on the straight and narrow! He has two sons, one of whom now lives in Spain. His interests include literature, ancient history, all religions, most sports, and movies. He is currently employed full-time as a funeral director. His books so far include *The Lost Files of Sherlock Holmes* (2007), *The Chronicles of Sherlock Holmes* (2008), *Sherlock Holmes and the Giant Rat of Sumatra* (2010), *The Annals of Sherlock Holmes* (2012), *Sherlock Holmes and the Unholy Trinity* (2015), *Sherlock Holmes: The Four Handed Game* (2017), and *The Illumination of Sherlock Holmes*, to be published 2019.

**Dick Gillman** is an English writer and acrylic artist living in Brittany, France with his wife Alex, Truffle, their Black Labrador, and Jean-Claude, their Breton cat. During his retirement from teaching, he has written over twenty Sherlock Holmes short stories which are published as both e-books and paperbacks. His contribution to the superb MX Sherlock Holmes collection, published in October 2015, was entitled "The Man on Westminster Bridge" and had the privilege of being chosen as the anchor story in *The MX Book of New Sherlock Holmes Stories – Part II (1890-1895)*.

**Arthur Hall** also has stories in the companion volumes, Parts XVI and XVII.

**Stephen Herczeg** is an IT Geek, writer, actor, and film-maker based in Canberra Australia. He has been writing for over twenty years and has completed a couple of dodgy novels, sixteen feature length screenplays, and numerous short stories and scripts. Stephen was very successful in 2017's International Horror Hotel screenplay competition, with his scripts *TITAN* winning the Sci-Fi category and *Dark are the Woods* placing second in the horror category. His work has featured in *Sproutlings – A Compendium of Little Fictions* from Hunter Anthologies, the *Hells Bells* Christmas horror anthology published by the Australasian Horror Writers Association, and the *Below the Stairs*, *Trickster's Treats*, *Shades of Santa*, *Behind the Mask*, and *Beyond the Infinite* anthologies from OzHorror.Con, *The Body Horror Book*, *Anemone Enemy*, and *Petrified Punks* from Oscillate Wildly Press, and *Sherlock Holmes In the Realms of H.G. Wells* and *Sherlock Holmes: Adventures Beyond the Canon* from Belanger Books.

**Christopher James** also has a poem in the companion volume, Part XVII.

**Kelvin I. Jones** also has a story in the companion volume, Part XVI.

**Steven Philip Jones** has written over sixty graphic novels and comic books including the horror series *Lovecraftian*, *Curious Cases of Sherlock Holmes*, the original series

*Nightlinger, Street Heroes 2005*, adaptations of *Dracula*, several H. P. Lovecraft stories, and the 1985 film *Re-animator*. Steven is also the author of several novels and nonfiction books including *The Clive Cussler Adventures: A Critical Review, Comics Writing: Communicating With Comic Book , King of Harlem, Bushwackers, The House With the Witch's Hat, Talisman: The Knightmare Knife*, and *Henrietta Hex: Shadows From the Past.* Steven's other writing credits include a number of scripts for radio dramas that have been broadcast internationally. A graduate of the University of Iowa, Steven has a Bachelor of Arts in Journalism and Religion, and was accepted into Iowa's Writer's Workshop - M.F.A. program.

**Michael Mallory** is the Derringer-winning author of the "Amelia Watson" (The Second Mrs. Watson) series and "Dave Beauchamp" mystery series, and more than one-hundred-twenty-five short stories. An entertainment journalist by day, he has written eight nonfiction books on pop culture and more than six-hundred newspaper and magazine articles. Based in Los Angeles, Mike is also an occasional actor on television.

**David Marcum** also has stories in the companion volumes, Parts XVI and XVII.

**Mark Mower** is a member of the *Crime Writers' Association, The Sherlock Holmes Society of London* and *The Solar Pons Society of London.* He writes true crime stories and fictional mysteries. His volumes of Holmes pastiches include *A Farewell to Baker Street, Sherlock Holmes: The Baker Street Case-Files*, and *Sherlock Holmes: The Baker Street Legacy* (all with MX Publishing) and, to date, he has contributed many stories to the ongoing series *The MX Book of New Sherlock Holmes Stories.* He has also had stories in two anthologies by Belanger Books: *Holmes Away From Home: Adventures from the Great Hiatus – Volume II – 1893-1894* (2016) and *Sherlock Holmes: Before Baker Street* (2017). More are bound to follow. Mark's non-fiction works include *Bloody British History: Norwich* (The History Press, 2014), *Suffolk Murders* (The History Press, 2011) and *Zeppelin Over Suffolk* (Pen & Sword Books, 2008).

**Will Murray** is the author of over seventy novels, including forty *Destroyer* novels and seven posthumous *Doc Savage* collaborations with Lester Dent, under the name Kenneth Robeson, for Bantam Books in the 1990's. Since 2011, he has written fourteen additional Doc Savage adventures for Altus Press, two of which co-starred The Shadow, as well as a solo Pat Savage novel. His 2015 Tarzan novel, *Return to Pal-Ul-Don*, was followed by *King Kong vs. Tarzan* in 2016. Murray has written short stories featuring such classic characters as Batman, Superman, Wonder Woman, Spider-Man, Ant-Man, the Hulk, Honey West, the Spider, the Avenger, the Green Hornet, the Phantom, and Cthulhu. A previous Murray Sherlock Holmes story appeared in Moonstone's *Sherlock Holmes: The Crossovers Casebook*, and another is forthcoming in *Sherlock Holmes and Doctor Was Not*, involving H. P. Lovecraft's Dr. Herbert West. Additionally, a number of his Sherlock Holmes stories have appeared in various volumes of *The MX Book of New Sherlock Holmes Stories.*

**Josh Pachter** (1951-   ) is a writer, editor, and translator. His short fiction has appeared in *Ellery Queen Mystery Magazine, Alfred Hitchcock Mystery Magazine*, and many other periodicals, anthologies, and year's-best collections. *The Tree of Life* (Wildside Press, 2015) collected all ten of his Mahboob Chaudri stories. He edited *The Man Who Read Mysteries: The Short Fiction of William Brittain* (Crippen & Landru, 2018) and *The Misadventures of Nero Wolfe* (Mysterious Press, 2020), and co-edited *The Misadventures of Ellery Queen* (Wildside, 2018) and *Amsterdam Noir* (Akashic, 2019). His translations of stories by Dutch and Belgian authors appear regularly in *Ellery Queen Mystery Magazine's* "Passport to Crime" Department. In his day job, he teaches interpersonal communication and film history at Northern Virginia Community College's Loudoun Campus.

**Tracy J. Revels** also has stories in the companion volumes, Parts XVI and XVII.

**Roger Riccard** of Los Angeles, California, U.S.A., is a descendant of the Roses of Kilravock in Highland Scotland. He is the author of two previous Sherlock Holmes novels, *The Case of the Poisoned Lilly* and *The Case of the Twain Papers*, a series of short stories in two volumes, *Sherlock Holmes: Adventures for the Twelve Days of Christmas* and *Further Adventures for the Twelve Days of Christmas*, and the new series *A Sherlock Holmes Alphabet of Cases,* all of which are published by Baker Street Studios. He has another novel and a non-fiction Holmes reference work in various stages of completion. He became a Sherlock Holmes enthusiast as a teenager (many, many years ago), and, like all fans of The Great Detective, yearned for more stories after reading The Canon over and over. It was the Granada Television performances of Jeremy Brett and Edward Hardwicke, and the encouragement of his wife, Rosilyn, that at last inspired him to write his own Holmes adventures, using the Granada actor portrayals as his guide. He has been called "The best pastiche writer since Val Andrews" by the *Sherlockian E-Times.*

**Jane Rubino** is the author of A Jersey Shore mystery series, featuring a Jane Austen-loving amateur sleuth and a Sherlock Holmes-quoting detective; *Knight Errant, Lady Vernon and Her Daughter*, (a novel-length adaptation of Jane Austen's novella *Lady Susan*, co-authored with her daughter Caitlen Rubino-Bradway, *What Would Austen Do?*, also co-authored with her daughter, a short story in the anthology *Jane Austen Made Me Do It, The Rucastles' Pawn, The Copper Beeches from Violet Turner's POV*, and, of course, there's the Sherlockian novel in the drawer – who doesn't have one? Jane lives on a barrier island at the New Jersey shore.

**Geri Schear** is a novelist and short story writer. Her work has been published in literary journals in the U.S. and Ireland. Her first novel, *A Biased Judgement: The Diaries of Sherlock Holmes 1897* was released to critical acclaim in 2014. The sequel, *Sherlock Holmes and the Other Woman* was published in 2015, and *Return to Reichenbach* in 2016. She lives in Kells, Ireland.

**Brenda Seabrooke**'s stories have been published in sixteen reviews, journals, and anthologies. She has received grants from the National Endowment for the Arts and Emerson College's Robbie Macauley Award. She is the author of twenty-three books for young readers including *Scones and Bones on Baker Street: Sherlock's (maybe!) Dog and the Dirt Dilemma*, and *The Rascal in the Castle: Sherlock's (possible!) Dog and the Queen's Revenge.* Brenda states: "It was fun to write from Dr. Watson's point of view and not have to worry about fleas, smelly pits, ralphing, or scratching at inopportune times."

**Shane Simmons** is the author of the occult detective novels *Necropolis* and *Epitaph*, and the crime collection *Raw and Other Stories.* An award-winning screenwriter and graphic novelist, his work has appeared in international film festivals, museums, and lectures about design and structure. He was born in Lachine, a suburb of Montreal best known for being massacred in 1689 and having a joke name. Visit Shane's homepage at *eyestrainproductions.com* for more.

**Mark Sohn** was born in Brighton, England in 1967. After a hectic life and many dubious and varied careers, he settled down in Sussex with his wife, Angie. His first novel, *Sherlock Holmes and the Whitechapel Murders* was published in 2017. His second, *The Absentee Detective* is out now. Both are available from Amazon.com.
*https://sherlockholmesof221b.blogspot.co.uk/*
*https://volcanocat.blogspot.co.uk/*

**S. Subramanian** is a retired professor of Economics from Chennai, India. Apart from a small book titled *Economic Offences: A Compendium of Crimes in Prose and Verse* (Oxford University Press Delhi, 2012), his Holmes pastiches are the only serious things he has written. His other work runs largely to whimsical stuff on fuzzy logic and social measurement, on which he writes with much precision and little understanding, being an economist. He is otherwise mainly harmless, as his wife and daughter might concede with a little persuasion.

**Kevin P. Thornton** has experienced a Taliban rocket attack in Kabul and a terrorist bombing in Johannesburg. He lives in Fort McMurray, Alberta, the town that burnt down in 2016. He has been shortlisted for the *Crime Writers of Canada* Unhanged writing award six times. He's never won. He was also a finalist for best short story in 2014 – the year Margaret Atwood entered. We're not saying he has luck issues, but don't bet on his stock tips. Born in Kenya, Kevin was a child in New Zealand, a student and soldier in Africa, a military contractor in Afghanistan, a forklift driver in Ontario, and an oilfield worker in North Western Canada. He writes poems that start out just fine, but turn ruder and cruder over time. From limerick to doggerel, they earn less than bugger-all, even though they all manage to rhyme. He also likes writing about Sherlock Holmes and dislikes writing about himself in the third person.

**Charles Veley** has loved Sherlock Holmes since boyhood. As a father, he read the entire Canon to his then-ten-year-old daughter at evening story time. Now, this very same daughter, grown up to become acclaimed historical novelist Anna Elliott, has worked with him to develop new adventures in the *Sherlock Holmes and Lucy James Mystery Series*. Charles is also a fan of Gilbert and Sullivan, and wrote *The Pirates of Finance*, a new musical in the G&S tradition that won an award at the New York Musical Theatre Festival in 2013. Other than the Sherlock and Lucy series, all of the books on his Amazon Author Page were written when he was a full-time author during the late Seventies and early Eighties. He currently works for United Technologies Corporation, where his main focus is on creating sustainability and value for the company's large real estate development projects. Learn more about the Sherlock and Lucy series at *www.sherlockandlucy.com*

**I.A. Watson** is a novelist and jobbing writer from Yorkshire who cut his teeth on writing Sherlock Holmes stories and has even won an award for one. His works include *Holmes and Houdini*, *Labours of Hercules*, *St. George and the Dragon* Volumes 1 and 2, and *Women of Myth*, and the non-fiction essay book *Where Stories Dwell*. He pens short detective stories as a means of avoiding writing things that pay better. A full list of his sixty-plus published works appears at:
*http://www.chillwater.org.uk/writing/iawatsonhome.htm*

## The MX Book of New Sherlock Holmes Stories
*Edited by David Marcum*
(MX Publishing, 2015-   )

"This is the finest volume of Sherlockian fiction I have ever read, and I have read, literally, thousands." – Philip K. Jones

"Beyond Impressive . . . This is a splendid venture for a great cause!
– Roger Johnson, Editor, *The Sherlock Holmes Journal,*
The Sherlock Holmes Society of London

*Part I: 1881-1889*
*Part II: 1890-1895*
*Part III: 1896-1929*
*Part IV: 2016 Annual*
*Part V: Christmas Adventures*
*Part VI: 2017 Annual*
*Part VII: Eliminate the Impossible (1880-1891)*
*Part VIII – Eliminate the Impossible (1892-1905)*
*Part IX – 2018 Annual (1879-1895)*
*Part X – 2018 Annual (1896-1916)*
*Part XI – Some Untold Cases (1880-1891)*
*Part XII – Some Untold Cases (1894-1902)*
*Part XIII – 2019 Annual (1881-1890)*
*Part XIV – 2019 Annual (1891-1897)*
*Part XV – 2019 Annual (1898-1917)*
*Part XVI – Whatever Remains . . . Must be the Truth (1881-1890)*
*Part XVII – Whatever Remains . . . Must be the Truth (1891-1898)*
*Part XVIII – Whatever Remains . . . Must be the Truth (1898-1925)*

### In Preparation
*Part XIX – 2020 Annual*

*. . . and more to come!*

# The MX Book of New Sherlock Holmes Stories
*Edited by David Marcum*
(MX Publishing, 2015-    )

*Publishers Weekly* says:

Part VI: *The traditional pastiche is alive and well . . . .*

Part VII: *Sherlockians eager for faithful-to-the-canon plots
and characters will be delighted.*

Part VIII: *The imagination of the contributors in coming up with variations on the
volume's theme is matched by their ingenious resolutions.*

Part IX: *The 18 stories . . . will satisfy fans of Conan Doyle's originals. Sherlockians will
rejoice that more volumes are on the way.*

Part X: *. . . new Sherlock Holmes adventures of consistently high quality.*

Part XI: *. . . an essential volume for Sherlock Holmes fans.*

Part XII: *. . . continues to amaze with the number of high-quality pastiches . . .*

Part XIII: *. . . Amazingly, Marcum has found 22 superb pastiches . . . This is more catnip
for fans of stories faithful to Conan Doyle's original*

Part XIV: *. . . this standout anthology of 21 short stories written in the spirit of Conan
Doyle's originals.*

Part XV: *Stories pitting Sherlock Holmes against seemingly supernatural phenomena
highlight Marcum's 15th anthology of superior short pastiches.*

# The MX Book of New Sherlock Holmes Stories
*Edited by David Marcum*
(MX Publishing, 2015-    )

# MX Publishing

**MX Publishing** is the world's largest specialist Sherlock Holmes publisher, with several hundred titles and over a hundred authors creating the latest in Sherlock Holmes fiction and non-fiction.

*www.mxpublishing.com* (USA)